Praise for *The Roaring Days of Zora Lily*

"A sensational novel… Brimming with emotion, romance, and dazzling prose, historical fiction readers will love this one!"

—Chanel Cleeton, *New York Times* and *USA TODAY* bestselling author of *The Cuban Heiress*

"An inspiring story of determination and talent set in the dizzying world of 1920s speakeasies, Hollywood film lots and Seattle high society. With an engaging heroine and colorful supporting characters, this captivating story makes for a delightful read from beginning to end."

—Shelley Noble, *New York Times* bestselling author of *The Tiffany Girls*

"Beautifully written and vividly drawn… Salazar skillfully weaves a tale of strength and ambition, of enduring friendship and romantic love, filled with an unforgettable cast of characters."

—Jillian Cantor, *USA TODAY* bestselling author of *Beautiful Little Fools*

"I found myself rooting for Zora every step of the way… Romantic, ambitious, and filled with adventure, Salazar swept me away to the roaring 20s."

—Nicola Harrison, author of *The Show Girl* and *Hotel Laguna*

"Jazz Age intrigue, rags to riches, smoky speakeasies, and the dark side of silver screen glamour—Noelle Salazar's latest, spun from a mysterious gown once worn by Greta Garbo, has it all."

—Judithe Little, *USA TODAY* bestselling author of *The Chanel Sisters*

Further praise for *USA TODAY* bestselling author Noelle Salazar

"Unforgettable."

—Pam Jenoff, *New York Times* bestselling author of *The Woman with the Blue Star*, on *Angels of the Resistance*

"Noelle Salazar shines a light on the grit and tragedy behind resistance work, never forgetting the humanity in her beautifully drawn heroines!"

—Kate Quinn, *New York Times* bestselling author of *The Rose Code*, on *Angels of the Resistance*

"From now on, I'll be recommending Noelle Salazar's book to anyone who feels beaten down by the status quo."

—*Forbes* on *The Flight Girls*

Also by Noelle Salazar

The Flight Girls
Angels of the Resistance

The Roaring Days of Zora Lily

NOELLE SALAZAR

Recycling programs for this product may not exist in your area.

ISBN-13: 978-0-7783-0520-0

The Roaring Days of Zora Lily

For questions and comments about the quality of this book, please contact us at CustomerService@Harlequin.com.

Mira
22 Adelaide St. West, 41st Floor
Toronto, Ontario M5H 4E3, Canada
BookClubbish.com

Printed in U.S.A.

For Zora.

Without whom neither this book nor I would exist.

1

Washington, DC, 2023

The fluorescent lights blinked on in a domino effect, one after the other, a faint buzzing sound filling the room as I stood squinting in the unnatural light.

I inhaled, taking in my small slice of heaven within the storied walls of the Smithsonian National Museum of American History. The long room with its high ceiling, soothing taupe walls, and wood floors—weathered in spots from years of conservators standing and pacing as they labored over the works of great minds—brought a sense of peace as soon as I stepped inside.

The museum had been my happy place since I was a little girl, when my mother would walk with me from our baby blue–painted row house on Capitol Hill, her slender fingers wrapped around my pudgy ones. We'd wander past sprawling parks, melancholy monuments documenting history, to the austere but magical facade housing wonders my six-year-old eyes could barely comprehend. By the age of eight I knew all the regular exhibits like the back of my hand, and waited anxiously for the monthly newsletter that arrived in our mailbox, telling us what traveling exhibits we could expect next. It was one such exhibit, a gallery of gowns worn by British royalty, that had burrowed itself inside me in such a way that a dream was born.

"I'm going to work here one day," I'd told my mother, pushing back a strand of dirty-blond hair as I stared up at a jewel-colored gown once worn by Queen Elizabeth the Second.

I was twelve.

I wanted to exist within these walls. It was my church, and I believed in its teachings wholeheartedly. I had drunk the water. Read the great books. And prayed to the gods of knowledge and creativity. I wanted to be part of whatever it took to bring history to life for others. And for the past nine years…that's exactly what I'd done.

I stared at the scene sprawled out before me.

"Sanctuary," I whispered, tucking a blond-highlighted strand of hair behind my ear.

Gleaming table after gleaming table sat covered in silk, satin, lace, and velvet. Gowns and dresses and blouses previously only seen on movie screens and in photographs now lay delicately in wait of tending to, their sparkle and sinew in contrast to the stark lights and tepid surroundings. Mannequins, my constant companions, stood at the ready, waiting for their moment.

Thread in every color imaginable, like a rainbow of rotund spool soldiers on a rolling rack, waited to be chosen. Needles in pincushions, strips of bias tape, shimmering appliqués, ribbons, seam rippers, clear drawers filled with buttons and clasps and snaps, and boxes upon boxes of straight pins, their colorful heads a happy bouquet of tiny plastic globes, were scattered across every surface, peeking from where they'd fallen to the floor, rolled beneath furniture, and stuck—I bent to pull a pink-headed pin from the rug beneath my feet—in a variety of inconvenient places.

The door clicked open behind me and I smiled.

"Good morning, Sylvia," a familiar voice said.

"Morning, Lu," I said to the one member of my team who, like me, couldn't wait to get to work.

Every day, my friend and fellow fashion-obsessed cohort, Lu Huang, and I arrived within minutes of one another, and a full half hour before anyone else. Working as conservators for the museum was a coveted get for us. A dream job that every morning caused us to rush from our respective homes, grabbing an insufficient breakfast on our way out the door, and wondering hours later why we were so hungry. We lost track of time constantly, surviving on coffee and bags of chips from the vending machine, and leaving friends and family waiting on us as we turned up late to holiday parties, dinners, and events we'd implored others to attend but couldn't possibly get to on time, and having forgotten to blend the concealer we'd hurriedly dotted on in the train, with paint under our nails and bits of thread or glue on our jacket cuffs.

In Lu I'd found not only the perfect work companion, but a kindred spirit. Over the nine years we'd worked together, we'd enjoyed laughing over our shared love of no-nonsense ponytails, and waxing poetic about old films and vintage fashion. We sat in her living room or mine, rewatching the movies that had shaped us and sharing stories of our schoolgirl walls plastered with images of iconic women of the silver screen, while our schoolmates favored posters of half-clothed men. So, when the idea for the newest exhibit started floating around our superiors' offices upstairs, we'd spent many a night poring over which films we'd choose if asked, and then deliberated, scrapped, and chose again until we had the perfect array.

Out of curiosity, we began to inquire with movie studios about the costumes we'd be interested in displaying, running into new obstacles with each call we made. Several times we chose a beloved film only to find half the costumes had been lost in a fire, were part of a decades-long legal battle, or were just plain lost—a travesty over which we consoled ourselves with a huge plate of nachos and a pitcher of margaritas. Eventually, the decisions about which movies to include boiled down to three simple things: Where were the costumes we'd need? Would they be available to us for the time required? And what kind of shape were they in?

Once we'd gotten the green light that the exhibit was on, we finalized our list, made the calls, gathered confirmations, and began the design for the wing the costumes would be shown in. And then we waited, barely able to contain ourselves as one by one the garments that would be featured in The Hollywood Glamour Exhibition arrived.

We chose two movies per decade, going back one hundred years to the 1920s. Every piece that had been worn by the female lead was sent to us from studios, museums, or estates. Once in our possession, my job as costume curator, along with my staff of seven, was to remove each gown or outfit from its protective garment bags or boxes, and go over it with a fine-tooth comb, looking for tears, stains, missing buttons, and the like. We'd been working for months. Some of the more intricate gowns needed extensive rebeading or sequin replacement, and many of the older pieces needing patching inside to hold the outside fabric together. In two cases we'd had to sew exact replicas of the linings, and then carefully fit them inside the original, giving it something to cling to, extending its life.

A pantsuit from the forties had lost an outside pocket and matching the fabric had been hell. The brim of an iconic straw hat that belonged to another outfit had been scorched by a cigarette and needed to be patched. Each garment presented its own set of unique problems, and we were giddy as we worked to solve each puzzle.

With our intention for each item to be viewed from all sides, it was crucial they looked as flawless as possible. Thankfully, my team were experts in their field, and excited at the opportunity to handle costumes worn by some of the most famous women in film history.

"Can't believe we're down to the final film," Lu said, running a finger over a strip of fringe hanging from a black evening gown. "I think this batch is my favorite."

I nodded, taking in the room of costumes from the 1928 film *The Star.* Each piece had been worn by the iconic Greta Garbo and was the epitome of elegance and class. And a notable diversion from the designer's usual style.

"It's so odd Cleménte changed her MO for this one film," I said, tilting my head as I took in the distinct wide neckline featured in each of the eight pieces. Even a blouse and jacket had been designed to show off the actress's collarbones. The pieces were alluring, but Cleménte had always been known for a more modest style.

Michele Cleménte had been a well-known designer in the '20s and '30s, her signature style demure, with higher necklines and longer hems. But for this movie, she'd completely diverged.

"It is strange," Lu said, frowning. "The studio must've wanted something exact."

"Then why hire her?" I asked. "Not that she didn't do a lovely job. The clothing is exquisite. I'd wear them all now."

"And look fab doing it."

I felt myself blush with pleasure at the compliment. Being tall and willowy had its advantages. Unfortunately for me, I had neither the opportunity nor the bank account to wear clothes as fine as the ones before us.

"Thanks, Lu," I said, bending to peer closer at the large white beaded star on the white satin gown that was to be the centerpiece for the entire show.

Aside from the star, the rest of the fabric had been left unadorned, letting the beaded element shine before one's eye went to the skirt, which fell in soft overlapping layers to the floor. It was a stunning piece of art. But a confusing one. Because it had no resemblance to any piece ever sewn before by Cleménte. At least not any piece I'd seen in my years of studying the different famous designers. It didn't have her specific way of hand sewing or her distinctive technique of tying off a knot, or even her tendency toward geometric shapes. But it was the neckline that really threw me off. Clemente had preferred to leave a lot to the imagination. It was her calling card during a time when everyone else was showing more skin. And yet for these, she'd completely gone off-script.

The rest of the crew arrived at nine on the dot and the quiet of the room rose to a dull roar as individual desk lights were turned on, loupes donned to scrutinize the tiniest details, and we all began to sew, glue, and chat our way through the day.

"Syl?"

I glanced up and winced as my back protested from having been bent over a table for the past hour. Lu stood, her coat over her arm, by the door. Everyone else had vanished.

"What time is it?" I asked.

"Nearly seven."

"Shit. How does that always happen?" I pulled the loupes from my head.

"You happen to be in love with a dress," Lu said. "That's how."

"Story of my life."

"Explains so much."

"Does it?"

"I mean, it definitely explains why you haven't had a date with a real live human in a while. Only—" She gestured to the mannequin beside me.

We laughed. She wasn't wrong.

Lu was the only person who truly understood me. The only person besides my sister who I'd ever allowed to see inside my guest room closet where dozens of scavenged vintage dresses, trousers, jackets, and hats hung, waiting to be delicately cared for like the ones I lovingly handled at work.

"You gonna stay?" Lu asked, watching me as I looked back at the dress spread out before me.

I rubbed my eyes and stared at the tiny white beads I'd been replacing. We'd named the dress The Diaphanous Star, and I'd been carefully sewing on one bead at a time for the past two hours. It was a delicate task as the fabric they clung to was nearly one hundred years old. I had to work slowly and thoughtfully to keep from shredding it.

"Yeah," I said, rotating my head. "I want to get this star done. How'd you do today?"

I glanced over at the black evening gown she was working on.

"I'm close," she said. "You can barely see the snag in the back now, and I should be able to replace the bit of fringe that's missing tomorrow."

"Perfect," I said, reaching over to wake my laptop and clicking on the calendar. "We are ahead of schedule, which bodes well should we have any catastrophes."

Lu knocked a small wooden box holding scissors inside it.

"Don't jinx us," she said and then waved. "See you B and E."

"See you B and E," I said.

B and E. Bright and early. We'd made it up one day after the youngest woman in our group rattled off a bunch of acronyms as if the rest of us should know what they mean. We used it constantly. She didn't think it was amusing. This of course made it that much funnier.

I pulled my loupes back down and resumed placing the beads that formed the shimmering star. Thirty minutes later I sat up, set the magnifying glasses on the table, and arched my back in a well-deserved stretch.

"Okay, you," I said to the dress. "Time to get you on a mannequin."

Sliding my arms beneath the gown, I lifted it carefully and carried it to the far end of the table where a mannequin with roughly Greta Garbo's 1927 torso measurements stood in wait, minus its arms which would be attached once I got the dress on it.

Unfortunately, the wide neckline made it hard to secure.

"You're pretty," I muttered, trying to keep the dress from slipping to the floor while I reached for one of the arms. "But a pain in my ass."

I clicked an arm into place, moving the capped sleeve over the seam where the appendage attached to the shoulder, and making sure the hand was resting just right on the mannequin's hip. Satisfied, I reached for the other arm and did the same on the other side.

"Not bad, headless Garbo," I said, straightening the gown and smiling at the beaded star glimmering under the lights.

I grabbed my notepad and made my way around the dress, writing down problems that still needed to be addressed. Loose threads, the unraveling second tier of the skirt, and a bit of fabric that looked like it had rubbed against something and was scuffed. There was a stain on the hem in back, and one of the capped sleeves sagged, leading me to investigate and find a spot inside where the elastic was stretched out of shape.

My eyes moved along every inch of fabric, bead, and thread, my fingers scribbling notes as I took in what was easier to see with the dress hanging rather than sprawled on a tabletop. As I scrutinized the neckline in back, I noticed the tag was exposed and reached up to tuck it in. But as I pulled the material back, the tag fluttered to the floor.

With a sigh, I bent to pick it up. I could leave the fix until morning, but as I had nothing but an empty apartment waiting for me, I began the task of detaching the arms of the mannequin and sliding the dress back off and onto the table.

"Always something with you ladies," I said, grabbing a needle and thread. "Can't complain, I guess. Hottest date I've had in a while."

But as I turned my attention to the spot the tag had fallen from, I frowned and pulled the dress closer, peering at a small, elegant stitch no longer than the length of the tag that had covered it.

"Is that…"

I grabbed my loupes and looked again, the stitching now magnified and leaving zero doubt that beneath the tag, in white thread and a beautiful freehand stitch, was a name—and it wasn't Cleménte's.

Sitting back, I removed my glasses and stared at the gorgeous dress with its beautiful wide neckline and capped sleeves, the beaded star, the tiered skirt that was so unlike Cleménte in style, and wondered aloud to the empty room—

"Who the hell is Zora Lily?"

2

Seattle, 1924

The slender gray thread slid snakelike across the back of my hand as I pushed the needle through the delicate remnants of fabric surrounding a tear I'd stitched only last week.

"Damn," I whispered as several more strands of the shredded material unraveled.

"Language," my mother muttered beside me, her own sewing brisk, almost savage as she stabbed her needle in and out of a seam.

I smelled the onion on her breath from the potato soup we'd eaten for lunch as she grumbled.

"It's not a ball gown, Zora. Work faster," she said as she moved to her old sewing machine to finish the piece she was working on. "You have more pressing matters to tend to."

But I'd promised my youngest sister, Eva, I'd stitch a heart-shaped patch this time to cover the worn knee. And I'd found the perfect bit of pink material in our scrap basket to do it. She didn't ask for much, and it was such a little thing to make her happy. Besides, a promise was a promise, as she'd reminded me, her big blue eyes wide with hope. It had nearly broken my heart. It seemed unfair a five-year-old should know so early in life to keep her expectations low. But such was life when you were born into poverty, your father was the town drunk, and all your clothes were threadbare hand-me-downs from your six older siblings, held together by patches. You learn quick and early to keep your sights low and your needs nonexistent.

"I'm nearly finished, Mama," I said, glancing at a gown hanging from a rack by the window. "I'll get to Mrs. Johnson's dress next."

I was excited to get my hands on the beautiful garment that looked so out of place in our rundown little house. It beckoned to me as the sunlight shifted through the window, the shimmering material undulating in between the shadows.

It had been purchased abroad and damaged on the trip home to Seattle. Told by the two well-known dressmakers in the city that the wait time would be at least a month, Mrs. Johnson had sought desperately for someone skilled enough to not only fix the torn sleeve and beading, but who could let out the cinched waist a touch to reflect the new, looser styles women were wearing. Her search led her to our door…and to me.

"You're Zora Hough?" she'd asked, barely able to disguise her disdain as she'd looked past me into the home where my two younger siblings were fighting over a headless doll and my father was stumbling through, his button-down shirt hanging crooked on his skin-and-bones frame while barely concealing his bloated belly.

"I am," I'd said, trying to block the scene behind me with my slight build as I frowned back at the stranger standing on our front porch wearing an expensive coat with a fur collar. Had she not known my name, I'd have reckoned she'd knocked on our door by mistake. "Can I help you?"

"I need a dress fixed. I took it downtown of course," she said, pressing her hand to the large pearls at her throat. Behind her, parked in front of our house, was a motorcar, the driver standing by in case I accosted his boss. "But they're booked for weeks. I need this done by next Saturday for a benefit. When I asked around, your name was at the tip of everyone's tongue. It's a complicated gown though." Again her eyes flicked past me, then down the plain blue frock I wore. "Are you sure you're… equipped for such work?"

"May I see the garment?" I asked.

It was a pale green, like the beginning of spring before sun and soil had mixed to give a plant's leaves its burst of color. It shimmered in the afternoon light, the ivory beads across the neckline and swaying from the shoulders sparking like tiny fireworks.

I noticed right away the ripped sleeve and beading that needed tending to, and nodded, refraining from touching the dress in case she should think my hands as dirty as she obviously viewed my house.

"The sleeve and beads are an easy fix," I'd said.

"I—" She'd frowned. "You're sure? The fabric is very delicate. You'd need to take your time so as not to tear it."

"I'm sure."

"Oh." Her dark eyes blinked several times and then she added, "Well, I was also hoping you could fix the waist."

She'd described what she wanted and I'd nodded and asked if I might take a closer look, holding up my hands to show her they were clean. At her nod, I took the hanger and held the dress up, turning it slowly, eyeing the cinched middle, and then handing it back.

"I can do what you want, but because the fabric is so fine, tiny holes will be left from the threads I cut. Others might not notice, but I can tell you have a keen eye and wouldn't miss them. If you'd like, I could remove the fourth tier of beads from either shoulder and scatter them, making a sort of constellation of camouflage."

She pursed her thin lips as she considered the idea, and then stretched them into a grin.

"I've been told by several women you are a magician with a needle," she said. "Do you really think it will work?"

"I wouldn't suggest it if I didn't," I said.

I'd fixed the torn sleeve and removed the tiers of beads that same evening. As soon as the heart patch was attached to the knee of Eva's trousers, I'd pull the stitches from the gown's waist. The entire job would be done a week before Mrs. Johnson needed it.

I slid my needle through the last stitch of Eva's patch and then jumped at the sound of someone pounding on the front door, narrowly avoiding piercing my skin. Mama wasn't as lucky.

"Dammit!" she said, the needle on the machine speeding up for a moment as her foot slammed on the pedal in surprise.

"Language, Mama," I said as I smiled and rose to answer the door, dodging her glare.

I stepped over the metal toy truck parked beside my chair, around the legs of my youngest brother, Harrison, who was in deep concentration trying to reattach the head he'd pulled off Eva's doll again the day before, which had been mine many years before, and jumped over a ball as it rolled across the tiny living space.

I reached the front door and pulled it open just in time to avoid the next barrage of knocking.

"I thought you weren't never gonna open up!"

I grinned into the anxious round face of my best friend, the ends of her newly bobbed blond hair swinging from beneath the beige linen cloche with off-white fabric flowers I'd made her for her last birthday.

"Sorry," I said, leaning on the door frame. "I was sewing."

She feigned surprise, pressing her hand to her open mouth, and I rolled my eyes.

"You on your way to work?" I asked.

"In this?" She waved a hand over the sleeveless peach frock with eyelet detailing along the hemline. "Heavens no. This is a daytime dress, Z."

I glanced down with bemusement at my own outdated dress with its built-in corset. Oh, the luxury of having dresses for different times of day.

Rose peeked past me into the house.

"Hi, Mrs. Hough," she singsonged, giving my mother a furtive wave before pulling me out onto the front porch.

"I'll be right back," I said over my shoulder.

"Zora," Mama warned.

"I'll only be a minute, Mama."

I closed the door and followed Rose to the street, away from the thin walls of our home, and out of my mother's earshot.

"Come tonight," Rose pleaded.

"I can't." I shook my head and laughed. I knew this was what she'd come for. Ever since she'd gotten a job dancing in one of the clubs downtown, she'd become relentless in trying to get me to come out.

It wasn't that I didn't want to. I did. Terribly. My heart ached with longing to see the lights of the city, hear the jazz music with the horns and bass Rose talked about, and see the clothes. Oh, how I longed to see what people wore out to this secret club she danced in. But my mother's disapproval of anything that involved alcohol or fun, combined with her constant reminder of my responsibilities, made it seem impossible.

"But Ellis is playing. You have to come. You've never heard him. You've never seen or heard any of it! The music…the dancing. The *boys*… Zora! You need to meet a boy."

I held my finger to my lips and looked back at the house to make sure my mother was still inside.

I'd never really had a boyfriend. When you're the poorest girl in school, no one wants to be your friend, much less your boyfriend. And that had been fine with me. I'd spent much of my school days trying to blend into the background, not wanting to speak up even though I knew the answers because in doing so, every eye would turn toward me and take in the cast-off clothing that had been my older brother's, modified with scalloped collars, and a drooping ruffle or two. At the age of twenty-one I'd only ever been kissed twice. Both times by a shabby fella called Gordon. I couldn't say they were kisses to remember. Except for the fact that they'd happened, I probably wouldn't remember them at all.

"Zora," Mama called. Rose pressed her lips together and I turned to see my mother now standing in the doorway of our house, arms crossed over her chest. She gave Rose a brief look before going back inside and closing the door loudly.

Rose, used to my mother, giggled and then turned her pleading blue eyes back to me.

Her face was free of makeup, a rarity these days. I missed her like this. This was the Rose I loved best. The one I met on our first day of fourth grade at Ballard Elementary after her family moved to town. She'd been all gangly arms and legs, her blond hair in two long braids she was constantly twirling, and the boys were constantly pulling on. Even back then she'd been mouthy and obstinate, telling them off and shooing them away. Unlike me, who never said a word out of turn and was a fearful rule follower. If a boy pulled my hair, I didn't say a thing. But when Rose came, that all changed. If she caught them or I told her someone had bothered me, she made sure they heard about it.

Her vibrancy was overshadowing. But I didn't mind. I flourished in the tough and scrawny shadow of Rose Tiller. I followed her everywhere, much to the dismay of my stern mother who would rather I play quietly inside than skip rope outside, noisily counting jumps and giggling when our ropes got tangled.

Our fathers were both loggers back then. Back before my

father's accident. Now her dad was the manager at the sawmill, and mine was often found drunk on whatever cheap and illegal booze he could get his hands on while my older brother, Tommy, worked to pay the bills so we could keep our home. But even with Tommy working at the mill, Mama and I had to take in sewing jobs because a family of nine was a lot to keep fed and clothed.

"It's Friday night, Z," Rose said, her rosebud lips forming a pout. It was no wonder she'd always had boys lining up for her. She was what my older brother, Tommy, and his friends called a stunner. "You're twenty-one. She can't *make* you stay home."

I could count on my fingers and toes the number of times we'd had this argument.

"I know," I said. "But there's a pile of work to get through and some of it is intricate stuff only I can do. Plus, I have nothing to wear to a club. Look at me."

I ran a hand down my drab, colorless frock. I could remember being a young girl and looking up at my mother wearing this exact dress. The fabric then was thick and velvety, but after years of wear and having been patched and sewn time and time again, it was now threadbare and fraying at the hems. I pulled at a stray thread, watching the fabric around it loosen as Rose persisted.

"What about your gray dress?" she asked.

"Rose." I grinned. "From the descriptions you've given me, my gray dress is fine for up here where the only place I go is to the market or the mill. But down there?" I shook my head. "No way."

"First of all, Jackson Street ain't uppity downtown. It's *down* downtown. Second, you're right. You'll stand out for all the wrong reasons if you wear that." She chewed her full lower lip, turning its natural pink shade a deeper hue. "I really don't understand why you don't sew yourself something. All those scraps have to amount to a dress, don't they?"

"Sure, if I want to wear a patchwork dress. Is that what they're all wearing to the clubs?" I laughed. "Is that what Mrs. Denny and Mrs. Fauntleroy go out to dinner in?"

"Well, no," she said, snickering. "But they might if you made it. It would be a masterpiece. The women would be lining the street to have one made."

"I highly doubt that. Nevertheless, it ain't gonna happen. Mama would never give me the time off to do it. If I've got time to sew for myself, I've got time to work through the pile and make us some money."

"Fine," she said, her eyes skimming up and down my body. "Tell ya what, it'll be a tad big on you since you're so thin, but you can wear that pink dress you fixed up for me. The one with the little ruffle at the hem in back?"

"Rose." I shook my head, my long, dark locks, so utterly out of fashion, swinging across my back.

I wanted to say yes. To throw caution to the wind. To assert myself with my mother and tell her I was going out and she couldn't stop me. At night I sometimes lay in bed beside my next-in-line sister, Sarah, in the bedroom we shared with two of our five siblings, and dreamed of dancing until dawn, my hand in the grip of a handsome young man, while wearing a dress I'd made just for me. Not something that had been handed down or made for someone else and tossed aside.

I had a stash of pictures I'd torn from Rose's mom's old magazines, and ads from the newspaper that I'd drawn over, reimagining hemlines and necklines and fabrics. I drew feathers on hats and bows on the shoes. There were ruffled collars, pleated skirts, and trousers with wide, swinging cuffs.

Beside the drawings were images of Coco Chanel, Clara Bow, and Josephine Baker. Each one's style inspiring something different.

But Mama didn't like the clothes that were popular now

and grumbled when we were asked to drop waistlines and raise hems.

"Indecent," she muttered as she sewed. "No corsets. Everything on display. What happened to modesty?"

How Rose thought I'd ever be able to sew something for myself with Mama constantly looking over my shoulder was beyond me. But I knew it wasn't just the style Mama hated, it was the new culture that had come along with it. Bawdy women making their own money and their own decisions, loud music (not that there was any heard in our house), and alcohol, despite Prohibition, that flowed day and night.

It was the alcohol in particular she didn't agree with. Ever since Daddy began stumbling in our door at odd hours after being who knows where, she'd grown increasingly hostile. I couldn't bring myself to tell her I wanted to go out.

"Come on, Z. Please?" Rose was pleading again. "Tell her you're staying over. You haven't done that in ages. Tell her it's for old times' sake. I have the night off and am watching the kids for my folks."

I chewed my lip. It could work.

"I promise it will be fun. And—" she lowered her voice further "—I can get us in to the back room at the Bucket."

"I don't even know what that is, Rose," I said.

She rolled her eyes. "It's a big deal, Z. That's what it is."

"I'll have to take your word for it."

"But you don't, because I can get us in."

She stopped talking then and stared at me, waiting for my final word.

"If I'm not at your house by seven I'm not coming," I said hurriedly.

She squealed and clapped her hands, then stood on her tiptoes to kiss my cheek as a pickup truck stopped in front of the house.

"Uh-oh. What are you two up to now?" my brother Tommy

asked as he jumped out of the back and reached in to remove a small bunch of kindling for the kitchen cookstove.

He ran a hand through his wind-mussed dark hair, slapped the side of the vehicle, and waved as the driver gave me and Rose a grin before rumbling off down the street.

"Heya, Tommy," Rose said.

"Hey, Rosie. Saw your mother the other day when she came by the mill to bring your dad lunch. How you doin'?"

"I'm good. How's Jennie?"

Tommy grinned, a pink flush washing over his handsome face at the mention of his girlfriend.

"She's good, thanks."

He waved at her, swatted me on the arm as he walked by, and hurried into the house, rubbing at tired eyes as he went.

"He's so grown," Rose said.

"I know. I swear he's twice the size he was when he left college."

"He doin' okay with that?"

I shrugged and looked back at the door my brother had disappeared behind. Tommy was smart. All he'd wanted since he was a boy was to learn. He wanted to know everything. When he got a scholarship at the University of Washington, he was over the moon. But then Daddy got hurt and the bills needed to be paid, so he quit school to get a job at the same logging camp that had nearly taken our father's life.

"I catch him reading through his old textbooks whenever he comes home for a night. It's like he doesn't want to forget anything he learned in case he ever gets to go back."

"I feel for him," she said. "Logger life is rough, and Tommy has so much more in him than all that." She reached up to hug me, whispering in my ear as she did. "Seven o'clock?"

"If I'm not there—"

"You're not comin'. Got it."

"What did that girl want this time?" Mama asked as I sat back down beside her and picked up Eva's trousers.

"She has the night off and her folks are going out," I said, tying a knot and snipping the end of the thread. "She asked if I could stay over. Help out, have some girl talk. We haven't done that in ages."

"Girl talk?" I could feel her eyes on me.

I smiled over at her.

"Oh, Mama," I said. "You know Rose. She's the same as she's always been. Silly and boy crazy."

"And loud," she said. "With too much stuff on her face."

"Well, there will be none of that tonight," I said. "Just snacks and games I imagine."

I stood and moved to Mrs. Johnson's dress, avoiding my mother's gaze. Truth was, Rose was right. I was an adult and could legally do as I pleased. But I knew Mama had a lot to worry about these days and I was happy to not add to the list.

"You'll be home in the morning?" she asked.

My heart skipped a beat.

"Of course. But not too early," I said with a laugh. "I might have to take advantage of a night without Sarah kicking me."

Her face relaxed into a soft smile then.

"That girl. She's been a kicker since day one." She patted her belly fondly. "Some days I swore she was going to kick her way out of me." She glanced at the dress I was standing before. "Why don't you leave it for tomorrow."

"I can start on the waist. I have time."

"I know what you're missing out on, girl," she said. "And I appreciate your dedication to this family."

My eyes filled as I smiled. She didn't often thank me. And she definitely didn't show much affection these days.

"Thanks, Mama. I love this family," I said.

"I know you do, Zora Lil. And we love you."

We jumped then as a thud shook the house, followed by a

scrape, a grumble, and the slamming open of my parents' bedroom door.

Mother's hand shot out and she steadied her water glass.

"Damn that man," she said under her breath.

The wilted form of my father emerged, his clothes from the day before rumpled as though he had spent a night getting trampled by car wheels. His face was bloated, as was his stomach, but the rest of him had wasted away.

"Good afternoon, Papa," I said, keeping my voice low so as not to assault his delicate state.

"Afternoon, girl," he rasped, running a knob-knuckled hand over my hair. "That heart for Eva?" He pointed to the pink heart on the trousers I'd left hanging over the back of my chair.

"Yessir."

"Yer a good sister."

"I try to be, Papa."

"The rest of 'em could learn a thing or two from ya," he said.

I nodded, trying not to choke on the alcohol wafting from his pores. My eyes watered and Mama shooed him away.

"There's soup on the stovetop," she said. "Get yourself a bowl. Maybe two."

"Gotta go out," he said, shrugging into his jacket.

Mama's fingers stopped moving and I held my breath. Harrison, still lying on the floor beside me, seemed to shrink in size.

"Where you off to?" Mama asked.

But my father didn't answer. He just swung open the front door, stepped outside, and closed the door behind him.

"Damn fool wasn't even wearing shoes," Mama said. She shook her head and gave a little chuckle. But I didn't miss the tear she wiped away.

3

Dinner was always a raucous affair when Tommy was home. He tried hard to make the absence of father unnoticeable, teasing the three middle kids, Sarah, Lawrence, and Hannah, and asking the smaller two, Harrison and Eva, what he called "Big Life" questions. At six and five, their answers were always good for a laugh.

"What will you be when you grow up?" he asked Harrison, who was making the most of the few boiled potatoes on his plate from the withering supply of spuds kept on the back porch.

"A lawyer!" Harrison said, to which we all widened our eyes.

"How do you know that word?" Sarah asked, tucking a wisp of chin-length hair behind her ear. I'd cut it for her the week prior when she'd come home from school in tears. "I just want to fit in!" she'd wailed, tugging on the braid she wore nearly every day. "All the other girls are cutting off their hair. Why can't I?"

I'd looked at her, heartbroken, knowing what it felt like to be a Hough. To go to school in unfashionable hand-me-downs. To eat meager lunches of sandwiches with no fillings, fruit too soft from age, and water from a well that had a brown tinge to it. And so I'd waved for her to follow me out to the back porch where I set out a chair and held up my fabric scissors.

"Really?" she'd asked, looking toward the house where Mama was sewing in her usual spot.

"It's your hair," I'd said. "And you're eighteen now, technically an adult, so..."

She'd plopped down in the seat, taken a deep, shoulder-lifting breath, and said, "Cut it." And so I had. When Mama got a look at her a good thirty minutes later, she merely shook her head and went back to her work, mumbling something about "shoulda stopped at one," which made Sarah and me laugh.

After Eva proclaimed she was going to be a street sweeper when she grew up, the conversation turned to other things, like could Sarah please, please, please get a new dress for graduation? Lawrence needed new shoes again. His feet had now surpassed the size of Tommy's, leaving him with no options for hand-me-downs any longer. Hannah, nervously chewing her strawberry-blond hair, mentioned quietly that her best friend Mary's birthday was coming up and she needed to buy her a gift. And Eva wanted a new doll, because the one she had was permanently headless after Harrison's last wrestling match with it.

Everyone looked from me to Harrison, the only two who hadn't chimed in with any needs.

"Looks like Harrison and I are doing just fine, right, buddy?" I said, running my hand over my little brother's soft brown hair.

"I want a truck," he said and we all laughed. He always wanted a new truck.

"Well," Mama said, looking anywhere but at Tommy, who provided most everything for us now. Even over a year into the arrangement she still felt shame for not being able to support us on her own. "I think I can cover a gift for Mary with some sewing money."

I looked to Sarah. "I know it might not be new from a store," I said. "But one of the dresses I took in last week had enough fabric cut off of it to fashion a whole other dress. The fabric is beautiful and the blue color would look amazing on you. I can make it any style—"

"I want it to be the new style everyone's wearing!" Sarah said, cutting me off. I nodded.

"I'll start on it tomorrow. I may even have a little sparkle to add to it."

"Anything you make from scratch is like getting it from a fancy store anyway," she said. "Thank you, Z."

"And I think I can manage shoes and a new doll," Tommy said. "But just. So everyone try to hold off on needing anything else, okay?"

After dinner we scattered as usual. Sarah helped Mama clean up the kitchen, Lawrence went upstairs to finish some homework, the youngest two pulled out a can of marbles and played with them on the threadbare living room rug, Hannah wandered off on silent feet to read or write or daydream, and Tommy and I went out front and sat on the porch steps like we always did when he came home for too-brief a visit.

"How's Jennie," I asked.

"Patient," he said with a wry grin.

"Her folks putting pressure on you?"

"Nah. Well, maybe a little." He shrugged. "They'd love for me to get back to school, get a good job, and for us to get married. Give her a home of our own for her to manage… Babies… Her pa likes to bring up other job opportunities I could look into. Something more 'suitable for a young man with a mind like yours.' But they're all jobs that require the schooling I gave up and…" He sighed and stared blindly across the street.

"I've been thinking of getting a job," I said. "Outside the house. Maybe something in town at one of the boutiques."

"Mama would never let you. You know what she thinks of downtown."

"I'm an adult. She can't tell me no."

"But she can make you feel guilty as hell every day for leaving her saddled with five kids and a pile of sewing that needs to get done fast to bring in as much money as possible."

"I don't understand why she hates the city so much."

"Alcohol. Women. Bad ideas." Tommy ticked the list off on his fingers. We'd heard it a thousand times from her. Downtown was no good. It was filled with people wanting things they didn't need and shouldn't have.

"There's plenty of alcohol in Ballard," I said. "Plenty of women. And more bad ideas than I can count on both hands and feet."

"But she knows the community here. She knows if one of her kids is up to no good, she'll hear about it. She feels safe in our little corner of the world. If Pa doesn't come home, she knows he's one of three places. If one of us gets hurt, she knows she can walk us over to Doc Truman. If someone doesn't come home when they're supposed to, she knows all the places to go looking." He looked over at me with a sad smile. "She wasn't always this way. So skittish. So housebound and eagle-eyed. Do you remember? Before Pa got hurt?"

"Yeah," I said. "I remember."

She'd been funny, her wit one of the best things about her. She could always get a smile out of someone, no matter how hard they tried not to be amused. And she was smart. Like most women her age, she'd hadn't finished school, leaving in the eighth grade, but she was rarely seen without a book in hand in those days. Now all her books had been spirited away to Hannah's corner of our shared room, and in their place were piles of clothes needing to be mended.

"Daddy's accident made her different," I said.

"No," Tommy corrected. "The accident made her tough. The drinking made her how she is now. Ashamed."

"I hate him for what he's done to the two of you."

"Me too. But I hate him more for what he's done to you."

"How do you mean?"

"Come on, Z. I know you'd like to go out on dates. To even be asked. You're a looker. I can't count how many times I've had to clock one of my friends on the ear for noticing. And I know you'd love to use that talent of yours to make the kind of life you deserve to have. You should be living downtown in a nice apartment, making fancy clothes for fancy people in a fancy shop. Not here, still sharing a bed with your sister in a house with no indoor plumbing on a street most people avoid."

My face went hot and I ducked my head.

"It's fine," I whispered.

"It's not. It's unfair that because of Father, people steer clear of us. No one wants their kid to be friends with the child of the town drunk—or their son or daughter to date her or him. You're young and smart, talented and beautiful. You deserve to get asked out. To have opportunities to dress up and experience more of life."

"And you don't?" I asked. "You belong in college. Not chopping down trees."

"It's not forever," he said. But by the tone of his voice, I could tell even he wasn't so sure about that.

"I really miss having you around all the time," I said, nudging him with my elbow.

"I miss bein' around." He nudged me back. "Maybe next weekend I'll try to get back earlier and we can take everyone to the beach."

"They'd like that," I said.

"Me too." He grinned, looking like he had when he was a little boy. "So, you goin' over to Rose's tonight?"

I pursed my lips and glanced toward the house. His eyes widened and he leaned in.

"Tell me," he said.

"She's working at the club tonight," I whispered. "I'm going with."

Tommy's grin turned impish. "Good for you, Z," he whispered. "Have a little fun for me too, promise?"

"Promise."

The pickup truck that had dropped him off a few hours earlier pulled up to the front of the house.

"Welp. There's my ride." He got to his feet, pulled me to mine, and wrapped his arms around me. "Have a good time, sis. But be careful. Don't go running off with the first slick-haired boy who promises you the world."

"I wouldn't think of it," I said, hugging him back. "Be careful out there in all those trees. See you next week?"

"See you then."

He held up a finger to the driver and then hurried inside. I smiled as I heard a rush of noise, everyone taking their turn saying goodbye, and then he reappeared, ran down the front path, hopped in the bed of the truck where two other young men sat, and they were off with a wave.

"What are you and Rose doing tonight?" Sarah asked from where she lay on our bed while I placed a nightgown and clothes for the following day in a small bag.

"Probably just some girl talk in our pajamas," I said, keeping my eyes averted as she had an uncanny knack for spotting a lie. But when I glanced at her, she was staring at Hannah, who was lying on her stomach on her and Eva's bed, her nose quite literally buried in a book.

"How does she fall asleep like that?" Sarah asked.

Out of the seven of us, Hannah stood out by practically disappearing into the woodwork. She was the quietest, always with a book in her hand and a far-off look in her eyes. She was the only one to inherit our father's pale red-gold hair and fair skin. While the rest of us turned a deep golden color in the sun, she merely turned a shade of pink before her skin rejected the idea of color and turned back to its beautiful shade of porcelain.

"I don't know," I said. "But whenever I see her like that, I think how wonderful it must be to get sucked into a story so deeply."

We stared for a moment longer, smiling at our younger sister, and then Sarah looked toward the door, her eyes widening, and pressed a hand to her mouth to keep from laughing too loud.

I turned to see what was so funny and found Eva, the youngest member of the family, wearing an old shirt and pair of trousers that had been Harrison's, an eyepatch I'd made her last week, and a glare with the one eye we could see.

"Where are you going?" she asked, taking in the bag I was packing.

"To Rose's house," I said. "Did you see the heart I sewed for you?"

Her expression changed, like storm clouds parting to expose the sun.

"It's perfect!" she said, and jumped on to the bed next to Sarah, nearly knocking my bag to the floor.

"Good," I said. "Try to make it last more than a week this time, okay?"

She scrunched up her tiny face but nodded, her mop of dark hair, uncombed and sticking up all over her head bouncing with every dip of her chin.

"Well," I said, latching my small suitcase closed. "That's everything I guess. See you ladies tomorrow?"

"See you!" Eva said before throwing herself at me in a hug and then racing from the room.

"Have fun tonight," Sarah said. "Don't do anything I wouldn't do."

"Can't get in much trouble at the Tiller residence," I said.

"Mmm-hmm," she said. I met her eyes. She knew. Maybe not where I was going, but that I wasn't being completely honest about my plans.

"I won't," I said.

"Be safe," she whispered and I nodded.

"You know me," I said. "Too responsible to be any fun."

"Well. Then maybe, for tonight, be a little irresponsible. You deserve it."

I leaned over and kissed her cheek, turned and kissed the top of Hannah's sleeping head, grabbed my bag, and waved as I hurried out the bedroom door.

4

The Tiller residence was exactly five streets away but might as well have been in a different city for how much nicer the neighborhood was.

When we'd first met, Rose had lived only one street over, her family of five nearly as poor as my family of nine. But her father had risen quickly in the logging business, and after a few years, the Tillers moved up in the world.

It never ceased to amaze me, the changes in my surroundings from street to street as I headed farther south and closer to the city. As I walked down our dirt path, I took in the patchy front yard and the house's faded white paint and sagging roof.

War and a pandemic had hit hardest in these little pockets of the city where money, already tight, became frighteningly scant. The houses here were old and shabby, and most slanted one way or the other as though tired of standing. There were lost shingles and siding, cracked windows, chimneys with missing bricks, and if they'd had a fenced yard, most of the boards were long gone now.

The streetlights, like the houses, still used candles to light the nights. And only one house, the Carters on the corner, had an indoor bathroom. They'd even thrown a party to celebrate when it was put in, letting everyone in the neighborhood have a chance at using the gleaming white toilet. Sarah threatened to run away and plead to be adopted by them she'd loved the experience so much.

The closer I got to Rose's house the lighter I felt, as if shedding the burden of poverty that clung to me from morning till night. It was still there, but lessened somehow with each footstep toward the well-painted houses with their well-kept lawns, and the smell of blooming flowers in the air, rather than the stink of damp and overgrown underbrush and rotting tree stumps that littered my neighborhood.

Painted white picket fences, little dogs sniffing at my feet as their owners walked them on actual sidewalks, and automobiles, washed and gleaming in the early evening sun.

I smiled, breathing in the air. Spring had finally come after a long, cold, and gray winter, and the signs of the new season were everywhere as tree leaves and flower buds began their slow bursts of color. I nodded at a woman pruning a shrub in her well-kept yard and she scowled, making me purse my lips as I tried not to laugh.

"You came!"

I looked up to see Rose running down the steps of the front porch of the Tiller house toward me. She threw open the gate, and then wrapped her arms around me. When she pulled back she was grinning so wide I thought her face might split.

I glanced down at the house three down with a wry smile. "Mrs. Roberts is her usually friendly self."

"She does the same to me all the time," Rose said. "She also says in a voice she pretends is a whisper that I'm too loud, too made-up, and too headstrong. Don't mind her. The rest of the neighborhood can't stand her."

She grabbed my suitcase then.

"Come on! We've got work to do!"

I noticed everything as we entered the house. From the pewter-framed mirror hanging in the entryway, the glass-topped coffee table with a matching end table in the sitting room, to the new geometric wallpaper in the dining room that perfectly complemented the new rug beneath the dining table.

How nice it must be to have new things, rather than items already worn down by the previous owner and given out of pity. The Tiller house was filled with modern furniture, vases of fresh flowers, and always a bowl of fruit for anyone to enjoy. I couldn't even remember the last time I'd had the satisfaction of biting into a crisp, shiny apple like the ones sitting in the bowl now. The last one I'd had was bruised in three spots and mushy.

"You know you don't have to ask," Rose said, catching me eyeing the fruit. "You're family."

"Well, hello, Zora," Mrs. Tiller said, looking up from the kitchen table where she was reading a magazine. Her hair, the same shade of blond as Rose's, was styled in a long bob, the soft curls hanging just below her jawline. Her dress was a fresh pale green, which she'd paired with a lightweight cream cardigan. She was the picture of the modern-day housewife. "How are you, dear?" she asked. "How's the family?"

The last part was asked not with the pitying tone so many others had, but with an empathetic one. Mrs. Tiller knew better than anyone about my father. She'd been my mother's closest confidant for years, though the two spent less time together after the accident, due to Mama's stubborn pride and obvious embarrassment.

"We're fine, Mrs. Tiller. Thank you for asking."

"I haven't seen your mother in ages. You'll tell me if she needs anything, right? More customers? I was thinking the other day I could put an ad in the paper for you ladies. It's guaranteed to bring in more business."

"That's very kind of you," I said. "May I get back to you on that? You know how Mama is."

"Proud as anything," she said. "As well she should be. She has much to be proud of. As do you. Fixing up a dress for Mrs. Johnson is quite the feather in your cap. I can't wait to hear her rave about it."

"Let's just hope she does."

"I have no doubts, Zora Hough. None at all. Now—" She waved a hand at us. "You gals go get ready for your night of girl talk." She winked and I smiled gratefully. Mrs. Tiller had always been a great secret keeper. So long as no one was getting hurt, she loved to be in on a plan.

"Let's find you a dress," Rose said as we entered her bedroom, which was the most girlish room I'd ever seen in my life, Mrs. Tiller having gone overboard when they moved in. "I think she decorated for herself," Rose had said when I first got an eyeful of the ruffled white curtains and bedspread, the pink lampshade, and frilly throw pillows.

She flung open the door to her closet and pulled out the pink dress she'd offered up when she'd come by, then another in white, and a last one in a slinky gray.

"Where on earth did you get this?" I asked, taking a bite of the apple I'd taken and running a hand over the gray frock.

"A girl at work. You should wear it. It would look fabulous on you."

As long as I'd dreamed of wearing something so fashionable, it was a bit racy for my first night out.

"I don't know," I said, looking at the other two options. They were lovely, but plain. I stared at the gray one again.

"I can see those wheels in your head turnin', Zora," Rose said. "I promise you. You won't even stand out. Girls wear much racier things than that."

"Really?"

"Really."

I pulled a pair of heels from the little suitcase I'd brought. "Will these be okay? They're all I have."

She stared down at my black, scuffed shoes.

"Don't worry. No one is going to be looking at your shoes. They'll all be looking at that face of yours."

I grimaced.

"Well, not if you do that!" she said, making me laugh. "Oh boy. I can hardly wait to paint you up."

I grinned. I had been waiting for this day for ages.

"Will you use powder and rouge?" I asked.

"I'll use much more than that."

"I won't look like a clown though, right?"

Rose placed her hands on her hips.

"Zora Hough. How dare you doubt my talent with makeup. You'll look fantastic. I'll only play up your features a touch. You don't need much more than that. You don't need anything at all. But you'll look out of place barefaced so have a seat and let's get started."

I sat at her pretty white vanity and tipped my face up to my friend. I'd always trusted Rose, even with some of her more outlandish ideas over the years. Like when she'd convinced me to sneak out her window in the middle of the night when we were thirteen so she could meet up with a boy from our class. Or the time I'd been lookout so she could steal us a piece of candy from the drugstore. At least this time we wouldn't be doing anything illegal. Or…

"Is it legal to be in the clubs?"

She snorted.

"The only thing not legal is the alcohol. But the clubs pay off the coppers in money and booze so they let us be. Sometimes they do a raid, but usually no one gets in trouble. It's more for show for the picketers than anything else."

It was her "usually" that made my stomach sink a little.

"Okay," she said. "Turn around. We'll start with your hair."

I breathed in her powdery perfume as she fussed over me, first brushing out my hair, then rolling up the back and pinning it here and there as she hummed a little tune and clicked her tongue while checking the final product.

Next, she moved to my face. I watched as she pulled the cap off a round stick of something flesh-colored.

"Is that pan stick?" I asked, having only seen ads for it in the newspaper.

"It is," she said, holding it up for me to see.

She smoothed it over my skin, wiping and dabbing while I relaxed, enjoying the feeling of having attention poured over me.

After the pan stick she grabbed a round container the size of her hand and pulled the lid off. A puff of dust rose in the air between us.

"Powder," she said. "To set everything. Close your eyes and hold your breath."

Next came a small flat compact, the contents inside pink. She swiped the pad of her index finger across the surface and patted it onto my cheeks. I watched her as she stood back, surveying her work, and then applying more before grabbing another container, this one rectangular and tin. Inside was a small block of something black. She wiped off a little angled brush and another that looked like a miniature hairbrush with a cloth and then poured a tiny bit of water from a glass vial onto the black cake and stirred it around some, making a paste.

I'd seen her wearing the black paint before, but hadn't seen how it was used and watched in fascination as she dipped the narrow brush inside and came at me. I flinched and leaned back. She laughed.

"If you do that while I'm applying it, I might get it in your eye."

"That's what I'm afraid of!"

"I promise I won't get it inside your eye if you stay still. I put it on myself every day."

I peered at her and then took a breath and tried to relax again.

"Okay?" she said.

"Okay," I said.

"Z?"

"Mmm-hmm?"

"I can't put it on you if you squeeze your eyes shut like that."

"Oh." I giggled and opened my eyes and blinked a few times. "Right."

The slender brush tickled my eyelids as she slid it across one, dipped the brush in the paste, and then slid it across the other. I watched her peer at me, her upturned nose wrinkling a little, her lips scrunching as she checked her work before dipping the brush a few more times to perfect whatever she was doing around my eyes. Finally she gave a nod, more to herself than me, and picked up the other brush and rubbed it in the paste before holding it up horizontally in front of my left eye.

"Blink," she said and I did, feeling the bristles brush through my lashes. "Again."

She did the other eye and then stood back one more time. Her face lit up.

"Nearly perfect," she said. "Now the lips." She opened a shiny gold tube and twisted until a cylinder of red swiveled into view.

She leaned in once more to apply the lipstick and then stood back, surveying her work.

"You look so glamorous, Z! The boys are going to be bugging me all night asking who you are. Wait until I tell them it's none other than Zora Hough. They won't even believe you're the same girl from Ballard High."

I cringed, my excitement for the night wilting.

"Will there be boys there I know?" I asked.

I'd never considered that and was now mortified. I couldn't go out in one of Rose's short dresses with my face made up like a clown. Or worse, a harlot, which is what I'm sure I looked like with how much makeup she seemed to put on me.

"Only a couple," she said. "Billy Hargrove and Stu Garwin. I see them and a few others out every so often. You'll know more of the girls. Millie, Ellen, and Jolene are always out at the clubs."

That might actually be worse. I'd never quite fit in at school, which was why Rose moving to town had been the best thing to happen to me. She wasn't fazed by the fussy girls in their fussier clothes. Their teasing about our lesser-than status never bothered her. Or if it had, she'd never shown it. She had always been a girl aware of where she stood socially and unafraid to challenge it or work harder for better. And I'd always been behind her, prepared to follow wherever her smart mouth took us. Until she'd applied for a job dancing. That's where I drew the line. I'd been afraid she'd think me a coward. Maybe rethink our friendship. But instead she'd said, "Good for you, Z. Don't do what's not you." And had been encouraging me ever since to take on my own sewing clients, rather than just mending whatever Mama handed me.

I looked up at her now, standing before me, hands on hips, waiting for me to take in the work she'd done.

"Are you going to look?" she asked, gesturing for me to turn and face the mirror.

Holding my breath, I turned.

"Well?" she asked when I didn't say anything, her big blue eyes anxiously looking from the me in the mirror to the me sitting before her.

"Oh." It was more breath than word.

"What did I tell ya?" she said, giving me a smug grin as she smoothed a hand over my hair.

I leaned closer to the mirror. It had felt like she'd used half the product in each little container, but in actuality, she'd used very little, accentuating the details of my face, rather than covering them up.

My cheeks looked flushed, as if I'd spent an afternoon in the sun, my lips a soft brown-red color, and the black on my lids and lashes made the irises of my eyes look more gold than brown. More honey than mud. The effect was...

"I look so glamorous," I said, turning my head from side to side as I took in my hair, which now looked as though it stopped below my ears.

"Damn right you do," she said, admiring her work for a moment more before waving me out of the way. "Now, scoot. I have to get ready and it takes me much longer to make up this face than it does to do yours."

I shook my head. Rose, with her creamy complexion, big baby doll blue eyes, cute upturned nose, and shining blond hair needed nothing at all to enhance her already alluring features. And even if she weren't so pretty, she had an effervescence I could only dream of having. She practically sparkled. In fact, with the shimmering champagne-colored dress she was planning to wear, she actually would sparkle. I was destined to always be eclipsed by the shining light that was Rose Tiller. And that was fine by me.

"Look in my second drawer for some stockings and roll garters and slip into that dress so we can see how it looks," she said as she powdered her face.

I nodded and did as she said, pulling open the drawer and sifting through the array of stockings inside.

"Which should I choose?" I asked, holding up a stocking with little blue flowers on it.

"Not those. Try one of the skin-colored pairs."

I pulled a pair of the silky stockings from the drawer and sat on the edge of a bed that had never been shared with a sibling. I slipped off my shoes and then slid the stockings on one at a time before pulling a roll garter over my knee.

"Uh-uh," Rose said, her reflection looking at me as she drew the line of her eyebrow down, elongating it by a good half inch. "Under the knee."

"Under?" I said, my eyes wide.

"If you don't want to seem a prude, they go under the knee."

"Rose," I said. "I hate to tell you this, but I fear I am a bit of a prude."

She snorted.

"Well, not tonight, my friend! Tonight, we're going to loosen you up a bit. Trust me. It will be fun. Have I ever steered you wrong?"

"Well…"

"Do not even mention that night we snuck out. What a waste. That boy couldn't kiss worth a damn."

"How could you know?" I asked, laughing. "You'd never even kissed a boy before that!"

"A woman knows," she said, giving me a saucy wink before turning back to the mirror.

By six thirty we were both dressed, our hair and makeup done, my stockings rolled beneath my knees correctly, my knees rouged in daring fashion.

"What on heaven's earth are you doing now?" I'd asked Rose as she'd lifted her skirt to rub rouge on her knees.

"It draws the eyes to the legs when one is dancing," she said as if it should be obvious.

"Is that necessary?"

"Yes. Yes it is, my sweet friend."

And so I let her rouge my knees too and then we stood side by side, admiring our reflections in the mirror.

"You look so glamorous, Z," Rose said, her eyes filling with tears.

Somehow, in this new style of dress with its shoulder straps and dropped waist, higher hemline and shimmering fabric, I did look glamorous. Like me, but a different version of me. I looked confident. Elegant. And maybe even a tad bit effervescent too.

I grabbed my friend's hand and squeezed.

"Thank you, Rose."

She gently dabbed at her eyes. "I feel like a proud parent."

She handed me a shawl dripping with fringe and grabbed her purse.

"You ready?" she asked.

I grinned at my reflection one last time.

"As I'll ever be," I said.

5

Rose was allowed to borrow her father's black Ford Model T one night a week. She saved that privilege for Saturday nights. As we left Ballard, I stared out the window, clutching the armrest as we bumped along, and watching the houses go by, noticing how dark the streets behind us looked compared to the ones closer to the city. Candlelight versus electricity. It made a hell of a difference.

I'd never been to the city at night. Only during the day when Mama deemed it safe. The last time I came was for my twentieth birthday. Rose and I had taken the streetcar in and Mama had given me enough money to buy a small gift for myself.

"I'd have bought and wrapped something myself," she'd said. "But I thought it might be nice if you went shopping with your friend and picked out something you knew you were going to like."

Besides the surprising little bit of money, she'd also fashioned me a cloche hat out of some fabric cut off the bottom of a dress a client had asked her to make shorter. The material was thin on one side, where it had dragged on the ground, but she'd made two fabric flowers to cover it.

That birthday had been one to remember. Rose had bought us both lunch and I'd found a beautiful bolt of fabric I planned to make a dress out of one day. As soon as I had the time, and Mama wasn't looking over my shoulder. It had been over a year now though, and still the fabric sat in its wrapping in the back of my closet gathering dust.

As we came up over a hill, I gasped, my eyes going wide like saucers as I took in the Smith Tower. It was Seattle's tallest building, finished eleven years before in 1914 and opened to the public on July Fourth of that year. Over four thousand people rode the elevator that day to the thirty-fifth floor, viewing The Chinese Room, furnished by the Empress Dowager Cixi, China's last empress, and the famous Wishing Chair. My parents took Tommy and me to see it, and I still remembered the excitement of the people around us, the dragon and phoenix carved into the chair, and the brass elevator that took us up and then down.

"Pretty, ain't it?" Rose asked.

"It looks like Christmas morning," I said, leaning forward in my seat. Though not any Christmas I'd experienced.

I was in awe of the streetlights, the lit-up signs, and even the traffic lights—there were so many. The headlights on the many cars shone like a constellation of stars, the rear lights sparking red like fireworks. Everywhere people were walking along sidewalks, calling out to one another, waving, hugging. There were groups large and small, laughter, the honk of car horns, and the ringing of bicycle bells.

"Zora." Rose laughed. "You're going to fall out of the car if you don't stop twisting around like that."

"I can't help it," I said, turning to look out the back window, my eyes following a group of women with little bands around their heads, some with feathers attached, some with ribbons. "I feel like I'm in another world. Why didn't you tell me it was like this? It's so exciting!"

"My dear friend," she said. "How I have tried."

She took a left, bumping over the streetcar tracks, and drove a few more blocks before pulling over and parking in front of a nondescript building.

"Is this it?" I asked, staring at plain facade and darkened windows.

"No." She laughed. "It's another block down. We're gonna hoof it a few blocks to the Bucket first, and then we'll head to the Alhambra. I'm not on for another two hours anyway."

She got out of the car, hurried around to my side, and opened the door.

"Miss?" she said.

I grinned and got out, linking my arm through hers and letting her lead me down the sidewalk.

"You're sure I look okay?" I asked, taking in the fancy attire of three women as we passed them and running a hand down the front of the dress.

Rose stopped and stood facing me. "You look perfect, Zora."

"Promise?"

"I promise."

We crossed the street, joined by throngs of people out enjoying the warm spring evening.

"Rose!" someone yelled from behind us.

She spun around and waved.

"Hey, Gus." Her voice turned flirty and I turned to take in this Gus fellow.

He was tall and good-looking in a way I'd never trusted. This was the kind of boy who had never given me the time of day. Blond hair combed too perfectly, a thin, straight aristocratic nose, and lips that curled into a self-satisfied smile. His clothes were expensive. Trousers and a thin-striped dress shirt, a jacket thrown over his arm, and a hat he tipped toward me.

"Who's your friend?" he asked, his eyes taking in every inch of me. I took a small step back and wrapped my arms around my waist.

"This is my best gal, Zora."

"A pleasure," he said, holding out his hand to shake mine.

I held in a sigh and placed my hand in his, squirming inside at the slight damp of his palm.

Rose linked her arm through mine again.

"You headed to the Bucket?" she asked Gus.

"I am."

As the three of us walked, Rose leaned over and whispered, "What do you think of Gus?"

I gave a polite smile back and said, "No."

While Gus and Rose exchanged gossip, I listened with half an ear, my eyes devouring the scene laid out before me.

There were dozens of people dressed for a night out, but the clubs Rose had told me about were nowhere in sight. I watched a couple ahead of us enter a drugstore, and a small group disappear inside a Chinese restaurant. A group of three women went down an alleyway, while two men knocked on the door of a barbershop that looked closed, but the door opened and they quickly stepped inside.

"Here we are," Gus said.

I looked up at the orange brick building he gestured to. The Louisa Hotel. I frowned at Rose as Gus steered us around the corner into an alleyway.

At my hesitation, Rose grabbed my hand, her lips curving into a secretive smile, her eyes bright. My heart sped up as I followed, stepping through the side door Gus held open and looking around the stairwell we now stood in.

I followed them a flight down, staring up at a myriad of murals as we descended. Beautiful large paintings of women and men of different ethnicities, dressed much like we were, covered the walls from top to bottom. Music notes. Musicians playing instruments, and glasses and bottles filled with drinks. It all depicted fun. Flash. And the promise of a good time.

At the bottom we stopped in front of a large black metal door. I could hear the music now, a faint but steady beat knocking against the other side of the door as if begging to be set free.

"There's a button under the railing," Rose said, pointing to the stair rail my hand rested on. "Press it."

I slid my hand beneath the polished wood and felt around until I found it, and then pressed and watched as a slender slot in the door opened. Gus slipped a card through and, after a series of clicks, the heavy door swung open.

I was hit by a wall of noise as I blinked, my eyes adjusting to the dimly lit space.

Music, voices, glasses hitting tabletops, laughter, and chair legs scraping against the floor as people got up to dance filled my ears and Rose pulled me inside and I tried to get my bearings, feasting on something that, until this moment, I'd only heard about but never witnessed.

The decor was black with flashes of red, the lighting from the iron chandeliers low. Tables covered in red tablecloths with candle centerpieces arced around a small dance floor and a black-skirted wood stage where the musicians were set up. Above us smoke hung in the air, low and heavy.

The scent of cologne and perfume, alcohol and sweat filled my nose while the music beckoned. A trumpet, bright and intense, took the upper register, while a saxophone, low and warm, cushioned and filled the in-between spaces. A piano flirted, but it was the bass…

It pulsed low and sultry, pulling me under its spell, urging me to come in, have a drink, find a partner, move…

Rose pulled on my hand and we began to weave through the crowd, careful not to step on toes or spill drinks.

I was tentative, almost wishing I could tuck into a far corner and watch the scene from a distance so I could take it all in without worrying about being seen myself in my borrowed, ill-fitting dress and scuffed shoes. But after a moment I forgot myself, focusing instead on the people around me.

And oh, the people. I tried not to stare, but it was nearly impossible. Never in my life had I seen so many different cultures under one roof socializing, drinking, and dancing together.

The women were painted up like us, rouged cheeks, lined eyes, and dark lips. Some of the men too I saw with surprise. I took in hairdos, makeup, jewels, bow ties, hats, and shoes. But it was the dresses that drew my attention. Fringes and sequins, feathers and beads, shoulder straps thin and wide, and necklines demure and plunging. Straight lines, draping, capped sleeves, high hemlines, satin, geometric patterns, pearls—so many pearls!—and more. I was mesmerized, making notes in my mind as I gathered and dismissed the details I loved, liked, and hated.

As we broke through the other side a woman called out, "Rose!" and we made our way toward a redhead sitting at a table next to the dance floor where couples danced so close, I was embarrassed to look. This wasn't just cheek to cheek, this was body pressed to body, and in some cases, mouth to mouth.

"Sit," Rose commanded and I sat beside the young woman who had waved us over. "I'll be right back!"

As Rose disappeared back into the crowd, the woman leaned toward me across the table.

"I'm Ginny!" she shouted over the noise.

"Zora!" I shouted back.

She reached across the table to shake my hand, and then turned her attention to the dancers while I admired everything from her soft auburn curls and the black shimmering band encircling her head, to the sexy draped neckline of her dress that revealed some, but not everything.

"What can I get you gals?" I turned in my seat to find a young Black woman standing beside me, hair in a sleek bob, lips painted a deep plum, her wine-colored dress shimmering under the lights. She stared at me, notepad in hand, pencil poised, an expectant look on her face.

I looked to Ginny who pointed to the empty mug in front of her. "I'll have another," she said.

The woman looked to me again and I felt my cheeks warm. I'd never had an alcoholic drink before and had no inkling how to order one.

"We'll take two beers," Rose said, sliding onto the chair next to me.

"You got it," the gal said, scribbling our orders and then moving on to the next table.

"They only serve one thing here," Rose said and then looked from me to Ginny. "Did you two meet?" Ginny nodded and then jumped to her feet as a man approached, one hand held out to her, the other gesturing to the dance floor.

"Ginny used to dance at the Alhambra but got a job at another club," Rose explained, scooting her chair closer to mine so she wouldn't have to yell as loud. "She's a beautiful dancer. She trained in New York as a ballerina."

Another young man approached the table and bent toward me.

"You wanna dance?" he asked. I winced at the familiar scent of alcohol on his breath and coming out of his pores. It reminded me of my father and I shook my head. He shrugged and looked at Rose who also shook her head.

"I made that mistake once," she said as he stumbled away. "He's always half-seas over and a little too handsy for my liking."

I wrinkled my nose and then sat up straight as the waitress returned with our drinks. Rose immediately took a sip of hers, but I stared at mine, unsure.

"You alright?" Rose asked.

I looked at her and she gave me a soft smile as she reached across the table and put her hand on my arm.

"You are not your pa, Z. You are not trying to drown your

anger and embarrassment in alcohol. It's one drink. I promise I won't let you get in a bad way."

"Will it make me feel different?" I asked, eyeing the dark liquid. I wanted to be like everyone else in this room, carefree and only focused on one thing—having a good time.

"It will," she said. "But not too different so long as you take your time and balance it out with water. And food! We'll make sure we get something in our bellies, as well. I can't get too tipsy myself or I won't be able to dance."

She nodded then, encouraging me to try a sip, and so I did, my eyebrows raising as the warm, bitter beer slid over my tongue.

"Whaddya think?" she asked.

"It's…different," I said, and she laughed.

"You'll get used to it. And we'll get you something tastier at the Alhambra. I promise," she said.

We sat and watched the dancers then, Rose leaning over from time to time to point out people she knew, dresses she thought I'd like, and making faux shocked faces as some of the couples danced in a racier style, making me blush into my drink.

Ginny returned with flushed cheeks, fanning herself with her hand after several rounds of dancing with different gentlemen every time the tune changed.

"My toes have been stepped on, my backside pinched, and I nearly got hanged by one of my necklaces," she said, plunking into her chair. "It was great!"

Rose's eyes met mine, which had been wide with horror until Ginny's last exclamation, and we laughed.

"So, what do you think?" Rose shouted to me as the band started another song, this one a quick tempo and drawing even more bodies to the floor.

"It's incredible," I shouted back.

"What do you think of the band?"

I peered through the bodies on the dance floor. Onstage was an all-Black band with a female singer in a sparkling red dress belting out a song in a deep, sultry voice. Behind her was a man on trumpet, one on trombone, a saxophone player, a guy on bass, and a pianist. I had nothing to compare them to, but from where I sat, they sounded spectacular.

"They're wonderful," I said.

"The one playing trumpet is Ellis," she said, her smile faltering a little. I turned back to watch the man who had captured my friend's heart.

He was mesmerizing. Eyes closed, body moving, he played with complete abandon, lost in the music. When he finally took a breath, the crowd hollered their appreciation and he flashed a smile, his eyes finding Rose. He winked and then placed the horn back on his lips and began to play again.

I could feel Rose's eyes on me, waiting. Waiting for me to comment. To pass some sort of judgment. Ellis was not what I'd expected when she told me a few weeks ago she'd met a boy and was quite possibly in love.

Coming from where we did, the poor part of town, it wasn't strange to share a classroom with kids of different colors and races. It wasn't odd to play together at recess or say hi when you ran into one another at the store. But in the wealthier parts of town, where Rose's family had moved and beyond, it had become less acceptable, and sometimes downright dangerous. Nice white people could turn violent at just the mention of such a relationship. And that's what worried me for my friend.

I could tell down here, within the confines of the club's walls, where some women dressed like men and danced with other women, some men wore more makeup than I did and danced with other men, and races mixed without hesitation, a love affair between Rose and Ellis wasn't any big thing. But what about in daylight out on the streets?

Maybe she knew something I didn't.

"He's really good!" I shouted.

Her eyes burned bright as she nodded, a huge smile on her beautiful face.

"Horsefeathers!" she said, clasping her hands in front of her chest. "He's the bee's knees."

As the night went on and I gingerly sipped at my drink, young men stopped by our table constantly, vying for our attention with offers of dances and drinks.

I shook my head time and time again, happy to watch Rose and Ginny dance instead. I wasn't ready yet. I didn't even know the steps, though they didn't look too hard. But I also didn't like the thought of dancing with a stranger, the idea of his hands in mine or on my body making me shudder.

"You having a good time?" Rose asked as she took her seat again after dancing with her friend Gus. She took a long sip of her drink, her wide blue eyes watching me over the rim.

"I am."

I took another small sip. My head was buzzing a little and everything had taken on a slightly blurred sensation, from the sound of the music to the sight of the faces around me. At first the feeling frightened me, but when another young man came by and asked me to dance and I declined, I knew I was still, mostly, in my right mind, and took comfort in that.

The music changed then, becoming slower and more seductive. I felt like a young girl witnessing something taboo as some of the couples danced with the man's front against the woman's back, swaying seductively, eyes closed. I blushed and fidgeted with the garter beneath my knee, the handle of my mug, trying to find something else, anything else, to rest my gaze on.

But a few minutes later the music picked up again and the bodies separated, swinging and kicking and twisting around the floor, as if the intimacy of the moment before had been merely a dream. And maybe it had. It was hard to tell with alcohol fuzzing my brain.

After a while the music stopped and the musicians left the stage, Ellis heading straight for our table as Rose stood to greet him.

"Ellis," she said, gesturing to me. "This is Zora. My very best friend in the whole wide world. Zora, meet Ellis Jones."

He was even better looking up close, and was dressed handsomely in a crisp white shirt and a beautiful dark gray vest and matching trousers with a sheen that glowed under the lights.

"How do you do, Zora?" He grinned and held out a hand. "Rose talks about you all the time."

I smiled and shook his hand.

"I'm sorry to hear she's been boring you," I said and he laughed. "It's a pleasure to meet you, Ellis. I'll admit I don't know much about jazz music, but from what I heard, I'm impressed."

"That's kind of you. But I did notice you weren't out on the dance floor."

"I don't know the dances," I said. "And, it turns out I'm a bit of a wet blanket."

At that he laughed so loud people at the table next to us looked to see what the commotion was about.

"You go at your own pace," he said. "Don't let anyone force you to do anything you don't wanna. Right, Rosie?" He put an arm around her shoulders and she grinned. It was then that I noticed those same people at the table beside us frowning and whispering as they stared at the two of them. Rose and Ellis didn't seem to notice, but my heart sank. Prejudice apparently made its way down the stairwell after all.

Ellis kissed Rose's nose and then held out his hand to me again.

"I have to get back to it," he said. "But I suppose I'll see you later at the Alhambra?"

"Will you be playing there too?" I asked.

"Nah. I just go to see my gal."

"Well then, I'll save you a seat."

He exchanged a look with Rose and then gave me a polite smile before kissing her cheek.

"It was a pleasure to meet you, Zora," he said. "Ladies."

With a last grin, he disappeared into the crowd.

We sat back down and I looked over at Rose who was watching Ellis's retreating back, a wistful look on her face. I didn't judge, but I had a feeling others did and, whatever she was dreaming up in that pretty head of hers might not come as easily as she was imagining.

6

"We'd better scram," Rose said as she hurried off the dance floor, her latest partner following close behind, clearly hoping to continue the pleasure of her company. She glanced over her shoulder at him as she grabbed her purse. "Not now, Sal." She waved him off. "You ready?"

I nodded and stood, picking up my own bag and waving to Ginny.

"Nice to meet you!" she called, giving us a wave.

I followed Rose through the dark club, weaving through cigarette smoke and bodies glistening with sweat, my body buzzing with the little bit of alcohol still coursing through my veins.

She waved and called out to people as we went, and then we were through the metal door and running up the stairs, our heels clacking on the steps, the sound of the music fading behind us before it was cut off by the heavy door thudding closed.

Outside, the quiet of the night and the cool, clean air jarred my senses.

Linking her arm through mine, Rose led me back the few blocks we'd come two hours before, and then turned down another alleyway past a small Japanese drugstore.

A back door this time, another staircase down—this one without murals—and yet another door, wood instead of metal.

Rose pounded three times and the slot in the door opened, a pair of sinister dark eyes peering out. A moment later the door swung open and a large man with slicked-back black hair in a navy pinstripe suit and a bright red tie stood staring down at the two of us.

I glanced at Rose nervously, my palms damp, and then jumped as the man shouted, his lips splitting into a huge grin.

"Rosie!" he said, enveloping my petite friend in a hug until I could only see a few of her blond curls. "I was beginning to think you weren't going to make it."

"You know I like to run in as last-minute as I can," she said with a grin and then pointed to me. "Frankie, this is my best gal, Zora. Zora, if you get into any trouble, Frankie will take care of you."

"Right as rain, Miss Rosie. You know I will. It's a pleasure to meet you, Miss Zora," he said, offering me his hand.

"It's lovely to meet you, Frankie."

He turned then to survey the room. "Looks like a twosome off to the right is leaving. Better hurry and grab the table. The crowd will be pouring in soon with the show about to start."

"Thanks, Frankie," Rose said. "Come on, Z."

The Alhambra was larger than the Bucket, the decor warmer, with tables covered in white, little gold lanterns lighting the center of each one, and brass chandeliers above, giving it an overall cozier feeling. I felt wrapped in the warmth of the music coming from the stage and the ambience of the lighting, the slow, almost hypnotic movements of the dancers on the floor, lost in the low, sexy moan of the saxophone.

"I go on in twenty," Rose said as I took a seat. "We have six numbers and then I'll be free for the rest of the night. Order a drink. I'll pay for it. I get a deal for dancing. And try to relax. Talk to people. Everyone's real nice here, I promise."

She turned to go, the club lights glinting off the beads of her dress, looking like the sparklers we lit on the Fourth of July.

I grabbed her hand.

"Wait!" I said.

"Yeah?"

"What do I order? Is it only beer again?"

She grinned.

"Try a Mary Pickford. It comes with cherries."

I raised my eyebrows and she laughed and hurried away with a wave.

I ordered my drink when the waiter came by and then turned my attention to the couples dancing while listening to bits and pieces of conversation nearby and praying no one would ask me to dance. A silly wish to have in a club that basically existed for two reasons: drinking and dancing.

"Care to dance?"

I looked up at the gentlemen proffering his hand before me, peering into a pair of familiar blue eyes, slicked blond hair, and small, turned-up nose. An uneasy feeling settled in my stomach. Ricky Wells.

"Hello, Ricky," I said, my voice flat.

His eyes widened.

"Zora?"

His eyes swung down my body and I shifted in my seat, pulling the neckline up and waiting for the disparaging comment that had always resulted from our meetings.

"You sure are a sight for sore eyes," he said. "How long's it been?"

I wanted to say not long enough. Ricky Wells had never been kind to me or my family when we were in school, making fun of my patched-up dresses and worn shoes. When my daddy got into the accident our last year of school, I overheard him telling his friends that folks as poor as us would surely be on the street soon, but his family could probably spare us a blanket and a pillow or two. It hadn't helped that his father was a policeman and had oftentimes been the one to bring my father home after finding him drunk and passed out in someone's doorway.

"Not so long that I've forgotten your kind offer of a blanket and pillow when my father was injured," I said, smiling brightly.

"I don't know what you mean." He took a step backward. "Nice to see you again," he mumbled before turning and nudging the two girls behind him to move along. I recognized them as well, hangers-on who'd joined him in tormenting me all those years ago.

"Who was that?" I heard one ask before he led her to the other side of the club by her elbow.

"Well done," a voice, deep and accented, said from behind me.

I turned, prepared to fend off another dumb boy, and found myself looking into a pair of eyes that could only be described as mischievous. Sparkling. And amused.

"I'm sorry?" I said, wiping the thin layer of sweat from my brow as my heartbeat picked up speed.

I remembered once hearing an older girl at school tell a group of us, "Girls, there are boys…and then there are men. And that—" she'd pointed to a broad-shouldered male jogging casually on the track as other, smaller boys shoved one another and laughed riotously "—is a man."

The gentleman sitting at a table alone behind me would never be mistaken for a boy. Even sitting I could tell by the fit of his jacket that he was well-built and tall. His wavy dark hair was slicked some, but not too much, giving him a rakish, almost dangerous look, and his pale eyes stayed respectfully on mine instead of sweeping over me like those of every other man I'd encountered tonight. He had an aristocratic nose, which was a tad crooked, making me wonder if he'd gotten in a fight in his youth, and his lips…

"I said well done," he repeated, nodding toward Ricky. "He's not a nice chap, that one. You did well to be rid of him."

The accent was British, and I could tell by the cut of his shirt and jacket that they were expensive. I wondered if they were designed by Brooks Brothers, or maybe even Gucci, and I was suddenly very aware of how inelegant and cheap I must look, despite Rose's pretty dress and my carefully painted face.

"We attended school together," I said.

"My condolences."

I couldn't help but notice the way his eyes crinkled in the corners when he smiled. My heart, racing a moment ago, nearly stopped. He was the most handsome man I'd ever seen.

A waiter placed my drink before me, nearly spilling it in my lap as he took in the man seated behind me.

"Can I get you anything, sir?" he asked.

"I believe you just delivered a drink to this young lady. Perhaps you should ask if there's anything more she needs first?"

"Of course," he said, almost falling over his feet as he turned back to me. "Miss?"

"I'm fine, thank you," I said, gingerly taking a sip of my drink and delighting in its light effervescence before plucking one of the cherries out by its stem.

The waiter gave a little bow and hurried off.

"Did he bow?" I asked.

"Indeed, he did."

"Are you…" I was suddenly mortified. The accent. The clothes. Was this man part of the royal family? I sat up a little straighter and plunked the cherry back in my drink, spilling a little as I did so.

"I can see your wheels turning," he said, his lips curving up on one side. "But I assure you, I am merely a common man."

"Somehow I don't quite believe you," I said, feeling plainer than ever as I fidgeted with the napkin beneath my drink.

"As we've just met, you are smart not to." Again with the half smile. "Actually, we haven't met, have we. How rude of me. Please excuse my appalling manners."

He stood and came around his table, his hand held out. I placed mine in it, inhaling sharply as my skin brushed against his calloused palm, his warm fingers wrapping around mine.

"Harley Aldridge," he said. "And you are?"

"Zora."

He raised an eyebrow.

"Just Zora?"

I was about to tell him my last name, but there was something about him, his playful nature maybe, or the accent and expensive clothes that made him seem so elegantly out of place in this underground Seattle club, that made me want to keep it to myself for now.

"Just Zora," I said.

"Well then, the mysterious Just Zora, it has been a pleasure meeting you. But now I must be going." He reached for his hat and coat, placed the hat on his head, and tipped it toward me. "I do hope you enjoy your evening."

"You're not staying for the show?" I asked. "Or the..." I gestured to the floor of dancing couples.

"No," he said, looking almost amused by the suggestion.

"Too lowbrow for you?"

"You assume a lot about me." He peered down at me, pausing as he seemed to consider what to say next. Rather than dismiss me as someone undeserving of an explanation, he continued. "I come here for business purposes. I then enjoy said business purposes—" he lifted the glass he'd been drinking from and then set it back down "—and the music. And then I take my leave."

"Sir!" The waiter was back. "Are you leaving? Can I get you anything else?"

"I am indeed leaving," Harley said. "In which case, I have no need for anything else."

"Of course," the young man said. "My apologies. Miss?"

I was hungry, but I shook my head. I didn't want to spend any more of Rose's money, and wasn't sure what the meager amount I'd brought would buy me.

"No, thank you."

"Are you sure?" he asked, glancing at my drink. "Another Mary Pickford?"

"No, thank you. The one is plenty."

"Well, if that's the case, when you're finished with your drink, I must ask you to move to a place at the wall to clear the table for our drinking patrons."

"Oh," I said, feeling my cheeks burn. "Of course."

But Harley shook his head.

"The lady will keep her table. Bring her a drink on me, and when she's done with that one, if she doesn't want another, bring her water for as long as she chooses to stay."

"Of course, sir," the young man said and then bowed as he had before and hurried away.

"You didn't have to do that," I said, my voice barely audible above the din.

"As a snob, I can easily identify another. But besides that, he was rude. You've ordered a drink, you've secured a table, why shouldn't you have a right to sit here all night?"

"Still," I said. "That was very kind, after I was less so to you. Thank you."

"No thanks needed. Enjoy it, and your night." He nodded down at me. "Until we meet again, Just Zora." And then, with a little bow that made me laugh, he turned and disappeared into the sea of bodies.

A few minutes later, as the floor was cleared for the girls to come out and dance, my drink arrived, followed by a tray of canapés, deviled eggs, and fruit cocktail.

"Oh no. I didn't order that," I said, shaking my head.

"From Mr. Aldridge," the waiter said.

I peered through the crowd and saw Harley speaking with

Frankie, the doorman. As he turned to leave, he glanced over his shoulder at me. The electricity I'd felt earlier crackled across the distance, and then he was gone.

"Oof," Rose said as she fell into the chair next to me some time later, crossing one leg over the other and slipping off a shoe to rub her foot. "My dogs are barkin'."

It was the quietest it had been since we arrived as the band made their way back to the stage after the cabaret show had cleared out.

"You were fantastic!" I slurred, my lips numb.

Rose peered at me, then noticed the two empty glasses nearby, cherry stems at the bottoms.

"Zora Lily Hough! You're zozzled!"

"I am not," I said. "Wait." I frowned, staring at her blurred face for a moment, and then nodded. "Yes, I think I am. But you were still fantastic. All that fringe and the beads…so sparkly."

Rose laughed and surveyed the table again, a look of worry shadowing her face.

"Did you order all this food?" she asked.

I shook my head. "Yes. I mean no. Don't worry. A nice man bought it for me."

Rose popped one of the ham canapés into her mouth as she took a look around the room.

"He left before the show," I said, trying to focus my blurred vision. "Very handsome. Maybe a prince. Definitely royalty. Definitely a snob."

"Zora, my love." She shook her head. "What are you talking about?"

"Harley."

"Harley?" Rose's eyes widened and she leaned forward. "Harley Aldridge? Zora, did Harley Aldridge buy you this food?"

"Yes. Prince Harley. Do you know him? He's handsome,

but a snob. Said so himself. Though he didn't really seem like one. He told the waiter I didn't have to leave the table and bought this food for me after all." I swept my hand over the tray of food that I'd only managed to eat a quarter of and nearly spilled my water, but Rose got a hand on it in time, snorting delicately as she did.

"Harley Aldridge is not royalty, but he might as well be. His family is rumored to be quite wealthy. I've heard they own property in Britain and all over Europe. You actually talked to him?"

"I did. Right after that stupid Ricky asked me to dance."

"I saw Ricky." Rose wrinkled her nose and then propped her chin on her hand, blue eyes wide. "Tell me what Harley said to you."

"He didn't say much. He made sure the waiter paid attention to me and warned me off of Ricky. He was nice."

"Nice?"

"Yes," I said, ignoring her probing gaze. "But also a little too…" I narrowed my eyes as I searched for the right word. "Too *much*."

"Too much?" she asked, giggling.

"Yes. *Much* too much."

"Okay. Definitely no more drinking for you tonight." She shook her head and then glanced at the tray of food again. "I can't believe Harley Aldridge bought you food. The man arrived in town two months ago and his name is on everyone's lips. Every woman I know is trying to land him, but no one can claim to have exchanged two words with him. And then here you are, your first night out in the big city, and he engages in conversation *and* buys you food and drinks. How do you rate, Zora Hough?"

I shrugged and took a bite of a canapé that had a swirl of some sort of yellow cream, the green sprig on top falling to my lap.

"Of course, I don't know why I'm so surprised," Rose said. "You are quite refined."

The music started up again and despite my protests, Rose dragged me to the floor where she taught me to do the Charleston and twirled me around until I was dizzy and holding on to her for dear life.

When a slow number came on, she pressed her cheek to mine and we laughed as we danced, our faces smashed together, her leading me badly around the dance floor, bumping into the other dancers and receiving dirty looks in return. At one point we narrowly avoided a young man and his date. He looked up from beneath his fedora and I realized he wasn't a man at all, but a woman in a wide-legged pair of trousers and a white button-down with flared cuffs. She winked and I grinned sloppily back and kept dancing with my friend.

We finished off the food, and by the time we climbed the stairs to leave, I was sweaty but sober once more.

"Well," Rose said as we stepped outside into the cool air and stopped to breathe it in. "What did you think?"

My body was tired but lit from within, memories of sparkling dresses and drinks, smoke hanging like a blanket from the ceiling, laughter and horns and the beat of a drum swirling in my mind.

Behind us the music played on, but the club was now at half capacity, most of the partygoers stumbling out around us.

"The clothes were amazing," I said and she rolled her eyes. "It was as fun as you promised it would be."

"Does that mean you'll come again?"

"One day," I said with a sigh, the guilt at lying to my mother nagging at me.

"She'll never know," Rose said.

I laughed. "Stop reading my mind."

"I've known you too long not to know exactly what's going on in that head of yours, Z."

I grinned and she gave me a hug.

"I'm glad you came," she said.

"Me too."

We drove home, Rose humming quietly as I stared out the window, watching the lights begin to fade behind us.

"Ellis didn't come," I said, remembering he'd said he would. I looked at her profile as she drove, wondering if it bothered her that her beau had broken his promise.

"It happens sometimes," Rose said. "The band starts drinking after they're done and one drink leads to another. I don't mind. He always makes sure he's there the next time."

"He's nice. He has a nice feeling about him."

"He does, doesn't he?"

"Just…be careful, okay?"

"Don't worry. Ellis wouldn't dream of hurting me."

"I don't mean him."

"Oh," she said, nodding. "You mean all those snooty white folk giving us dirty looks."

"It's not just them, Rose. It's people like Ricky and…" I'd noticed some of Ellis's musician friends and the women I assumed were their girlfriends looking at the two of them at the other club like they didn't approve. I was worried they'd make trouble for the couple.

"It's fine," Rose said. "I promise. Please don't worry. We can handle the looks and the things they say."

"They say things? Like what?"

"Never you mind. We have it in hand."

I pursed my lips, worried that Rose was avoiding something she shouldn't be. But what did I know?

As we drove past my street, I leaned forward to look down the road to my house, reveling a bit that I wasn't inside asleep in my bed like usual, but out living my life with my best gal. But as I looked for the familiar plain wood house, ice filled my veins.

"Rose," I said, gripping her arm.

"Hmm?"

"Rose. Stop the car."

"What?"

"Stop the car!"

She hit the brakes and I braced myself on the dashboard. We looked down the street to my house where several cars, including at least two police cars, were parked in front.

"Z?" she said.

"Go!"

She cranked the wheel and swung the car around, skidding to a stop behind one of the many cars.

We hurried out, slamming the doors and running across the yard, up the steps, and through the front door to a wall of people, their backs to us as they stood silently in the sitting room facing what I assumed was my mother getting bad news about my pa.

"Zora?" Sarah whispered from behind me.

I turned and met my sister's eyes, which were red and puffy from crying.

"Daddy?" I whispered and Rose grabbed my hand.

She'd known how I'd dreaded this day, assuming it would come sooner or later. There didn't seem much choice the way he drank so much, came home at all hours, and had run up tabs all over town.

But Sarah shook her head.

"Zora?" my mother said from somewhere in the crowd. "Is that you?"

The bodies parted and I stared at my mother…sitting beside my father on our tattered old sofa. Her gaze swept over me and I shrank a little as Rose moved in closer, offering support as Sarah's hand wrapped around mine.

"What's happened?" I asked, confused by the sight of my father who looked more sober than I'd seen him in months.

My mother's face crumpled then, and she pressed a fist to

her trembling lips as Pa put his arm around her, his own eyes wet with tears.

"I'm sorry to be the bearer of bad news, miss," one of the officers said. "Earlier this evening there was an accident at a logging camp up north. Your brother Tommy was killed."

I didn't realize I was falling until my knees hit the floor.

7

The funeral for Thomas Alcrick Hough took place on a damp and gray Saturday afternoon, seven days after the accident. It was attended by our immediate family, a couple dozen men from the logging camp and sawmill, his girlfriend, Jennie, and her parents, and Rose's family.

The pastor, a man who had known Tommy his whole life, spoke of Tommy's hard work, kind spirit, and loyalty to both his friends and family.

"A good man willing to give up his education to care for those he loved."

Daddy shifted his feet at the words and Mama leaned into him. I wondered if it was to comfort him, or to hold him up. I could smell the alcohol from five people away.

As the plain wooden coffin was lowered into the ground, both Jennie and my mother broke down in sobs, and Harrison and Eva, clinging to Mama's legs, began to wail. Sarah and Hannah stepped forward to comfort them, but I found myself unable to move, my hand clasped around Lawrence's arm as it had been for the entire service. I glanced up at him now and found his eyes red-rimmed and staring at the coffin where the big brother he'd revered lay inside. As it disappeared into the earth, he took in a long, shuddering breath and I wrapped my arms around him.

"I'm so sorry, Lawr," I whispered.

I was sorry for him. For me. For all of us. For the brother we'd lost. For the future ahead, certain only in its hardship.

I looked then from one sibling to the next, the responsibility of feeding them all, clothing them all, heavy on my shoulders.

"It's going to be okay, Z."

I smiled at the smell of Rose's signature scent and let it wash over me as I reached a hand for hers and she laced her fingers through mine.

Lawrence kissed my head and gave Rose a small nod before jogging off to fetch Harrison who had run across the small cemetery, chasing after a squirrel.

I turned to my friend and searched her wide blue eyes, looking for answers. For strength to draw from. Something that would get me through this next part. Because I was positive I wouldn't be able to get through it without her.

"I don't know how we're going to do it," I said, worriedly watching Hannah lift Eva into her arms and cradle her there. Eva at five was sturdier than Hannah at thirteen, who was a slip of a girl that we oftentimes joked might blow away on stormy days.

"We'll figure it out," Rose said, squeezing my hand. "There are good jobs for young women out there. I promise we'll find one for you. Mama's been asking around and she's already found a couple things you might be interested in."

"She has?" I looked past my friend to her mother who was talking to mine and grasping her hands.

"She wasn't going to bring it up today," she said and gestured to the gravesite.

"Of course."

"But perhaps tomorrow you can come by for lunch."

I nodded and looked toward the grave where Jennie was

kneeling, shoulders shaking, her parents standing on either side of her. She and Tommy had been going steady since their last year of high school. When Pa had his accident and Tommy dropped out of university to become a logger, her father tried to convince her to stop seeing my brother. But she wouldn't have it.

"I will be a logger's wife. A scholar's wife. A clerk's wife. Or even a trash collector's wife!" Tommy had told us she'd shouted at her father. "I don't care what he does for work. I only care that he's decent and kind and that he loves me, because I love him!"

We'd already adored Jennie, but her unabashed and defiant love for Tommy that day made her an unofficial member of the Hough family.

"I wonder what she'll do now," Rose said, her voice low. "Her whole future was wrapped up in Tommy."

"I suppose she'll do like the rest of us," I said. "Try to move forward as best she can, but without the best part of us." My voice broke then and the shock of his death hit me like it hadn't before, my knees threatening to give, a pit of despair opening in my belly and threatening to swallow me whole. I was racked suddenly and violently with tears and Rose pulled me to her, hugging me fiercely as I cried on her shoulder.

When my tears finally subsided, I pulled away and looked up into the face of Jennie, her own face red and streaked with tears. We hugged for a long time and then she said she had to go.

"You're not coming to the house?" I asked. Rose's mom had organized food for anyone who wanted to come by and give their condolences. There were pictures of Tommy set around the living room and some of his favorite items, all of which had made me want to run and hide and pretend this wasn't happening. That he'd be back any minute. That he'd just gone out with friends.

But he wouldn't be. And he hadn't. And every time that knowledge returned, it hit me like a punch to the gut.

I gave Jennie another hug and she promised to come by soon, but for some reason it felt like a lie.

After she wandered across the cemetery with her parents, I gave Rose a sad smile.

"I need a minute," I said and she nodded as I stepped away to stand alone beside Tommy's grave, staring down at the box in which his broken body lay,

"I miss you already," I whispered. "I wish I'd known when you left that day it would be the last time I'd see you." I sucked in a breath and swallowed, willing myself not to cry. "I can't believe you're not gonna pound on my door tomorrow morning and scare me to bits and tease me about all the boys I don't even like. You and Rose have always been the only ones who really saw me. I don't know what I'm going to do without you. I love you, Tommy."

I couldn't say more, choking on tears that were like waves pushed forth by an ocean of sorrow.

I dropped my little bouquet onto the plain wooden coffin, watching as the flowers I'd picked that morning from a hillside we'd run up and down as children scattered across the surface. My shoulders and head heavy, I turned to find Rose waiting for me, my youngest sister's hand clutched in hers.

"Ready?" Rose asked.

"Ready," I whispered.

Back at the house I sat in a corner with Rose, keeping watch over Eva and Harrison who were eating cookies a neighbor had brought, and playing with the new doll and truck Rose's mother had bought for them.

"It will help keep them distracted while the grownups talk," she'd said to Mama when she'd tried to refuse the gifts.

After a while, the six of us Hough siblings that were left drew like magnets to one another, huddling together in our small living room. Rose, whom we'd adopted long ago as honorary sister, sat along with us.

I listened as she chatted with everyone, asking them questions about their school year, what they were looking forward to doing this summer, and if any one of them could touch the tip of their tongues to their noses—which prompted some much-needed laughter.

When it was time for her to go, she reluctantly stood and hugged each child goodbye before turning to me.

"I am going to help you through this. I swear it."

"I know, Rosie. Thank you."

She held me for a long moment, her familiar perfume washing over me like a salve.

"Come by for lunch tomorrow. Mama's expecting you," she said and kissed my cheek.

8

At one o'clock the following day I had lunch at the Tillers' house, where we ate sandwiches filled with meat and cheese, drank tea, and devoured a small plate of cookies while Mrs. Tiller told me about a family looking for a new nanny.

"The Harringtons are a prominent family," Mrs. Tiller said, stirring a small cube of sugar into her tea and stirring delicately. "They came from New York two months ago and the nanny they brought with them ran off with a boy back to New York last week. They have two young kids and are desperate. Mr. Harrington works in finance, and his wife has a hand in nearly every organization the city offers. The pay is exceptionally good but..."

"But what?" I frowned.

So far it sounded great. I'd been helping take care of my younger siblings for as long as I could remember. I could change a diaper, make meals, and sew a torn hem.

"It's live-in."

"Live-in?" My brow furrowed.

"Yes. So you can get up with them in the morning. You'll have evenings and weekends off."

"Evenings *and* weekends?"

"As I said, they're prominent. As in wealthy. Very wealthy. They employ a nighttime nanny and a weekend nanny, as well. It's perfect for you, Zora. You can use the evenings to design and have your weekends free to sew, come home and see your family, or—"

"Or come out with me!" Rose said, causing Mrs. Tiller to chuckle and shake her head.

My mouth opened and closed as I considered the position. Live-in meant moving out of my own home. Live-in meant not as much freedom in some ways, exceptional manners at all times, probably another shared room, little to no privacy, and definitely no deciding at one in the afternoon to have a quick lie-down. Unless it was the weekend.

"All meals are included," Mrs. Tiller continued. "And if they go on vacation, they'll take you with them."

She was trying to wrap it up like a gift now. And it was. If I got the job.

"Oh. And you get your own room."

Now that was a gift.

"How do I apply?" I asked.

"Mrs. Harrington is expecting you at three."

I looked down at my dress and then back up at Rose and her mother.

"You can borrow something of mine," Rose said.

Mrs. Tiller looked at her watch. "You haven't much time if you want to catch the streetcar into town. Rose—"

But Rose was already on her feet, pulling my hand.

Ten minutes later I was in a pale blue dress with a dropped waist and white collar. I wore a simple ivory cloche with a satin rosette on the side, and a slightly too-small white pair of heels Rose found in the back of her closet.

"You look lovely," Mrs. Tiller said when I came down the stairs. "Best hurry now. You don't want to be late."

"Thank you, Mrs. Tiller," I said. "I promise I won't embarrass you."

"I wouldn't have recommended you if I thought you would, dear."

Four minutes before the hour I stood on the doorstep of a gothic Victorian home, staring at the impressive front doors before me. I was intimidated by the sheen of the paint, the little lion head door knocker, and the large light fixtures on either side. Even the greenery sitting in ornate urns unnerved me. We kept flowers in a few small chipped pots, but these were the size of my younger brother, Harrison.

I lifted the heavy knocker and tapped it twice, then stepped back, my hands clasped in front of me, and waited.

The gentleman who opened the door a moment later had a neatly trimmed mustache and was tall, thin, and wore a crisp black suit. I smiled hesitantly and he grinned in return, his manner less stuffy than the clothes he wore.

"Miss Hough, I presume?" he asked.

"Yes, sir," I said.

"Please come in." He stood aside. "I'm called Smith. May I get you something to drink while you wait for the lady of the house?"

I glanced down at the pale dress I wore, afraid in my nervousness I'd spill anything I was handed down the front of it.

"No, thank you," I said.

He nodded and led me to a large brightly lit study.

"Please have a seat. Mrs. Harrington will be along shortly."

"Thank you, Smith."

"My pleasure, Miss Hough."

He held up crossed fingers, gave me a wink, and closed the doors behind him.

I barely dared sit, afraid I'd leave a crease on the surface of one of the chairs when I left or somehow sat in the wrong spot. I chose the far end of a sofa and tried to make myself light as a feather while staring in awe at the opulent room. My hand brushed lightly over the soft velvet of the emerald-colored fabric beneath me, my neck rotating as I took in each item and piece of furniture adorning the space. It was unlike any room I'd ever been in, from the sofa I perched on, to the plush dove gray armchairs across from me, several mirrors hanging from the walls, and paintings I didn't understand. All the tables in the room were glass-topped, and behind me were shelves upon shelves of leather-bound books in an array of colors.

"Miss Hough?" a woman's voice asked and I shot to my feet, taking in a diminutive woman who looked not much older than me.

"Yes, ma'am."

"I'm Mrs. Harrington." She walked to me and held out a dainty hand, her pale fingers reminding me of Hannah's, though she wore several rings on hers, and Hannah's were often covered in ink that had rubbed off on her skin from the pages of the books she read.

As we shook hands, I took in the champagne-colored day dress she wore with its modest neckline, long sleeves, and lace overlay. It was elegant, refined, and the fabric expensive. Nothing less than what I'd expect from the lady of this house.

She motioned to the little sofa I'd risen from. "Please. Sit. Tea?"

As she asked, an older woman in a starched uniform arrived with a delicate-looking tea set and placed it on the table before us.

"No, thank you," I said as the maid took leave and Mrs. Harrington poured herself a cup. She carefully placed a single sugar cube inside the hot liquid, the sound of her tiny silver spoon reminding me of a tune from a music box I heard once as it brushed against the sides.

She was Southern, she told me as she sat, hailing from Savannah, Georgia. As did her husband. They'd met when she'd been formally presented at the traditional debutante ball.

"He was the kind of man who stood out. Elegant, handsome…a real charmer." She gave me a little grin. "All the girls were jealous when he asked me to dance."

She was kind, showed glimpses of a wicked sense of humor, and was a bit fussy, constantly straightening the cuffs of her sleeves, crossing and recrossing her legs at the ankles, patting her hair, twisting her rings, and fluffing the throw pillow beside her.

"We moved to New York shortly after marrying," she continued, taking a sip of tea. "But Jonathan liked the idea of coming out West. He wanted to be part of helping Seattle grow, and he has the mind to do it. I was just beginning to learn a bit of the business myself when the nanny up and left. Thankfully we have the other two nannies to fill in until we find another permanent girl, but one's older and not quite up to the task of caring for the children full-time, and the other doesn't want the daytime responsibilities."

I nodded my understanding and she went on.

"The children are…" She shrugged her slim shoulders and laughed, a tinkling sound that reminded me of a spoon against crystal. "Well, they're children. That about says it all, doesn't it?" I smiled. "I understand you have younger siblings?"

"I do. Five of them."

"Gracious!" she said, pressing a hand to her breast. "Your mother must be a saint. The patience she must have. Perhaps I should have her over for tea and ask how she manages?"

"She manages by delegating. She's quite clever, my mother."

"She must be," she said and clasped her hands in her lap. "Well, I understand from Mrs. Tiller you don't have references other than what she and your mother can tell me. I normally require at least three professional referrals, but I'm in a bit of a pickle and I trust Mrs. Tiller implicitly. Plus, I have a good feeling about you." She lowered her voice then. "But if my husband ever asks me in front of you, I will lie through my pearly whites and tell him there's a list a foot long of people singing your praises." She winked then and took another sip of her tea, blanching prettily. "The tea has grown unpalatably tepid. How about I give you a tour of the house, let you meet the children, and show you where your room would be, should you decide to take the job, and inform you of the rules of the house. You can tell me all about you and your experience as we go, but from what I've been told, we'd be lucky to have you, so please do think about it. And please consider saying yes."

"Yes, ma'am."

The house was enormous and I wondered how she managed in her fancy heeled shoes when my lower-heeled ones had begun to rub around my ankles by the time we climbed to the third floor.

I lost count of the bedrooms after five, each decorated in a different color scheme, as well as the sitting rooms, of which there were at least four. There were dozens of wall sconces, lamps tucked in every corner, window coverings in a variety of expensive fabrics, and flower arrangements displayed prominently in nearly every room. The kitchen, outfitted in the newest appliances, looked as though it could feed an army, the dining room like it could seat them. And I was positive the nursery, consisting of the children's two rooms, a play area and the nighttime nanny's room in between, and a bathroom, was bigger than the entirety of my parent's house.

"The children are outside getting some fresh air," Mrs. Harrington said as she stopped to look out a window, adjusting the tasseled tiebacks and removing a piece of lint before turning and smiling at me. "Which means tormenting the neighbor's dog. I'll show you where your quarters would be and then we'll go find them."

My quarters, should I accept the job, would be up a narrow staircase to the third floor.

"There are three bedrooms up here, a small sitting room, and a large, shared bathroom," she said and then opened a door and waved me inside.

"Oh," I said, trying not to gape at the pale blue and white decor, the filmy white curtains waving in the breeze of an open window, and the large bed that would be only for me.

There was a small sitting area off to one side, a large armoire, a vanity, a separate writing desk, and in the bathroom a tub I was positive I could stretch the full length of me in and still have room.

"Is it to your liking?" she asked, and I nearly laughed at the worried look on her face.

"It's lovely."

"Wonderful." She clapped her hands. "Let's find the children."

Madeline and Willem, four and six respectively, were giving the weekend nanny a run for her money as they bolted along the fence line, antagonizing the neighbor's dog that was barking up a storm.

"What did I tell you?" Mrs. Harrington said. "Every day they bother that poor dog. The last girl did nothing to dissuade the behavior. Mrs. Larson, who usually works the weekends only, can't keep up. I'm hoping, if you take the job, that you might find other uses for their energy?"

"My youngest siblings used to do something similar. I have several tricks up my sleeve to help keep them occupied."

We watched them for another few minutes, and then Mrs. Harrington called them over to meet me.

"Zora, this is Mrs. Larson, the children's weekend nanny. And this is Madeline and Willem. Children, this is Miss Zora."

"Good afternoon, Mrs. Larson," I said, nodding to the harried-looking older woman, her gray hair coming loose from the bun at her nape, before taking in her charges. "Hello, Willem and Madeline. It's very nice to meet you both."

"Hello, Miss Zora," Willem said.

There was silence as we all waited for his sister to respond in kind.

"Madeline?" Mrs. Harrington said.

Her brother elbowed her and I pressed my lips together at the younger sibling's look of indignation. I could tell she was the scrappier of the two, and would happily retaliate were there not three pairs of adult eyes on her.

She took in a little breath, gave a little huff, and presented me a begrudging greeting. While her mother and nanny discussed a detail about the afternoon schedule, I suppressed a laugh as Madeline shot her brother a look. Eva and Harrison would've been in an all-out war, regardless of the audience. I was impressed by this little girl's ability to suppress her anger. But wondered if there'd be payback later.

"Shall we return to the house?" Mrs. Harrington asked.

I gave a nod, bid the children and Mrs. Larson goodbye, and we walked back across the yard, Mrs. Harrington listing again all the duties she'd expect from me.

"Morning wake-up, have them dressed before breakfast—they'll try to convince you not to make them, but please don't give in, it will make getting Willem off to school on time that much harder. While he's gone, depending on this weather that can't seem to make up its mind, you will either take Madeline for a walk or do a quiet activity inside. Reading time, lunch, nap time, and then Willem will return. Another walk or bit of play outside, and then dinner, after which they'll need to be sent straight upstairs to be bathed by the night nanny."

"They bathe every day?" I asked as we entered the house and I followed her back to the study.

Her eyes widened slightly and then she caught herself, the surprised lines in her forehead smoothing as she remembered not everyone, especially not the young woman in borrowed clothes standing before her, had opportunity to bathe daily.

"Yes. Every day. You'll have your evenings free after the children have had their supper, and of course the weekends off, as well," she said. "I shan't work you to the bone, you'd quit on me. When the children were babies, I only employed one nanny at first and learned rather the hard way that working one person twenty-four hours a day, seven days a week, is actually quite cruel. Even five days is a lot. But I suppose you've been doing all that to help out your mother, so you well know that having time to yourself is not only a necessity, but crucial for one's peace of mind."

"I do indeed."

She went to her desk, an ornate piece of furniture with flowers engraved in the wood, and pulled a single sheet of paper from a drawer.

"These are the house rules," she said, handing me the list. At her expectant gaze, I skimmed through it. "The most important items are probably quite obvious to you. No stealing, and no guests. Not even family members. We must set a precedence in our home. If everyone were allowed to invite guests and something were to go missing… Well. It's best not to even have to consider the consequences. Don't you agree?"

"I do," I said, reading the note at the bottom of the page that stated going against any one of the rules was grounds for dismissal.

We walked to the front of the house then and said goodbye on the front porch.

"When will you let me know?" she asked. "I'm keen to have a new nanny straightaway and, while I've interviewed a few other women, there's something quite nice about you, Miss Hough. You have a pleasant disposition and, I don't know why, but you feel trustworthy."

"Thank you," I said. "In all honesty, I'd be a fool to say no. I need the work. But also, I think I'd do well at it."

Mrs. Harrington clapped her hands together, a hopeful look on her face.

"Is it settled then?" she asked.

I took in a long breath, looked up at the enormous, elegant home, and then at the lady of the house.

"It's settled," I said.

"Oh!" She grabbed both my hands in hers, squeezed, and then quickly let me go, a pretty blush lighting her cheeks as she straightened her cuffs and adjusted her watch. "I'm sorry. How undignified of me. I've been so worried finding another nanny would be terribly hard, but that Mrs. Tiller sure knows her people. I'll make sure to find her again should I have other needs."

"She'd be most honored," I said. "When shall I start?"

"Is the day after tomorrow too soon?"

"That sounds fine."

"Wonderful."

Rather than return home on the streetcar, Mrs. Harrington insisted her driver, Charles, take me.

"I'll return for you in two days' time," Charles told me as he pulled up to my house and got out to hold the door open for me. "Say nine o'clock?"

"I'll be ready," I said.

"You have a good day, miss."

"I think I just might." I smiled.

And somehow, despite the reason I had to go in the first place, it had been a good day.

9

"Two days?" Mama said, her eyes moving from the dirty dishes left from lunch on the dining table, the kitchen beyond where a bucket of soapy water was waiting for someone to grab the mop and clean the floor, to the sitting room where old toys that had been passed down from one kid to the next were scattered.

"It'll be fine, Mama," Sarah said, appearing like magic from the shadows as she always seemed to. She wiped her hands on the apron she wore and bent to pick up the ball Harrison had rolled her way. "I'll take on Zora's chores and Hannah can do mine."

"Huh?" Hannah said, glancing up from the book her nose was buried in at the sound of her name being spoken.

"I don't know," Mama said, chewing her full lower lip.

At first glance she was a plain woman, but I remembered looking up to her as a little girl. How I'd loved to run my fingers through her long, pale brown hair that she wore down more often than not in those days—until baby Sarah was born and the mere idea of leaving her tresses free of the tight knot she began wearing it in seemed unfathomable.

She had wide hazel eyes, which Tommy, Hannah, and Harrison had inherited, a smattering of pale freckles one wouldn't suspect were there until you got up close to her, high cheekbones, a small, straight nose, and lush lips I imagined boys had dreamed of kissing when she was in school. But her appearance went unnoticed these days, mostly due to her constantly furrowed brow, pale skin, the shadows beneath her eyes, and the hard line of her set jaw as if always in wait of bad news.

I noticed now the lines on her forehead, the gray in her hair, and the leanness of her body—always taking less food so that her children would have more. But she was strong too, despite the lack of nutrition. In spirit and in body. Lillian Hough had been born a fighter. No matter what life served up, she dealt with it head-on.

A sharp snore from the couch startled me and I looked over at the diminished yet bloated form of my sleeping father. I sighed, saddened by the state of him, the man he'd become after knowing the man he'd been. He, unlike my mother, was not a fighter. At least, not since the accident. Shame had wounded him far worse than the rogue log that had pummeled him.

I wondered if Harrison or Eva would ever remember how he'd carried them on his strong shoulders and swung them to the ground so easily with one arm. How dashing he'd seemed when he'd come home bone-tired from the logging camp, with a twinkle in his eye and a bag of treats he'd picked up on the way, laughing at Mama as she tut tutted him for spoiling us, before turning away with a grin on her face. Or would they only remember this version of him? The way he grunted every time he moved as if it were hard just to exist. How his face was always red, his skin aged and haggard, his eyes watery, lips cracked, hair greasy, alcohol seeping from his every pore. It saddened me to think this shell of a man was all they'd be able to conjure in their mind one day when they thought of their pa. But it also angered me. They deserved so much better than this weak soul who had succumbed to his vanity. Who couldn't bear to face hardship and so had drowned it in the illegal drink he sought out every day no matter the hour and despite his lack of funds to purchase it. He owed everywhere and for the past two years Tommy had settled his debts. But now… Now it would be up to me.

"Two days, Mama," I said. "I know it's soon, but they need the help and we need the money. The sooner I get to work, the sooner I can help with the bills."

She waved a hand, as if brushing off the very hard fact of our poverty. "We don't need—"

I reached for her hand and held it tight in my grasp.

"We do."

Her eyes met mine then and my chest ached as I watched a tear trace a lone path down her cheek. I'd seen my mother cry three times in my life. Once late at night after father's accident when she didn't think anyone was still awake. The second time when Tommy died. And now, as she relinquished the idea in her head that a miracle was going to keep me from having to support the family now.

"It should be me," she said, her voice a rasp.

"Just keep sewing," I said. "Teach Sarah. She's good but she can get better."

"And faster," Sarah said.

"I'll come home on the weekends to help out," I said. "But between Sarah, Lawrence, and Hannah, you should have enough help to keep the house clean, get food on the table, and have the little ones looked after."

She nodded and wiped the tear from her face.

"You're sure about this, Zora? I hate to think of you living in someone else's house, tending to their every need, being treated like you're less than they are. You're not and you never will be. I can try to figure something else out. I just need time to think."

"This is a great opportunity, Mama. I promise I'm okay with it." I ignored the twinge of guilt as an image of a room of my very own with a bed I didn't have to share flashed in my mind.

"I'm sure there will be parts I don't enjoy, but there's no part of the job I can't handle."

"If they treat you badly, you quit and come straight home, understand?" Mama said. "Your misery is not worth the money they pay you." She reached for my hands this time and held them tightly to her chest. "Promise me."

"I promise," I said, meeting her pleading gaze. "Now, I'm going to wash up and Sarah and I will get dinner started." I looked to Hannah, her eyes flying over the words on the pages of the book she read. "Hannah can help too. And then tonight and tomorrow I'll finish up the sewing jobs waiting for me."

"What will I tell the women who come looking for you to fix their fancy gowns?"

"Tell them I'm only available on weekends now. If they can't wait, they can find someone else."

The next two days were a whirlwind, Sarah following me and Hannah following her as chores were written down and demonstrated and then performed by the girl they were being passed on to.

"But I can't reach!" Hannah said, holding a feather duster and staring up at a corner of the living room.

"If you don't," Sarah said, "spiders will form webs there and make a home."

Hannah shuddered. She hated the eight-legged creatures and screamed bloody murder anytime one had the misfortune of crossing her path.

"Fine," she said, looking around the room. I smiled at Sarah as our younger sister dragged Mama's step stool from the kitchen, climbed up, and gave the duster a twirl before stepping back down with a huff and another shudder.

As us older children divvied up the household tasks, Eva decided she wanted a job, as well.

"I can do stuff too!" she said, tiny hands on tiny hips, a wet rag leaking through the hand-me-down overalls that had been passed down from Harrison the year before.

"You bet you can," I told her, giving a stern nod as I removed the rag she'd taken from the dirty mop water. "Let's see, what can Eva do, gang?"

A few minutes later, armed with the broom, she set off to sweep the front porch.

"Harrison?" Sarah asked. "Do you want a job too?"

"No thanks," he said, rolling a truck across the floor.

On the eve of the day I was to leave home for the very first time, I sat with my suitcase open on the bed before me, staring at the sad state of my belongings.

"You won't be very far away," Sarah said, her voice soft as she stood in the doorway looking at me.

"It's not that," I said with a wry smile. "Just look at what I have to bring into that fancy house!"

She snorted and plunked down on the other side of the case, taking a look at what I'd packed.

"It's grim indeed," she said. "Want to borrow my green sweater?"

"But then what will you wear when the weather turns?"

She shrugged. "I have your old blue one."

"I packed that," I said and she reached over and smacked me on the arm.

"You'll be making money in no time," she said. "And didn't you say there's a uniform?"

"There is, but what if I want to meet Rose and go out? You know how people are."

"I do," she said, giving a sad smile.

All our lives we'd been teased for wearing the same clothing over and over again.

"Is that a new dress?" someone would ask, and then elbow their friend and laugh. "Oh no. You wore the same thing yesterday!"

It was mortifying and had happened nearly my whole life. But despite being used to it, I didn't want to be seen leaving the fancy Harrington home wearing the same dress every time. It was demeaning, no matter what Mama said.

"Other people's opinions aren't our business," was her motto.

"And yet she gets angry when we don't take hers into account," Tommy had mumbled to me once, causing me to laugh so hard I choked on a mouthful of peas at the dinner table.

Tommy.

I sighed. What would he think about all this?

"It won't last," Sarah said, reaching across the suitcase and squeezing my hand.

My eyes filled with tears. That was Tommy's line. I nodded. "It won't last," I said.

Smith arrived with the car at nine on the dot the following morning and the entire family, minus Pa, saw me out the door.

"You'll be home Saturday?" Mama asked.

"Friday evening if I can," I said.

She sniffled. "I never imagined I'd lose you like this. I figured some silly boy would steal your heart. That's what should've happened."

"Oh, Mama."

"Never mind." She gave her head a little shake and then hugged me to her. "You'll do fine. Just do as you're told and keep your head down. And remember your manners."

"I will, Mama. I promise I'll make you proud."

"You always have."

I hugged everyone else in turn while Charles put my suitcase in the trunk, and then he opened the back door and I climbed in and waved as we drove away.

"You've a fine family, Miss Zora."

I smiled, watching them out the back window. Mama was herding the younger two, Hannah wandering around the side of the house, a book in her hands, and Lawrence and Sarah were still standing in the street, watching me go.

"They're the best part of me."

"Nah," he said. "They're *a* part. But not the best part."

"How do you know?"

"No other person should ever get credit for being the best part of who you are. They may have helped shape you, lent you ideas, shown you other possibilities, but you are *you*. Simple as that. Know your worth, girl. Because the world you're going to will make you feel small if you let it. Don't let it. Don't let *them*."

We pulled up to the Harrington estate a little while later and I watched as Charles opened the trunk of the car. My suitcase looked tiny inside it, swallowed by the opulence of its surroundings.

"Don't forget what I said," he whispered, handing me the case. As my hand wrapped around the handle he held fast until I met his eyes. "Promise me."

I looked at the suitcase, up at the massive house before us, and then at Charles.

"I promise."

And with that, I walked up the back steps of the great house and over the threshold into my new life.

10

"Miss Zora! Watch!"

The days were now filled with pleas of this nature. *Miss Zora, watch! Miss Zora, look! Miss Zora, can you get that? Miss Zora, get the ball!* Always with a tug of a small hand on the hem of my starched pale blue nanny's uniform, the toes of their shiny shoes stepping on mine, leaving scuffs for me to buff out as soon as my shift ended.

I smiled and pressed a finger to my lips, then nodded at Willem to proceed in showing me his new acrobatic feat—which ended in him tumbling over sideways and his younger sister Madeline falling over with unrestrained laughter.

Even though we were outside, the elder Harringtons preferred that their children weren't too loud. Coming from a household where one had to shout just to be heard over everyone else, I was constantly amused by this. But in this house, everything was quiet and tasteful. There was no running, no heavy walking, no smacking of lips, or slurping from cups or bowls.

I'd always been self-conscious around those with more than me, but now I found myself nervous about how loud my steps were, how hard I closed a door or cabinet, and how I chewed and swallowed.

It amazed me how well the children took to these stringent rules. I couldn't imagine myself at their age not having a hearty laugh, or one of my other siblings regaling the rest of us with some noisy bodily function. But the Harrington children were well-behaved and well-mannered—with a healthy dose of mischief they saved for when they were out of earshot of their parents.

Despite being intimidated by my surroundings, the many breakable vases and statues begging to be knocked over by any small misstep or wayward elbow, the furniture that looked as though it had never been sat upon or had a drinking glass put on it, the spotless rugs and gleaming wood and tiled floors, I'd gotten into the routine of the household and my job easily enough.

In the mornings I woke a good hour before the children and set about choosing their clothes for the day from their large walk-in closets. A dress for Madeline, and button-down shirt and trousers for Willem. They were to look proper at all times. No stained knees, cuffs, or shoelaces. If he came home from school untidy, I immediately set out something clean for him to change into.

After they woke, used the facilities, washed their hands and faces, had their hair tidied, and got dressed, we quietly—no stomping please—made our way to the dining room where they took their breakfast with their mother and Mr. Harrington, if he hadn't already left for work.

While they dined on fine china beneath the sparkling light of a crystal chandelier, I hurried to the dining area just off the kitchen that was set aside for the help.

It was easy work, but exhausting, and I relished my evenings alone in my room, just me and my sketchpad, or one of my siblings' articles of clothing that needed mending. I sometimes brought a few items back with me from my visits home that needed more than a simple fix. I'd sit in the armchair in the corner of my room, a snack I'd brought up from the kitchen beside me on the round end table, and breathe with the rhythm of my needle piercing and sliding through the fabric.

The first few days in the Harrington household were pleasant enough as I got to know the rest of the staff. The head maid, Mrs. Beckwith, was a kindly woman with a neat auburn bun at her nape, perpetually rosy cheeks, and a uniform so stiff with starch, it was a wonder it didn't break whenever she moved. The butler, Smith, was in and out at mealtimes. Charles, Mrs. Harrington's driver, had the least time to dally, but could often be found holding court at the far end of the table and regaling whoever would listen with tales of where he'd taken the lady of the house the day before.

The night nanny, Evelyn, and the weekend nanny, Mrs. Larson, were seen the least. Evelyn's job was the most lenient, consisting of sleeping in a small room between the two children's should one wake and need water or soothing from a nightmare. Her days were free and she often flitted in to grab a quick bite in the morning before heading out to meet with her friends, her mother, or her beau. Rumor was her fiancé had died in the Great War and her parents couldn't take her back in. She'd lived in a boarding house and worked washing dishes for another family before the Harringtons moved to town and hired her.

Mrs. Larson arrived early Saturday morning and left late Sunday evening after getting the children off to bed. We'd only crossed paths a handful of times. The first the day I'd interviewed, the second so she could instruct and train me, and only haphazardly after that.

I got along well with everyone, except the younger of the two maids, with whom I suspected trouble was on the horizon. Of what nature, I couldn't be sure, but it was clear from the first moment I met Elsbeth Pritchard, her sapphire eyes sweeping from my head to my clothing to my shoes, a look of disdain on her pretty but pinched face, that she didn't like me. I was further convinced by her line of questioning that came at me like small daggers.

"What family did you work for before coming here?" she'd said almost immediately upon us meeting, arms crossed over her chest, eyes squinted.

I'd glanced to Mrs. Beckwith who sent her eyes skyward and shook her head.

"I didn't work for another family," I said, feeling my face warm at my lack of experience in such a household.

"I'm curious how then you got the job. Not just anyone can work for the upper echelons of society without having experience or an important connection of some sort. Are your parents acquaintances of the Harringtons?"

I nearly laughed at the question.

"I—um… I was recommended by the mother of a friend."

"The *mother* of a *friend*?" Her eyes moved over me again. "What's your surname? Would I know your family?"

If I were Rose, I would've laughed and fired off a stinging retort. But I wasn't Rose. I was just a girl from the wrong side of town once again trying to fit in somewhere I very clearly didn't.

"You wouldn't," I said, my voice soft.

"I suppose the Harringtons must be trying something new. Maybe it's charity. Or perhaps you owe a favor?"

When I didn't answer she sniffed delicately, brushed her hands down the front of her uniform, and stalked on silent feet from the room.

"Don't mind her," Charles said. "She's been here five months and is quite put out that her efforts to succeed Mrs. Beckwith haven't played out."

"She seems…nice," I said, dabbing at the sweat on my upper lip as he chuckled.

"If nice means conniving, then you're spot on."

"Do you think I have anything to worry about?" I asked,

chewing my lip and staring at the door Miss Pritchard had disappeared behind.

"She doesn't want your job. She can barely stand being within twenty feet of the children. But I wouldn't put it past her to make your job harder."

"Why?"

"Of that, I am not sure. Her motives are a mystery. But the last girl to fill your shoes wasn't nearly half as pretty or sharp and Elsbeth ran her off quite quickly."

"I thought the last girl went back to New York to be with her boyfriend."

He folded his newspaper and stood. "That was the story she gave Mrs. Harrington. But we all knew it had something to do with—" He motioned to the door Miss Pritchard had disappeared behind. "My advice to you? Don't keep anything of value in your room, don't say anything too personal about yourself, and have your clothes sent out to be cleaned. It's an extra expense, but if she gets her hands on them, they most likely won't be returned in a condition you prefer."

"My clothes aren't all that nice to begin with," I said with a grin.

"Not all that nice and unwearable are two different things."

"But—how does she get away with it? Wouldn't Mrs. Harrington find out?"

"One would think. But Miss Pritchard can be very convincing. And no one else ever sees her do the misdeeds."

"Clearly you know though."

"I do. It turns out I'm easily ignored. Dismissed. Unimportant. People find it easy to say the most outrageous things around me, either because they think I won't tell, or I'm so inconsequential they don't think anyone would believe me if I did."

"That's awful."

"Ah, but is it?" He winked. "It affords me the knowledge to tell you to watch your back, does it not?"

"Did you warn the last girl in my position?"

"I did not."

"How come?"

"Because like Miss Pritchard, she wasn't very nice."

"Why have you told me?"

"Because you, Miss Zora, are like me. You come from nearly nothing. You work hard, have good manners, and treat others with respect, no matter who they are or what they come from. And that, my dear girl, will get you far in life. Not to mention in my good graces." He winked.

"How come *you* don't say something to Mr. and Mrs. Harrington?" I asked.

"About Pritchard?"

I nodded.

"Biding my time, girl. Biding my time." And with that, he patted my shoulder and swung out the door.

Forewarned, I refrained from adding my laundry to the collection basket set out for me each Friday. Instead, I scrubbed my uniforms in the bathtub when I bathed, hung them to dry, and pressed them myself. Whatever clothing I wore home for the weekend I cleaned when I returned Sunday evening. When I partook in community meals, I spoke about nothing personal, smiling and nodding and laughing along as other people shared, but keeping my own stories to myself. No one knew how many siblings I had, or that I spent my evenings drawing dresses, blouses, and hats. I was quiet, polite, and as far as they knew, had no interests or friends. And as for having anything of value in my room, well, unless she found rocks, pictures drawn by my siblings, and a chipped glass vase valuable, I couldn't imagine she'd take anything. Though, a few days after Charles and I talked, I did wonder if she might take my sketchbooks. The very idea made my heart skip a beat and so when I woke the next morning, I padded in my bare feet to the small writing desk and removed them from the drawer, placing them instead in the space between the wall and the headboard of my bed.

While I enjoyed my job and most of the household staff I spent my time with, it was a relief to leave every weekend.

"Headed home?"

I smiled at Mrs. Larson as she herded the children out of their rooms and pointed down the hall, watching as they obediently headed for the stairs. It was only when she turned her attention back to me that I saw Willem pull Madeline's braid and Madeline yank the back of his shirt free of his trousers. I pursed my lips in an effort not to laugh.

"I am," I said, falling in beside her in the wide, airy hallway.

"Any plans while you're there?"

I gave her a sideways glance and she smiled. Despite her strict style, she was a sweet woman with three grown children of her own. Out of all the household staff, only she and the nighttime nanny knew what I got up to on the weekends, as we often exchanged small talk intermixed with details about the children in our brief talks before one or the other of us took charge.

"Just to help out," I said.

"More sewing projects?"

I'd only told her I helped Mama with projects, not that it brought in extra income for our busy household, or that I knew anything more about sewing other than fixing hems and tears. Mentioning the need for money was personal, and not something I wanted to get back to Miss Pritchard, who I could feel constantly waiting to pick up any personal crumbs I accidentally dropped.

"Always," I said.

"Your family must go through clothes on a tear," she said as we hurried down the stairs after the children, who had picked up speed at the heavenly smell of baked goods wafting through the house.

"We are a busy bunch," I said.

"Isn't that how it always is," she said and then gave me a wave as she disappeared through the door to the dining room.

I exited the house through the servants' door on the side and ducked my head against the rain. Hurrying down the brick path, I breathed in the scent of Mrs. Harrington's roses as I went. They were prize-winning blooms, I'd been told, and I didn't doubt it as I had never seen such full and vibrant flowers in all my life. I touched a pale yellow petal as I rushed by, and then lifted the metal latch on the gate and stepped through to the sidewalk on the other side.

"Just Zora?"

I turned in surprise and found myself looking up into the handsome face of Harley Aldridge, the man I'd met the night I'd gone to the clubs with Rose.

The night Tommy died.

It was hard to believe it had been just over a month. It felt as if it were a lifetime ago. So much had changed so fast. But the wound left by his death was still raw to the touch, and seeing Harley made the memory of the police cars in front of our house come flooding back.

"Mr. Aldridge," I said, giving him a nod and then, on a whim that would've made Rose proud, I dipped into a shallow curtsy.

His mouth quirked on one side.

"I'm never going to live down the actions of that imbecile, am I," he asked, his warm British accent settling cozily around me.

"I'm afraid not," I said, feeling my face warm at my impromptu joke.

He was even more handsome in the daylight, cloudy as it was, his eyes catching the light, his dark hair curling slightly from the damp in the air over the collar of his light tan suit jacket.

A drop of water fell from a leaf above, landing on my cheek, and he gestured for me to join him beneath his umbrella.

But standing beneath an umbrella with a man I only knew by name, and barely that, felt a bit too familiar. Sure, Rose would've done it without a second thought. But I wasn't Rose.

"Thank you," I said. "But I have to run."

He didn't move, the umbrella still poised, waiting for me to stop being foolish and take cover.

I sighed and stepped forward, trying to ignore the little flutter that arose in my belly as I stood inches from him, the warmth of his body reaching for mine.

"You're friends with the Harringtons?" he asked.

"I..." I looked down at the sidewalk between us. "I work for them. I'm their nanny."

I waited for the polite response laced with disdain as he realized he was talking to a mere servant.

"Why, that's splendid," was what he said though, and I looked up as he leaned in. "Unless they're awful to work for and Maddie and Wills are little terrors when company isn't around. Come on, tell me the truth."

I laughed, completely disarmed. No wonder all the ladies at the club swooned over him.

"They are lovely employers. And the children are very well-behaved. Are you good friends then?" I asked, noting his nicknames for the children.

"We are," he said. "I met Jonathan when he and Mirabel were in London for their honeymoon eight years back. We wrote back and forth for years and would meet up in New York or Europe when our schedules allowed."

"That sounds lovely."

His eyes flitted over my face and he gave me another smile, but this one seemed a bit less bright, finally realizing, I assumed, that he had better things to do than talk to a poor servant girl.

"It was," he said, his voice soft. "Have you ever been?"

I snorted indelicately.

"I think we both know the answer to that."

"I've no idea what you mean, Zora..." he trailed off, a question at the end of his sentence, and I smiled.

"Zora Hough," I said.

"Miss Hough." He inclined his head. "So, no trips to the South of France or drinking wine in Tuscany?"

"If only. But you are a true gentleman to assume I've led such a life."

"Well, as a gentleman, I must insist you let me walk you to wherever you're going. I would be letting my countrymen down were I to let that beautiful hat get ruined."

I touched the cloche covering my hair and grinned.

"It's a kind offer," I said. "But it's unnecess—"

"Nonsense. It's miserable out here today and only getting worse. Please?" he said. "I'll feel a cad if you don't allow me to be of assistance. Plus, they might take my British citizenship away."

"They'd do that?" I asked, my eyes wide in feigned shock.

"Off with my head."

There was something conspiratorial in his eyes. His teasing different than the torment I'd received from other boys in my life.

"Well, we can't have that now, can we," I said and nodded down the street. "I'm headed for the streetcar."

"The streetcar," he said, his brow furrowing. "Right. And where might that be?"

I couldn't help it. I laughed. Of course, this man with his square jaw, wearing his elegant suit jacket, the rain hardly daring to touch his trousers and shoes, didn't know where the streetcar was.

I pointed. "Four blocks that way."

"Well then, let's be on our way, shall we?"

He offered his arm and I was about to decline when a loud clap of thunder shook the air and I grabbed hold, glancing at the sky with trepidation.

"Perhaps we should move at a quick clip?" he asked. I gave him a grim smile, nodded, and we were off.

At the corner we stopped, looking for a sign of the odd car driving by. As I stepped off the curb to cross the street, I glanced over my shoulder at the Harrington house. In the drawing room window stood Elsbeth Pritchard. My stomach turned. Despite all my best efforts to not let her know hardly a thing about me, I'd just given her something to use. It wouldn't matter that Harley Aldridge was nothing more than an acquaintance. She would find a way to use it against me, of that I had no doubt.

11

As soon as I returned to my room in the Harrington house the following day, I noticed a rock missing from my desktop. Since there were only three, each one picked for me with meticulous concentration by my youngest brother over the past couple of years, it was easy to spot that the smooth red pebble was gone.

I was perplexed, but with no other difference in my routine, I could only conclude that Miss Pritchard had seen me with Mr. Aldridge and, for reasons known only to the young maid, that brief meeting had warranted an attack. A small one, but one she assumed would cause me pain.

I quickly determined it would only feed into her satisfaction should I confront her, or if she heard me asking around to the others. And so, despite losing the small stone, which Harrison had told me with great seriousness he thought had come from another planet, I kept quiet as if I hadn't even noticed its absence.

It was during my sixth week on the job that Mrs. Beckwith interrupted me while I enjoyed a break from running after Madeline with a lunchtime meal.

"There is someone here to see you, Zora," she said.

"For me?" I asked, regretfully setting down my sandwich. It was filled with two kinds of meat, cheese, a thick slice of tomato, and some kind of spread that had made me moan out loud the first time I'd tasted it.

"Cook is a wonder, is she not?" Smith, the butler had asked, a satisfied smile beneath his mustache as if he himself had made it.

Mrs. Beckwith nodded and motioned toward the side door.

I hurried to the door and pulled it open, grinning immediately at the familiar face on the other side.

"Took you long enough," Rose said, smiling in the sunlight, her big blue eyes, free of makeup, were wide as she took me in from head to toe. Without the eyeliner, rouge, and mascara I'd grown so used to seeing her in, she looked like a teenager. This face was the Rose of my childhood. The Rose of schoolyard jump rope contests (I always won), and wild blackberry eating competitions (she claimed that title).

"You look adorable," she said.

I lifted one side of my uniform skirt and curtsied.

"What are you doing here on this gorgeous spring day, and how did you know to come to the side door?" I asked.

"My friend Millie works for the Dennys. I know all about side doors." She gave me a wink and I shook my head.

"I don't even want to know about what other side doors you've been frequenting, Miss Tiller."

"You're probably right about that!"

I clapped a hand over my mouth as her face went from teasing to pleading.

"Come out tonight," she said.

"Oh, Rose." I sank against the door frame. "I don't know. I'm going home tomorrow for the weekend and—"

"You go home every weekend! Your mother can't need you that much with the money—"

My eyes widened and I shook my head, then tilted it toward the room I'd just come from.

"Sorry," she mouthed.

"Mama's trying to tuck some aside," I whispered. "She's never been able to save anything and now she can."

"Are you at least saving a little for yourself?"

"I am," I said. I had my sights set on a small sewing kit I'd coveted since the first time I'd seen it in the window of the fabric store near my parents' house. That and maybe a new dress. Or a pair of shoes. Perhaps a coat.

"Good. Then you can come out tonight!"

I rolled my eyes, but I was tempted, remembering the music, the drinks, everyone dressed up so glamorously, the glimmer of the lights dancing across the surface of people's drinks...

"I have nothing to wear," I said. "No makeup. No idea how to do whatever it was you did to my hair before."

Rose waved a hand. "I'm staying at my friend Jessie's tonight. She has a tiny apartment three blocks from the Alhambra. You can borrow something of hers, I already asked."

I chewed my lip. I wanted to go and she knew it, a wide grin spreading across her face.

"I can't be out too late," I said.

"Of course not," Rose said, backing away, already knowing she'd won.

"How do I get the dress?"

"I'll come by and fetch you around six. We'll get ready at Jessie's. I'll do your hair and makeup."

Before I could say another word, she turned and disappeared behind the branches of the blooming shrubbery along the garden path.

After I handed the children off, I hurried out of my uniform and got in the bath, quickly washing my hair and body before dunking the starched dress in with me and giving it a good scrub too.

My body wrapped in a towel, wet hair sending rivulets of

water over my shoulders and down my arms, I wrung out the uniform, placed it on a hanger, and left it above the bathtub to dry. I'd iron it Sunday night when I returned from my parents' house.

At five forty-five, I stepped lightly down the back staircase and peeked into the kitchen where Cook was standing before a large, steaming pot, her cheeks red from the heat.

"Stew?" I asked, sniffing at the air, my mouth watering. I wouldn't have time to eat much before Rose showed up.

"Soup," she said, giving the broth a taste. "Damn fine soup too, if I do say so myself."

"Any bread to go with it?"

She tilted her head and I looked to the far counter where a tray of rough-shaped biscuits sat cooling.

"May I?" I asked.

"Take two," she whispered. "But don't let anyone else know I said that."

"Thanks, Cook."

"Nothin' to thank me for, hon. I didn't see anything."

I grinned and wrapped one of the rolls in a napkin and shoved it in my purse, then grabbed another and took a huge bite, waving as I made my way down the hall to the servants' side door.

"Where are you off to?"

I jumped at the sound of Pritchard's voice and turned to find the young woman sitting alone in the corner, a book in her hands.

She was pretty, though I'd never tell her that, her straight chestnut hair cut in the bobbed style that was all the rage, nose small and straight, blue eyes bright, belying the look she was giving me.

"Out," I said.

"That much is obvious," she said, closing her book with a little snap. "Which is why I posed the question *where* are you off to. As I was already certain you were headed out."

Besides the fact that she was nosy. And a thief. And acted as though she were better than the rest of us. It was the way she talked to me that made me angriest.

"I wasn't aware I had to inform you of my whereabouts," I said, giving her a tight grin as I worked to keep my voice level.

"I get the feeling you aren't aware of many things," she said. "But you're right. You don't have to tell me. I was just curious and being friendly."

I nearly snorted but held it back. And though I was in no way interested, I found myself asking—

"Why?"

"I happened to notice your little interlude with one Mr. Harley Aldridge the other day."

"And?"

"I thought it very timely is all."

I held in a sigh. "I ran into him on the sidewalk. He insisted on walking me to the streetcar since it was raining and I didn't have an umbrella."

"Mmm," she said. "Well, one would hate to see you get your heart broken."

"Whatever do you mean?" I asked, understanding just fine, but wanting to hear her poisonous words for myself.

"You're not his type, Zora. Anyone can see it. Even you aren't that stupid."

"And what is his type?" I asked, clenching my hand around the handle of my purse. I wasn't the least bit curious, but I was angry that she would say such a thing and dying to hear her interpretation of a man I was sure she had no real inkling about.

"Someone from a respectable family, to start with," she said, studying my face. But I gave nothing away as I waited for her to go on. "Someone with fine manners and good breeding, who knows about the finer things in life. Who can appreciate them. I mean, what do you know about keeping a staff to run a household? Or how to furnish a home appropriately? All the lunches and parties that need to be thrown. The dinner menu to keep up on. The clothing to wear." At that last one she sent a disparaging glance down my worn dress to my scuffed shoes.

"Not that it's any of your business," I said. "But I have no interest in Mr. Aldridge. And not for the reasons you so helpfully listed. As it turns out, he's not *my* type."

"Let me guess," she said. "You like them a bit rougher around the edges, with dirt under their fingernails from a hard day's work, and the scent of sweat on their skin?" She shrugged. "I guess one can't blame you when that's all you've known."

I bristled but kept the smile on my face. Just as I was about to respond there was a knock at the door. Turning, I pulled the door open and smiled gratefully at Rose, who had impeccable timing.

"Ready to go?" she asked, glancing past me and giving Pritchard an undeserved Rose Tiller smile. "Hiya."

"Hello," Pritchard said, getting to her feet, her gaze flicking over Rose and dismissing her with a smirk.

Rose looked at me and raised her eyebrows. She'd heard about the young maid during one of my weekends home and I watched her sweet smile turn dangerous.

"We should hurry," she said, her voice a decibel louder than it had been previously. "I hear Harley has offered to buy drinks for the entire club tonight."

My mouth opened, unable to believe her gall. I'd pay for that later, Pritchard would make sure of it. But in this moment, I didn't care.

"Well, then," I said. "Let's be off, shall we?"

And with that, I closed the door and raced, laughing, beside Rose all the way to Jessie's place.

12

The club was just how I'd remembered it, the music, stifled by the thick door, drifting up the staircase low and beckoning. Then the burst of sound as the door was opened, before we were swallowed, swimming through the smoke and perfume-scented air that was the sparkling belly of the Alhambra.

I was less intimidated this time, but barely, holding fast to Rose's hand as she followed Jessie through the crowd, the lights undulating across the metallic fabric of their dresses as they waved to people they knew, kissed cheeks, all while still moving us along until we broke free on the other side.

"Looks like we're outta luck on a table," Jessie said, peering around the room. "Let's check the back."

She was a petite girl with an admirably curvy figure, eyes the gray-blue color of the sky on a stormy day, lush lips, light olive skin that gleamed under the lights, and dark blond hair cut in the stylish bob nearly every woman was wearing these days. Outspoken, sassy, with a love of teasing, she was a slightly darker version of Rose, which I told my friend.

"We joke that we must've been separated at birth," she'd said.

The back room was a departure from the front, with a bar at

the far end and low jewel-colored tufted sofas and chairs perfect for lounging…and necking. The three of us found a place to stand at one end of the bar and I took in the scene, catching sight of a few familiar faces from my past seated around the room.

Rose waved down one of the two bartenders and we ordered drinks. By the time I was halfway through my Mary Pickford, the anxious feeling I'd been holding on to since my encounter with Miss Pritchard had faded.

"Wanna dance?"

I looked up into the warm brown eyes of a handsome young man with slicked-back blond hair and an easy smile.

My face grew warm and I shook my head.

"I don't know how," I said, glancing over at Rose who was watching the exchange with great interest.

"Nothin' to it," the man said. "I can teach you."

"My friend Rose is a wonderful dancer," I said, pointing to her.

"I know," he said, shooting her a grin. "I've caught her show. But I would like to dance with you if that's alright?"

There was a commotion then near the entryway and I could see Rose from the corner of my eye leaning forward to see what was happening.

"Aldridge," the man before me muttered. For some reason my heart began to beat faster.

I set my glass on the bar.

"You sure you can teach me to dance?" I asked.

His smile was blinding.

"I can at that," he said, holding out an arm.

The beat was quick, the movements fast, and I was out of breath with one rotation around the floor. But I was having fun and he was a fine distraction from Harley, who I was determined to not even look at. I didn't need any more trouble with Elsbeth Pritchard. I wasn't sure if she liked him, or if she just didn't like the thought that I was gaining ground on what she considered her turf, but I needed my job and wasn't willing to risk it for the attention of a man who would never be interested in a girl like me anyway.

When the song was over, my partner asked for another dance.

"Thank you," I said. "But I think I'll sit this next one out."

"What's your name?" he asked.

"Zora."

"I'm Gil."

"Nice to meet you, Gil."

"May I call on you to dance again?"

"You may," I said, surprising myself.

"I'll check back soon then," he said before wandering off.

"He's handsome," Rose said, bumping her elbow against my arm.

"He's okay," I said.

"Just okay?" She laughed. "You shoulda seen all the women watching him as he walked over to talk to you. I daresay he rivals Harley even."

I would never admit to how vehemently I disagreed with that statement. Gil was handsome indeed. But no one rivaled Harley in the looks department. His was the kind of face one saw on big picture screens. And not because it was pretty, but because it was handsome in a way that felt almost dangerous. The way he looked at a person with those eyes, making you zero in on him, and only him, until you were lost.

"Zora?"

I blinked and looked at Rose who was waving a hand in front of my face.

"There you are," she said.

"Sorry," I said.

"Thinking about your handsome dancing fella?"

"No. About your show. What time do you go on?"

She checked her watch then searched the dance floor for

Jessie. "Shoot! We gotta go. You should come find a place to watch in the other room."

"I will. Have fun!"

She gave a little shake of her hips. "You know I will!"

As she hurried away, I followed at a slower pace, finding a spot to watch from against the wall and waving down a waiter to order another drink. When it came, it was delivered not by the waiter, but by Harley.

"Your drink, miss," he said, holding out a glass brimming with alcohol, two cherries bobbing on top.

I tried not to smile. I hated that he had the same effect on me that he did on everyone else.

"I had no idea you worked here, Mr. Aldridge," I teased, careful not to touch his hand as I took the drink.

"I find it useful to try all types of careers. Keeps one informed and humble."

"You do seem to be the very humblest."

He gave me that mischievous smile of his and I found myself delighted to have amused him.

"You cut a rug with the best of them," he said, changing the subject as he turned toward the dance floor. "And your gentleman friend looked quite taken with you."

"Did he?"

"Indeed."

"I didn't notice."

"I think, Miss Hough, that part of your charm is the way you play naive to the most obvious of flirtations directed at you."

I was about to respond when I heard my name being called and looked around Harley to find Rose hurrying toward me, an anxious smile on her face.

"There you are— Oh. Mr. Aldridge. Hello," she said, her face flushing red. "I'm sorry to interrupt, but I need to borrow my friend for a minute. Zora, can you come with me?"

I glanced at Harley and then my drink.

"Shall I hold on to that for you?" he asked and then turned to Rose. "Will you be bringing her back?"

"I will," she said. "We just have a costume situation and Zora's the only one who can help."

"Oh," I said, and placed my glass in Harley's outstretched hand, my fingers brushing his and sending a streak of lightning through my veins that I tried to ignore. "Of course. Thank you, Harley."

"I want to hear all about *that* later," Rose said as she pulled me through the crowd and down a hallway behind the stage to a cramped and hot room filled with half-dressed women, racks of dresses, mirrors framed in lights, and more makeup and sparkles than I'd ever seen before. "This is Zora," she announced. "She's come to save the day. Betty, where's your dress?"

Betty, a tall gal with legs for miles and wearing only her underclothes, held up the offending garment.

"The straps have both gone," she said, her eyes red from crying.

"Stop that," said a woman bent toward one of the lighted mirrors, turning her face from side to side. She was unusual-looking, with high cheekbones, a square jaw, luscious wide lips, and eyes that reminded me of a cat. I was positive I'd never seen anyone as beautiful and watched as she stood and handed Betty a tissue. "Or you'll have to redo your face and we don't have time for that too."

"Is there a sewing kit somewhere?" I asked, taking the dress and sitting in the chair someone offered.

"Here," Rose said, handing me a small brown case.

I rummaged around until I found what I needed and the room went quiet as I threaded the needle, fashioned a knot to one end of the thread, and got to work. It took barely more than a couple of minutes for me to reattach both straps, cut the thread, and hand the dress back to Betty.

"Rose said you were fast," she said, taking the costume, her eyes welling again. "Thank you."

"Betty!" the rest of the women yelled.

"Sorry. Sorry," she said and wiped her eyes and hurried into the dress.

When I returned to the main part of the club, my heart skipped a beat to see Harley talking with another man, my drink still in his hand. He caught my eye and gave me a little smile that turned my knees to jelly as I walked toward him.

"Here you are," he said, handing me my drink as the other man gave Harley a nod and left.

"Thank you," I said. "You didn't have to keep holding it though. I'm sure you had better things to do."

"I assure you, I did not."

Unsure how to respond, I bowed my head and took a sip.

"Were you able to help with the costume?" he asked.

"I was," I said, just as the music came back on and the dancers filled the stage.

"Well done, you."

I shrugged. "It was a simple fix."

"I'm sure for the woman whose performance you saved, it was more than that." He checked his watch then and grimaced. "Regrettably, I must go. I hope you enjoy the rest of your evening, Just Zora."

And with that, he bowed deeply, winked, and made his exit.

I pressed my lips together hard, but it didn't work. Had the music been any quieter, the whole room would've been treated to my loud peal of laughter.

The Harrington house was quiet when I entered, the only sound coming from the direction of Mr. Harrington's study, where he often entertained friends and colleagues in the evenings, a couple of the men always staying later than the others.

I peeked in the kitchen and found a plate of leftover biscuits. Nibbling one, I returned to the hallway where a single light three stories up illuminated the back staircase. I slipped off my shoes and hurried to the third floor, my feet a whisper on the hardwoods as I padded to my room, careful to avoid the one area that squeaked.

My bedroom door closed behind me, I turned on the lamp on my bedside table, and pulled an old nightgown from the bureau before carefully taking off the dress I'd borrowed from Jessie's extensive collection and hanging it up. I gave it an admiring look. When I'd asked her about returning it, she'd waved a hand at me.

"Keep it," she'd said. "It looks better on you than it ever did on me."

It was a lovely frock, but would be even better once I got my needle and thread into it. The bottom hem was practically pleading with me to raise it a couple inches and cinching the sides for a more interesting silhouette. And straps instead of the capped sleeves would make the unforgiving material less hindering when dancing.

With a happy yawn, I went to the bathroom to wash my face and hands and brush my teeth. I was patting my face dry in the mirror when I noticed the uniform I'd left wet and hanging over the bathtub was facing the wrong direction from how I'd hung it. An ugly feeling deep in my belly crept its way up my body as I walked toward the garment, my eyes taking in the back, looking for something amiss. Finding nothing, I reached up and turned it around.

I sucked in a breath.

Down the front was a long, jagged gash, made by a dull pair of scissors or perhaps a knife. And as if that wasn't enough, there were several spots that looked like the threads had been cut, pulled, and tied so that there were odd gatherings of fabric here and there.

There was only one person who would do such a thing, and I knew why. Pritchard clearly had her sights set on Harley. In her mind, he was her ticket out of a life of servitude, and despite my declaration that I had no interest in him, she felt threatened. Rose's jibe surely hadn't helped. I'd have to find a way of letting her know he really was all hers. I had no claim to him, nor did I intend to try and find one. And even if he were interested in me, no man was worth losing this job.

My happy mood ruined, I took the damaged dress and hung it in my room to continue drying through the night. In the morning I'd pack it and take it home with me to fix. By Sunday when I returned, no one would be the wiser, and I'd have come up with a solid plan to let Pritchard know Harley was all hers.

13

"I'll want you to bring the children in after their dinner," Mrs. Harrington told me. "They'll need to be bathed and dressed in the clothing I've had Mrs. Beckwith iron, and then, once they've made their rounds, you can take them to the kitchen for a treat and up to bed."

The Harringtons were throwing their first party since I'd moved in and I'd been asked to stay the weekend to help with the children.

"Mrs. Larson is simply wonderful, but not suited to this kind of work," Mrs. Harrington explained, giving me an apologetic smile. I took to mean that Mrs. Larson did not clean up quite as well as I did. Somehow the woman always had a stain on her uniform and unkempt hair by midday that she didn't bother to tidy. "I adore her," Mrs. Harrington had said. "But she's not suitable for company and you—" her gaze swept over my neat hair and pristine uniform "—are always a picture, my dear."

"Do we have to go?" Madeline asked moments before I was to bring the children downstairs to the party. I held out my hand for the pencil she was drawing with and nodded, giving her a sympathetic smile. She was a picture in a pale pink dress and gleaming white shoes.

"It's only for a little while," I said, kneeling before her and tucking a stray curl back in place. "Afterward you get to go to the kitchen where Cook has a special treat for you."

"And me too?" Willem asked, pulling at his bow tie.

"And you too," I said, removing his hand and straightening his tie and vest before stepping back and surveying them both. "Now. Are we ready?"

At their solemn nods, we made our way downstairs.

The party at the Harringtons' set the house ablaze with lights, laughter, and music. I had never seen it so alive or so filled with people. It reminded me of a scene in the first motion picture I'd seen when I was just ten years old.

The city of Ballard was the first of the smaller Seattle area cities to get not one, but three theaters for showing films. The lines to see a show in those first weeks were around the block, and I'd had to wait a frustratingly long time for Ma to finally give Pa a yes to take us. I remembered sitting in the soft seat, my father on my right, Tommy to my left, staring at the large screen as we watched Mary Pickford smiling and drinking from a sparkling glass while wearing a stunning dress I couldn't look away from. It had been amazing.

But this was better.

Hearing glasses clinking, silverware placed on plates or digging into dessert goblets, cups placed on saucers, and the swish of silk and satin as the women moved about gracefully felt surreal. Dreamlike. And not a little bit intimidating as I glanced down at my neat-as-a-pin uniform I'd starched extra for the occasion.

Waiters, hired for the night, whisked by with platters of food and drinks bubbling their effervescence, the bottles coming out of Mr. Harrington's private collection. And in the middle of it all were the hosts, dressed to impress and smiling and making conversation graciously with all their guests.

There were oohs and aahs as I led the children to their parents, the lights of the chandeliers playing off the gems and beads of the women's dresses and drinkware as we went. A wink here, a flash there, a shimmy. There was a familiarity to it all. It had the essence of the clubs downtown, but less frenzied. Less hectic and hot and humid.

And less colorful. In a way that struck me uncomfortably.

It was never more apparent, as I took in the sea of white faces, how unequal the world still was. On Jackson and King Street, amid the Japanese corner markets, Chinese restaurants, and Black-owned hotels and clubs, there was an ease to the people shopping, talking, and strolling. A joy. An acceptance of their fellow man and woman. Of course, there were still those who didn't feel that way. Who came it seemed to merely stare and whisper and vocalize their disapproval, but despite that, it was like being in an entirely different world from the one I was now standing in.

As I stood out of the way, my back pressed to the elegant gold and cream wallpaper, I took in the guests of this great house, who were doing their best to stand out, just as the patrons of the clubs did. The clothing here may be more expensive, but in many ways it was also more over-the-top. The number of jewels was the same, but at the clubs, most of the baubles worn were fake. Here? I couldn't imagine any one of these women walking in wearing something that didn't cost her husband a month's worth of my salary. Probably more.

The men were debonair, and most were married. If they were looking for a good time with someone other than their wife, they were discreet about it, unlike at the clubs where I'd twice been told some man was on the hunt while his wife was off flirting with someone across the room.

While I waited for Mrs. Harrington's signal to fetch my

charges and exit, the back of a woman appeared suddenly in front of me, so close I could smell her familiar too-strong rose-scented perfume.

"Appetizer?" I heard Pritchard ask, proffering a tray of food to the guests. Apparently I wasn't the only one getting overtime pay this weekend.

I kept my smile in place and was about to sidestep out of the way when a voice whispered in my ear, "I wouldn't eat anything off that tray if I were you."

I glanced over and then quickly looked away, pursing my lips in amusement at the sight of Harley, dashing in a tuxedo, standing beside me, a look of innocence on his face as if he hadn't said a word.

"Couldn't if I wanted to," I murmured back.

He frowned then and looked flustered for a moment, a pink hue coloring his cheeks.

"I'm sorry. I didn't mean—"

I snorted delicately and shook my head. "It's okay. I'm not offended."

Pritchard wandered off then, her head swinging left and right before disappearing into the next room.

"Thank god," Harley said. "She's hard to hide from once she's got her sights on you."

"You were hiding?" I asked, trying not to laugh. "Behind her?"

"I figured the only way I could lose her was to never be in front of her. So far it's working. I just keep circling as she does. Keeps conversations with others brief as well, which I find terribly helpful at these things."

"You aren't enjoying yourself?" I chanced a quick look up at him and found his smile as forced as my own.

"It's tedious," he said. "The accent makes people inordinately interested in me. The women flirt and the men are uneasy—because of their wives flirting. Usually in full view of their husbands. The women question me relentlessly, wanting to know what females on my side of the world wear and eat. As if I know. And the men want all my thoughts on business affairs and politics. As if by being British I am an expert in such things."

"You mean you're not?" I teased.

"I am not." He chuckled. "Though of course, I do have expertise in other areas."

It was the way he said it, his voice husky and low, that made my knees weaken.

I was about to say more but Mrs. Harrington raised a single finger, her signal for me to retrieve the children.

"That's my cue," I said, stepping forward to take charge of the children once more. "I wish you luck, Mr. Aldridge."

As I turned toward the staircase, I caught sight of Pritchard reentering the room from the direction she'd left earlier.

"Make haste," I whispered as I slipped past Harley, tilting my head toward the young maid.

He didn't even look, just turned in the same direction I was going and hurried ahead of me with a "thanks" over his shoulder.

A few nights later the house was filled with boisterous noise once again as Mr. Harrington had one of his men-only nights, something he put on once a month. For the monthly soiree, a dozen or so friends and colleagues were invited over to discuss business, politics, and the like while being served from his private stash of alcohol and eating what Cook called her "gin soakers."

"Soaks the booze all up so they're safe to drive home," she told me as she placed a plate of freshly baked croissants and other bready treats on a tray and hurried out the door.

I followed at a slower pace on my way to Mrs. Harrington's personal study to have a quick word about the next week's activities for the children.

On my way back out, I found Harley being ushered in by the butler, who promptly disappeared.

"Well, hello again, Miss Hough," Harley said, bending in a slight bow.

"Good evening, Mr. Aldridge. How are you tonight?"

"Better now," he said.

"An evening with the men undoubtedly boosts one's spirits," I said, enjoying watching one side of his mouth lift in amusement.

"Exactly what I meant," he said. "And what plans have you this evening? It's a bit late for going out."

His brow was creased with concern and I laughed softly.

"Have you not just arrived here for an evening out yourself?" I asked.

"I have. But it's different."

"How so, Mr. Aldridge?" I said, tilting my head and crossing my arms over my chest as I waited to hear about the differences between men and women that I was sure was about to come.

"I do wish you'd call me Harley," he said, avoiding my question.

"And I do wish you a good night." I curtsied then, willing myself not to smile, and hurried down the hall, nearly running into Pritchard who was coming from the opposite direction.

"Watch out!" she said as our shoulders brushed.

"You're too late," I muttered and then swore under my breath.

"Excuse me?" she asked, stopping in her tracks and grabbing my wrist. "What did you say?"

I stared down into her eyes, glad to have a bit of height over her, my mind racing for a way out of what I'd said.

"I said you're too late. Mrs. Harrington has retired to her room for the evening."

"I wasn't— I mean—"

She was caught in a trap. Mrs. Harrington forbade female staff of a certain age to be in this part of the house when men-only events were happening. She'd heard stories of staff and men mingling after wives had gone to bed. It was a stipulation listed in my contract, and as such, I knew it was in Pritchard's, as well. If Mrs. Harrington wasn't around, neither were we to be. Pritchard had no way of knowing whether it was true that the mistress of the house had gone upstairs, but she risked getting in trouble if she went to check the study.

"Then what are you doing here?" she asked. "I could just as easily tell the mistress where I saw you coming from."

"She and I just finished a meeting. She went up as I headed this way." I looked down at my arm. "Can you remove your hand please?"

She released me, but not before digging her nails in and practically hissing at me.

"Harley Aldridge has no interest in you. Your status makes a relationship between you two impossible."

I wanted to say likewise, but knew any retaliation would only make my situation worse, and my employment in the Harrington house tenuous. I bit my tongue and instead sighed with faked resignation.

"I am aware, Miss Pritchard. Will that be all?"

Her eyes narrowed and she took a step back.

"Have a nice night," she said and turned on her heel, leaving me alone in the hallway.

For reasons I couldn't explain, tears welled in my eyes. They weren't from fear of losing my job. Not from the nails that had dug into my arm, or the blatant threatening nature of Elsbeth Pritchard. They were tears for something else I wasn't prepared to admit to. A tiny hope that had somehow been lit—and that I desperately needed to extinguish.

14

A few nights later I sat nervously on a streetcar as it glided through town and I stared out the window, anxiously gripping the seat in front of me as I gazed at the buildings in hopes I'd recognize one or two, afraid I'd miss my stop.

I'd never gone downtown alone before. Never put makeup on myself, or fixed my hair the way Rose had for me when we were going to the clubs. But tonight I'd done all three in a desperate attempt to show Pritchard that not only was I not interested in Harley, I'd made plans to go out knowing he'd be at the Harrington house.

It had taken two tries to get the mascara right, having blinked before it was dry and leaving messy black splotches under my eyes. The rouge went on okay. I dabbed a little on at first and then added more until I looked sun-kissed and not clown-like as I'd feared I would. And then I had a go with the lipstick. It was a shade of red the salesgirl assured me was not only all the rage, but looked divine on me, as well. I wasn't so sure, but the up-and-down I got from Pritchard when she saw me on my way out the door, followed by a glare, led me to believe I must look okay, because she looked like she wanted to murder me.

"Does she ever go out?" I'd asked Charles a few days before after finding Pritchard once again reading in the room off the servants' dining area.

"Why would she?" he'd asked. "What she wants comes here."

"She'd have a better chance at socializing with him outside of the house."

"And you know that how?"

I'd shrugged. "I've seen him out is all."

"I imagine he frequents the clubs quite a bit. A handsome, young, single man like that? Probably a lot more fun out there then at the stuffier parties he probably feels obligated to attend up on this hill."

"I imagine you're right," I'd said.

Pulling myself from the memory, I stared past my reflection in the streetcar window, watching the buildings go by. I realized I still didn't know much of the city at all. Just a few of the surrounding streets by the Harringtons' house and a bit of Jackson Street. Mainly the alleyway where Jessie parked when we went to the clubs.

I was always being led. I felt proud that this time I'd taken the lead. But that wouldn't matter if I ended up missing my stop and going right back to where I began.

And then I saw it. The little corner Japanese grocer the Alhambra sat beneath. I scooted to the edge of the seat, preparing to stand and ask the driver to stop. But there was no need. The car slowed and, sighing relief, I got to my feet and hurried out onto the sidewalk.

The summer sun that had stretched the light late into the evenings was long gone, and I pulled my coat tight around me as I crossed the street to the alleyway leading to the club. It seemed darker than it had previously and I wondered if I was wrong to have come. There weren't many people about and a girl alone at night in the city was never a good idea.

But I was here, and the next streetcar wouldn't come for an

hour. Squaring my shoulders, I hurried into the shadows and around the building to the door in the back.

As soon as I pushed inside I could feel the music coming from below. I let out a long exhale and then gasped as a voice snapped at me.

"You comin' or goin', hon?" a woman said.

I turned and found myself face-to-face with three women, no hair out of place on any of their heads, the red lipstick on their lips in stark contrast to their pale skin, and each one of them looking me over in a way I'd seen all my life.

Like I didn't belong.

"Sorry," I said, my voice low as I shuffled out of the way.

They brushed past me and went down the stairs, their heels clomping on the steps, echoing around me as I followed at a distance.

One of them knocked and the slot slid open. A moment later, so did the door.

"She's not with us," one of the women said, jabbing her thumb in my direction.

Frankie looked past them to where I stood, leaning against the rail. His smile stretched across his face.

"Zora!" he shouted above a saxophone solo.

He reached a thick arm between the women, his hand outstretched as he effectively moved them to either side of the stairwell, making space for me to walk through.

"What are you doin' standin' there like these regular folk?" he asked. "Get in here!"

Each of the three women's expressions went from disgust to surprise to curiosity to—much to my delight—embarrassment, having just registered the slight delivered by the host. Once again their eyes took in what they could see about me. The subtle makeup, so unlike their own, the unpolished hairdo, and the coat that had seen its best days ten years before when it had belonged to someone else. And yet, here I was, being ushered into one of the city's most popular clubs like I was somebody.

"Thanks, Frankie," I said, taking his hand.

"Rose didn't tell me you were comin'," he said, using his body to shield me from being knocked by the other patrons.

"Thought I'd surprise her."

"And what a great surprise it is, Miss Zora. Shall I find you a table?"

He let his hold on the door go then and I heard one of the women exclaim "Oh!" as it bumped into her, just as someone else shouted my name.

"Zora!"

I smiled at the dark-haired woman weaving her way through the crowd toward me, a giant grin on her beautiful face as she joined me at the table Frankie led me to.

Lorraine Darling was the star of the show Rose and Jessie danced in, and had been friendly to me ever since I fixed the straps on Betty's dress. Everyone who came to the Alhambra knew who she was, and I reveled in this moment, knowing the three women who'd snubbed me were watching this all play out.

"Heya, Lorraine," I said, taking in her catlike eyes lined in black charcoal, the sparkly black band with three long feathers around her head, and then her dress—a layered number with a nude slip beneath a sheer black beaded sheath, giving the illusion that you were seeing more skin than you actually were.

"Hiya, darlin'," she said and pulled me to her, kissing both my cheeks, her perfume wrapping around me in a sweet cloud. "That boy was lookin' for you again. He's cute, that one. But I'd hold out for the other." She winked and I shook my head.

The boy she referred to was Gil, the handsome young man who had asked me to dance over a month ago and seemed to find me every time I went out, which was a lot this past month as I tried to prove a point to Pritchard.

The other one she mentioned was Harley. No matter how

much I denied it, she, Rose, and Jessie all thought he had his eyes on me, which irritated me to no end since I didn't want anyone, most especially Pritchard, to get the idea in their head that he liked me. Which was why I always made sure any interactions Harley and I had were brief should anyone be watching and word somehow got back to the young maid. But aside from the missing rock from Harrison and the slashed uniform I'd fixed so well one would have to take a magnifying glass to it to see where it had been cut, I'd only suffered one more attack: a scratch across the toe of the first pair of brand-new shoes I'd ever had.

"You're sure you didn't get that while out dancing?" Charles asked when I showed him.

"This is the first time I've taken them out of the box since I bought them," I said.

I was angry. Not because they weren't in pristine condition—I fully expected after one night in the clubs they'd be full of marks and dents. But it should've been me to put the first mar on them. Not her.

As with everything else though, I'd let it go.

"But if you keep letting her do these things," Rose had said when I'd told her, "it'll only get worse."

I knew she was right, but had no idea how to address the situation, other than to try and show her I wasn't a threat to her precious fantasies of locking Harley down. Which I was doing by going out as often as I could. Perhaps if she saw I had a social life, she'd assume I was trying to meet men who weren't Harley. And so, much to Rose's delight, I went with her down to Jackson Street two to three times a week now. And every morning I'd recall my night out to whoever was in the help's dining room, including the dances I'd done and the men I'd done them with.

"That Carl sure can spin a girl," I'd say.

"Freddie is an angel."

"Joe and I danced seven times. My feet are absolutely aching!"

Most of the time it was an outright lie. Sometimes a small embellishment. And while I wasn't sure if my methods for making Elsbeth Pritchard think I wasn't interested in Harley were working, in the past few weeks nothing else had gone missing or gotten ruined.

The upside to frequenting the clubs was the new friends I'd made. Like Lorraine.

"Do you know if Gil's still here?" I asked her now, looking through the crowd for him.

"Unsure, doll. He seemed anxious to find you though so I can't imagine he left. Unless he went to check another club."

"We usually see each other here," I said, scanning the room and spotting him with his usual group of friends in the far corner. "There he is."

He saw me at the same time, his face lighting up as he patted the arm of the guy next to him and got to his feet.

"Yep, he's a handsome one," Lorraine said. "Watch out for him."

"Because he's handsome?" I asked with a laugh.

"Exactly," she said. And with another wink, she disappeared in a flurry of sparkles.

"You're here!" he said, leaning down to kiss my cheek before sitting in the chair Lorraine had just vacated. "Rose said you weren't coming."

"Last-minute change of plans."

"I'm delighted."

I inhaled with pleasure. He was kind, good-looking, and attentive. The kind of boy I assumed I'd have married if I came from a smaller, cleaner, and more well-to-do family. The kind of boy that made a good wage, cute babies, and expected dinner to be ready when he got home from work.

"He looks like the kind of boy who only does it one way," Jessie had said last week when we were getting ready at her place.

The comment had elicited a howl of laughter from Rose

and me. I may not have had sex yet, and had admittedly garnered a prudish stance on the subject much of my life thanks to my mother's adamant warnings over the years that a woman should wait until after marriage, but thanks to Rose and Jessie, who had, I'd learned a lot about what to expect—and what to demand. And also how good it could be—and how waiting might actually be the foolish thing to do. All of which had made me think that perhaps waiting, as I'd been told time and time again was the "right" thing to do, perhaps wasn't "right" at all.

"You gotta know what you're getting into," Jessie said. "That's what they do! Don't let anyone tell you sex is only for making babies. And do *not* let any man get away with—" She threw herself on her bed then and mimicked humping while Rose laughed and I covered my face, feeling my cheeks warm. "Zora! You have to look. This is not good sex. You need..." And with that she turned over and mimicked something else that made Rose slide off her chair, her laugher now silent, shoulders shaking, while I lifted the skirt of my dress like a curtain over my eyes.

It was a different sort of education than the one Rose and I had received briefly behind the school by an older girl who drew terrible illustrations of what she'd seen her parents doing. We'd been fourteen at the time and, despite the rudimentary drawings, we'd been shocked.

"And that's how you get babies," the girl had said, to which Rose replied, "That's not how I'm gettin' babies," before shaking her head, grabbing my wrist, and pulling me back to class.

Regardless of whether Gil made love in a way Rose and Jessie found acceptable, or whether he did it like they suspected (with his eyes closed, his kisses too wet, and a lot of fumbling about), I didn't really care and wasn't planning to find out. His interest in me provided two things: safety from the feelings I denied I had for Harley, and proof for Pritchard that there actually was someone else and her designs on Harley were safe from me.

"So," Gil said, giving me his most charming grin. "You wanna dance, Miss Hough?"

"I'd be delighted."

The problem though was that Gil was no Harley. He didn't have that air of sophistication, quick wit, or hint of mystery about him. No quirk of his lips when he was amused, or way of looking at me that made my entire body grow warm as something in my center squeezed in an unbearably delicious way. But he was charming, if not a little bland. Solid. Steady. And he always made sure I had water to sip, or something stronger if I wanted. He walked me to whoever's car was driving me home, and when we danced he protected me with his body from arms and legs flying about. By anyone's standards, he was a solid choice for a boyfriend were I to choose to have one, which I hadn't yet. Because I feared that if I did, those looks and quirks and smart replies from Harley would stop—and though I knew that's what needed to happen for the sake of my job, and that they likely meant nothing, I wasn't prepared to let them go.

15

"A little too much fun last night?"

I opened my eyes and glanced up at Mrs. Beckwith standing at the far end of the dining table with a sympathetic smile. I nodded then winced and closed my eyes again.

"I think the poor dear got a batch of bad gin," I heard Cook say, her voice low. "Here you are, Zora."

There was the soft clunk of a drinking glass on the table and I peeked with one eye and gratefully grasped it and brought it to my lips.

"I don't think orange juice is going to cure her," Mrs. Beckwith said.

"Course not. But orange juice with a splash of the mister's vodka will help."

"Thank you," I whispered, taking a sip and letting the sweet, slightly tart juice slide over my tongue and down my throat.

I'd been out every night for the past three, each time partaking in one particular drink. But last night it had tasted different. Rose had warned that sometimes it happened. A bad batch that didn't rear its ugly head until later, inducing vomiting, or a raging headache. Or both. I was glad I didn't vomit, but the headache felt like I'd been hit over the head with a brick. Probably hadn't helped that I hadn't sipped it. I'd tipped my head back and drunk it in one gulp.

"Zora!" Gil had exclaimed and then laughed. "Well then. Cheers!" And he'd tipped his own head back and done the same. But when he'd offered another, I'd said no. The one drink hadn't gone down as smoothly as others had on previous nights, burning my throat as it went.

Gil hadn't asked why I'd thrown back the drink, and so I didn't explain. I wasn't even sure I could if asked. All I knew was, I'd looked up and seen Harley come in the door, devastatingly handsome as usual, and ushering in a beautiful woman beside him. At first I thought she just happened to arrive at the same time, but then he turned and bent to whisper something in her ear and she'd smiled up at him, making my stomach turn over. Next thing I knew, my drink was gone.

"You want another?" Cook asked me, pointing to my now-empty glass of juice.

"Please," I whispered and she went back to the kitchen.

"How many drinks did you have?" Mrs. Beckwith asked.

"Just the one," I said. "It burned something awful and sat in my stomach afterward like poison."

"Cook is right. Sounds like a bad batch. You still planning on going to your folks today?"

I nodded and winced at the movement. "Yeah. I have to help Mama."

"You're a good girl, Zora," Cook said, placing a fresh glass of juice before me. "Always going home to help out. I hope they appreciate you."

"They do," I said, managing a smile. "And it's nice to see my siblings."

"How many you got?" Mrs. Beckwith asked.

I was always so careful not to divulge too much about my family, even as the others nattered on. But I wasn't comfortable doing the same. Not with Elsbeth Pritchard around, just waiting for me to offer up information she could somehow use against me.

"A couple," I said, taking a sip and then carefully getting to my feet. I lifted the glass. "I'll bring this back down when I leave."

In the safety of my room, I pulled my new valise from beneath the bed and began to pack. I only ever took a few items. Something to sleep in, clothes for the following day, and my toiletries. I made quick work of it and then sat on my bed, sipping more juice and remembering the night before.

Previous to Harley arriving, I'd been having a good time. I'd been summoned to the dressing room again, this time to fix a sagging line of fringe, the women regaling me with hilarious anecdotes of their dancing beginnings as I worked.

Gil was as charming as ever, arriving in a playful mood, teasing and flirting, making me wonder if perhaps I should give serious thought to being his girlfriend. It was unfair that I'd compared him to someone else all this time. Hadn't I hated being compared to others all my life? And so I'd set my reservations aside and let him pull me onto the dance floor time and time again, and even dancing to a couple of slow songs, despite feeling like they were just a chance for people to get away with touching one another in public.

And then Harley had arrived with that woman. She was glamorous and well-dressed in a fur-lined coat, understated black dress, and tasteful jewels. And she suited him much better than I ever could. Not that I ever thought about such things. In response, I'd swallowed the drink Gil had ordered for me and immediately felt its effects, the lights blurring and the talking and laughter and music overlapping into a sound I could barely comprehend.

But it was fine. Until it wasn't. Until Harley was suddenly standing before me, his face etched with concern, his eyes brushing over my face and lingering on my lips…

Or had they? Had I just imagined that part in my haze?

"Zora?" he'd said. "Are you alright?"

"Mmm-hmm." I'd nodded, taking a step backward and bumping into Gil who was talking to a friend and turned in time to catch me as I stumbled.

"Oh," Gil said, seeing Harley. "Mr. Aldridge. We haven't yet had the pleasure of meeting. I'm Gilbert Parkinson. My father is Robert Parkinson. He speaks very highly of you." He reached a hand out to shake Harley's, but the other man just stared at him for a moment before giving him a curt smile.

"Of course," he said. "Please give your father my best. Are you with Miss Hough?"

"Yes," he'd said at the same time I said, "No."

I'd laughed, remembering myself and all the reasons I needed Gil.

"I mean yes," I'd said. "He is. We are." I frowned and shook my head a little. "Sorry. I'm feeling a little…strange."

"How much have you had to drink?" Harley asked.

"Just the one drink." I'd hiccupped and covered my mouth.

"You're sure?"

I'd crossed my arms over my chest. "Yes. I'm positive. Ask—" I'd pointed to Gil, momentarily forgetting his name.

"She's telling the truth," he'd said. "She's only had the one." He'd pointed to my glass and Harley picked it up, sniffed it, and drank what was left.

"She needs to go home," he'd said, placing the glass back on the table.

"No, I don't!"

"You do. That's a bad batch of gin and you're more than likely going to be sick. Something you'd probably prefer to do in your own bathroom rather than in the ones here." He'd looked to Gil again. "Do you have a car?"

"I don't. But my—"

"Never mind. I'll take her." He held out an arm. "Zora?"

"What about your friend?" I'd slurred, turning to look for the woman and watching in fascination as the room tilted.

"What frie— Oh, right. Hang on." He'd pulled out a chair and sat me in it, then disappeared into the crowd.

"You'll be okay with him," Gil'd said, kneeling beside me. "My father talks highly of him. And lord knows the women love him. You should feel honored he's offered to take you home. Make sure you thank him. A man like that…with the connections he has. He could probably get you a better job than the one you have now. One more suited to—"

Harley was back and Gil had immediately gotten to his feet.

"I've informed the staff about the gin," Harley had said. "Hopefully the damage won't be too bad. Glad it wasn't any of my product."

"Your…" I'd frowned, not understanding, and then took the hand Harley held out, trying to ignore the jolt of electricity created by his skin touching mine.

"Shall we?" he'd asked.

"Yessir," I'd said and then turned to Gil. "Good night."

"G'night, Zora. See you Friday?"

I'd waved without answering and let Harley steer me out of the club, up the stairs, and into the fresh air where a light rain had begun to come down.

"Here." He'd stopped to pull his jacket off. I'd stood facing him, watching him lean forward, the warmth of his body intoxicating as he wrapped the jacket around me, pulling it closed under my chin. "Is that better?"

I'd nodded and then remembered, "My coat! I left it inside."

"It'll keep. I can come back tomorrow for it and drop it by the house."

But I shook my head.

"You can't," I'd said, and began removing his jacket as the rain came down harder. "And you can't take me home tonight either. If Elsbeth sees you she'll try and ruin another uniform, or something worse, and I'll lose my job and have to move back home and I'll fail them. All of them and—"

"Whoa," Harley had said. "Zora. Slow down. What are you talking about?" He'd moved to wrap the jacket back around me, this time buttoning the top button to secure it. "Who will ruin another uniform?"

And so I'd told him. Stumbling over my words as I explained about the warnings from Charles about Miss Pritchard, the small retaliations by her after seeing me talking to Harley, her cruel words, and my worries of being fired.

"I can't lose this job," I'd said, a tear wobbling on my lower lid. "My family needs the money. So she can't see me being driven home by you. And you can't bring me my coat. She thinks I have a thing for you and no matter how many times I tell her I don't, and how many ways I try to prove it, she—"

"Is this why you haven't been around the last few times I've come to the house? And why you were curt the last time I saw you there?"

"I wasn't—"

"You were." His voice was soft and I was surprised to see he looked hurt, a droplet of rain, like a tear, tracing a path down his cheek to his jaw.

I'd sighed and nodded. "I'm sorry. But she's always listening. Always watching."

"And you're afraid she'll tell a lie and get you fired?"

"Yes. At least, that's what she did with the last woman who had my job." I'd frowned and looked up at him. "Did the last nanny flirt with you? Were you the reason she lost her job? Because Pritchard is quite determined that no one else should even look your way."

But Harley shook his head.

"I never met the last nanny," he'd said. "And to be perfectly honest, I never noticed Pritchard until she made herself be known—and then promptly knew I should keep my distance.

She's the kind of woman who will twist your words and shape other people's opinions of you depending on her mood. I don't like hearing she's a threat to your employment. What can I do to help, Zora? Shall I talk to Jonathan? Mirabel?"

"No," I'd said. "I appreciate the offer, but that would only make things worse. I think, other than not talking to me when you come by the house, maybe asking her to marry you should solve the problem."

He smiled gently.

"That's not possible though, Zora."

"It could be."

"No," he'd said, his face serious as his eyes swept over my face, stopping to linger on my lips. "It's not."

It took one step for him to reach me.

He'd reached for my face and then hesitated, a look of uncertainty in his eyes. Whatever inhibitions I'd had were somehow lost in the moment, and I put my hands on his and pressed them to my cheeks, gasping at the feel of his skin touching mine.

His thumbs ran along my cheekbones and as his eyes met mine again, he lifted my chin and lowered his mouth.

One breath. One beat of my heart and I knew no other man would ever compare to Harley Aldridge.

And because of that. Because of the woman he'd left inside the Alhambra. Because I wasn't a suitable match. And because having him was too big a risk, I'd known I had to stop this kiss, even though it physically hurt to pull my lips from his.

He'd looked down at me, searching my eyes, and then nodded, dropped his hands and stepped away.

He'd driven me home without a word and parked down the street like I asked. When I'd handed him his coat, he'd wrapped his hand around mine and we sat there in the car, the rain thundering down around us, staring at one another in the dark.

"Zora—"

"Thank you for the ride, Harley," I'd said, and then slipped out the door and ran the entire way to the Harringtons' house.

I could still feel his lips on mine when I woke in the morning. Could feel his body, warm and strong against mine. I'd never felt desire before. Not until last night.

Not until Harley.

16

Since Charles had to run errands for Mrs. Harrington the following morning, he offered to drive me to my parents' home.

"Thank you," I said, my hand on the door handle as we pulled up to the house. The pounding in my head had finally abated, but my nerves were frazzled, and my skin tender, remembering the way it had felt to have Harley pressed against it. "I'd have been soaked walking from the streetcar stop."

"Of course, Zora. I hope you have a nice visit."

I hurried out of the car and ran up the front path to the house.

"Hi, Mama," I said as I came in the door, finding her in her usual spot in front of the sewing machine. I sniffed at the air, thick with the scent of something baking. "What is that I smell?"

"Hannah just pulled a cake out of the oven."

"A cake? What's the occasion?"

"There's never an occasion."

I turned at the sound of Sarah's voice laced with irritation. She was carrying the laundry basket and shaking her head.

"Hannah and her book club found a book a couple weeks ago that had a recipe in it. They just had to try making it. When it turned out well, they went in search of another book with a recipe, until someone told them they could just check out a book filled with recipes from the library."

"Or raid my recipe box," Mama said. "Which they did. And now they've been trying out recipes every few days, depending on what ingredients they can get their hands on."

"And do they turn out well?" I asked.

"It's a four to one ratio," Lawrence said, hurrying down the stairs and coming in for a hug.

"Four being good?" I asked and the three of them shook their heads. "Well, whatever was made this morning smells delightful."

"They always do," Mama murmured.

"I keep trying to convince them to move on to something else," Sarah said. "It's a waste of perfectly good ingredients. But three of the girls have part-time jobs so they replace anything they use. I can't complain about that."

"And yet," Lawrence said. "She does."

Sarah smacked him on the arm as I laughed and headed for the kitchen.

"I'm going to make some tea," I said. "Mama? Can I get you some?"

We worked quietly, side by side, as we always had. Every so often I'd catch her watching me, her eyes flicking over my hair, my face, the blouse and trousers I wore, the new shoes...

"You look well," she said. "Healthy. Happy. They still treating you okay?"

"They treat me very well, Mama."

I knew she worried. There were rumors of young women getting taken advantage of. Worked to the bone. Accused of stealing or worse. But the Harringtons were lovely people. Fair and respectful.

"I would tell you, Mama," I said. "I promise."

"Good girl," she said. "And are you getting time to sketch? Mrs. Gordon came by this week to pick up a garment and asked if you might make her another dress for a party she's throwing for Mr. Gordon's work. She was hoping to see your book."

I thought of my sketchbooks, tucked behind the headboard of my bed for safekeeping at the Harringtons' house.

"Nearly every night," I said.

The inspiration I'd gotten from what the women wore to the clubs, what I'd seen in town when I'd had time to check out the shops, and even Mrs. Harrington and her friends' wardrobes, had prompted several new designs. New collar shapes, hemlines, sleeve adornments, and drape work. There were nights I sketched until I fell asleep, waking in the morning to find my face pressed to the paper, my pencil wedged uncomfortably beneath a collarbone or arm. Before getting out of bed, I'd flip through what I'd drawn and then tuck the books away, wishing I had the time and fabric to sew the designs into reality.

"I'm happy to bring my books home next weekend for her to look through. I'm not sure how much time I'll have to work on anything though. Do you know when the party is?"

"I'll certainly find out."

Three hours later I was on my fifth garment and second slice of cake.

"It's no fair you missed all the terrible attempts," Sarah said from where she was up on a ladder hanging a new pair of curtains she'd sewn for the front room.

Below her, Harrison sat on the sofa, his brow gathered in the middle as he read a book for school, his feet resting on a toy truck. I grinned and glanced at Eva from across the table where I was working. She had grown a lot in the past few months, her limbs long and thin like mine, her hair turning a pale, burnished copper color our mother said was the exact color our grandmother's had been. She was a bit of a mystery to me, my youngest sister. Quiet like Hannah and me, but authoritative like Sarah when she wanted something. She didn't have much interest in sewing, reading, or fashion like her older sisters, making me wonder what she'd end up doing with her life.

"Maybe she'll just get married and have a family," Sarah had said a few weeks ago when we'd sat watching her from the back porch. She'd been sitting on the swing Tommy had made, staring up into the willow tree it hung from and not saying a word for hours to anyone.

"Maybe," I'd said. "But for some reason, I don't think so."

Something was happening behind the eyes of our sweet Eva, and I was excited to find out one day what it was.

Every weekend it seemed another small change had occurred in one of my siblings. They'd grown taller, thinner, stronger, wiser. They were outgrowing the tiny house they'd been born into, their long limbs stretching across the furniture and filling doorways.

Harrison's baby face had begun to slim, and Hannah had curves where she hadn't before. Sarah's features had become elegant. Lawrence was so manly now, his shoulders wide and strong, his strides long. But it was the baby of the family I noticed the most. Little Eva no longer dragged a headless baby doll along behind her, the head in her other hand, having fallen off again. Now she wandered, her eyes staring off into the distance, as if contemplating deeply the world around her.

The only one who hadn't changed was Pa. It was hard to see the closed door of my parents' bedroom at midday, or hear him shuffling in in the middle of the night. The smell of alcohol seeped from his every pore and I had to make an extra effort not to look at Mama whenever he made an appearance, scratching at his scraggly beard, his hair unkempt, looking confused like he didn't know a one of us.

My role in the house had changed drastically, now that Sarah did all my old chores, looked after the little ones, checked to see if Mama needed anything, and made sure the doors were locked at night after everyone was in bed. The one place I'd always felt I belonged was starting to make me feel like I no longer did. And I wasn't sure what to do with that feeling.

Even the list of things that were needed by household members, dolls and trucks, new dresses and shoes, usually rattled off over dinner, had changed. The money I brought home was more than Tommy had been able to provide, and thus the needs were taken care of without having to prioritize and negotiate. It felt good to be able to give enough, but also made me feel left out.

After dinner, and the subsequent cleanup, Mama sat with the basket of family clothes that needed mending.

I sat beside her but she shooed me away.

"Go play with your siblings," she said. "They miss you."

"You don't?"

She looked up at me and her chest rose as she took in a long breath.

"Zora Lily Hough, you will never know how very much I miss having you here daily. But you were never going to stay anyway. If you hadn't found this job, you'd have married and moved away." She looked away for a moment and I was surprised to see her wipe away a tear.

"Mama?"

She shifted in her seat as though gathering herself before turning back to me.

"When I saw you that night—the night Tommy died," she said, her voice low. "I knew what I'd done to you. The life I'd kept you from. The life you might've had were it not for my own fears." She blinked and a tear fell to her blouse. "You looked so beautiful. So grown and capable. And I knew. I knew in that moment I'd lost not only one child, but two."

I leaned forward and grasped her hand. "But you haven't lost me, Mama. I'm still here."

She smiled then, raising a calloused palm to my cheek.

"In body, but I can see the stars in your eyes, Zora Lily. In spirit, you've flown away. You've seen a bit of the world now.

You know what's out there." She dropped her hand and straightened her shoulders then. "As you should, because that's how life is meant to be. And so I cope the only way I know how. With a needle and thread."

She raised the hem of the skirt she was sewing. It was a floral fabric I knew well, as it had once been mine, but in the form of a dress. The bodice of it had worn thin before the bottom, so Mama had removed the top, trimmed off the shredding hem, and made a skirt for Hannah. Clearly, by the state of it now, it was on its last legs and about to take one final turn with the last of the Hough girls.

I returned to the dining table and sat down as Lawrence began to shuffle a deck of cards, a pretend cigar in his mouth.

"What's your game, doll?" he asked Eva who giggled from across the table.

My gaze moved from one sibling to the next, and then to the familiar surroundings. The shabby little house with all its creaks and groans and worn surfaces. The dishes and lamps that didn't shine under crystal chandeliers. Plain white walls that had yellowed. The meager decorations that had been gifted long ago—a ceramic vase, glass candle holders, books that now kept the sofa from tipping where one foot had broken off—were chipped and tarnished with age. There was no plush furniture. No rugs so thick you could lose sight of your toes within the fibers. But there was noise and laughter and a connection one just doesn't find when family members live with too much space between them and servants are in charge of baths and dressing and bedtime stories.

Maybe I didn't quite belong here anymore, but I'd hang on for as long as I could.

The following Monday I brought Willem and Madeline down for their dinner and then parked myself at the servants' dining table with Mrs. Beckwith and Charles, who were discussing some piece of gossip from the weekend.

"You're going to have to serve yourselves," Cook said, poking her head in. "The Harringtons have just had an unexpected guest arrive."

"Who is it?" Pritchard asked from the corner armchair where she was reading and ignoring the rest of us.

"That handsome Mr. Aldridge," Cook said, and I could swear a blush colored her already red cheeks.

Pritchard was instantly on her feet.

"I've forgotten to clean the stair rails," she said with a guilty look at Mrs. Beckwith. "They'll have my pretty little head for that if they notice. Don't hold my dinner."

"As if we would," Charles mumbled under his breath. "And didn't I see her wiping down those rails this morning on my way out the door?"

"Indeed, you did," Mrs. Beckwith said with a roll of her eyes as she got to her feet and headed for the kitchen.

I followed her, fretting at this unprecedented turn of events.

"Do you think I should fetch the children?" I asked Mrs. Beckwith, taking the plate she held out to me.

"They'll call for you if they need you," she said.

And they did, just as I'd shoveled a pile of potatoes in my mouth.

"Zora," Cook said, waving at me from the doorway. "The missus is asking if you might bring the children to the kitchen to finish their meal. They're apparently dominating the dinner conversation with tales of the three of you dancing in the music room this afternoon. Something about a shimmy?"

I felt a blush creep up my face, set my fork on my plate, and got to my feet.

"Delightful," I said while Mrs. Beckwith snorted laughter.

I hurried through the kitchen, stopping to check one of the

hallway mirrors for crumbs on my face and dress, and then reached for the dining room door.

"What do you think you're doing?"

I turned to find Elsbeth glaring at me from where she stood lingering in the hallway, feather duster in hand.

"My job," I said and pushed through the door.

"Oh, Zora, there you are," Mrs. Harrington said, a small, amused grin on her face. Her cheeks had the slightest hint of pink, a telltale sign she'd had a glass of wine. "The children were just telling us how much fun they had with you today."

"So I heard," I said, smiling at my bosses and purposely avoiding the other member of their party. I moved to pull back Madeline's chair. "It was a jolly good time though. Willem and Madeline have great taste in music. And we had fun dancing and learning to keep time, didn't we, children?"

"Yes, Miss Zora," they said, sliding from their chairs.

As I picked up Madeline's plate and glass, the dining room door opened again.

"Elsbeth?" Mrs. Harrington said and my heart sank. "Is there something you need?"

"I thought Zora could use the extra pair of hands," she said, rounding the table to pick up Willem's dishes that were set next to Harley's. "Good evening, Mr. Aldridge."

"Good evening, Miss..."

As he trailed off I dared to take a quick peek at him and then glanced at Elsbeth who was clearly trying to keep the frustration off her face at his not remembering her name.

"Pritchard," she said. "Elsbeth Pritchard."

"Hmm," he said and turned back to Mr. Harrington.

Ducking my head so that she wouldn't see me smile, I picked up Madeline's napkin and gave Mrs. Harrington a nod.

"Enjoy the rest of your meal, ma'am," I said and then turned to my young charges. "Come along, children. Rumor has it, Cook's made one of your favorite desserts tonight."

With wide eyes the children ran from the room.

"Well done, Zora," Mr. Harrington said with a laugh. "You certainly know how to appeal to their sensibilities."

"Dessert is never not enticing," I said.

"Agreed," Harley said, his voice lowering in such a way that I got the feeling his idea of dessert and the kids' were very different.

"Good evening," I said to no one in particular and headed for the door.

But as I turned my foot caught on something hard and I found myself careening forward, watching in horror as the plate and the food on it went flying until it, the drinking glass, and I hit the floor hard.

"Oh my goodness," Mrs. Harrington said. "Zora!"

The sound of chairs scraping against the floor filled my ears as tears blurred my vision, the shock of what happened replaced by the pain of my knees hitting the hardwood floors and my left hand landing on a shard of plate, splitting the skin, blood smearing in a long, red stripe.

"Jonathan, help her up," Mrs. Harrington said.

"I've got her," Harley said, his hand, warm and gentle on my arm. "Zora—Miss Hough. Let me help you."

"Is she okay?" Elsbeth asked, kneeling beside him. "Shall I get a bandage?"

"I'm trying to determine that," Harley said. "Perhaps you could give me some room?"

"I— Of course," she said. "Just let me know. I'm happy to fetch—"

"Elsbeth," Mrs. Harrington said. "Perhaps you could take Willem his food and get Madeline a new plate and a fresh serving?"

"You want me to take charge of the children?" she asked, failing to keep the disappointment out of her voice.

"I would like you to make sure they have their dinner, and then you may retire for the evening."

"I can come back and help."

"That will be unnecessary," Mrs. Harrington said.

"Yes, ma'am," she said, pasting a smile on her face and stalking from the room.

"I think she's going to need stitches," Harley said, pressing his napkin to the wound on my hand. "Sorry," he whispered when I winced.

"I'll call the doctor," Mr. Harrington said and rushed from the room just as Mrs. Beckwith appeared with a bucket of soapy water, a scrub brush and some towels.

"Oh no," she said. "Zora dear, are you alright?"

"Yes," I said. "More embarrassed for my klutziness than anything else."

"No need to be embarrassed," Mrs. Harrington said. "Doc Judson will get you fixed right up."

"Thank you, ma'am."

"Not at all."

The doctor arrived thirty minutes later. By then my blood had soaked through the rag and Harley had requested his dinner be given to me "to keep her strength up."

Once I was stitched, the process of needle going through skin not nearly as satisfying as a needle sliding through fabric, the wound was covered with a bandage and I was given instructions on how to care for it.

"Come see me in a week," Dr. Judson said, packing up his bag.

"Thank you, Doctor," I said, and then Mr. Harrington walked the doctor to the door.

"If you need the day off tomorrow, Zora, just say the word," Mrs. Harrington said. "I'll call on Mrs. Larson to come in."

"Thank you, but I should be fine." I turned to Harley then. "Thank you, Mr. Aldridge. You were very kind."

"Anytime," he said and then laughed. "But please try not to hurt yourself too often."

"I'll do my best. Especially since I ruined your dinner. And then ate it!"

He laughed and Mrs. Harrington covered her mouth, her eyes wide.

"Oh my goodness. She's right. You haven't eaten, Harley."

"I suppose that's what I get for turning up unannounced. I'll scrounge up something at home."

"Nonsense. I'll have Cook wrap up something to take with you."

"That would be lovely, thank you, Mirabel," he said and then looked down at me. "Is there anything more I can do to be of service to you, Miss Hough?"

"You've done plenty. Thank you."

He nodded and then followed Mrs. Harrington to the kitchen. With a sigh, I limped to the door they'd just gone through, staring at the floor as I went, remembering the feeling of my toe catching on something before I went sprawling.

But there was nothing there. What had been there was long gone, having taken the Harrington children to the kitchen and then undoubtedly pouting the entire way up to her room afterward. I knew without a doubt Elsbeth had tripped me. I had no idea why she'd done it. Maybe only to hurt me. Or perhaps she'd hoped I'd get in trouble for being so graceless. For breaking dishes and spilling Madeline's food. Certainly, she hadn't expected Harley to come to my rescue.

As I limped down the hall, my knees aching as I passed where I could hear Harley still talking with Mrs. Harrington while Cook packed up food for him to take home, my anger at Elsbeth grew. Even if I were making a play for Harley, her treatment of me was uncalled for. He wasn't hers. She had no claim to him.

I entered the help's dining room and reached for the stair rail leading up. But as I did, my gaze landed on the coat rack near the side door where Elsbeth's favorite scarf hung. Clenching my hands into fists, I limped to it and brushed my fingers over it. I wanted to rip a tear in it. Take shears to it and cut it to shreds. Use it to clean the floors. But I wasn't that kind of girl. I didn't take revenge. That was something Rose would do—and had in the past—but it wasn't me.

I turned away and started back for the stairs, wobbling and nearly falling, catching myself with my stitched hand on the table.

I gasped, tears spilling from my eyes first from the pain, then from anger. Exhaling, I spun around as fast as my aching knees would allow, hobbled to the coat rack, and pulled the scarf from its hook. Without stopping to think of the reasons I shouldn't, I opened the side door, cringing as wind and rain flew at my face, and stepped outside, dropping the scarf in the muddy puddle off to the side of the walkway. I watched with satisfaction as it floated, and then slowly, inch by inch, was swallowed by the murky water. With a huff, I stepped inside and closed the door.

17

“It must’ve slipped off when you came in yesterday,” I heard Mrs. Beckwith say the next morning from where I had paused in the stairwell. “It was quite blustery out.”

“I’m sure you’re right,” Pritchard said a moment later, glancing at me as I stepped into the room.

My knees ached and my hand was swollen and red beneath its bandage.

“Do you know anything about this?” she asked, her eyes narrowed as she held up the soiled scarf.

I frowned. “What is it?”

“My scarf. My most favorite scarf. Gifted to me by my father.” Her face was stone-like, her eyes fierce.

I shook my head. “That’s dreadful. But no, I don’t. I’ve been a little preoccupied.” I raised my injured hand and then eased myself into one of the dining chairs.

“Can I get you some coffee, dear?” Mrs. Beckwith asked me.

“If you wouldn’t mind,” I said. “I’m going to be a bit slow for the next few days I’m afraid.”

“However will you keep up with the children?” Cook asked, setting a bowl of food before me.

“Thank you.” I smiled gratefully. “I stayed up last night for a bit and came up with some activities that will keep them entertained and learning, and me mostly in one place."

"Smart girl," Mrs. Beckwith said, setting my coffee down and pouring in a bit of cream. "Just let the rest of us know if you need help. We're happy to do what we can."

We ignored Elsbeth, who mumbled something under her breath before excusing herself to go soak her scarf.

Rose turned up at lunchtime, bundled against the cold in a beautiful camel-colored coat and matching cloche with a bright red felt flower on the brim, and horrified to see the shape I was in.

"I heard it wasn't good," she said, taking my hand gently in hers. "But I didn't realize just how bad."

"You heard how?"

She wiggled her eyebrows up and down and gestured for me to come outside.

I grabbed my coat, wrapped the sandwich I'd been about to eat in a napkin, and led her to the gazebo at the far end of the garden where we sat on a bench and she handed me a small package the size of my palm from her purse.

"A little bird told me," she said, her voice low. "Brought this by the club last night and asked me to give it to you. Said he didn't want to cause any more trouble so soon."

My lips parted as I took the package, turned it over, and then looked toward the house before putting it in my pocket.

"There is just something about that man," Rose said, her eyes dreamy.

"Don't let Ellis hear you say that," I said with a laugh.

"Oh, he knows. He said even he has a crush on Harley Aldridge. Unfortunately, for the rest of us mere mortals, he only has eyes for you."

"What?" I said, leaning back. "He does not."

"Z. You are pretty but daft."

My mouth dropped open and she laughed as I felt my face

warm and shook my head, pulling out the sandwich and handing her half.

"It's not true," I said, taking a bite. "He's friendly, that's all."

"Have you ever seen him be so nice to anyone else like he is to you?"

"Sure," I said. "He was being awfully friendly to that woman in the club the other night."

"The one in the gold dress with the red jewel in her headband?"

"You saw her," I said. "See? I don't know why anyone would think he likes me when he can be with someone as refined as her. She's the perfect sort of woman for him."

"If only she weren't related to him," Rose said.

"What?"

"That was his sister."

"How do you know?" I asked, forgetting my sandwich for a minute.

"After he took you home that night, he came back and introduced her to the band. One of the guys told me afterward. Apparently she was only in town for a few days."

"Oh," I said.

"Oh indeed."

"Still. That's the kind of woman someone like Harley belongs with."

She gave me a look that read like disappointment.

"What?" I asked.

"It's that kind of thinking people have about me and Ellis. He should only be with a certain kind of people—as should I."

"Oh, Rose, I didn't mean—"

"I know *you* didn't, Z. But it's the truth. People see us out and they look at us like...like we don't belong. Like it's wrong. Why does it matter to anyone who we love? Shouldn't it only matter to the two people involved?"

"I'm so sorry, Rose."

"It's fine. I'm just feeling sensitive about it today. Some boys gave us a hard time when he walked me to Jessie's car last night."

"Which boys?"

"Bobby, Ricky, and Verle."

I shook my head. Those boys had been causing trouble since we were kids. Picking on others, bullying, and getting into physical altercations nearly every recess for our entire school career together.

"Why am I not surprised," I said, taking the last bite of my sandwich and brushing off my hands. "Verle Waldrip is the very worst. And those other two...they'll do anything he tells them to. Can't Frankie do something about it?"

"Probably. If I told him," she said. "Which I won't. He has enough to deal with. I don't want to ask him to leave his post just to walk us out."

"The club should hire someone then. To stand watch at the doors. It would be safer for you gals anyway, leaving so late at night. I hate that alleyway. It's too dark and quiet when everyone's inside."

"Ah, it's fine. Nothing ever happens out there. Just a bit of peeing behind the trash bins. Maybe a bit of vomiting when someone's had too much. A little necking..."

"Maybe," I said. "But that night I came alone, I was spooked walking by myself. I think you should at least mention it to Frankie or the owner."

"I'm not sure Harry will fork out more dough just to keep us safe, but maybe... Speaking of Harry forking out money. Lorraine spoke to him about you tending to our costumes. She thinks you should get paid for it. As do I."

"It's fine," I said, waving a hand. "It was just a couple of times and they were easy fixes."

"Z, I know fixing beat-up costumes isn't your dream, but if you're doing it, you should get paid for it. And you could always tell a future employer."

"Tell them what? That I stitched some fringe once? They won't be impressed."

She rolled her eyes. "No. But they might be if they knew the club employed you."

"But it doesn't."

"If Harry gives you some money, it does. Also, our regular seamstress is never around when we perform. Up until you came, we were keeping our costumes together with pins until she could get to them. Which isn't often. You should see how many dresses are barely holding it together. It's a wonder they don't fall off us every night."

"I mean," I said, letting the idea run through my mind. "I don't mind running back there and helping out. And if Harry wants to pay me..."

"What if we asked him to pay you for more than that?"

I frowned. "What do you mean?"

She stood then and held out a hand to help me up. "Nothing. Yet. Lorraine has some ideas. I'll let you know. Now, you'll come down as soon as you're healed?"

"You know I will."

She tapped my pocket. "And I want to know about *that* soon."

I bit my lip and nodded, my stomach fluttering with wonder at the thought that Harley had sent me a gift.

After dinner was consumed and the children had been passed along to Evelyn, I limped up the two flights to my third floor bedroom, stepped out of my uniform and hung it carefully on its hanger, then used a hand cloth to clean my face, neck, chest, and under my arms before slipping a nightgown over my head and padding to bed.

I reached behind the headboard and felt around for a minute until my fingers brushed the corner of the package from Harley that I'd tucked out of sight, should Elsbeth once more find herself in my room, looking for something to steal or ruin.

Sitting on my bed, I set the little box in my lap and stared down at it. The wrapping was elegant and the paper unlike any I'd ever seen before with silver vines that weaved their way around one another. I pulled one side of the white satin ribbon holding it all together and then pushed the edges of the paper apart, careful not to wrinkle it, and revealing a white box inside. Holding my breath, I lifted the lid.

Nestled inside was a fine gold chain, the charm hanging from it a glass rectangle surrounded by a delicate metal frame. Inside was a tiny bouquet of pressed flowers. I lifted it and found a note beneath.

> I am not in favor of the temporary. In lieu of a fresh bouquet to say I hope you feel better soon, something that will last a lifetime.
> ~Harley

It was too dangerous to wear it. Elsbeth would notice it immediately and question me. I'd have to keep it hidden. But for now. For tonight…

I undid the clasp and limped to the vanity, taking a seat and watching my reflection as I put it on. It hung beautifully between my collarbones, the tiny bright pressed flowers like a happy little omen. When I got in bed, I wrapped my fingers around it and smiled. I would only wear it while I slept, the thought of having something given to me by Harley against my skin bringing a sense of peace and happiness I didn't quite understand, but didn't want to question.

The rest of the week went by at a snail's pace, my lack of mobility keeping me from enjoying the usual running around with the children as I watched from the sidelines, coming up with races to keep them engaged, and wearing them out for the less strenuous and quiet things later in the afternoon. We played old games, made up new ones and, when my body was particularly tired and sore, I did as I was told and asked for help. Thankfully, Cook was game for some little helpers in the kitchen.

"Today," she said, wielding a wooden spoon, a smudge of flour on her nose. "We are going to make a cake."

Sugar was spilled, eggs dropped on the floor, and milk splashed. Somehow, Cook kept her wits about her and a smile on her face through it all and, in the end, the children were excited to see the finished cake rounds that emerged from the oven and set aside to cool.

"A job well done," Cook said, bestowing each child a frosting flower she'd made while the three of us watched in awe.

"Amazing," I said as she handed me one, as well. "I almost don't want to eat it." I caught the eyes of Willem and Madeline and winked. "Almost," I said again, and popped the little white flower in my mouth while they giggled.

By the end of the week the bruises on my knees had faded to a terrible yellow green. My hand still ached, but no longer stung nearly as bad, thanks to some ointment the doctor had dropped by with a package of fresh bandages.

"Keep it clean like you are and it should be good as new in no time," he said.

I hadn't seen Harley to properly thank him for his help that night, and for the thoughtful get-well gift. Not that I knew how to properly thank someone for such a lovely present. Of course, when I made the mistake of saying that aloud to Rose when she'd come by to check on me that Friday afternoon, she had several lewd ideas that made me blush to a temperature I hadn't known existed.

"Rose!" I said, elbowing her in the ribs, which only served to make her laugh harder.

We were sitting in the gazebo again, our new unofficial meeting spot for when she came by. It was cold, the November gray and gloom heavy in the sky, threatening rain as a low rumble of thunder rippled in from the west.

"I suppose you're not up for coming out tonight," she said, taking in my bandaged hand.

I shook my head. "No. The wound is still quite sore, and my knees look a fright." I lifted the hem of my uniform and she made a face.

"No one will notice if you rouge them," she said.

"I'll come next week," I said. "I promise."

"I suppose it just gives you more time to work on new designs. Anything you want to share with me yet? Or maybe sew for me? Anything that would look good on a stage?"

I laughed. "I have tons of new drawings, but no time to make anything when I'm at my folks', and no sewing machine to use while here. They probably wouldn't let me bring one in even if I could afford one."

Rose's brow drew together in a frown.

"Zora, it's your dream. There has to be a way." She gestured at the beautiful house before us. "This is not what you're meant for. Maybe if Harry agrees to pay you to fix up our costumes, you could ask him for time on the sewing machine. It just sits in the back room not being used most of the time anyway."

The prospect of bringing my own designs to life was exciting, but I didn't want to get my hopes up. And the only time I'd have to use it would be right after I got off work at the Harringtons', when the club would be swamped, and on weekends, when I needed to be home.

"We'll see," I said.

"We will." She got to her feet and kissed the top of my head. "Give your family my love?"

"Of course."

But rather than go home after dinner like I'd planned, I found myself wandering my room in a slow circle, sketchbook in hand as images of necklines, collars, sleeves, ruffles, scallops, beads, cutouts, and fringe swirled around in my head. What Rose said that afternoon had stuck with me. While I played with the children, every detail I'd taken in from every person I'd encountered since being brought on staff, since frequenting the clubs, since taking walks with the children, encountering neighbors, and running errands in town came back to me. One after the other, sometimes several at once, a barrage of design elements my fingers physically ached to alter and create crashed into one another in my mind, begging to be contemplated, drawn, and reworked until they made sense.

This was how a new design always started for me. Too many ideas drifting like snowflakes, a blizzard of concepts, until they settled and then a gust of inspiration kicked up one I could grab on to and expand upon.

I sat at my desk and stared down at the cover of my sketchbook, running my palm absently across it, the bandage catching at the edges as I tried to focus. I flexed my hand, still sore from my fall, grateful it wasn't my drawing hand, and then opened the book to a blank page and began to draw.

I worked late into the night, revisiting old designs and drawing them fresh on new pages, adding updated details, modernizing dresses and trousers and coats I'd drawn a year before. With each sketch I imagined the type of woman who might wear it. A Jessie, a Rose, a Lorraine… Mrs. Harrington, Mrs. Beckwith, Cook. Even Elsbeth.

It was after midnight when I finally stopped, exhausted but exhilarated as I flipped through the pages. I'd updated fifteen previous designs and added twelve fresh ideas. I had no idea if Rose was right, but I knew something in me came alive when I created. I knew that I became a version of myself that I liked. One filled with determination and hope. Hope that others would see my designs one day and love them, and determination that I would not give up on this dream and would have a shop of my own—even if it took years to make come true.

"Even if it takes decades," I whispered.

18

"Zora!" Rose's voice could be heard across the club, even with the band in the middle of a song.

I grinned and held out my arms and she rushed into them, nearly knocking us both over before standing back and taking in my outfit. It was another Jessie castoff. A red frock I'd added layers of fringe to after my mother had gone to bed for the night the weekend before.

"You look stunning," she said, motioning for me to spin. "I want it!"

I grinned and shimmied my hips a little, blushing at my own actions as she threw her arms around me again.

"I'm so glad you're here," she said, her eyes bright, the lights above making them sparkle. "It's been ages."

"It's been a week and a half," I laughed. But it had felt like ages to me too and I drank in the room with its flickering candles, elegant white tablecloths, and drinks served in sparkling glasses, hungry for the sights and sounds I'd come to love.

"How's your hand?" she asked, gingerly lifting and inspecting it.

"Not bad."

"And your knees?"

"Craving a dance," I said.

She gasped and pressed a hand to her chest. "May I do the honors, Miss Hough?"

"You may, Miss Tiller."

She pulled me to the dance floor where we spun one another and laughed as we forgot who was supposed to be leading whom and kept bumping into one another. Afterward we found a spot in the back room on a purple sofa where she talked about Ellis and I grinned at her absolute adoration of the man.

"He's so romantic," she said. "Always bringing me flowers he's bought from the market and homemade treats made by his landlord's wife. Last week he borrowed a friend's car and drove us out to the lake for a picnic. He's saving up for a car of his own and I can't wait. It'll probably take a while, but once he can afford one, he's promised to take me away for an entire weekend."

"Can't he get a loan from the bank? I've heard that's what people are doing these days. Seems he could—"

But Rose's cheeks colored as she shook her head.

"No," she said, her voice harsh. "Apparently the bank doesn't loan money to many Black folks. At least not ones that aren't makin' money hand over fist and can offer a little something in return."

"That's terrible."

"It's criminal, is what it is."

"Well, he sounds dreamy, Rose. And I can't wait to hear all about that weekend away one day. I'm sure he'll make it happen."

"I really love him," she said, but as she looked past me, a cloud passed over her face.

"What's wrong?" I asked, turning to see what she was looking at, my stomach flipping at the sight of our old schoolmates, Ricky, Bobby, and Verle, coming through the door. "They still giving you trouble?"

She pasted on a bright smile. "Not really. Come on, let's get ourselves some drinks!"

I frowned before letting her pull me up from the couch and to the bar, but as we passed the three men I noticed Ricky look her up and down and then elbow Verle and whisper in his ear. The look on his face as he too took a turn looking at my friend made me feel sick. Something was brewing there and it wasn't good.

Gil showed up later in the night, his face radiant as he hurried toward me.

"Zora," he said, taking my hands in his. "It's so wonderful to see you back. Did Rose tell you I asked about you? Poor thing probably wanted to run every time she caught sight of me."

"She did tell me. Thank you for inquiring."

"I've missed you." He lifted my hand gently then, turning it over and surveying the bandage. "Does it hurt still?"

"A little, yes."

"I'll be sure to be gentle with you." He winked and, for some reason, it wasn't as thrilling as it had once been. In fact, when Rose had told me he'd been asking after me, I'd felt a sense of dread.

I shoved the feeling aside though. He was kind and decent and I was flattered to have his attentions. Besides, being with him gave me authenticity when telling Elsbeth I had no interest in Harley. Of course, it would've looked even better had he come himself to check in on me, instead of just sending word via Rose, but perhaps he'd thought it improper. Regardless, he was here now, smiling down at me and asking me to dance.

I came back the next night. Breathing a little easier as I shed the prim and proper restrictiveness of the Harrington house for the loud and uninhibited atmosphere of the Alhambra. The smoke, the lights, the dresses, the music, and the freedom to laugh as loudly as we wanted.

"Come with me to the Club Royale after the show to see Ellis," Rose shouted at me as we danced cheek to cheek, ignoring the boys whooping and hollering at us.

"The what?" I asked, pulling away with a frown. "I thought he worked at some place called the Bucket."

She laughed. "Club Royale *is* the Bucket. The Bucket of Blood. It's a nickname. Cuz of the dark-colored beer. You'll come, yes?"

"Of course!"

She beamed and spun me around.

Again I was asked to assist in a quick fix, this time one of Lorraine's costumes.

"She needs to get paid, Harry," Lorraine said as she pulled me past him to the dressing room.

I ducked my head as he said, "Okay, okay. I hear you, Lorraine."

"A gal's gotta get paid for her hard work," she said to me before handing me a white dress with the seam holding one side of the zipper on coming undone.

After I fixed it, I got out of the way so the women could finish getting ready. But instead of turning left back to the main part of the club, I turned right, hurrying down the hallway to the back room where I flicked on the light and got an eyeful of the lone sewing machine and bolts of fabric, fringe, and sequins. My fingers itched. What I could do with all that material…

On my way out I passed Harry.

"Hey," he said. "Zora, is it?"

"Yessir."

"Here."

He held out a hand and I stared at the money in it.

"Thank you," I said, taking it and putting it in my purse.

"We'll talk," he said, and as I weaved my way through the bodies, the lights sparking off dresses, headpieces, and drinks, I couldn't stop smiling. The money in my purse felt like possibility, not desperation. I had done the work by choice, not because the one or two extra dollars would mean the difference between having something to put between bread slices for lunchtime sandwiches or not.

As soon as the show was over and Rose and Jessie had changed out of their costumes, we hurried up the steps of the Alhambra, ran through the alleyway, and hoofed it the couple blocks to the Louisa Hotel.

I'd forgotten how much darker and smaller the Bucket was compared to the Alhambra. And hotter. It was like going into a humid cave with black-on-black geometric design on the walls and red glass candleholders. It was more sultry than soft. Sexy as opposed to romantic. And the clientele was decidedly less whitewashed, with the Black musicians allowed to mix with the guests rather than only being allowed onstage, the guests coming in a variety of ethnicities, and genders sometimes hard to decipher. It was an entirely different atmosphere, the kind of place where anyone belonged.

As soon as we entered, Rose waved to Ellis, who was onstage dressed in a handsome light gray suit, tapping his toe to the beat. He grinned and waved back with his horn, and then the three of us squeezed into a booth with a couple I recognized from the Alhambra, and a redheaded woman I'd never seen before.

"I'm Inez," she said.

Inez had dyed red hair, thick-lined dark eyes, and full lips painted a brick red that had stained the cigarette she was smoking. Her navy dress clung to large breasts that heaved as she pulled in a breath of smoke that she then exhaled into rings above the table before holding out her hand to shake mine.

"Zora," I said, placing my hand in hers.

Her dark eyes went wide. "So you're Zora. Rose here says you're a whiz with a sewing machine. Did you make that?" She pointed the cigarette at my dress.

"No."

"But she altered it," Rose said. "You should've seen it before."

"Is that what you do for a living?" Inez asked. "Sew clothing?"

"I hope to have a dress shop one day. But for now I work as a nanny for—"

"The Harringtons," she said, cutting me off. "That's right. Rose told me that too. What a great get. That house is spectacular and—oh!" She slapped the table, making us all jump. "He's here!"

June, the woman on the other side of Inez, rolled her eyes as my own met Rose's in confusion.

"Give it a rest, Inez," June said. "He ain't interested. He's never been interested and—"

"Oh my god, he's coming over," Inez whispered, causing us all to turn and look to see who "he" was.

Rose's foot tapped mine and my breath caught as a familiar voice greeted the table.

"Good evening," Harley said, smiling at everyone in turn before his eyes met mine. "Miss Hough."

"Mr. Aldridge," I said, trying and failing as usual to keep the grin from my face. "What brings you here?"

"Business. And you?"

"Also business," Inez said. "We're in the middle of a very important meeting right now, as a matter of fact."

"Are you now?" he said, raising his eyebrows at her before turning his gaze back to me, the corner of his mouth rising. "Perhaps I can be of some assistance. I'm very good at making business decisions. May I?"

He gestured to the spot beside me and, after quickly meeting Rose's gaze across the table, I looked to Inez who scooted over, leaving me just enough room to slide a few inches and give Harley a spot to sit. But just barely. His thigh pressed against mine and, hard as I tried to pay attention to what he said next, his words were lost in the sensation of his body touching mine.

He stayed and talked for a good hour, buying us all a round of beer and entertaining us with stories of London. He was polite, charming, had a delightfully wicked sense of humor, and made sure to include everyone in the conversation.

When the music stopped, he set down his still half-filled mug and stood.

"This has been lovely, but I must be going. Thank you for letting me join you," he said before turning to greet Ellis with a handshake. "That was a fantastic set, El."

"Thanks, Harley. You leavin'?"

"I am. Business. You know how it is."

"I do at that. Good to see you, man."

But as Ellis slid into the booth beside Rose, Harley lingered.

"Miss Hough," he said. "Do you have a minute?"

"I—of course," I said, glancing at Rose before taking the hand Harley offered, inhaling as my palm met his. "Is everything okay?" I asked as we walked toward the front of the club.

"I was going to ask you just that," he said. "How's the hand?"

"Mostly healed," I said, showing him the smaller bandage now covering it. "Thank you again. For everything."

"I did what anyone would do."

"Maybe. But not everyone would send a necklace the next day."

"I noticed you're not wearing it. Is it not to your liking?"

I felt my cheeks warm. "It's beautiful," I said, my voice low. "But too dangerous to wear. If Elsbeth saw..."

He nodded. "Of course. How thoughtless of me."

"But I do wear it to—" I stopped, ducking my head.

"You wear it to what?"

I stared down at my shoes, feeling suddenly vulnerable.

"To bed," I said. "I wear it to bed. Every night."

I risked a look up at him and felt my knees buckle as he beamed back at me.

"Go out to dinner with me," he said.

I sucked in a breath, desperately wanting to say yes but shaking my head no.

"Harley, I can't."

"Is it merely because of the maid?" he asked. "Or is it something else. That boy who's been following you all around the Alhambra?"

"I'm not interested in Gil."

"So then it's the maid."

"Yes."

"It would only take my mentioning that she's an annoyance to me when I come by to be rid of her, and it wouldn't be a lie. They've seen how she is around me."

I shook my head. "I can't let you do that. She's my problem."

"Well, she's become mine now too." He scratched his jaw, taking in the room for a moment and then looking back at me. "So, if not for her, you would let me take you to dinner?"

I hesitated and then nodded.

"Then meet me somewhere. Or I'll pick you up down the street from the house so she won't see you."

"And then what?" I asked. "We'll just keep doing that? Forever?"

He smiled. "If it means getting to see you, I'll do whatever I have to."

My lips parted as I tried to come up with a response, my eyes taking in everything from his eyebrows, to his nose, to his jawline, and finally, his lips. Whatever the feeling was coursing through my veins, I had never felt it before. No other man possessed whatever power Harley did over me. It was like my body was made for him. It instantly turned on in a way it never did around anyone else. It hummed. It burned. And it ached in places that made me want things I'd never imagined wanting. It was this odd combination of danger and safety when I was near him. Safety that he would always make sure I was okay. Danger that I'd somehow lose myself when with him.

"One dinner," I said.

"That's all I ask for. For now." That grin. My heart raced.

"I'll meet you at the corner behind the house."

"Tomorrow night?"

I wanted to say it was too soon. But I knew if I waited, I'd find a way to back out.

I nodded. “Tomorrow night.”

He took my chin in his thumb and forefinger then and leaned forward, his lips brushing my cheek before whispering, “Good night, Zora.”

I watched as he left, stopping to chat with the club’s owner, Mr. Woo, on his way out.

“That looked like an interesting conversation,” Rose said from where she’d suddenly appeared beside me.

“He asked me to dinner.”

“I knew it!” she said, her voice an excited squeal.

“Shhh,” I said, waving a hand to quiet her.

“I knew it,” she whispered in my ear, and then with a last look at Harley, I let her pull me back to the table and our friends.

19

He was waiting at the corner as promised. Standing beneath an umbrella beside a handsome car so shiny it reflected the lamp post he was parked beside and thunderous clouds above.

"Miss Hough," he said with a bow. His eyes, shaded beneath the shadow of the umbrella, sparked with mischief, belying the overly courteous tone of his voice.

"Mr. Aldridge," I said, curtsying in response, unable to keep the smile from my face.

He opened the passenger side door and I closed my own umbrella and set it on the floor as I got in.

My palms were damp and I ran a hand over my hair as I waited for him to round the car and join me inside. We hadn't been alone since the night he drove me home, and the small dark space of the vehicle's interior felt particularly intimate.

I kept my eyes forward on the gleaming front panel while he stowed his umbrella in the back and got in beside me.

It was quiet, the only sound the rain's pitter-pat on the car. I watched the droplets on the windshield gather and form rivulets that then streamed down the glass, all too aware of Harley's proximity to me.

"Zora?" Harley said, his voice soft.

"Mmm-hmm?"

He chuckled. "You are going to look at me sometime tonight, yes?"

I held my breath and turned my head, taking in every inch of his handsome face as he took in mine, his eyes lingering on my lips before meeting my gaze once more.

I couldn't explain the rush of sensations that came over me. I was awash in nerve endings firing at every level like little bursts of starlight. With as little experience with men as I had, no one was more surprised than I when I reached for him.

He didn't hesitate, enfolding me in an embrace that made me feel both secure and desired, his lips soft but firm against mine. The searing bolt of electricity that shimmered down my spine as Harley's lips parted mine, his tongue ever-so-sensually tasting my own, caused a small wanton moan to escape my throat.

I was almost embarrassed. But not enough that I stopped. Instead I pressed closer as he shifted in his seat so that his chest pressed against mine.

"Hello," he whispered against my lips.

"Hello," I whispered back, running my palm along his jaw and thrilling at the feeling of his whiskers biting into my skin.

"I would very much like to stay right here doing just this for the rest of the evening, but as this is our first date, I feel the gentlemanly thing to do is to take you to dinner as promised."

"And you are nothing if not a gentleman, Mr. Aldridge."

"I do like to think so."

I moved away from him, feeling my cheeks burn as I wondered what he must think of me while straightening my hat and pulling my coat back into place.

"Zora?"

"Yes?" I stared down at my hands clasped in my lap.

"I hope it's not too forward to say this so early on, but I quite fancy you."

I grinned and peeked over at him, my heart threatening to burst through the navy dress I'd borrowed from Rose.

"As it so happens, I find your timing to be impeccable," I said, winning a shy smile in return.

"Good. Because I've been wanting to tell you for ages."

He started the car then and drove us into the city.

Being with Harley was like being in a fairy tale. Upon seeing him enter the front door, the staff at the restaurant immediately assembled to greet us, seat us, and present us with a variety of delicious appetizers that they placed before us on silver plates while we decided what to order. And because I was with him, I was treated like I was someone who mattered. Like my needs were important too. It was the first time I felt like a woman, rather than a girl.

"You're treated very well," I said, following his lead and placing my napkin in my lap.

I was very aware of the crystal, the delicate dinnerware, and the number of utensils before me. While the Harrington household displayed similar items, they were not a part of my everyday life, and thus I was daunted, paying close attention to how Harley handled himself around such things.

"I'm a good customer," he said.

"You come here often then?"

"Mostly for business. And I brought my sister here when she visited."

"She's lovely, your sister."

"She is. And likes to play the big sister role." He rolled his eyes and I laughed.

"Be nice to your big sister," I said. "Our role isn't always an easy one."

"I do wish the two of you had met. I imagine you'd get on well, both of you being overbearing older sisters and all."

I feigned outrage and he laughed and leaned forward, placing his elbows on the table and resting his chin on his hands, his blue eyes rapt with a look no man had ever dared send my way.

"Tell me about your siblings," he said. "I want to know everything. Have you one? Two? Ten? Do any of them look like you? Are you all close? Who steals what from whom?"

The sounds and people around us became a blur of happy noise as I told him the good, the bad, and the tragic of the Hough family tree. He listened, his expression changing with each new bit of information as courses were served, plates and bowls came and were cleared, glasses filled, and dessert was presented in beautiful gold-rimmed porcelain cups.

"They sound lovely," he said when I finally finished. "I hope one day to meet them all."

"Me too," I said softly. But I couldn't imagine it. Harley did not belong in my world. And I was an imposter in his.

"And how are things at the Harringtons'?" he asked, changing the subject. "Is Elsbeth treating you any better after that vicious little stunt of hers?"

"You know!" I said, my eyes wide.

"That she tripped you? Of course. There was no other explanation."

"I could've tripped over my own feet."

"No," he said, taking a sip of his tea. "I've seen you dance. And I saw the smug look on her face. It wasn't hard to figure out what happened."

"Do you think the Harringtons know?"

"They may suspect, but unfortunately neither of them was looking when it happened."

I shook my head. "She's going to get me fired—I just know it. She's kept her distance since that night, but I wouldn't put it past her to start in on me again as soon as the bandage comes off my hand. And if she catches wind of this..." I gestured to him and me. "It won't bode well for me. She believes you belong to her."

"I've never understood women like her, and I've known a few. Please be careful."

He began peppering me with questions again, curious about what I liked to do in my spare time, what I was passionate about, what I wanted out of life, and what I saw myself doing in the future.

"Are you happy running after other people's children? It's a noble calling. But do you want your own one day? A husband? A house near the water? A pony or a herd of sheep to tend to? Tell me your dreams, Zora Hough."

I bit my lip, shyness washing over me as I twisted the napkin in my lap.

"Oh," he said. "I'm intrigued now. Spill it, Z."

I grinned at his use of Rose's nickname for me and then took a breath.

"I want to own a boutique," I said.

"A boutique?" he asked, sitting back, his eyes widening. "What kind of boutique?"

"Women's clothing."

"Would you procure the clothing from someone?"

"No," I said, my voice low. "I would sell *my* clothing."

I told him about sewing with my mother and the sketches I'd drawn over the years. How I'd designed for women referred to me by people who knew about my talent.

The waiter came and I paused as Harley paid the bill. He gestured for me to continue as he helped me up from my seat, into my coat, and walked me out onto the sidewalk.

When we reached his car he held up a hand.

"I hate to interrupt," he said. "But if we go to a club like I'd planned, I won't be able to hear more and I want to hear everything. It's forward of me to ask if you want to come back to my place. Would it be very unromantic to sit in my car? We can find a nice spot to park. Or if you'd rather just go home, that's fine too. Perhaps we can do this again. If you'd like to."

"I'm not ready to go home yet," I said, my voice soft. "I'd love to see where you live."

I could feel Rose cheering for me from wherever she was. But I wasn't looking to have anything happen. I was merely curious about the mysterious Harley Aldridge everyone talked about, but no one seemed to know too much about.

"Would you?" he asked and I laughed.

"Harley. You must know you're quite the intriguing figure about town. Everyone knows you, but no one seems to *know* you."

"And what will you tell them once I set you loose inside my home?" He peered teasingly at me.

"Not a thing," I said. "This mission is to satisfy my own personal curiosity."

"You won't tell a soul what you find there?" he asked, taking a step forward, a small smile on his lips.

"Not a one," I whispered, my heart beating hard in my chest.

He tilted his head in a little bow.

"It would be my pleasure to have you then, Miss Hough."

It was the way he said it, making the innocent sound wickedly sinful, that made me shiver in anticipation.

Harley lived in a handsome house five blocks from the Harringtons'. It screamed bachelor with its dark wood paneling, rich mahogany furniture, and spare but elegant decor.

"Have you traveled a lot?" I asked, walking around each room of the first floor, looking at a globe here, a framed map there, and several other items that looked to be from far-off places I could only dream of visiting.

"Some, yes," he said, handing me a glass filled with a deep burgundy wine.

I sipped and kept walking, running my hand over a wallpaper in dark brown with metallic gold fan shapes from ceiling to floor.

"Did you pick all this yourself?" I asked.

"I did," he said. "Is it to your liking?"

He asked like he cared. Like it mattered what I thought. I turned to look at him, watching him as he watched me.

"It's beautiful," I said. "Masculine and spare in some places, and then ornate in others. And yet—" I stopped next to a photograph of a younger version of the man before me, pictured with a girl I now recognized as his sister. "I feel like it doesn't give me a sense of you at all. It's all very nice. Very rich in color and texture and choice, but…who *are* you?"

"I could say the same of you," he said, gesturing to a plush navy sofa.

"How do you mean?" I asked as I sat, taking a sip of my wine before placing it on a glass-topped table. "I am what you see. Decidedly *not* fancy. My clothes are mostly secondhand. I work as a nanny and live in someone else's house. And the money I make is not my own to do with as I please."

"And yet you tell me you can sew beautiful things and dream of having your own shop," Harley said. "You wouldn't have such a dream if you didn't think you could do it. Most dreams start because the person knows they have a knack. A talent. And so what if you wear secondhand clothing. You do so with a grace that makes it seem entirely original to you. Not only that, *you* wear the clothes, they don't wear you. Not many people can say that. Most look as though they are in costume trying to fit in." He set his wineglass down and laced his fingers through mine. "You walk around thinking you don't fit in. The truth of it is—you don't. Not entirely. But you think that's a bad thing. That it makes you invisible. It doesn't. It makes you stand out. Which is how I noticed you. I couldn't *not* notice you. I saw you the moment you stepped inside the Alhambra and I haven't stopped thinking about you since."

The room was silent, save for the sound of my breath as I stared at him and he stared back.

He reached for me at the same time I reached for him, and

we folded into one another as if we'd done it a thousand times before. His hands on my skin lit my insides on fire, his mouth silently asked things only my body knew the answers to, and his tongue turned all thoughts to gasps and murmurs that strung together meant only one thing: yes.

"I should take you home," Harley said, his voice hoarse as he pulled away and rested his forehead against mine.

But I shook my head. "I don't want to go home. Not yet."

"Zora," he whispered. "I'm not sure I can remain gentlemanly if you stay a minute longer."

"Harley," I said. "I'll be disappointed if you do."

He kissed me deeper, longer, and with a longing mirrored by my own as I pressed myself against him, frustrated, wanting to be closer.

Eventually he pulled away and stood, holding my gaze for a long moment before offering his hand. I took it without hesitation, and he led me upstairs to his bedroom where a large four-poster bed covered in an emerald quilt sat elegantly off to one side of the room.

Having always been a slender, almost gangly girl, my clothes hanging off my body and hiding any curve I may have had, it was a wonder to watch Harley's eyes as he undressed me.

"Jesus, Zora," he said under his breath as he slid one strap of my dress off my shoulder, then the other, skimming the garment down my body and watching me step out of it. "You are stunning."

No man had ever seen me in only my slip, tap pants, and bra. And certainly not wearing less. As much as I wanted this. As much as I physically ached for him. I was also, suddenly, very nervous, my legs shaking beneath me.

"Harley," I whispered, placing my hand on his chest.

He looked down at me, the blue of his eyes darker than I'd ever seen them, the desire blatant, making my knees weak and the center of me sear with want. But whatever he saw in my eyes made him take a small step back, and that one tiny movement was all it took for any nerves I was having to disappear.

I reached for him, arching against him, feeling the heat of his body through his clothes as my fingers dug into his hair, bringing his mouth down to mine. His moan sent a wave of need through me and he wrapped his arms around me and crushed me to him.

"Just say the word and I'll stop," he said, and then backed me up to the bed.

I stood, watching as he undressed himself, my eyes taking in every inch of his body with curiosity and hunger. I'd never seen a man naked before, and Harley's body was something to behold.

He was tall and muscular, his skin a light shade of olive that gleamed beneath the light of the lamp on the bedside table. My eyes traveled over him as he moved toward me again, his muscles flexing as he first removed my slip, then my tap pants, and finally my brassiere, leaving me to stand before him naked and trembling with the slightest bit of fear and a need I'd never felt before.

I inhaled, wrapping my arms around his neck as he ran warm hands down my back and over my hips to my thighs. He scooped me up into his arms and delivered me to the bed, lowering his body over mine, kissing me until I was breathless, my hands roaming tentatively over his skin as his kisses moved lower.

My entire body was quaking by the time his lips reached the inside of my hip, my hands clenching the quilt beneath me.

"Do you want me to stop?" he asked, looking up at me.

"Please no," I said, my voice jagged. He gave me that grin that made my heart race and then parted my legs and bowed his head once more.

20

"You either got in very late or very early," Mrs. Beckwith said as I hurried into the kitchen to grab a cup of coffee before waking the children.

"It was both," I said, keeping my eyes on the dark liquid in my mug so as not to meet the older woman's gaze. She was a stickler for figuring out what we'd been up to without us saying a word.

"I don't know how you do it," she said. "I could never have stayed out so late and been up to run after children in the morning."

"It's good to be young," Cook said, giving me a wink.

I took the freshly baked biscuit she held out for me and yawned, covering my mouth with my forearm as the older women laughed.

"Best get a move on," Mrs. Beckwith said. "The house is about to come alive."

I drank the last of my coffee, set the mug on the counter, and hurried back up the stairs, eating as I went.

Back in my room, I slipped into the bathroom to tidy my hair, splash my face with water, and then wet a cloth with cold water. Leaning on the countertop, I lifted my uniform and slid the cool cloth into my undergarments, pressing it to my sore center.

Thanks to Rose and Jessie, I knew how not to get pregnant, and thankfully Harley was prepared for such things. They'd also told me varying ways to please a man, and myself. But in all the girl talk that had happened inside the walls of Jessie's small apartment, neither of them had mentioned just how sore a woman might get after her first time. Followed closely by her second and third. And while Harley had tried to be gentle, being with him, moving with him, had brought out something primal in me, and sometimes we forgot about my inexperience as the moment overwhelmed us.

But as I replayed bits of my evening with Harley, the way his hands had felt on me, his skin against mine, the delicious ache of my body taking in his, I decided, undoubtedly, that it was worth the little bit of discomfort I felt today.

I watched the time ticking away at my wrist and, with a sigh, washed the cloth out, hung it over the towel bar that was mine, and put on my apron as I walked with clipped steps to wake the children.

"Good morning," I sang, entering Madeline's room. She was the easier of the two to wake, Willem always benefitting from those extra seconds I gave him. I pulled open the curtains and sat on the bed beside the dark-haired girl, laughing as I always did at her tangle of curls splayed across the pillow. Soon they would be tidied and trailing down her back in one fashion or another, but currently they resembled a small bird's nest.

After both children had dressed, I set about giving Willem the task of cleaning up the toys he'd pulled out after he'd been tucked in for the night while I fixed Madeline's hair. When both of them looked like an ad for a child's clothing boutique or a trip abroad, I led them downstairs.

"Good morning, Zora," Mrs. Harrington said, looking up from a small stack of cards on a silver tray beside her plate.

"Good morning, ma'am," I said.

"Morning there, Zora," Mr. Harrington said, folding his newspaper and waving to the kids to come greet him with a hug.

"Good morning, sir," I said and then waved to the children. "Have a good breakfast."

Elsbeth was seated in the servants' dining room when I arrived and I saw her dour expression take me in from head to toe as she always did.

"You look tired," she said. "Better be careful. All your late nights will catch up with you. No man wants a worn-looking woman."

I wanted to say no man wants a sour-faced one either, but I bit my tongue.

"I'll be sure to take that into consideration," was all I said.

"You'd do well to listen to me. You may not be a viable candidate for the Harleys of the world, but there's someone out there for you, and he'll want you to look your best."

I reached for another biscuit and tried not to laugh. If she only knew where the Harley of our world had put his tongue last night.

When my workday was finished, I freshened up and changed into a clean dress, dabbing on the faintest bit of rouge and lipstick, before grabbing my purse and going back downstairs.

"I see you aren't taking Elsbeth's advice," Mrs. Beckwith said with a smirk.

"I guess if any man has an interest in me, he's gonna have to take me with bags under my eyes and blisters on my feet."

I could still hear her laughter as I hurried down the garden path to the gate.

My heart quickened when I saw him, standing just as he had the evening before beside his car, though this time without the umbrella.

"Miss Hough," he said as I approached. "You are a vision."

"Mr. Aldridge," I said. "You flatter me."

"It's all true."

"Where are we going?" I asked as he took us in a different direction than the night before.

"You ever been to Doc Hamilton's Barbecue Pit?"

"I haven't."

"Then you're in for a treat."

The Barbecue Pit was hopping. Cars lined up down the street and when we reached the front a doorman opened my door while another man took Harley's keys. It seemed awfully elegant for a place with "pit" in its name.

"Good evening, Mr. Aldridge," the doorman said. His sandy hair was combed neatly to the side, his tuxedo complete with tails. "It's good to see you again."

"And you, Bill. This is Miss Zora Hough," he said, gesturing to me.

"Miss Hough," Bill said. "It is my honor to know you. Welcome to the Barbecue Pit."

We were seated in a booth, one of many, that surrounded a large dance floor with a bandstand at the far end. A band played and the smell of barbecue was in the air. My stomach grumbled.

"What is this place?" I asked. Rose had never mentioned it, and she mentioned a lot of places.

"Doc Hamilton owns several dining establishments. This is his finest."

I took another quick glance around, trying not to be obvious at the shock of seeing several prominent faces. "Is that—"

Harley turned to see the direction I was looking in.

"Mayor Brown and his wife? It is. The Olmsteads are here tonight too," he said, nodding in the direction of the police sergeant and his wife.

After dinner, a delicious meal I wouldn't soon forget, we went to Harley's house again and sipped wine sitting on opposite ends of his navy sofa, our shoes slipped off, feet tucked under us as we talked about his childhood this time. His dreams for the future.

"I'd like to have something of my own as well," he told me.

"The furniture business is my father's, and while it's been good for me, providing me with all this—" he waved a hand "—it's not mine to do with as I please."

"What would you do?" I asked.

"I have my hands in a few different things now. But not anything substantial. Not anything I'm proud of. They are ventures mainly to make my own money on the side and not feel so under my father's thumb. I don't know what I'll do in the long run. I'm here to figure that out. In fact—" he looked at his watch "—we should probably make it an early night tonight. I have a morning meeting tomorrow."

"Oh," I said. "Is that why…"

I stopped, feeling my face grow hot as I looked away.

"Is that why what?"

"I was worried when you… When we came back here and you didn't kiss me… I thought perhaps last night wasn't…that I wasn't…"

My face burned. I couldn't say it. Couldn't admit that since we'd come to his house, every minute that had passed without him making a move to touch me made me think I hadn't been good enough the night before and maybe he'd kept our date tonight merely out of kindness.

"Goodness. Zora." He looked flustered as he placed his glass on the table beside him and slid toward me on the sofa and took my hand in his. "I'm so sorry. To be honest, I was a bit worried I'd come off as an animal if I brought you here and took you to my bedroom again. I love being with you like that. But I also love being with you just like this."

A small grin worked its way onto my face then and I ducked my head.

"I am a bit relieved," I said. "I'm a bit…" I felt my face warm. "Uncomfortable, shall we say?"

"Oh dear," he said, his cheeks coloring. "Oh, Zora, I'm so sorry."

And then we laughed, quietly at first, the humor of the moment growing until our peals of laughter filled the room.

"I truly am sorry," he said when we'd finally stopped and he'd pulled me to him where I now lay, curled against his chest.

"You have nothing to be sorry for. I enjoyed every second. But had you wanted to tonight, I might have cried. Both because I wanted to, but also from the pain if we had."

"Please know you can always tell me. We never have to do anything you don't want to. I love just having you here. I love the way it feels with you in my home. The way you fill this space with me. The way I feel after you go, knowing you've been here, touching my things, getting to know me, being in my life." He grew quiet then and I glanced up at him, frowning when I saw the worried look on his face.

"Harley?"

"I should be honest with you," he said. "About the other business I'm involved in. In case you want to change your mind about me. About us."

He rubbed a hand over his jaw, whiskers scratching against skin. I remembered that particular sensation from the night before and felt a raw need deep inside.

"Tell me."

"I'm a bootlegger," he said. "I'll be the first to admit it's not the safest move I could've made. Thankfully most of the cops are corrupt and just want a little of the product to keep their mouths shut and their eyes averted, but you never know when an attitude might change in lieu of another. Someone faithful to me today could turn if someone else offers them a better deal. And if that other person wants me out of the way, I could get arrested."

"So why do you do it?"

"Pride?" he said. "Stupidity? At first I was just curious. I had the means. All these furniture trucks and shipping crates going across the country and coming in from abroad. I started taking note of how trucks were searched when they were stopped. And then I started small, gaining confidence with each shipment that came in unscathed."

"And your father?" I asked. "What if he found out? Would you get in trouble for using his business as a cover?"

Harley laughed. "My father is a businessman first and foremost. I told him my idea and he was happy to turn a blind eye to it, so long as he got a cut of the profits. Money makes people do strange things sometimes."

"Money makes people do desperate things sometimes as well," I said. It was something I knew all too well.

He pulled me to him and kissed me. "What you're doing for your family is honorable, Zora. You should be proud of yourself. You could go off and get married and leave them all to fend for themselves."

"I'm not as selfless as you think," I said. "After years of sharing a bedroom and a bed? The thought of having my own room, making enough money to save a little for myself, and having enough food for second helpings made taking the job an easy choice."

"Taking a husband and keeping your own house is something you could've chosen too though. And would've given you a certain amount of freedom," he said. "You are selfless, Zora. Wanting to benefit a little from the situation personally doesn't change that fact."

I nodded and then peered at him. "Do the Harringtons know?"

"Dear god no. Jonathan would probably find it entertaining. He might even want to dip his toes in. But Mirabel would have my hide for that, so I keep it from them. I think it's best."

We ended up talking long into the night, sharing kisses in between thoughts, and holding hands while divesting ourselves of secrets we'd kept hidden and buried from others.

After that night, we met nearly every evening. If the weather was nice we'd go for a walk before dinner. If it wasn't, we tucked into a restaurant we knew and loved, or tried out a new one, sampling the menu and sharing bites of food.

On Friday nights we went to the Alhambra. The first time Harley suggested it I was nervous. What would it be like to walk into the club on the arm of the most eligible man in town?

"You look worried," he'd said as we walked down the alleyway. He'd stopped, taking in my expression. "Tell me what's bothering you."

"People are going to look at us. At me. They'll think I don't belong with you. And I probably don't. You're handsome and rich and kind and—"

"You think I'm handsome?"

I grinned. "You know you are."

"I know nothing of the sort. Tell me again."

"Harley Aldridge, you are very hard to look at."

He feigned shock and then kissed me hard.

A moment later he pulled away and tipped my chin up with his finger and looked deep into my eyes, making my breath catch.

"You belong, Zora. You belong in this place. And you belong with me. Remember when we had dinner at the Barbecue Pit?"

I nodded. No one had said an unkind word to me there, even though I was certainly the most inexpensively dressed one. Even Doc Hamilton himself, when he'd come to greet us, as he apparently did every guest to visit his establishment, hadn't given my attire a second glance. He'd been friendly and welcoming. Period. But the Alhambra was different. People were more inclined to whisper and gossip.

"Who cares what anyone else thinks," Harley continued. "They're all here pretending to be something they're not. Don't let them fool you."

"Why are you so wise?" I asked, leaning into him.

"Because I am British."

I laughed, but after a moment grew serious, remembering the years of awful comments I'd endured silently.

"If they say anything," he said, his voice lowered, "I want to know."

"I'm afraid you'll start believing them," I said, my voice small.

"I'm afraid you've been believing them for far too long. It's time to start believing in how *you* think about you."

We made a splash. There were looks. Of surprise. Of jealousy. Of suspicion. I overheard women talking in the bathroom, saying I was only after his money. He overheard men telling one another that he was only after me because I was an easy lay. The words were hurtful, but I watched the way he ignored them, letting their opinions pass by him like they didn't matter. Because he didn't believe them. And so I took note, breathing through the looks and comments, quieting my mind against others' opinions of me until there was nothing but silence. Peace.

Possibility.

21

"She's looking at me again," I murmured to Rose over the rim of my glass, the lights of the joint swirling in the alcohol under my nose in a mesmerizing kaleidoscope.

"Of course she is," she said, over her own drink. "She's horribly jealous and a right fat cow."

"Rose!" I said, covering my mouth as I laughed.

We were tipsy, having arrived at the Alhambra early to watch the band warm up and noticing two women across the club staring at us and whispering.

"Isn't he dreamy?" Rose said, staring at Ellis, who was onstage filling in for the usual trumpet player.

"He is. And absolutely in love with you."

"He is, isn't he?" she said. "I adore him. He plays me like he does that horn, you know. All fingers and lips."

I nearly spit out my drink as she laughed, loving the reaction.

"Hello, ladies," Lorraine said, plunking down beside me and taking a sip of my drink.

"How are you feeling?" I asked.

She'd been unwell the past couple of weeks, and hadn't been able to perform, leaving Rose and Jessie to fill in for her.

"Tired," she said. "But happy to be back." She checked her

watch. "Shoot. Gotta run. I promised Al I'd meet him at the Shiner for dinner before the show. Ciao, ladies!"

The band finished up and Rose waved for me to follow her backstage through the narrow hallway filled with racks of costumes, instrument cases, extra chairs, and low-hanging smoke, to the band's dressing room across from the nook where the club sewing machine sat. As always, my eyes went straight to the back door, which also served as the "Blacks Only" entrance, reminding me that, though many of us were friendly with the band, the rest of the world wasn't always friendly with them.

"Hey, girl, you slummin' it back here with us tonight? Where's your fancy man?"

I froze where I stood, my eyes on Rose who had planted herself on Ellis's lap.

"Stop givin' the girl a hard time, Jerry," one of the other guys said, poking him in his portly belly.

"I'm just playin'!"

"Jerry," Ellis said, shaking his head and waving for me to take the empty seat beside him and Rose. "He's kidding, Zora. Ignore him."

"Jerry lacks manners," the trombonist, a tall spindly man named Hal said, a wide grin on his face. "Talent too."

"Hey now," Jerry said, shooting a playful glare at his bandmate before turning back to me. "Sorry, Zora. I'm just playin' with ya. We love Harley. He's a good cat." He set his saxophone in its case, pulled out a deck of cards, and sat his heavy frame down in the seat Ellis had saved for me. "Wanna play?"

"Jesus, Jer," Ellis said.

"What?"

"Zora does not want to play one of your terrible made-up card games," a man said from the doorway, leading us all to turn and take him in.

Oscar Holden was the leader of the band, playing piano, singing, unless they brought in a guest singer, and sometimes gracing the crowd with a clarinet solo that had to be heard to be believed.

"Good evening, Oscar," I said, smiling shyly at the musician.

He was dressed, as always, to impress. And impress he did. Oscar Holden was a presence. Cropped hair, a friendly smile, warm inviting eyes, and talent oozing from his every pore and fingertip. I took in his white tuxedo jacket and starched shirt, black trousers, and red pocket square, the burst of color understated but demanding to be seen—like the man wearing it.

"Evenin', Zora," Oscar said and pulled a chair from a stack by the door. "Here you go."

"You aren't falling for that gentlemanly act, are ya, Zora?" Hal asked, waving his flask at Oscar.

I shrugged. "I call it like I see it, Hal. And I sure didn't see you getting me a chair."

The room erupted in laughter.

"You're alright, Zora," Jerry said, shuffling his deck of cards.

I still went home most weekends, but more and more I made excuses, hurrying in later and later on Saturdays and leaving as early as I could get away with on Sundays. Oftentimes I took some of the sewing work with me to finish up after my shift with the Harrington children ended. Other nights I took it to Harley's house where we'd eat dinner and then he'd sit on one end of the couch with paperwork, listening to a radio show Elise Olmstead put on, while I sat on the other with a needle and thread. It was cozy, peaceful, and had started to plant ideas in my head of what life could be like.

"Are you okay?" he asked one particularly cold winter day as he hurried to help me after I slipped on the sidewalk and nearly fell.

We still met on the corner, hiding from Elsbeth who never missed a chance to bring up his name and remind me I wasn't worthy of his time.

I laughed and stomped the snow from the toes of my shoes.

"I'm fine," I said, my breath rising in a cloud between us.

"That you are, Miss Hough," he said, giving me that one-sided smile of his.

He opened the door for me and, as always, I gave a quick glance back toward the house. I was still always on guard about my relationship with him, never divulging to anyone on the Harringtons' staff who I was with when I went out, letting them assume I was meeting Rose and Jessie. So far no one had asked about my whereabouts. I was just another young woman about town in these exciting times of jazz music and gin joints, rouging her cheeks and knees, and flashing bits of skin in a display that was unheard of just a few years before. They paid me no mind and were often amused by the stories I told of a night out with my friends, never suspecting that in between those glimpses into my exploits were kisses and dances danced lost in Harley's eyes, capped off with hours in his bed as we sought one another in the dark again and again.

But a few mornings later my careful omissions and sneaking out to meet Harley caught up with me.

"I saw you," a voice hissed from behind me as I followed the children from the second floor down to the first.

I turned to see Elsbeth, her face stony, eyes narrowed with hate so fierce I nearly tripped and had to grab the handrail to keep from falling.

"Excuse me?" I said, my voice low. I noticed the children had stopped walking and I pasted on a smile and gestured for them to keep going. "Hurry along. Breakfast is waiting."

"I saw you with *him*," she whispered.

"I've no idea what you're talking about," I said, before breezily adding, "Have a nice day!" But my heart was pounding, sweat rising on my skin and dampening my clothes.

"Good morning, everyone," Mr. Harrington said as I ushered the children into the dining room. "Zora? You okay? You look pale, dear."

"Yessir."

I put a smile firmly in place. I didn't want to leave knowing Elsbeth would most likely be waiting for me in the servants' dining area. But I had no choice.

"Good morning, Zora," Cook said when I pushed through the door to the kitchen. "Coffee?"

"Yes, please," I said, hoping she couldn't hear the waver in my voice.

When I took my cup into the staff dining room, Elsbeth was sitting in the spot I usually occupied.

"He's just using you," she said, shaking her head as though pitying me. "It's what these great men do while they bide their time searching for suitable partners. They find playthings. Women of no consequence. Easy prey. You're fooling yourself if you think you're anything more. It's not as if he'll marry you." She laughed as though the thought was ludicrous. "You're nothing to him because, simply put, you're nothing. You come from nothing and you will always be nothing."

She said the words while sipping her tea, her voice never wavering from its low and steady pitch, watching me, waiting for me to say something.

They were ugly words. Words I'd heard before in some shape or form. Words I'd even told myself. But for some reason this time they didn't sting. Perhaps because the person saying them was poison herself.

Perhaps because I was beginning to believe something else. And *in* something else.

Me.

But also Harley. Harley and me. Elsbeth was wrong. Marriage had come up. A fleeting mention one day when Harley handed me a key to his house and told me I could come and go as I pleased. He considered it mine too.

"Until we're married and find a place of both our choosing," he'd said with that grin of his before going to the kitchen to make us dinner.

Elsbeth let out a loud sigh and got to her feet when I didn't rise to her insults.

"Well," she said. "Don't say I didn't warn you."

I went about my day with the children as though nothing had happened. I smiled, sang songs, played games, and organized brief and cold outings outside in the yard, after which the three of us returned inside with pink noses, frozen fingers and toes, and a hankering for Cook's warm milk drink, laden with cinnamon and lightly sweetened with one sugar cube. We sipped from our cups at the kitchen counter, laughing as we peered at one another through the steam.

But when the day was done and I hurried along the sidewalk to meet Harley in our usual spot, I burst into tears as soon as I got close enough to see his waiting smile.

"Zora? What's happened?"

He pulled me to him and I breathed in his scent, pressing against him, his body warming me through my layers.

"Tell me, little love."

But all I could do was bury my face in his lapel.

"Come on," he said. "We'll have dinner in tonight."

While he cooked and I watched, admiring his forearms and hands as he sliced vegetables and threw them in a pan like a professional cook, I told him about my encounter with Elsbeth.

"She's really on a tear, that one," he said, pouring some wine into the pan, the sizzle and steam that followed breathing a delicious scent into the air.

"You're sure you never had a moment with her?" I asked. "Something she misconstrued. Or one you don't remember, but she thought meant something important?"

He laughed and looked at me from the corner of his eyes.

"I do not get around so much that I can't recall names and

faces, my love. Also, I have manners. My mother made sure of it. I don't flirt with..." He stopped then, his cheeks turning a deep shade of red that made me smirk.

"What's that, Mr. Aldridge? You don't flirt with whom?"

"I am not *normally* one to take up with members of a friend's staff."

"And why am I an exception to that rule of yours, kind sir?" I asked, getting out of my chair and leaning my hip against the counter next to him.

"For starters, we met before you had that job. And aside from that..." His eyes swept over me and he put down the spoon in his hand and traced the neckline of my dress with a single finger. "You are too delicious to resist."

He kissed me slow, teasing me until I dug my fingers into his hair with frustration. I wanted more, and I wanted it now.

Having grown up in a household where displays of love were infrequent, and never being with a man before Harley, it was sometimes shocking to me how uninhibited I was with him. I undid his belt and pants and slid my hand down until I found what I wanted.

"Jesus," he whispered, pushing me against the counter, his hands skimming my thighs, raising the hemline of my dress and slip. I wore nothing under it and when he realized that, he groaned, lifted me so that my legs wrapped around him, and carried me to one of the dining room chairs where he lowered himself, and me onto him.

The food was burnt by the time we remembered it, but we merely laughed and picked at the charred dinner, sipping wine and sharing a fresh loaf of bread he'd picked up that afternoon.

"I've half a mind to ask you to stay and drop you off at the house in the morning," he said. "Maybe walk you to the door and kiss you for Miss Pritchard to witness before I leave."

I grinned and raised my face to kiss him.

"You're terrible," I said, with a laugh. "You do that and I'll be out of a job."

"I promise you, Zora, the Harringtons won't care about us dating."

"Maybe not. But Elsbeth will, and then she'll get me fired. She'll tell them I stole something and they'll find it hidden in my room."

"People may have believed her antics before, but we'll know the truth, and we'll make sure others do too."

I sighed as his hands slipped around me. I hoped he was right, but he didn't know how vindictive Elsbeth was. And, despite the calm in her voice, there was a storm brewing inside her, and I was on its path.

Weeks went by without incident. Christmas came and went in a magical rush of snow flurries and beautifully wrapped presents from the Harringtons, some of the girls at the Alhambra, my parents, Rose, and of course, Harley.

"Do you like it?" he asked. It was unlike him to be unsure and I laughed as I twirled in the new coat that hung like a dream and was the most elegant thing I'd ever owned.

"It's gorgeous, Harley," I said, sinking to the floor and tucking my whole body into it, making him laugh. "And so warm. You shouldn't have."

"It's perfect on you," he said as I admired the beautiful lining and ran my hands over the fabric.

"One day I'll make coats like this," I said. "But better."

I'd shown him my sketchbooks, pulling them from their hiding spot one evening and spiriting them out of the house, wanting to share with him what I could do. He'd been impressed. But not just that, he was inspired.

"You need a shop," he'd said. "I'll buy one for you! It'll be a smash."

But I'd laughed and told him no. That was too much and I wasn't ready. Yet.

"I can't get ahead of myself," I said. "What I need is to start sewing the creations I've designed. And I need people to buy them and wear them. If only Harry would get back to me about the sewing machine in the back room. If I could just get some time on it..."

Harley got up from his seat and gestured with one finger. "Come with me. I have one more gift for you."

"Harley!" Besides the coat, he'd already given me a lovely pair of shoes, a beautiful bangle with a fan-shaped clasp, and a dressing gown for when I slept at his house.

I followed him down the hall past his office to a small sitting room that previously housed only an elegant burgundy settee, a small table beside it, and a desk. But now...

I gasped and wrapped my hands around Harley's arm. "Is that—"

"It is," he said, and pressed his hand to the small of my back, urging me forward.

In front of the window where the desk had been, a brand-new sewing machine now stood.

"It's mine?" I whispered, barely daring to touch its sleek body.

"It's yours."

I stared at it a second more and then launched myself at him, feeling his laughter reverberate through me until he set me back down, his expression serious.

"In case you haven't noticed," he said, "I do so love you, beloved woman of mine."

I sighed and melted into him.

"Oh, Harley. I love you too."

"Merry Christmas, Zora."

"Merry Christmas."

22

"Evenin', Mr. Aldridge," the bartender said, having seen Harley and immediately rushing over. "An old-fashioned?"

"Yes, please, Marvin. And the lady will have—"

"A Mary Pickford?" Marvin's eyes met mine and I smiled.

"Yes, please, Marvin," I said.

We'd arrived early to the Alhambra and, since it was quiet still, took a seat at the bar in the back instead of our reserved table near the dance floor where I liked to sit so I could have an unobscured view of my friend when she performed.

"You're here!"

I pulled my eyes away from Harley's at the sound of Rose's voice and watched her hurry through the club, the chandeliers above sparking off the red beading of her dress like miniature fireworks, a look of distress on her face.

"What's wrong?" I asked.

"Milly's strap broke and Carla's hem is unraveling. Can you help?"

"Of course," I said.

Harley stood as I slid off my barstool.

"Save the day, my love," he said.

With Rose's hand around my wrist, we maneuvered through

the tables, hurried across the gleaming hardwood dance floor past Harry, and strode down the backstage hallway into the women's dressing room.

I coughed, breathing in the cigarette smoke, face powder, and perfume that hung in a swirling cloud above.

"Can you fix it?" Milly asked, holding a limp strap in her hand while Rose held out the sewing kit.

"Go finish doing your makeup," I said, shooing them all away. "I'll be done in a jiffy."

As the women returned to their mirrors, I stitched and knotted and snipped as fast as I could.

"These will hold for a few wears, but you'll need to get your seamstress to fix them as soon as you can to make sure nothing catches on it again," I said when I was done, handing the women their garments.

Carla and Rose exchanged a glance.

"What?" I asked, sliding the needle into the fabric.

"Barb's on a bender," Carla said. "She often is. That's why our dresses are such a mess all the time."

"A couple months ago she sewed one of Lorraine's sleeves closed. There was no place for her to put her arm through!" Rose said.

"Does Harry know?" I asked.

More glances between the women.

"He does," Lorraine said, "and we've all begged him to hire you, at least part-time. But he's a cheapskate. He pays her a monthly salary and then ignores the fact that she disappears for a lot of those months and the fact that our costumes are falling apart."

I frowned as I put away the needle, thread, and scissors and closed the sewing kit. Maybe I should be the one to talk to him.

"Have a good show, ladies," I said and hurried from the room.

Harry was at the podium talking to Frankie when I emerged from the back. I caught Harley's eye in the back room and held up a finger to let him know I'd be with him in a moment, and then took a breath and headed toward the owner of the club.

"Harry?"

He turned and gave me a friendly smile.

"What do I owe ya this time, Zora?" he asked, digging in his pockets for some cash.

"I'll get to that," I said. "I heard Barb's…not feeling well at the moment. And the women's costumes are practically falling off them, not to mention they could use a few new ones. There's a ton of fabric in the back and…the truth is, you'd be doing me a favor. I need experience. Designing and sewing for the Alhambra could give me it. I can work for cheap and I promise when Barb is feeling better I'll hand over the reins. But while she's out—"

"How cheap?" he asked.

"Not that cheap."

I turned at Harley's voice.

"I'll make you a price list," I said. "Different charges for different jobs. Sewing on buttons, fixing a strap, raising a hem, and sewing something from scratch. It'll be fair for both of us. And I get to use you as a reference later."

"When can you start? Lorraine won't stop goin' on about the gals at Doc's getting some new costumes. If you can get her off my back, I'd be thrilled."

"I can get measurements from the women tonight and start drawing something up tomorrow. Run designs by you next week?"

He held out a hand. "Deal."

As I walked with Harley back to the bar he squeezed my hand.

"Well, look at that," he said. "You're on your way."

I couldn't stop smiling the rest of the night.

The next night when I arrived at Harley's house, I found a clothing rack beside my sewing machine.

"Where did you get it?" I asked, running my hand along the cold metal bar.

"Clothing store downtown. I asked if they had one I could buy and they didn't. But I'm a good customer so they shifted some things around and here we are."

"It's perfect, Harley. Thank you."

"Anything for my rising star."

Every night that week Harley picked me up on the corner and drove me to his house where he made dinner while I designed and stitched up a dozen or so dresses I'd brought over from the club. Most had holes from wear, hems that had unraveled and been hand sewn into place, patched up straps and sleeves, missing detailing, and the gathered stitching I'd heard about.

I ripped apart seams and resewed them, replaced missing beads, sequins, and fringe, adjusted hemlines, reinforced straps, and revised one set of costumes that were a bit outdated—all on my brand-new, all-mine sewing machine.

It was a much newer model than my mother's, and took a while to get used to the quieter hum, faster stitching, and the many switches.

"It's more complicated than my car!" Harley said at one point as I peered from the instruction manual to the machine.

But I loved it. And once I got the hang of it, stitching up the costumes became a breeze.

When I showed up one Friday evening with an armful of finished dresses, the women squealed, finding their garments and checking them over from neckline to hemline before hugging me one by one.

"Zora doll, you're a genius," Lorraine said, standing in front of the dressing room's one full-length mirror and admiring the side slits and lower neckline I'd added to one of their costumes. "I thought this one had had its day but you've given it new life."

"Well?" Harley asked when I rejoined him in the main room.

"They're ecstatic," I said, just as a tray of drinks and a platter of food was delivered to our table.

"On the house from Harry," the waiter said.

"Well done, you," Harley said, raising a glass.

I grinned and clinked my own against his, thrilled that for once I was responsible for the drinks and food on the table.

The next two weeks were a flurry of meetings with the women as they worked on new routines and I threw them ideas for costume designs and fabric colors.

Life was busier than ever as by day I ran after Madeline and Willem, the evenings I spent having dinner with Harley, and our nights were split between sewing and hanging out at the club.

"Are you happy, my love?" Harley asked on a rare night of staying in while drawing lazy circles on my arm with his finger, my head resting against his chest.

"I am."

I looked up at him and smiled, inhaling, feeling something I hadn't in a very long time, and certainly never in my adult life.

Peace.

"And you?" I asked.

"Quite honestly, Zora? I've never been happier in my life. You are a dream I never imagined could come true."

"I never thought someone like you could exist," I said. "And if you did, I certainly never imagined you could love me back."

He rolled me onto my back then, that little grin on his face that made my body respond in ways I couldn't put words to.

"Oh, but I do," he whispered, trailing kisses down between my breasts. "I do… I do… I do…"

A few nights later, drunk off time spent with Harley, I hurried down the sidewalk to the Harringtons' house, arms crossed over my chest as a barrier to the wind, and nearly ran straight into Elsbeth who was waiting at the side gate.

"I see you refused to heed my warnings," she said, nodding up the street to where Harley was just now driving away. "I hope you know he's telling everyone what an easy lay you are. You're the talk of the town, and not in a good way. All the men know and are taking numbers for who gets you next. I'll be surprised if you have a job tomorrow morning. The Harringtons aren't going to want some floozy taking care of their children. You should probably pack your things now."

With that, she turned on her heel and left me standing in the darkness, shaking. I turned and looked back to where Harley had been parked, but he was gone.

"Shit," I whispered into the wind.

I knew this was coming. Elsbeth had been quiet for far too long, though she'd made sure I saw her watching me. I'd varied the times I left the house to meet him, in hopes I'd miss her on my way out in case she ever followed me and saw me get in his car. Most evenings it worked, but sometimes I wasn't so lucky. And while it made me nervous as to what I'd come home to, I couldn't stop. I loved him.

With a sigh, I pushed through the gate and entered the house.

It was quiet, the usual lights left on, creating a dimly lit pathway from the entryway up the back stairs. I slipped off my shoes and padded upward, avoiding the two steps that creaked and smiling when I reached my room, where a picture of a little girl holding hands with a bigger girl had been adhered to the door. Madeline loved to leave me hand-drawn gifts.

I turned the knob and pushed the door open, frowning as something on the other side slowed its movement. Glancing down at the floor, my stomach turned over. The little bit of light coming from the hallway sconce showed a smear of something dark on the hardwood floor. Stepping over it, I slipped into the room and hurried to the lamp on my bedside table, pulling the chain to turn it on.

On the other side of the door, sitting inside my room, was a large dead rat.

I blinked. Message received.

It was disgusting, but if she'd expected me to scream and wake the house, she was wrong. My life had started in a logging camp and moved to a neighborhood where bathrooms were still outside the house and rats were an unfortunate but common housemate. And thanks to the feral cats the roamed around, I'd cleaned up more "gifts" left on our front porch than most. So the sight of this one, though disturbing to see among the pristine and beautiful decor, didn't make me bat an eyelash.

Stepping back over the blood, I went to the closet where cleaning supplies for the top floor were kept. I scooped the rat into a dustpan and took it outside, tossing it behind a shrub. Grabbing a scrub brush and a pail, I filled the latter with water and soap and went to work, scrubbing the hardwood until it was clean, and then rinsed everything out in the bathtub, put the tools back where they belonged, and cleaned the tub. When I was finished, I washed up, changed into my nightgown, and got in bed. Only then did I allow myself to cry. Not because I was scared or sad, but because no matter where I went, there was always someone who made sure I knew I didn't belong.

23

In the morning I went through the motions as usual. I woke, washed my face, pulled my hair back into a bun at the nape of my neck, and got dressed in my uniform.

Knowing Elsbeth would be waiting for me to come get my morning coffee before I woke the children, I put it off and sat on my bed, watching the clock. When it was nearly time, I put on my apron, smoothed my hair, and went downstairs to the second-floor nursery.

"Good morning, my dears," Mrs. Harrington said a half hour later when I ushered the children into the dining room. "We have a special surprise for you. You're going to eat breakfast with Cook in the kitchen. She's whipped up something extra special for you today."

I moved toward the door, but it opened just then and Cook entered with a jolly smile and her usual pink-cheeked appearance from working over a hot stove and oven.

"Follow me, children," she said.

As they ran past her, her eyes met mine for the briefest of moments. But instead of the worried or disappointed look I'd expected, she gave me a small grin and a wink, confusing me further about what was going on.

"Zora?" Mrs. Harrington said. "Will you have a seat, please?"

I looked from her to Mr. Harrington, unsure what to say, and with a nod, took the seat she'd motioned to.

"We know you've been seeing Harley Aldridge," she said, looking from me to her husband.

I took in a long breath, my heart sinking as my faced warmed and I tried to keep the tears from my eyes. Elsbeth had finally done it. She'd gotten her way and I was out of a job.

"Yes, ma'am," I said. There was no point in lying.

"He had a word with me after that incident in the dining room," Mr. Harrington said. I looked up, surprised. Harley had never said a word to me about speaking to his friend. "He told me his intentions with you, and I told him as long as it didn't interfere with your work here, we had no problems with it." He shrugged. "As far as I can tell, he's lived up to his promise. You are professional, timely, and the children are not only exhibiting daily the skills you've taught them, but they adore you. We are more than happy with the work you are doing and we'd like to offer you a raise."

"I—" I looked from him to his wife, who was smiling. "Are you sure?"

"Do you not like money?" Mr. Harrington asked, laughing.

"Of course but..."

"Yes?"

Confused, I looked from husband to wife and back again.

"You thought Miss Pritchard had gotten you in trouble," Mrs. Harrington said. "I will admit she tried. Which is why we're having this conversation after having an even briefer one with her. Elsbeth sees herself owed more by life. She likes to stir up trouble." She grinned. "You can imagine her disappointment when she found out not only do we know about the relationship, but support it, as well."

I exhaled. "Thank you, ma'am. Sir." I nodded to Mr. Harrington.

"We realize she can be hard to work with. We should've warned you. I hope she hasn't done anything too terrible?"

I thought of the dead rat in my room. I could tell them, but would that make me no better than her? Besides, I'd won. And if she did anything now, the Harringtons would know she was just doing it out of spite and it would more likely be her job on the line, not mine.

"Nothing too terrible," I said.

I bid them good morning then and made my way to the kitchen where Cook was waiting for me with the children.

"Here she is!" Cook said as I entered the kitchen a minute later, the underarms of my uniform damp from nerves. "We've saved you some breakfast, haven't we, children?"

I sat beside them and smiled at Cook as she passed me a plate of fresh-baked thick-cut toast slathered in butter and homemade jam.

"Good morning, Zora," she said.

"Isn't it just?" I said and took a large bite, the weight I'd been carrying on my shoulders dissipating into the bread-scented air.

"She's a cow," Rose said, furious after I'd told her and Ellis about the rat.

It was early and we were sitting in the Alhambra while the staff buzzed around us lighting the centerpiece candles on each table, sweeping the floor, and wiping down the bar.

"Calm down, you," Ellis said, squeezing Rose's hand. "Sounds like Z took care of herself."

"Of course she did," Rose said, pouting prettily. "Still. That girl deserves a taste of her own medicine."

"I'm sure karma will take care of that," Lorraine said from where she'd been quietly sitting, listening, and smoking a cigarette. She blew a perfect smoke circle and sat back in her chair, pointing to the dress she was wearing. "Zora, doll. Think you could take this in for me? It's gotten loose and it's my favorite. But it damn near falls off me these days. I'll pay of course. Whatever you say."

"I'm happy to," I said.

"You're a love," she said and got to her feet. "See you cats later."

She made her way to the front door, waving to the early evening patrons as she went, smiling and doing her Lorraine Darling act, which wasn't much of an act at all. She was always gracious.

"She okay?" I asked Rose who was watching her as well while Ellis chatted with Oscar, who'd come over looking for his red bow tie, which seemed to be missing from their dressing room.

"I don't know," Rose said. "She says she is. But she can't be, right? She so slim and tired all the time."

"And she hasn't said anything about it?"

"Just that she's trying a new diet."

"I'm worried about her."

"Join the club. Oh!" She nearly jumped out of Ellis's lap, her eyes wide. "I forgot to tell you! A man Lorraine knows is coming to the club tonight. He's from Hollywood." Her entire body seemed to sparkle with mention of the famous place we'd only ever read about in newspapers. Rose had been dreaming of going there since seeing her first film and learning it had been made there.

"What's he coming here for?"

"Apparently he's from Seattle, but he's been working in Hollywood for a few years now. On *films*." Rose stomped her blue shoe–clad feet, the satin ribbons keeping them on undulating beneath the lights while Ellis and Oscar laughed at her excitement.

"Rosie's gonna be a movie star," Ellis said, smiling up at her. "I told her she could go right ahead, so long as she doesn't forget us little people."

"Oh, you," she said, sitting back on his lap and kissing him. "I'd never forget you." She looked back to me. "Lorraine says he's looking for talent. Dancers for a new film!"

"Well," I said. "If there was ever a face that belonged on the big screen, it's yours."

"That's what I told her," Ellis said.

Rose shot to her feet again, a look of panic on her face. "I need to get ready!"

She was gone before anyone could say a word, hurrying out of sight backstage as the rest of us laughed.

Harley arrived a while later after a long day of work.

"Hello," he said, taking a seat beside me, his eyes weary but full of love.

"Hello," I said, leaning in for a kiss. "Missed you."

"You have no idea, Zora Hough, how very much I've missed you."

"I may have some inkling."

"I think you just might." He kissed me again and then waved down a waiter. "I hear there's some Hollywood chap coming in tonight. I hope you aren't starstruck and run away with him to the glitz and glamour of Los Angeles."

I laughed. "I think that's more Rose's style than mine," I said. "And how did you hear that so fast? You just got here."

"Frankie told me."

"Of course," I said. Everyone raced to be the first to tell Harley any news that was sure to make a stir.

"Think Rose will head to Tinseltown if he offers her a job?"

"I do," I said, spying her across the room, shoes in hand as she perched on the edge of the stage while Ellis got set up for the night.

He had recently taken over for the former trumpet player and had been joining Oscar at some of the other clubs in town. The Jungle Temple (No. 2) was a favorite spot, and Rose and I had convinced Harley to take us once after an hour of begging and promising not to stay long.

"Fine," he'd said, throwing his hands up. "But those road-houses are known for getting rowdy and I will not risk the two of you getting hurt. We go for one set and then I'm taking you both home."

Ellis had agreed. The roadhouses up and down Highway 99 were famous for fights breaking out, prostitution, and raids. But also some of the best music around.

"Do you think he'd go with her?" Harley asked now, watching Rose and Ellis too.

"I don't know. They love each other, but he's got a good thing going here. I'm not sure he'd leave it. Even for her."

He leaned over to kiss me once more just as a flurry of movement grabbed my attention and I turned my head, causing him to kiss behind my ear and making us both laugh as Rose threw herself into the chair beside me.

"He's here!" she whispered loudly before racing away again.

"She's subtle, that one," Harley said.

Lorraine, followed by Rose, Jessie, and a gaggle of some of the other dancers, led Mr. Hollywood, as Harley had dubbed him, to our table a few minutes later.

He was medium height, thin, with light brown hair and eyes that darted around to each of us, seeming to take in a lot in the few seconds each of us had his attention. His suit was expensive, the ring on his pinkie finger too large, and he had an air about him like he knew he was important and was waiting for that to be acknowledged, his chest puffed out, chin tilted up, a smile on his face at all times.

"Ladies," he said and then looked at Harley. "And gentleman. I'm Dean Billings. A pleasure to meet you all."

Harley gave him a nod, the smile on his face amused. I squeezed his hand and he squeezed back.

Dean Billings had indeed grown up in Seattle and had spent most of his life there until moving to California ten years ago at the age of twenty-two.

"Music, acting… I love it all," he said. "I needed to be in the town creating the magic I'd only read about in the papers."

He was charming, and handsome in a forgettable sort of way, no one feature standing out to make you stop in your tracks or elbow your best gal to take a gander. It was his prowess, his confidence, that were his most attracting qualities. That and the very fact that he was connected to Hollywood.

"You're a pretty girl," he told me after the dancers had gone backstage to prepare for their entrance. He looked to Harley as if waiting for a jealous reaction. But Harley knew me too well to think I'd be enraptured by this man. "Do you dance too?"

"I don't," I said.

"Shame," he said and then turned his attention to the dance floor as the music started.

"Whadja think, Dean?" Lorraine asked when the show was over.

"As good as you promised," he said. "Those two on either side of you especially."

I grinned at Harley. He was talking about Rose and Jessie.

"You gonna offer 'em jobs?"

"Well, I suppose I'm gonna have to if I can't convince you to come."

"Would if I could, doll," she said. "But I'm too old for all that nonsense."

"You're still as gorgeous as ever, my dear."

"You're sweet," she said. "But a liar. All you Hollywood types are the same." She gave him a saucy wink and we all laughed, but I knew there had to be a lot of truth to what she said, which made me worry for Rose. I knew if she was offered a job by this man she would probably take it without a second thought.

"Gotta do what I have to, to get what a film needs," Dean said with a small shrug. He put a hand on Lorraine's slender shoulder then, rubbing the strap of her dress with his fingers. "This is lovely. Where do you ladies get your costumes? I may have to hire them away from this place too."

Lorraine pointed to me.

"You've been sitting with our costume designer all evening. Zora took over a couple months ago and she's been a wonder."

"You designed this?" he asked me.

"And made it," I said.

He took a step away from Lorraine and twirled a finger, watching Lorraine do a slow spin, the lights sparking off the red fabric, sequins, and slender strips of gold I'd sewn on to sway with the dancers' bodies.

"It's exquisite," he said and looked at me again. "We should have a conversation. I was only half joking when I said I might have to hire away whoever designed it. Would you have any interest designing for the film industry?"

"I'm not sure. It's not something I've ever thought of."

"Well maybe you should. You are a talent, Miss..."

"Hough," I said.

"Zora Hough," he said, squinting his eyes. "Not much of a ring to that but we can work on it."

I looked to Harley and could tell he was trying not to laugh.

Dean looked at his watch. "I have to be off," he said. "I have another club I want to check out tonight." He looked to me and held out a hand. "I'll be in touch. Harley?" He shook Harley's hand next. "A pleasure, sir. I hope to see you both again soon. Lorraine, dear? See me out?"

I watched his retreating back, my mind a cocktail of excited thoughts and ideas as the band struck up a lively song and bodies weaved through the crowd to get a spot on the dance floor.

"Well," Harley said. "He's a whirlwind."

"Indeed."

"What did you think about what he said?"

"Honestly?" I looked into his beautiful blue eyes, the sight of him never failing to make my heart race. "It sounds ludicrous. One of those things people say but don't mean."

"And if he does?" he asked, worry creeping into his gaze.

"Then I guess you and I will have some things to discuss," I said. "Like where we'll live."

"I do declare, Miss Hough." He sat back and pressed a hand to his chest. "Are you suggesting we run away and shack up in sin?"

"You have a problem with that, Mr. Aldridge?"

He stared down at me, his gaze so intense, for a moment I was worried I'd said something I shouldn't have.

And then I saw it, that cute quirk in the corner of his lips that slowly melted in a smile, causing my blood to race.

"Not at all, my love," he said. "Not. At. All."

24

"You have to come," Rose said from where she was lying on Jessie's bed, dressed only in rolled stockings, white satin tap pants, and a brassiere. "Can you imagine the fun we'd have?"

"It's true," Jessie said, pulling a purple scarf from the lampshade it was thrown over and tying it around her neck. She frowned at her reflection in the full-length mirror, untied the scarf, and threw it back on the lamp. "We'll get to see movie stars every day on set, eat food brought in for us, and go out every night."

I grinned from where I sat out of the way in the corner of Jessie's studio apartment, reveling in the scents and sights that filled the small space.

Jessie Droney, I'd learned in the past couple of months, was really Jezebel Diaz. She'd spent her early childhood in her parent's hometown of Madrid, Spain, but the family moved to America when she was eleven, first to Texas, then to Northern California before making their way to West Seattle where her parents and two younger siblings still lived.

She'd told me her secret one night when Harley had to work late and I'd come over for dinner with Rose, marveling when Jessie served dish after dish of foods I'd never seen or heard of before, pronouncing their names in a beautiful accent.

"How do you know how to cook all this?" I'd asked, causing her and Rose to exchange a glance.

"It is my heritage," she'd said, and then twirled away from the table, spatula in one hand, dishtowel in another, and did a dance the likes of which I'd never seen before. "As is flamenco."

After years of watching her parents struggle to find good jobs, she'd decided early on to lose her accent as fast as she could.

"By the time we got to Seattle, I sounded American. And it helps that I come from a line of fair-haired Spaniards." She pointed to her blond hair and blue eyes. "At first my parents were appalled I hid my heritage, but I was desperate. We were treated differently here. People would see us and be friendly, but as soon as my father opened his mouth and rattled something off in Spanish, they would be put off. I became angry with them for not even trying to learn the language. Why come to America and not learn how to speak English? Despite their stubbornness, they finally began to appreciate that my learning helped not just me, but them, as well. It does make me feel bad sometimes. I look at other immigrants who can't hide in plain sight like I can and are treated poorly. Like they are less than. I feel guilty. But we're all just trying to survive."

Since that day, she'd taught Rose and me some Spanish words. Specifically naughty ones.

"Whisper that to Harley in bed," she'd said after rattling off a particularly lewd string of words in Spanish before translating it to English, making Rose howl with laughter and causing me to nearly choke on my drink.

I loved being with the two of them. Loved how alike they were, but still so different. But mostly I loved how eagerly Jessie had taken to me and included me, honoring the friendship Rose and I had created so many years before in the dusty schoolyard of our youth.

I leaned back now, watching as the two of them changed outfits yet again, making myself scarce so as not to get run over or have garments thrown on top of me. As it were, I had two dresses lying across my lap, a hat Rose had discarded on my head, and a coat on the chairback behind me. At my feet were a pile of shoes.

It was all because of Dean Billings, who was rumored to be returning to the Alhambra for tonight's show. The news had sent Jessie and Rose into a tizzy, as they wanted to make sure he saw them in their best clothes should he arrive early.

And so I'd watched as they slipped into one outfit, posed in the mirror, posed for one another, asked my opinion, ignored it, and pulled the garment off again.

I had to admit, it was fun. It had been weeks since I'd joined them at Jessie's before going to the club.

After a while, Rose sighed and sat heavily on the bed, sending several garments sliding to the floor.

I peered at her. I'd noticed she'd seemed a little off today. Her smile a little less bright. Her energy seen but not felt. As though she were faking her enthusiasm, but I had no idea why.

"You alright, Tiller?" I asked.

She rolled over onto her stomach and propped her bare face up on her hands. I loved her like this. Natural, her freckles showing, eyes wide and bright and unhindered by a frame of black cakey makeup.

"Ellis is sad I'm so excited about this Hollywood thing. He supports me, no matter what I choose, but he's unhappy I'd go without him."

"Why doesn't he go too? I'm sure there are plenty of bands that would love to have him."

"That's what I said. But he loves his bands. And Oscar. He doesn't want to let any of them down. He said their time ain't up yet. And then..."

"And then what?" I asked.

"Verle, Bobby, and Ricky are still giving us a hard time."

"Still?" I frowned, my skin pricking with anger.

Rose nodded and her eyes filled with tears. I got out of the chair and sat beside her.

"What did they say?"

"Just more hateful things. Terrible things. Stuff about whites and Blacks mixing. About it being dirty. It was embarrassing. And frightening."

"Did they threaten you? Did they threaten Ellis?"

But she didn't respond, she just laid her head down on her arms.

"We need to talk to Harry," I said.

"I have," Jessie said. "So has Lorraine."

"And?"

She sat on the other side of Rose and shrugged. "These club owners are all about one thing. Money. As long as those boys aren't disrupting that, he doesn't care much. They haven't started any fights or made a scene, so to him, they're just children playing schoolyard games."

Maybe, I thought, but I was worried all the same.

"We'll make sure you're safe," Jessie said, patting Rose's back. "I promise."

"Hollywood?"

Mama sat staring at me, her mouth open as she tried to register the news I'd just told her.

"But—"

"Nothing's for certain, Mama," I said, ripping out a stitch so I could take a hemline up. "It's an idea that's being thrown around is all."

As I normally did on the weekends, I'd come home to my parents' house to help with the sewing. There had been a few occasions when I'd begged off so I could stay in with Harley, or go shopping downtown with Rose and Jessie, hitting our usual spots, and every so often peeking into the upscale Carman's, a large store that sold beautiful women's apparel, and the place they bought their stockings.

"But Zora…the money? Would it be more? Less? I'd hate to think of you giving up your place at the Harringtons for less. Not just—" She stopped, her cheeks reddening, and I reached for her hand.

"I'd never take the job if it were for less than what I was making now. But the talking hasn't even gone that far yet," I said. "And it might not. The whole idea could amount to absolutely nothing, and probably will."

"And if it isn't?"

"I don't know, Mama," I said.

I flew through a pile of easy mending, raised three hems, shortened a pair of sleeves, and added a ruffle to a hand-me-down dress for a neighbor. At four I set my needle in its pincushion, stretched my back and stood.

"I'm gonna go for a walk, Mama," I said.

She nodded, her mouth full of straight pins, eyes focused on the skirt she was sewing.

It was comforting but strange walking down the street of the neighborhood I'd grown up in, breathing in the familiar air, taking in the houses I knew so well.

Everything looked smaller suddenly, and I found myself noticing every little detail. A fence that had been torn down in lieu of new shrubbery. A fresh coat of paint on a house. A new car in an old driveway. Missing shingles and bicycles sprawled in yards.

The sagging roofs looked saggier. Barren yards, bereft of grass. Scattered toys, stacks of wood left out in the rain, and tilting porches.

This was home. This was where I had belonged for so long I knew how many steps it took me to walk from the corner to our front door. And yet, it didn't feel quite like home anymore. Nowhere did. I felt untethered.

I walked to the end of the block and kept going, heading toward Sunset Hill Park.

It looked the same. And I felt the same standing in my favorite spot. It had always seemed like the edge of the world as I stared out over Shilshole Bay, the Olympic Mountains in the distance, craggy and snow-tipped. How many times had I stood here contemplating life, crying at being bullied, the wind wiping away my tears. Crying because I was hungry. Crying because Tommy was gone.

I sank to the damp ground, gathering my knees and resting my chin on them, thinking of what had become of my life in less than a year. The Harringtons, the job at the Alhambra, Harley...and now the possibility of Hollywood. It was strange and wonderful and confusing. Before my life had been filled with hardship, but it had been solid. I'd known who I was and where I stood in the world. Now the world had opened up to me, and I felt as though I were off-kilter, and scared I might fall.

Three nights later Dean was back at the club with an offer.

"We'll set you up in an apartment with Rose and Jessie, and pay the first two months' rent while you ladies get your feet under you. There will be some long hours and a few weekends here and there, but not too many. But who cares? You'd be designing for the stars. Hollywood's darlings. Your creations on the silver screen." He slid a folded piece of paper across the table to me. "And this is what we'd pay you."

I glanced at Harley and then picked up the paper and looked at the number inside. It was double what I was making at the Harringtons' and the Alhambra combined. I refolded it and set it down.

"When do you need to know?" I asked.

"I leave two weeks from next Monday," he said and got to his feet. "I hope you'll be joining us."

I looked past him to where Rose and Jessie were standing just off to the side of the stage, watching us, huge grins on their faces.

Us.

"And if I have other living arrangements?" I asked.

He looked to Harley and then back at me.

"Then just let me know," he said and, with a nod to Harley and a tip of his hat to the girls, he left.

"Did you say yes?" Rose asked as she and Jessie ran over.

I shook my head. "No. Not yet anyway. I have a lot to think about. I can't just up and leave the Harringtons with no nanny."

"Don't they have two others that could step in?" Jessie asked.

"What about Sarah?" Rose asked.

I grinned. We both knew my younger sister hated taking care of any kids that weren't her siblings.

"Nice try," I said.

"Think of the money you'll be making. Sarah wouldn't want you to miss out on that."

"I'll think about it. It's an amazing opportunity. But the timing might not be right and I have to make sure I'm doing the responsible thing."

I looked over my shoulder at Harley then and smiled softly. I knew he'd have to shift a lot of things to come with me. We'd been talking about it ever since the possibility had arisen. He was willing to do it, for us. But probably wouldn't be able to come down until a few months after me so he could make sure the manager of the furniture company had everything well in hand. The bootlegging business would take a hit though. He wasn't comfortable leaving that in someone else's hands and without him around to make sure things were being run properly, he didn't think it was wise to keep it going and wasn't sure he wanted to start from scratch somewhere else. On top of that, he'd had some recent issues with the business when one of the trucks and a boat had gotten sidelined and searched. And then there were the recent threats from another bootlegger who didn't like an out-of-towner infringing on what he thought was his turf.

"Are the threats serious?" I'd asked.

"I don't think so. But people do strange and drastic things sometimes when they think they're right. I have my staff keeping eyes and ears on things."

"What could they do to you?"

He'd smiled and pulled me to him. "Don't fret, my love. It's most likely all a bunch of bluster."

I'd hugged him tight, reassured, but also hoping that his confidence wouldn't make him overlook something he should be more concerned about.

The music started up then and Rose and Jessie, excitedly discussing everything they wanted to see once they arrived in Hollywood, hurried backstage to get changed. I glanced at the stage and saw Ellis staring after her, a sad smile on his face.

"Long-distance relationships are hard," Harley said, taking my hand.

I nodded, having had the same thoughts and comparing them to Harley and me. Harley, who was willing to leave a town he'd done so well in in order to be with me should I ask him to.

And it was in that moment that I realized I wouldn't ask him. Because while it would probably be exciting and a tale to one day tell my grandchildren, Hollywood wasn't the dream. Seattle was. Seattle and a little boutique I was starting to believe I could one day really have.

"What are you grinning about?" Harley whispered in my ear.

"The future," I said

"Yours?"

"No, Harley. Ours."

25

The band was on fire, the dancers moving around the floor as the lights above made beads, sequins, and fringe undulate like waves in an ocean of excess and booze.

I was tipsy, forgoing my usual one drink for two and a half thanks to Lorraine, who'd been absent for most of the week and unable to celebrate both Rose and Jessie accepting the offer to dance in Hollywood, and my decision to stay.

I'd told Mr. Billings my decision after the girls had told him theirs.

"A shame," he'd said, looking past me to where Harley stood at the bar chatting with the bartender. "The boyfriend doesn't approve?"

I grinned. How like a man to assume a woman's decisions were determined by anyone but herself.

"He does. Wholeheartedly. But Hollywood isn't my dream."

"I respect that," he said. "If you change your mind, I'm but a mere phone call away."

I took a sip of my drink and watched Lorraine take a large gulp of hers.

"I'm so glad you're not going," she slurred.

I was happy to see she had a little color in her face, her cheeks not quite as gaunt. Wherever she'd gone to get some rest, it had clearly helped.

"Want another?" she shouted, pointing to a tray of drinks that had just been delivered.

I shook my head and held up the one I was still working on.

"So?" she said. "You're other hand's free, ain't it?"

I laughed, feeling the sensation reverberate through my body. I didn't often get drunk. Didn't like the feeling of losing control. But I felt safe here with these people. *My* people. Rose and Jessie and Lorraine pulling me out to dance, and Harley, waiting for me always when I came back to the table.

I took the drink from Lorraine but then set both down and leaned into my boyfriend.

"You okay?" he asked, running a finger lightly down the nape of my neck, making me shiver.

"I think I've had a touch too much to drink," I said.

"You going to be sick?"

"No. But I do need to use the ladies'."

I stood up and immediately fell back down in my seat, laughing so hard I hiccupped.

"Rose," Harley called, pointing to me. Her eyebrows raised. "She needs to use the bathroom. I think she could use a hand."

Rose took one look at me and laughed. "Well, I'll be, Miss Zora Lily Hough. I do believe you're zozzled."

"And how," I slurred, letting her pull me to my feet.

We weaved through the crowd, the movement of the bodies combined with my feet hitting the floor with each exaggerated step making me feel like I was on a boat. Except I'd never been on a boat. But I had been on a horse-drawn wagon, and someone once told me the two things felt similar.

Holding tight to Rose's hand, I saw a familiar face in the crowd. Gil. I'd never given him much in the way of explanations when I'd stopped showing up at the times I knew he'd be at the club. But when I professed feelings of guilt over it,

Jessie had waved a hand and said, "He never staked his claim. That's on him. Besides, I think he's got the picture." I'd pursed my lips, my face warming as she alluded to my involvement with Harley that hadn't been missed by a single soul. And certainly not Gil.

In the bathroom I splashed water on my face while Rose fixed her lipstick in the mirror beside mine.

"You're sure havin' fun tonight," she said, glancing over at me and grinning.

I looked in the mirror, grinned at my reflection, and hiccuped again, the sound echoing through the bathroom.

Our laughter bounced off the walls.

We headed back out, my hand in Rose's again as she led me down the hallway to the main room of the club.

"Hey, Rose!" I heard a male voice call out.

Her pace quickened, causing me to trip as I tried to keep up. I turned my head and saw Verle and his friends staring after us.

"Rose?" I said.

But she wasn't listening, too intent on putting as much space between us and them as possible.

"Everything alright?" Harley asked when we returned, looking with concern from me to Rose.

"I'm not sure," I said, staring at my friend. But if she was still bothered by the brief interaction, she was covering it well with a bright smile and a big, long sip of what was left of my drink. I noticed Verle, Ricky, and Bobby leaving and caught her eye.

"They're leaving," I said.

"Good," she said, without looking.

Since it was Friday night, we stayed late, enjoying the ambiance as the crowd thinned, people moving on to other clubs or heading home for the night, and leaving us with a calmer, more intimate experience.

"Where's Harley?" Rose asked. She had changed into her day dress and Ellis was waiting for her as always in the doorway to the backstage area, instrument case in one hand, his jacket in the other.

"Talking to Harry," I said, walking with her over to Ellis. "You guys going somewhere else or heading home?"

"Home," Rose said, leaning in to hug me. "My toes are screaming."

"It was a great show. Have a good weekend, you two."

"G'night, Z," Ellis said, giving me a wave before turning his attention to Rose.

I wandered back to our table, noting Harley at the back bar, the few stragglers left, and two members of the band still sitting in their seats on the stage, quietly working through a piece of music and chatting in between notes.

Grabbing my purse, I threw my coat over my arm and headed for the door.

"You leaving, Miss Zora?" Frankie asked from where he stood by his podium.

"I am," I said, stifling a yawn. "Will you tell Harley I'm waiting for him outside? I need the cool air."

"You got it, miss. See you next week."

"Thanks, Frankie."

I slowly scaled the stairs, tired, my feet aching, my belly in need of food. I was staying at Harley's that night and couldn't wait to get there, picturing the fresh loaf of bread and jar of jam he'd purchased the day before that would taste so good after all that dancing, and would sop up whatever alcohol was left in my stomach too.

My shoes clicked against the hardwood floor as I walked down the empty hallway to the door leading outside. I pushed it open then stepped through, frowning at a strange set of sounds as the door swung closed behind me.

In a flurry of movement I was yanked to the side, a hand clamped over my mouth, and my arms pinned painfully behind my back as I was half dragged into the dark behind the building.

"Where's Harley?" a voice asked in my ear, hot breath and spittle spraying my cheek.

"Right behind me," I lied into the hand.

"Hurry up, boys," he said. It was then that I saw what was happening, my eyes adjusting to the darkness. I screamed into the hand and tried to break free, but I was just held tighter.

We were tucked out of sight behind a set of large trash cans and crates filled with empty bottles. Ellis was being held down on the ground as another man punched him repeatedly. His trumpet case lying on the ground beside him, open, the pieces strewn about on the pavement. A few feet away Rose was pinned against a wall, her back to her assailant, a hand over her mouth as he lifted her dress and tried to get her undergarments out of the way, his own pants pulled down just enough to get the job done.

"No!" I screamed, throwing my head back in hopes of catching my own captor in the chin. But he just pulled my arms back harder and my knees nearly gave at the pain in my shoulders.

Between the horrible wet, smacking sound of Ellis being punched, and Rose's pleading turning to whimpers as she began to lose the energy to fight, I felt something I knew I never wanted to feel again. A helplessness that ached to the very core of me. I would rather die than see any of this happen.

The man holding Rose shouted to the guy hitting Ellis.

"Leave him, he's done. Come hold her for me. Quick!"

He turned his head then, finally giving me a view of his face.

Ricky.

Whatever was left of what I'd drank that evening bubbled up and spewed hot and putrid from my lips.

"Ugh!" the man holding me yelled, unclamping my mouth long enough for me to scream.

"Help!"

"Shut her up!" Ricky shouted.

But as the hand moved back into place over my mouth, I

found I had enough room to do what I'd tried earlier. This time when I threw my head back, I made contact.

"Dammit!" the man yelled, releasing me.

I pitched forward, falling to my hands and knees, my head ringing, the pavement digging into my skin.

But all I could think of was Rose.

Scrambling to my feet, I lurched toward her, but my legs gave and I fell again. The door slammed behind me and I watched in confusion through the dark as another pair of legs appeared. Then another. There was shouting, a crash, and Rose, whimpering as she sank to the ground.

"Rose," I said, but the sound was barely more than a whisper. And then someone was lifting her into their arms.

"Zora."

I blinked.

"Harley?"

"Let's get you out of here."

I reached up and then gasped, letting my arms fall back to my sides, my shoulders screaming in pain.

"Don't," Harley said. "I've got you."

I sagged against him as he carried me out of the alleyway to the street, and then into the passenger seat of his car.

"I'll be right outside the car if you need me," he said. "Just have to take care of some business."

I nodded, turning sideways in the seat and resting my cheek against the soft, cool fabric. It took a minute before I realized there was someone whispering in the back seat and I peeked around to find Rose, her face streaked with makeup, her hair in a disarray, and Ellis lying across her lap, bloodied, his eyes swollen shut, a stream of blood dripping from his nose and mouth onto her knee.

"Is he…?" I was afraid to ask. Afraid to know. Afraid to be witness to such brutality. And my friend… "Rose. Are you…"

But she didn't say a word. Didn't answer me. Just kept her head bowed over Ellis, whispering and crying softly into his hair.

The driver's door opened suddenly, making me jump, and Harley got in.

"Frankie and Harry are staying until the police get here. I'm going to take the rest of you to the hospital."

"No," Ellis whispered. "No hospital."

I turned to look at him, breathing a sigh of relief that he was alive and awake.

"Don't fight me on this, Ellis," Harley said. "You could have injuries we can't see."

"No," he said again. "I won't go."

"Baby," Rose said.

"No," he said more forcefully and began to cough.

"He hates hospitals," she said. "It's a long story. He'll probably fight you if you try and take him."

"He's in no shape to fight me," Harley said, running a hand through his hair. "Fine. I'll take him to my place and call the doctor to come see you all there."

"I'm fine," I said. "Just scraped up a little."

"Me too," Rose said.

"Rose." I looked around the seat at my friend.

"He didn't—" Her eyes filled with tears and she looked out the window. "I'm fine."

Several minutes later we pulled up to Harley's house. He hurried out of the car to help Ellis, Rose limping around the back of the car to assist.

"Let me," I said, gently moving her aside so I could assist Harley in getting Ellis into the house.

Inside, we put Ellis on the couch, propping his head on one of Harley's fancy velvet pillows and pulling the throw blanket from the chair in the corner and spreading it over his bloodied body.

"I'm going to call the doctor," Harley said. "Zora, why don't you get Rose and Ellis some water."

When he returned, I was alone with Ellis, watching his chest rise and fall and listening to his labored breathing.

"Where's Rose?"

"Bathroom," I said. "Is the doctor coming?"

"He's on his way."

"You gotta get her outta here," Ellis mumbled.

I glanced at Harley who shot me a worried look.

"What do you mean, El?" he asked.

"Rose. You gotta get her out of here. I don't want her to hear what the doc has to say."

"Ellis—"

"Please, Harley," he said, his one eye that wasn't swollen shut imploring. "Please."

"Where does she live?"

"Ballard," I said and looked at Ellis. "Can she stay at your place? It's closer."

"Nah. Not without me with her. It isn't safe."

I chewed my lip, thinking.

"I could sneak her in the Harrington'," I said, musing over the idea. "She could stay in my room all day and then I could sneak her out tomorrow night after everyone's gone to bed." I looked to Harley. "Can you get word to us how Ellis is doing?"

"Of course. But are you sure?"

"She's my friend. What choice do I have?"

"I'll vouch for the situation if need be," he said and I nodded. I may need him to indeed.

"What's going on?" Rose asked, returning to the room.

"Rose, baby," Ellis said, reaching out a hand that clearly had a few broken fingers. "Come here."

She didn't want to go. Didn't want to leave his side. Wanted to hear what the doctor had to say. Harley and I left them as he whispered to her and wiped away her tears, leaving streaks of his blood on her skin. When the doctor arrived, Rose put on a brave face.

"I'll be back tomorrow night," she told Ellis, leaning down to kiss his forehead.

"I'll be waiting for you."

While the doctor examined Ellis, Harley took Rose and me to the Harringtons', parking near the side gate and helping each of us from the car.

"You run into any trouble," he said. "Have Jonathan call me."

I nodded, kissed him, and then led Rose to the house while saying a silent prayer that no one in the house was awake.

As usual at that late hour, the house was silent, save for the ticking of the clock in the servants' dining room.

We slipped off our shoes and hurried up the stairs as fast as we could to the safety of my room.

"What do you need?" I asked when we were safely inside.

I'd never seen Rose look small before. She'd always been bigger than life. A presence. A force of power, laughter, and love. Nothing ever seemed to get her down. Until now.

She stood just inside the door, dress torn, hair knotted, scratches, bruises, and blood on her arms and neck. I wasn't sure if it was hers or Ellis's and feared what the rest of her looked like. The parts beneath the dress. I feared for her heart, her mind, and her precious soul.

"Rose?"

"I want to be clean," she whispered. "I can smell him on me."

I closed my eyes for a moment and then nodded. "Come on. I'll draw you a bath."

I helped her undress, watching her carefully as I knelt and undid the straps of her shoes and then stood to help her out of her dress, which was easy as the zipper was torn open. I slid the straps off her shoulders and carefully pulled her dress, camisole, and tap pants down so she could step out of them.

The marks on her arms and neck were nothing compared to

the brutality marking her hips, buttocks, and thighs where she had been held on to so tight it had broken her skin.

She gasped as she reached back to undo her brassiere and I stood.

"Let me," I said, brushing her hands away. She sagged in response.

I helped her into the tub then, watching as she sank down to her chin, eyes closed, the water rocking with her every breath. She looked like the saddest porcelain doll I'd ever seen, with black eye makeup streaked down her cheeks, her lipstick smeared, a pale bruise just beginning to show on her cheekbone.

"Rose," I said, but she shook her head.

"Don't," she said. "I can't, Z." She shuddered. "I can still feel his hands on me."

Her lip trembled and she squeezed her eyes shut tighter, tears gathering in the corners before streaming down her face to the water below. She reached for my hand, gripping it tight, and that's how we stayed until the water grew cold.

We slept like we had as girls whenever I got to sleep over at her house—facing one another, hands clasped between us. She fell asleep almost immediately, her breath slowing, the rise and fall of her body easing from wakefulness to somewhere I hoped brought her peace. At least for tonight. I feared what tomorrow would bring. What news of Ellis would come.

As I drifted off to sleep finally, my own body worn, my emotions raw and heartbroken for Rose and Ellis, I thanked the universe once again for the blessing that was Harley. That he'd been able to help stop what was happening. That he was strong and had loyal friends who didn't hesitate to help. That he was able to get us out of there to somewhere safe. I wasn't sure what I'd done in life to deserve him, but I knew I'd never take my good luck for granted.

26

I awoke and dressed as quickly and quietly as I could so as not to wake Rose who'd had a fitful night of sleep, tossing and turning and even crying at times.

My body ached as I pulled on a blouse, a pair of trousers over the bandages covering my bloodied knees, shoes, and a jacket, pulling the cuffs of the sleeves over my scraped hands before hurrying from my room to the kitchen.

"Mornin'," Cook said as I poured myself a cup of coffee.

"Good morning," I said, nearly scalding myself as I took a sip. "Oh!"

"It's hot, Zora. Just like every morning," Mrs. Beckwith said with an impish grin as she slowly sipped her own coffee from her usual spot at the dining table.

I looked from her back to Cook and over to Charles who raised his own cup and went back to reading the newspaper before him. No one looked at me strangely. No one knew I'd broken the rules and brought someone into the house.

I poured a second cup, grabbed two biscuits from the basket, and tucked an apple in my pocket.

"I'll be in my room all day if anyone needs me," I said to anyone who was listening.

"Not going home this weekend?" Mrs. Beckwith asked.

"No," I said and went back upstairs.

I sat with Rose all morning while she fell in and out of sleep, turning and moaning, frowning as she slept, crying silently when she woke.

She barely said a word as she sipped at the coffee, picked at the biscuit, and didn't bother with the apple at all. At ten I checked the hallway to make sure Mrs. Larson wasn't around and then ran her another bath. We both grimaced at the sight of her bruises, which were even darker than they'd been the night before.

"I wish Harley would get a message to you," she said. "Not knowing how Ellis is is maddening."

"I'm sure he's resting, just like you are."

The moment the words were out of my mouth there was a knock on my bedroom door.

"I'll be right back," I said, pressing a finger to my lips.

I hurried to my bedroom and opened the door.

"Mr. Aldridge is here," Mrs. Beckwith said with a grin. "He's asked to see you."

"Oh," I said, running a hand over my hair. "Thank you. I'll be right down."

I shut the door and rushed back to the bathroom.

"Harley's here," I said and then watched in horror as Rose quickly sat up, nearly sending a small wave of water over the edge of the claw-foot tub, her face contorting with the pain the movement caused her. "I'll be back as soon as I can. Please don't try to get out without my help. Promise me."

Defeated, she nodded and lay back once more, closing her eyes, her tears mixing with the bath water.

"Harley," I said, a worried smile on my face as I walked across the grand foyer to meet him.

No one else was around, that I could see, but I didn't trust we weren't being watched, or at the very least listened in on. Harley must've suspected the same.

"Zora, my love," he said, and then leaned down to kiss my cheek and whisper in my ear. "Everything go okay last night?"

I nodded.

"How's our friend?" I asked.

He frowned and my heart dropped.

"He's got a long road ahead of him. Some broken ribs, a broken nose, a few fingers… Doc seems to think he'll be okay though. Lots of rest for now. He'll stay with me for the next few days so I can keep an eye on him, and then I'll take him home where Rose can dote on him."

"She'll like that."

"And how is she?" he asked, lowering his voice again.

"A bit beat up, but nothing seems to be broken. Except maybe her spirit. She's mostly worried about him."

"Well, let her know Ellis is going to be okay. That should help."

"And tonight?" I asked.

"I'll meet you both by the gate. Eleven okay?"

"We'll see you then."

He kissed me then and I saw him out, watching as he walked down the front path to his car. With a last wave I shut the door and hurried back upstairs to my friend.

Thankfully there was no one about when Rose and I crept down the stairs and out the side door to Harley's waiting car.

"Everything okay?" he asked as we got in.

I nodded.

"How are you, Rose?" Harley asked as he drove away from the house.

"Anxious to see Ellis. How is he?" she said.

He glanced at me and I gave him a small smile. Rose hadn't said much, even though we'd spent the entire day in my room together. Every time I'd broached the subject of the attack, her body stiffened. But from the little she had said, I got the impression that what was taken from her was only her sense of safety and the feeling of being powerless. Which was no small thing, but better than what else could've been taken.

Harley had brought Ellis to his own home at his request. He was resting in bed when we arrived, four men and a woman, whose faces I found familiar, sitting around the kitchen and living areas.

Without a word, Rose left Harley and me at the front door and rushed down the hall to see her boyfriend.

"This is Zora," Harley said, introducing me to the crowd. "Zora, this is Roger, Bill, Charles, Jamie, and Drea."

I smiled and nodded, taking the hand of one, a tall Black man, as he approached.

"Nice to meet you, Zora. I'm Roger, Ellis's older and better-looking brother." He winked and we all laughed. "Bill and Drea are our younger siblings. And I think you may have seen Charles and Jamie around?"

I nodded. Charles was a musician and had played with Ellis at the Bucket of Blood where Jamie was a frequent visitor, standing out for his sharp and slightly flamboyant suits. He was usually in the company of a pretty blond-haired woman. I wondered where she was now.

"It's nice to meet you all," I said.

"You're the one who makes all those dresses?" Drea asked. Out of all of Ellis's siblings, she looked the most like him.

"I am."

"You've got a good eye on you. I might have to hire you to make me one."

"I'd be happy to. Where is that one from? It's beautiful." I asked, admiring the periwinkle fabric, dropped waist with wide band that wrapped around her hips, and pleated detailing on one shoulder.

"Got it in San Francisco. It's a Hilda Steward."

"It's very elegant."

Roger pulled out a chair for me then, and he and Harley

and I took a seat around a small kitchen table where a vase I recognized from where it used to sit on Rose's dresser sat in the center.

Charles, Drea, and Bill returned to the living room, while Jamie took the remaining seat at the kitchen table. It wasn't until I saw them under the kitchen light that I realized the person I'd assumed to be a man had eyebrows made fuller with makeup, a soft shadow rubbed across their jaw with what I assumed was the same caked black stuff I'd learned to use to line my eyes. They caught me watching, winked while I tried not to appear flustered at my naivete.

I sat quietly, sipping a soda Drea got for me and listening to Harley talk to Roger and Bill about his side business, not understanding until they started discussing locations that the two brothers worked for Harley.

The small clock on a shelf chimed that it was midnight. I yawned and Harley gave me an apologetic look.

"We should go," he said.

"I'm just going to go tell Rose," I said, getting to my feet. But then she reappeared, a wan look on her face and a grateful smile as Harley got up to give her his seat.

"Thanks," she said.

I watched as Ellis's family took turns giving her hugs and squeezing her shoulders.

"What can I get you?" Drea asked. "Tea with honey?"

Rose nodded. It was interesting seeing this part of her life. She'd told me how Ellis's siblings had been wary of her at first, wondering at her intentions with the up-and-coming musician. But her love for him was clear. Even they couldn't deny it. And eventually they accepted her, taking her under their wing whenever she showed up at the Bucket and inviting her to family gatherings. It would have been easy for them to blame her for what had happened to Ellis, but it was clear they never would.

With the kettle on, Harley and I said our goodbyes.

"If you need anything," Harley said to Rose, "just send word. I've stocked the cupboards and paid next month's rent so Ellis doesn't have to worry about trying to get back to work before he's ready. The doctor will be by the day after tomorrow, and I'll be checking in every day until he's on his feet. And if you want, I'll bring Zora by in the evenings."

"Thank you, Harley," Rose said and looked at me with a soft smile.

"Any news on the guys that did this?" Roger asked.

"I'm going down to the police station tomorrow to make sure those boys aren't getting out anytime soon. And Harry has denied them further access to the club and spread the word to other clubs."

"It's about time," I said.

We left then, Harley driving me back to the Harringtons'. He pulled up to the curb, turned off the car, and pulled me to him.

"You okay?" he asked.

I sighed, sinking into him. I didn't know how I felt. I hadn't had time to think about me, my concerns lying with Rose and Ellis.

"I think so."

"Can I do anything for you, my love?"

"Just help our friends."

Harley and I spent the next week checking in on Rose and Ellis. We came by in the evenings after both our workdays were done and made dinner, sometimes for the four of us, sometimes for whoever else came by too. Roger and Drea were constant presences, the four of us standing around the kitchen talking and laughing quietly until Rose joined for a while before getting Ellis's dinner back to the bedroom where they ate together.

On Saturday, Harley had to work for part of the day so I got myself to Ellis's on my own, stopping at a corner market for flowers and trying to ignore the curious looks as one of the only white faces in the neighborhood.

"Zora," Rose said, her big blue eyes filling with relief when she saw me.

I hugged her long and hard.

"Come in, come in," she said, taking the flowers and filling the vase on the table with water.

"How's Ellis?" I asked, taking a seat at the kitchen table and looking around the empty room.

"You just missed the doctor. He's doing well. Everything should heal up just fine, but it will take some time, of course. And he's worried about his fingers. Only one on his right hand is broken, but three on his other hand are. He can't play his trumpet until they're all healed." She jumped up then and retrieved a plate of cookies from the counter. "Lorraine brought these by yesterday. She came over to check on us and tell me Dean Billings said if Jessie and I are still interested in Hollywood, we can come when I'm feeling better. Production got pushed back so there's time."

"That's wonderful," I said.

"Yeah," she said, her voice low. "I didn't tell Ellis. I can't imagine leaving him now."

"But do you want to go?"

She shrugged, reaching out to fuss with the flowers I'd brought.

"Rose?"

She sighed and dropped her hands to her lap. "I do. You know I do. It's an amazing opportunity. But how can I leave him now?"

"Rose. You've taken amazing care of him and he's going to be alright. But if this is something you want to do. Something you *need* to do, then you should do it. And if he loves you, he'll understand."

She nodded but didn't meet my eyes.

"How are *you* doing, Rose? Are you—"

"I'm fine."

But she wasn't. I knew my friend, and I could tell.

"Are you sure Ricky didn't—"

"He didn't," she said, meeting my gaze, her eyes hard. "I promise. I would tell you, Z. You know that. But…I was terrified he would. I've never felt so powerless or so scared. I—" Her voice broke then and she put her head down on the table and began to cry.

I hurried to her, holding her as her body shook. Until she was spent and sagging against me.

"I'll come back this evening," I said. "Okay?"

"Thank you, Z."

"You don't have to thank me, Rosie. You'd do the same for me."

Two weeks later, the first signs of spring in the air, Rose opened the door to Ellis's apartment with barely any evidence on her person of the brutality she'd endured, though anyone who knew her well could see the scars left on the inside reflected in those big baby blues of hers.

"You packed?" I asked.

She'd finally gone back to her parents' the week before to get some of her things and visit with them. She hadn't been home since the attack, calling and telling her mother she'd picked up some extra shifts at the club and would be staying with Jessie for a while.

She smiled and waved me inside. "Not yet. Two more weeks."

"How did they take it?"

"They're worried."

"I'll just bet."

"Heya, Zora," Ellis called from where he was sitting on the sofa.

"Heya, Ellis." I smiled, happy to see him out of bed. "How are you feeling today?"

"Same as yesterday, but look." He lifted a hand and moved one of his bandaged fingers.

"Ellis! That's great!"

"I'll be playin' in no time," he said.

"Damn right you will, baby," Rose said.

"Just in time to distract me from you leaving me."

"Oh, Ellis..." She sat beside him, her eyes welling with tears.

"I'm kidding, Rosie. Stop that," he said, gently pulling her to him.

He went to nap after a while and Rose and I curled up on either end of the sofa to talk.

"He's being really sweet about it," she said. "I mean, he gives me a bad time every once in a while, but he supports my decision."

"Have you two talked about what you'll do?"

She shrugged. "We're talking about making a clean break of it. He doesn't think it's fair to either of us to stay together when we don't even know when we'll be able to see each other again. And he has no idea when or if he'll want to come down there. At least not without the guarantee of a job."

I nodded. "That sounds very sensible, even if it is heartbreaking."

"I stopped by Jessie's yesterday," she said, her face brightening. "You should see her place. She's bought so many clothes, she can't fit them all in her suitcases."

I laughed, that sounded just like something Jessie would do.

After a while I said my goodbyes, took the streetcar back up the hill, and walked the last few blocks to Harley's.

"How are they?" he asked when I arrived.

He was sitting at his desk, frowning at some paperwork, but looked up when I rested a hand on his shoulder. He pushed his chair out to make room for me and I slid onto his lap, resting my head against his.

"They're getting there," I said and kissed him.

He sighed against my lips, his chest rising and falling.

"I love you, Zora Hough," he murmured. "Have I told you that lately?"

I grinned. "Once or twice."

"Good. I will never stop and I will always make sure you're taken care of."

My grin faded and I leaned away from him, studying his face.

"What's happened?" I asked.

"Nothing."

"Harley." My voice was a warning.

He shook his head. "I've just heard some things. Could be nothing but…maybe not."

More threats. That's what he was talking about.

"Have more trucks been hit?" I asked.

He hesitated then nodded. "Couple guys got hurt this time." He pointed to the radio. "Hey, I need to…"

"Aunt Viv?" I asked and he nodded. "Go on then."

"Aunt Vivian" was the evening radio show he listened to every few nights. At seven fifteen every night a woman called Aunt Vivian read bedtime stories for children. At first I'd found this odd, a grown man sitting and making notes while listening to children's tales. But then he'd explained. Aunt Vivian was actually Elise Olmstead, wife of Roy Olmstead, a lieutenant for the Seattle Police Department. It was widely known that he did bootlegging on the side, and it was rumored she left codes in her stories. Times and places, among other things, to alert a select few in the business of shipments and arrivals of product, as well as where cops on the make were purported to be.

As it happened, the rumors about the codes were true. Harley had met Elise, a fellow Londoner, when he'd arrived the year before, and they'd all become fast friends. Often the two men helped one another out. If Harley was short a truck, he called Roy. If Roy needed a boat, he called Harley. And the tips Harley got about police raids came straight from the lieutenant. But that meant he had a target on his back too. Because of that, the two men had been meeting more often to discuss alternative transportation options and routes.

But their efforts came too little too late.

Two nights after we'd sat there anxiously listening to Aunt Viv, I hurried out the servants' door to find Harley standing by the garden gate, a worried look on his face.

"Harley?"

"Roy's been arrested."

We'd had plans to go to the Alhambra, the first time since the attack on Rose and Ellis, but as soon as the words were out of his mouth I knew we wouldn't be going.

"What?" I said, following him to the car he'd left running at the curb. "When?"

"This afternoon," he said, once we were both seated inside. He sat staring out the windshield at the city spread out below us. "Elise came by my office in tears. Apparently they're talking about making an example out of him."

"How?"

"I don't know. Keeping him locked up for a long time?" He turned to me. "Zora. Elise thinks I could be next."

Goose bumps rose on my arms as fear pricked up my spine.

"You're frightening me," I said, my voice quiet.

"I'm sorry," he said, pulling me to him. "But I've prepared for this."

"What do you mean?"

"I've set up an account for you."

"An account?" I frowned and looked up at him. "What kind of account?"

"A bank account. After Elise came to see me, I went straight to the bank. There is now an account in your name with plenty of money for anything you need. For quite a while."

"Harley, no." I tried to pull away but he clasped our hands between us.

"Please don't tell me no." He sighed and let go of me, sitting back in his seat and rubbing his eyes. He looked tired. But it was the worry I saw there that bothered me the most. "I probably shouldn't tell you this, but I was planning to ask you to marry me soon. If I'm in jail, I can't do that. And maybe you wouldn't want to anyway. Who wants to be betrothed to a crook?"

I couldn't respond at first, a multitude of sensations, good and bad, racing through my body.

"You're not a crook, Harley," I finally said.

"What would your parents think?"

"My pa doesn't have a leg to stand on, and my ma would understand."

"So you're saying..."

"I'm saying, if you ever decide to ask me, I plan to say yes."

He peered at me. "Can I get that in writing?"

"Tell me where to sign, Mr. Aldridge."

He kissed me. Hard. And then drove us to his house.

Several hours later, I was sleeping deeply from being so well loved, when Harley gently shook me awake.

"Zora," he said.

"Yes?" I whispered, my eyes still closed as I reached for him in the dark.

"Zora, my love. They're here."

I blinked my eyes open, frowning up at him, confused. And then I heard it. The pounding on the door downstairs.

"Harley?" I said, sitting up and clutching his arm.

"Get dressed, my love," he said. "I promise. No matter what, it's going to be okay."

But it wasn't. It wasn't okay at all.

27

The following day was a Sunday and after waking on the sofa I'd spent the rest of the night on, I changed my clothes and hurried to the Harringtons' house where I made a beeline for Mrs. Harrington's office.

"Zora?" she said when I entered.

Her eyes took in everything. The hat covering my unkempt hair, my blotchy face, and the way I was twisting my fingers. She motioned to the sofa.

"What's happened?"

I told her everything and when I was finished, she sat for a moment staring at me, her lips parted as she took it all in. After a moment she stood, her eyes looking everywhere but at me, a frown creasing her brow as she tried to make sense of what I'd just told her.

"And he's in jail now?" she asked and I nodded, watching as she spun a pale gold bracelet around her slender wrist. "Dammit, Harley," she whispered before meeting my eyes once more. "I'll fetch Jonathan. He'll know what to do."

She returned a few minutes later with Mr. Harrington in tow. When he'd heard the tale too, he did as his wife had moments before, blindly staring while absorbing the information he'd been told.

"What was he thinking?" he finally said and then shook his head and gave me a gentle smile. "Try not to fret just yet. I'll go down to the police station and see what I can find out."

He gave my shoulder a squeeze, kissed his wife on the cheek, and hurried from the room.

"Have you eaten?" Mrs. Harrington asked, adjusting the bracelets on her arm so they were just so.

"No. I'm not hungry."

"Well, while I support doing what it takes to stay svelte, one must keep up appearances, you know, you're almost too thin. Go to the kitchen and ask Cook to whip you up something at my request. You're going to need your strength if the news isn't good. I'll call for you when Jonathan returns."

The news was worse than I could've imagined. For Harley, and for Roy, the latter of whom was charged with an eight thousand dollar fine and four years in prison. But Harley…

"He has to what?" Rose asked.

We were sitting at Harley's dining table. I'd returned from the Harringtons' and immediately called the line to Ellis's building, crying into the receiver to his landlord's wife, barely able to make words when Rose finally got to the phone.

"I'm coming over!" she'd shouted before hanging up.

Her blue eyes were wide as she took in the information, her lips parted much like Mrs. Harrington's had been only a few hours ago, as though she wanted to say more but couldn't find the words.

"They're making an example of him and Roy," I told her, repeating the words I'd heard from his attorney. "All thanks to Ricky."

"Ricky?" Rose said and involuntarily shuttered. "What's he have to do with it?"

"Apparently, he thought he'd get back at Harley for smashing his nose in when he helped save us. So he—"

"He told his policeman daddy," she said, finishing my sentence. "The bastard."

"They started following Harley the day after Ricky went to jail. Saw him meet with a couple of his men. Saw a couple of the trucks. A delivery..." I closed my eyes, trying to keep from crying.

"What's going to happen to Harley now?" Rose asked.

"He has to return to England," I said, my voice flat, still unbelieving. "They'll release him tomorrow and then he has until the end of the week to be on a train to the East Coast. From there he'll take a ship to England. He'll have a policeman who will travel with him to make sure he goes. At his own expense."

"For how long?" Rose asked.

"Two years." I swallowed a sob. "He can't come back for two years."

I put my head down on my arms, letting the emotions wash over me, pulling me under, threatening to drown me while Rose rubbed my back, telling me it would be okay.

But I didn't see how.

As promised, on Monday morning Harley was released. An officer drove him home where I waited on the front porch, Mrs. Harrington having given me the day off so I could be there when he arrived.

He looked tired, his clothing wrinkled, but no worse for wear.

"Zora," he whispered into my hair, and then we walked inside and closed the door.

"You could come with me," he said later that day as we clung to one another on the sofa in the sitting room.

But I couldn't. London was too far from my family. What if I couldn't find a job there? I couldn't and wouldn't ask Harley to support my family.

But it was more than that. I was scared.

I loved Harley, but we weren't married. What if one or both of us decided the relationship wasn't working? I'd have to find my way back on my own. And the truth was, I wasn't ready to leave my family so far behind. I'd never known a day I couldn't just jump on the streetcar and hurry back to the safety and comfort of my parents' home. I would know no one but Harley in London.

And then there was my dream, which resided in Seattle. This city was where I wanted to expand on the roots so deeply implanted here. This was where I wanted to grow the idea I'd had since I was a girl. If I left, I may never come back. I may allow myself to get swallowed up in the excitement of a new place and new people, and forget what I wanted. For me.

Of course, these thoughts then made me wonder if I really did love Harley after all. Because if I did, wouldn't I just say yes and go with him?

But as I looked at him now, his eyes so full of love… I knew without a doubt I'd never loved anyone more.

"Or we'll wait it out," he said. "If you want to?"

At the sound of the uncertainty in his voice, I placed my hand on his cheek.

"No if," I said. "I'll wait for you, Harley."

"You could go to Hollywood with Rose in the meantime," he said. "Work for the movies? It would certainly help when you want to open your own shop. All the experience you'd get?"

But I shook my head. "I don't know. It's not as far as London, but it's still far. And what if I hate it there?"

"Do you hate sunshine and the ocean and palm trees?"

I shrugged. "Well, two of those I've never seen."

"Zora. Take the money I set aside for you. Go do something exciting while I'm gone. Get even more experience. Make some new friends. And when my two years are up, I can either meet you here or there, whichever you choose."

But I didn't want to talk about it. Didn't even want to think about it. All I wanted was to be with him now, as much as I could, for as long as we had.

Every night after work for the rest of the week, I slipped out the garden gate to find Harley waiting for me with a bouquet of flowers, a loaf of fresh bread, a cake, a necklace with a bird charm. Always a gift of some sort.

"You don't have to do this, you know," I said as he clasped the necklace around my neck.

"Of course I don't. But I love it. I'd buy you everything if I thought you'd let me."

"I don't think you'd like me that much if I were the kind of woman who would let you buy her everything."

"That's true," he said, and leaned forward to kiss me before opening the passenger door.

As we drove off, I saw Elsbeth standing in the doorway of the servants' entrance. Maybe Harley was right. Maybe I should give Hollywood a chance.

That Friday we stayed up long into the night, talking, making promises, laughing softly, and making love.

"One day," he said, sliding his fingers through mine and bringing my hand to his mouth so he could kiss it. "One day I'm going to take you to Italy."

"What will we do there?" I asked, shivering as his kisses moved up my arm.

"We'll visit small brightly colored towns, drink wine and eat pasta, listen to music, and sit on our balcony every morning in our dressing gowns, drinking coffee and falling even deeper in love."

"Promise?" I asked.

"That's an easy promise to keep," he said, and then rolled me onto my back.

He left at ten the following morning while I stood on the porch beside the man who worked as the manager of the furniture company under Harley. Wallace was a quiet man I once suggested was a ghost, the way he would enter and leave a room on silent feet, one minute there, the next gone. While Harley was away, he'd be overseeing the business, making sure the bills were paid on Harley's house, and overseeing that the car was serviced, the maid that would be coming in once a month still was paid, and that I had whatever I needed.

"You let Wallace know what you want to do with the house," Harley said, kissing the tip of my nose. "It's yours to live in if you want, or you can close it up and we'll reopen in two years' time."

I nodded, unable to say much of anything, my heart pushing against my breastbone, threatening to burst from my chest.

I wrapped my arms around his waist and he held me tight.

"I should be going with you," I whispered. "I'm a coward."

"No. You're a woman who loves her family and is honoring an obligation."

"Do you think I don't love you as much as them?" I asked. I'd spent days worrying about this. But I'd made them a promise and I couldn't let them down.

"I know you love me. Almost as much as I love you."

I heard the teasing in his voice and peeked up at him.

"You'll write to me?" he asked.

"All the time."

One of the two officers that had come for him cleared his throat then and Harley sighed.

"Zora," he said, his mouth lifting in that crooked little grin that had been driving me wild since the day I met him.

My eyes filled with tears.

"Yes, Harley?" I choked out.

He gave me one last, long kiss, looked deep into my eyes, and then he was gone. Sliding into the back seat of the car, the slam of the door reverberating through my body, a last glimpse of his handsome face as they drove away.

Wallace and I stood side by side for a long moment.

"Miss—" he started.

"I'll figure out something for my sewing machine," I said.

"And then I'd like you to close up the house. We'll reopen in two years."

"Yes, miss," he said and then offered to drive me back to the Harringtons'.

"Thank you," I said. "But I think I'll walk."

It was the longest walk I could ever remember taking, each step taking me farther from Harley's house sending a shock of grief up through my body. I was glad it was Saturday and I could just go up to my bed, crawl under the covers, and not get up again until tomorrow. But when I came in the door, I knew instantly that's not how this day would go.

"There you are," Mrs. Beckwith said, her voice hushed as she gestured for me to follow her, placing a finger to her lips as she pulled me out of sight into the hallway.

"What's happening?" I asked.

"Elsbeth," she said. "She's been on a tear since she woke up."

"About what?"

"About you. Said you harbored a friend here a while back."

Ice ran through my veins and I closed my eyes. She had seen me bring Rose into the house. And now she had her moment. Harley was gone. There was no one to speak up for me.

"It's not true, is it?" she asked.

"I can explain," I said.

"Indeed you'll have to."

Mrs. Beckwith and I jumped at the sound of Mrs. Harrington's voice.

"Zora," she said, her voice soft but stern. "Please come with me."

Without Harley there to verify my story, it was my word against Elsbeth's. And this time, she was the one in the right.

"I've been told you brought someone into our home without our permission," Mrs. Harrington said, taking a seat on the sofa in her study.

She hadn't asked me to sit this time.

"Is this true?" she asked.

I took in a breath and nodded.

"Why did this happen?"

And so I told her. About the attack on Rose and Ellis. How he was afraid of what the doctor would say about his condition and so he'd wanted her to leave. How she was hurt and had nowhere to go, her parents' home too far away, and how I'd offered to take her back to the Harringtons'. How I'd kept it a secret because I knew I was breaking a rule.

When I was done she sighed.

"Zora. As you can imagine, this puts me in a very unfortunate position. We have rules and we expect them to be adhered to. That rule in particular we will not bend on. It's imperative we know who comes into our home. People of our stature…well, others look for ways to harm us. To take from us. I can't have my staff bringing in anyone they please right under our noses while our children sleep. And you signed a contract promising you wouldn't."

"Yes, ma'am," I murmured. "I'm so sorry."

"And Harley knew?"

"He drove us here."

She nodded and I could see she was torn. On the one hand, I was an excellent nanny to her kids. On the other, a precedent had to be set. If I got away with this, then who was to say someone else wouldn't try? I could've put her family in danger, and that was unforgivable.

But I knew as I stood there, an image of Rose bruised and battered in my mind, that I'd do it again should she need me to.

"I'm so mad you've put me in this position," Mrs. Harrington said, twisting the lace overlay of her dress. "But rules are rules. And if I let you break them, then others will think they can to. I'm so sorry, Zora."

I was surprised to see her eyes fill with tears.

"You have nothing to be sorry for," I said. "I'm the one that's sorry. It was a horrible decision to have to make. But even though it was the wrong one for the household, it was the right one for my friend, and I stand by my decision."

My heart ached as I wondered what I'd do now.

"Shall I pack my things then?"

"Why don't you stay through next week," she said. "To give me time to try and replace you. Which, mind you, will be nearly impossible. If only you'd just asked us."

"If I thought I could have, I would have."

She nodded and I excused myself then, taking my time walking up the stairs, my mind filled with questions. What would I do now? Where would I go? Who would hire me after this?

I knew I could stay at Harley's, and the money he'd left me would provide for a long time. But I didn't want to sit alone in his large empty house, living off him while I waited for his return. And while the Alhambra job paid decent money, it was only part-time and most of the job was the same thing I'd been doing with my mama for years, stitching holes and sewing on buttons and zippers. Harry didn't fork out money often for new costumes so I wasn't getting to create nearly as much as I would've liked.

Harley had mentioned once that I could offer my sewing services to some of the other clubs, but they had their own seamstresses. I would need to figure something else out.

"Why don't you start sewing the designs from your books?" Rose asked one night when I met her at Jessie's apartment for dinner.

I'd thought about that too. With the money from Harley and what I made from the club, I could spend my days at home working on my designs. But then what? How would I get them sold? I wasn't ready to open a shop yet.

I finished out the week at the Harringtons' with a smile on my face and a heaviness in my step, avoiding Elsbeth's satisfied grin as much as possible. The children were sad to see me go. We'd had fun together. But I promised them their next nanny would be just as fun, and that I'd visit one day so they could show me all the new things they'd learned.

As the clock struck six that Friday, I said goodbye to Willem and Madeline, thanked the Harringtons for the opportunity to work for them, and went upstairs to place my uniform in a laundry bag and grab the two suitcases I'd packed early that morning.

While Charles carried my belongings to the car, I said goodbye to the staff.

"You'll be greatly missed," Mrs. Beckwith said.

"Come by and see us sometime," Cook said, handing me a basket filled with freshly baked muffins.

I hugged them both and waved goodbye as I followed Charles out the door, Mrs. Harrington insisting I let him drive me wherever I was off to next.

"Where to?" he asked. "Home?"

I rattled off an address and he nodded, shut the door, and rounded the car to the driver's side.

Ten minutes later I stood on the sidewalk outside an apartment building. Grabbing my two suitcases, I climbed to the second story, walked down the hallway, and knocked on the door.

"Zora!" Jessie said.

"Z's here?" Rose yelled from inside. I heard her steps pounding across the floor as she ran to see. "Z!" She launched herself into my arms and I laughed as I tried to stay upright. "We're just doing some packing and then we're going for a drink at the club. Wanna come?"

"I'd love to," I said. "But also…"

"Yeah?"

I'd taken a quick trip home to my parents' house two days earlier to tell my mother about Harley and what I was thinking of doing next.

"I thought you didn't want to go to Hollywood though," Mama had said. "You said it wasn't your dream."

"I know. But maybe that's okay for now," I said. "I'll probably never have the chance to do anything like this again, and it could be a diversion while Harley is gone. Plus, it can't hurt to tell future clients I designed clothes for a film."

She'd given me her blessing, but suddenly, as I stood in the doorway of Jessie's apartment staring into the eyes of my best friend, I started having second thoughts. Maybe Rose and Jessie wouldn't want me to join them after all. Maybe their plans weren't big enough to include another person. Maybe…

I sucked in a breath and blew it out.

"I was wondering if I might come with you to Hollywood."

I was positive their screams could be heard for miles and I smiled apologetically at their neighbors as they opened their doors to see what was going on.

"Sorry," I mouthed to an old woman across the hall. She shook her head and slammed the door and I turned back to my friends. "Is that a yes?"

"Yes!" they shouted, and Rose pulled me inside.

An hour later the three of us caught the streetcar downtown. As the two women chattered the entire way to Jackson Street, I sat back, listening with half an ear, watching the city go by, and remembering my first streetcar ride alone into town. How nervous I'd been. How little I'd known the city, and how afraid I'd been to miss my stop. I had changed so much since that day. And I imagined whatever came next would change me even more.

But I was ready for it. I'd chosen it.

"What are you smiling about?" Rose said, breaking through my thoughts.

I grinned.

"I'm going to Hollywood."

28

Los Angeles shone like a jewel encased in a setting like none I'd ever seen before.

Ornamental light fixtures lined streets I'd only read about in the newspaper. Palm trees swayed high above, the warm spring evening air scented with blooming flowers. And in the distance, the sparkling waters of the Pacific beckoned.

"Welcome to Hollywood," our driver, Sophie, shouted.

In front of us, high up on a tree-covered hill, was the iconic Hollywoodland sign.

Jessie and Rose squealed, but I just stared. I'd never imagined seeing it in person. And doing so now made a nervous thrum zip through my veins. Was I right to have come here?

I glanced to my left at Sophie, a tall blonde with ice-like blue eyes, the longest eyelashes I'd ever seen on a human being, and gams for miles. Like Jessie and Rose, she'd been hired to be a dancer for the upcoming movie, and had been tasked with picking the three of us up from the train station and giving us a tour.

When we'd seen her, standing out from the crowd with her perfectly coifed hair and painted lips, holding a sign with our names on it, we'd stopped and stared.

"I guess Mr. Billings got my telegram," I'd murmured as Rose squeezed my hand.

In addition to the telegram to Mr. Billings, I'd sent a letter to Harley detailing what had transpired with the Harringtons, and the last-minute decision to join Rose and Jessie in California after all.

"I'm scared," I'd written. "But maybe you were right. The experience will be valuable, and perhaps it will make the time pass faster as I wait for your return."

I'd promised to write as soon as I arrived and got settled, but had already written two letters on the train ride down, wanting to share every moment of the journey with him that I could.

Sophie had driven us straight to our new apartment first.

"We'll drop off your things and then go for a little tour," she'd said, dangling a ring of keys. "I have a company car and a wad of cash to show you ladies a good time for the next two days until we're needed on set for fittings and..." She looked at me. "Well, I guess you'll be part of that."

"I hope so," I said. "Otherwise, I have no idea why I'm here."

It took us four trips to get all our things inside the small but bright and friendly apartment the three of us would be sharing. Since I was a last-minute addition, one of the two bedrooms had a pair of single beds set up.

"You and me, kiddo?" Rose had asked and I'd nodded, grateful. I knew my decision had thrown a bit of wrench in their plans, and had offered to find my own place, but neither of them would hear of it.

"It's gonna be a blast," Jessie had said, her blue eyes shining.

After a quick look around, the three of us oohing and aahing over the bathroom, the sitting room, the tiny kitchen, and even a little balcony that led to—

"There's a pool!" Rose shouted, gripping the rail and pointing, Jessie and I clambering in next to her to see.

We changed into fresh clothes, touched up our makeup and

hair, and piled back in the car for what Sophie called her "Sophie's Special" Los Angeles tour.

Spring in Los Angeles was warmer than in Seattle, the clear sky streaked with pinks and oranges.

"Oh, I could get used to this," Rose said, putting her hand out the window.

While she drove, Sophie told us all the gossip. We learned which star had been caught leaving the pink Beverly Hills Hotel with a married producer, and where the cops hang out after hours—and sometimes while still on the clock.

"Stay away from King Eddy's," Sophie said, pointing to a piano store. "The saloon is down below and if you don't want cops questioning what you know about whosit and whatsit—don't go there. Besides that, the men are questionable."

"I'm certainly not looking for a man," Rose said. "Questionable or otherwise."

I looked over my shoulder and stole a quick glance at Jessie, who was watching our mutual friend fidget with the charm hanging from her necklace.

"Keep an eye on her out there, will you, Z?" Ellis had asked.

I'd reassured him I would and was determined to make good on that promise.

We drove by the Los Angeles Biltmore Hotel, staring, our mouths open at the opulent front doors, fancy doorman, and even fancier cars lined up out front.

"Most days of the week you'll find Cecil B. DeMille, Mary Pickford, or Gloria Swanson having lunch or dinner in the hotel's Gold Room," Sophie said.

I turned in my seat to see Jessie and Rose exchanging wide-eyed looks.

"That's the Townhouse." Sophie pointed at what looked to be a grocer. "And the Apes is over there. We'll head there tonight. Dean got us in for tonight's show."

"What kind of show?" Jessie asked.

"Showgirls. Feathers, sequins, the whole bit. Johnny Otis leads the house band and it's spectacular."

Spectacular didn't cover it. We sat near the back of a large room, our meal brought out to us on silver platters, drinks flowing as if there was a fountain in back that never stopped, and watched in awe as the most beautiful women we'd ever seen swayed and kicked and winked, their bright white smiles flashing at us from behind massive, feathered fans.

At one point Rose turned to me, her face alight with wonder, stars in her eyes. I grinned. She was hooked, and I wondered in that moment if she'd ever go back to Seattle. She squeezed my hand and let out a little squeal, and then froze as a trumpet solo began, her smile disappearing as she turned to watch the musician now standing center stage.

I leaned toward her. "You okay?" I asked.

She nodded, still watching and listening. When he finished, she gave me a sad smile.

"I miss him."

"I know."

Their goodbye, she'd told me on the train to California, had been agonizing, neither wanting to let the other go as they hugged, but knowing they must.

"I really love him," she'd told me. "And I know he loves me too. But what we both want for our careers is just too different. He wants to settle down in Seattle. Make the music scene as big as he can with Oscar, get a real following, maybe open his own club one day. And I want...more. I've never seen anything outside Seattle. I want to know what else is out there."

"Hollywood seems like a good place to start then," I'd said.

I looked at her now, wearing one of the sparkly new dresses she'd bought for her new life in Los Angeles, her hair held back on one side with a beaded clip, her blue eyes bright with possibility. I'd known from the first moment I'd seen her back in grade school that she was gonna go places, and now I was watching it happen.

During the intermission, Mr. Billings stopped by our table. "You ladies enjoying your evening?"

"Mr. Billings!" Jessie said. "It's amazing. Thank you for organizing this for us. And for sending Sophie. She's a wonderful tour guide."

"You're very welcome," he said. "I'm glad you're enjoying yourselves. I thought it would be good for you ladies to see what you will be emulating for some of the movie's dance numbers."

"Do we get to have costumes like that?" Rose asked, staring at the now-empty stage.

"Indeed," he said and then looked to me. "Which makes me glad you changed your mind, Zora. We're going to need your eye for detail."

I grinned and felt Rose nudge me under the table.

"I'm delighted to be of assistance," I said. "I can't wait to get to work. I have so many ideas."

"Wonderful." He smiled and then took a step back and tipped his hat. "Enjoy the rest of your evening, ladies."

The following morning I was the first to wake. I turned on my side and grinned at Rose who was lying on her stomach, her head beneath her pillow. She'd been sleeping like that for as long as I'd known her.

We'd gotten home after one and had wandered the apartment shedding shoes and clothes and hairpins and searching the cupboards for food before heading to our respective beds and falling asleep.

We didn't have to report to work until the following day and thus, Sophie had told us as we'd tiredly pulled one another from the car, she would be back at eleven to take us to the beach.

"It won't be the summer experience. It's not quite warm enough for that. But if you're going to live in California," she'd said, covering a yawn with her hand, "we have to at least visit the beach."

Digging through one of my suitcases, I found the butter-yellow, lightweight day dress I'd purchased at the end of last summer and changed in the bathroom. When I came out, Rose was awake and sitting on the edge of her bed rubbing her eyes.

"My head hurts," she said.

"You did have three drinks," I said.

"I couldn't help it. Those...what did they call them?"

"Marinades," I said.

"Yeah. Those marinades were delicious."

"And strong."

She nodded, winced, and then got on the floor and started digging through her own suitcase.

Sophie arrived at eleven on the dot, looking fresh and ready for the day in a baby blue dress with white polka dots, a straw hat, and strappy sandals I immediately wanted a pair of.

"You ladies ready?" she asked.

We piled in the car and were off, breathing in the California air, and smiling all the way to the Casa del Mar Hotel in Santa Monica, where Sophie handed the car off to the valet and led us through the grand lobby with its twin grand staircases, large potted plants, huge chandeliers, and giant pillars, and out the other side.

Across a patio with a pool, down a path, and we were at the beach, staring at the sand, the water, and several people lying about on sun chairs beneath striped umbrellas.

"Ladies?" Sophie said, grinning at the three of us, our eyes wide as we took it all in. "You coming?"

We returned to our new apartment that evening, slightly sunburned and very tired from walks on the beach, splashing in the cold Pacific Ocean up to our knees, and lazing in the sun. Los Angeles felt a world away from Seattle. Everyone seemed shinier, happier, and I wondered if it was because of being constantly bathed in sunshine instead of the gray I'd grown so accustomed to.

"I'm going to have to set some rules for myself," Jessie said from where she was lying on the sofa, a deep purple number that screamed Hollywood glamor in our otherwise spare but lovely apartment. "I cannot go out every night or I'll never make it to work on time the next day. Or..." She sat up. "Maybe I can go out every night—I just have to make sure I'm home before midnight. What do you girls think?"

Rose looked at her from where she was kneeling on the floor, searching one of the lower cupboards for a pot.

"I like the sound of the second plan. Z?"

"You two will have to tell me all about your exploits on our way to work every morning. I don't plan to go out often. I need to be awake if I'm going to be designing and sewing for a movie."

"You'll come out sometimes though, right?" Rose asked.

"Sometimes," I said. But it made me sad to think of going out to the clubs without Harley, even though he'd encouraged me to do just that when he'd called me before boarding the ship to England.

I'd paced his house for hours that morning, waiting for the call he promised would come, and running for the phone when it finally rang. In my rush, I'd knocked the receiver to the floor and then told the operator eagerly that yes, yes I would accept the call. My knees had buckled at the sound of his voice in my ear.

"You're okay?" he'd asked, and I'd lied, not wanting to tell him yet that I'd been fired, knowing he'd want to try and fix it and would feel helpless when he couldn't. Saving it for my letter.

We didn't have long to talk. Just enough time to tell one another how very much we loved each other, that we'd wait and we'd write often. He told me to go out, have fun, and make connections where I could. And then there was a flurry of goodbyes and I love yous before he was gone and I was standing with the receiver in my hand, the operator asking if I needed to place another call.

"No," I'd whispered, and finally hung up.

To get off on the right foot, Rose, Jessie, and I all stayed in our second night in town, taking turns bathing, helping one another set our hair, and unpacking our clothes into the bureaus and closets, my meager number of outfits quickly swallowed up by Rose's abundance.

Afterward, I sat on my bed with the new stationery set I'd purchased in the hotel lobby, and wrote a letter to Harley, telling him about our arrival, Sophie, the show we'd seen, our tiny apartment, the beach, and how beautiful the sky was.

"I still don't know if I'll stay past this movie, but I can see why people want to come here. It's like being in another world."

"I can't believe we're really here," Rose said the next morning after we were granted access to the MGM lot and followed a security guard down a quiet street between large buildings boasting signs for movies we recognized and others that were in production.

As we walked, we passed men and women in an assortment of costumes, people rushing by with clipboards, a woman pushing a rack of clothing that looked like it was from another planet, and several young men in caps carrying food, cameras, and a number of other items.

"Here we are," the security guard said, pointing to a door with a small plaque beside it on the wall.

Studio number five.

"Do we…just go in?" Jessie asked.

He nodded and left us and we stood for only a moment more before Rose reached out and opened the door.

Sophie saw us as soon as we entered and hurried to introduce us to the other dancers, several of the extra actors, the cameramen, and so many other people with strange job titles that I quickly got confused and stopped trying to remember.

It was amazing to see the sets that were being constructed, the bright lights above nearly blinding us as we weaved around people and cords and any number of things we'd never seen before.

"Okay," Sophie said after showing us around. "Rose and Jessie, go on back to the rehearsal space. Zora, I'll show you where you'll be working."

I grinned. I'd been dying to ask and was a little sad Rose and Jessie weren't coming to see what I assumed would be a large office space to sketch and sew and do fittings in.

"We'll come get you at the end of the day," Rose said.

"Have fun, girls," I said and waved before turning to follow Sophie down yet another hallway.

At the end of the hall were two doors with nondescript signs on the wall next to them reading Sewing Room 1 and Sewing Room 2.

I frowned as she pointed to the second one.

"This is you," she said, a bright smile on her face.

My heart sank. This was not the room of a designer. It was exactly what it said it was. A sewing room.

Inside the too-warm room were three sewing machines. In front of two of them was a pair of older women working diligently, heads down, straight pins in mouths, their focus on the costumes they were mending. They barely looked up to see who had come in.

Along the back wall were three racks of clothing, one labeled Done, and the other two sitting in wait.

In one heartbreaking instant I realized I hadn't been asked here to design like I'd been led to believe. I'd been asked to do the work I'd always done. The work I'd grown up doing while sitting beside my mother day in and day out.

I was here to mend other people's work.

The sketchbook in my hand felt suddenly heavy. Silly.

Pointless.

The fantasies I'd had of picking out fabric, measuring actors and actresses, and having my name on garments worn on the silver screen were dashed in the blink of an eye as shame, embarrassment, and disappointment filled me from the toes of the fashionable shoes I'd bought thinking I was on my way up in the world, to the cloche that was making my head sweat in the small, dingy room.

But, I reminded myself, these clothes weren't just any clothes. They weren't just a few frocks worn in secret clubs beneath ground level. These costumes would be worn by actors and actresses and seen on big screens across the country. It might feel like the same kind of work, but it was definitely a step up and a major stride in the right direction for what I wanted to do with my life.

"All good?" Sophie asked, taking a step backward as if to escape the dreary surroundings for the bright lights of the set.

Taking in a deep breath, I threw back my shoulders, smiled, and stepped inside.

29

"You're sure you can't come?" Rose asked, checking her hair in the oval mirror she'd bought with her first paycheck and hung by the front door. "You haven't gone out in weeks!"

I looked up from where I sat on the sofa, hand sewing a jacket cuff for one of the extras. We'd been in Los Angeles a month and a half and, while Jessie and Rose had gone out nearly every night since we'd arrived, I'd stopped after the first couple of weeks.

My schedule was nothing like theirs. Not only did the sewing room need to keep up with mending costumes, we had to measure and sew new ones, rip apart old ones, and reconfigure per a set of specifications we were given that didn't always make sense.

When we'd first arrived, I'd gone along on the nights out, not understanding that the to-do list I was given was meant to be done in a single day, and anything that didn't get done in the sewing room would need to go home with me. I'd been rolling the work over into the next day and by the end of the second week, it was made quite clear to me that I was behind.

"I don't understand why you are so slow," the designer, Michele Cleménte, said to me in front of the other two seamstresses in the room, after I'd been there for two weeks. She picked up the garment I'd just finished and looked at the stitches. "Your work is good, but it needs to be faster. This should've been done two days ago."

Humiliated, I apologized, and promised I'd catch up. Which meant no more going out, the amount of work on my daily list like nothing I'd ever done before.

I gave Rose a tired smile now, admiring the new dress she'd bought on her lunch hour that day.

"This jacket has to be done for tomorrow's rehearsal," I said. "You ladies have a good time though."

"We can wait for you," Jessie said, entering the room in a navy blue frock and matching beaded headband. Her skin was lightly tanned from weekends lying by the pool or going to the beach, giving her a beautiful glow.

"Thanks," I said. "But once I'm done with this, I have that." I pointed to the cloth bag at my feet filled with several more pieces to mend.

She frowned and met Rose's eyes.

"It's not fair," Rose said.

I shrugged, the motion drawing my attention to the tightness in my neck and shoulders. Every night, for the past few weeks, I'd sat in this very spot, or on the balcony, or in my bed, sewing until midnight or beyond until it was all done.

"Mr. Billings did say there'd be long hours," I said by way of excuse.

"Yeah, but he also said you'd be designing, not stuck in a room with those two old crones," Rose said, hands on hips that had become even more slender thanks to all the rehearsing.

"Betty and Ruth are lovely," I said, my eyes back on the task at hand.

"I'll just bet. What do you three talk about anyway?"

I refused to look up as I answered. "Important things. How production is going. What we need to work on next. The list is long." I peeked up at her and tried to keep the grin from my face as I continued. "They tell me about their ungrateful kids, their ungrateful grandkids, and don't get me started on their husbands!" I said the last part while shaking a fist, mimicking the women and making Rose and Jessie laugh.

"That's what I was afraid of," Rose said. "What's Harley got to say about it?"

I sighed. His second letter had come a few days ago. A response to the one I'd sent him, telling him about the job, and admitting what I hadn't in my first few: that it wasn't what I'd been told, and I was no more than what I'd been before. A seamstress, mending other people's work.

His reply had come with beautiful words of reassurance, sweet professions of love, and anger at "That Dean Billings. Those Hollywood types are all the same. Glittering words to cover blathering lies."

I glanced down at my apron where the letter sat nestled in the pocket. I'd reread it several times, the comforting words bringing a tiny bit of peace to my otherwise unchallenging and long days.

"He reminded me that I can always go home," I said. "That his house is mine and I can sew my designs and figure out what I want to do next from there, including opening a shop of my own. But I'm not ready to do that yet, and when I am, I want to use money I've earned myself."

I stabbed the needle through the fabric of the jacket.

"He also reminded me I can come stay with him in London and return to Seattle with him when he's allowed. Or I can stay at my folks' and look for another job if that's what I want to do."

"Do any of those ideas sound good to you?" Jessie asked.

I shrugged. "I just want the life I had. Before Harley left. It was good and I was happy. I felt like I was starting to get somewhere. Like I was getting closer to my dream. But now..." I stared down at the cuff in my hands. "I feel like I'm going backward. Or maybe to the side. I feel stuck. And horrible for complaining because the money is so good."

I waved them off then, urging them to go, have fun for me, and to tell me all the juicy gossip in the morning.

"I love you, Z," Rose said, planting a kiss on my head. "It's going to be okay. I promise."

I smiled up at her. "I love you too, Rosie. Now go. Have fun. One of us has to."

Preproduction for the film went on and on. The motion picture was to be MGMs first "talkie," and with the exciting opportunity came a number of issues, from lighting to microphones to sound being relayed correctly.

But the technical issues weren't the only problems. The actors were ripping through their costumes in rehearsals, and since there were dozens of actors with dozens of costume changes, it felt like the sewing room was on a carousel of unending restitching, mending, and hemming. And to top it off, every few days or so the costume designer, the newly minted "darling of design" Michele Cleménte, would come by with a fresh batch of ideas she'd mocked up that we were then supposed to make, only to have them tossed aside and a new batch brought in days later.

"Sorry, darlings, I'd do it myself but I'm up to here outfitting Garbo," she told us one day before disappearing in an invisible cloud of perfume.

"She's a piece of work, isn't she?" Ruth said.

Betty mumbled something rude and the three of us laughed before exchanging long sighs as we reached for the new set of costume ideas.

As usual, I brought my work home with me, as well as a paper sack full of food from the commissary. I ate out on the balcony in the late evening sun, a cool breeze ruffling my hair, which I still wore unfashionably long, despite Jessie and Rose constantly nagging me to cut it. But I loved being able to pull it back. And Harley loved pulling it loose and wrapping it around his fingers, the memory of which stuck with me whenever I contemplated cutting it.

I took a bite of my sandwich and sat back in one of the two chairs the three of us had chipped in to buy. Two chairs. Not three. The balcony wasn't big enough for three with the little table Rose had found and brought home. Sometimes I woke in the middle of the night and came to the kitchen for a glass of water. I'd find Rose and Jessie sitting out there, sharing a cigarette and rehashing stories of their night. Neither of them ever sat out there with me. Three chairs would've been a waste of money.

Down below, two of the dancers from the studio were lying on sun chairs. Another was doing a lap in the pool, while still three more passed a ball around, trying to keep it from falling in the water.

I couldn't count how many times I'd been invited to join in on numerous outings, gatherings at the pool, drives to the beach, and evenings out at the clubs. They were a friendly bunch. But I'd had to say no so many times, the invitations had slowly waned until they'd finally stopped. The last time I'd been asked anywhere and had said no, I'd overheard someone inquire with the woman who'd asked, "Who is she?"

"No one," she'd said.

I finished the sandwich, brushed off my hands, and pulled out the first garment of the night that needed mending. As I shook it out, Harley's latest letter fell out.

It had only arrived two days before, but I'd read it so many times the corners were already bent and the folds worn.

We'd exchanged several letters by then, a new one arriving from him every couple of weeks. There was a phone in the main office, but the line for it was always out the door and the sign-up list on weekends was always filled. I missed his voice, but I didn't mind writing and receiving letters. His were always filled with love and encouragement, and reminders that if I didn't want to stay in Los Angeles, I didn't have to. But as comforting as the words were, they'd also begun to make me feel worse, as below them were more words. Words of how he was doing (healthy, well, keeping busy), and how business was thriving. He'd already taken a trip to Paris.

"The people are quite elegant there," he'd written. "Fashionable. And funny in their disdain for the silliest things. You'd love it. I imagine you here, taking in the clothes and then sitting in a park on a blanket, sketching until dusk, unaware that the day has gone until you realize you're drawing in the dark."

It was meant to show me he was thinking of me. But all it did, as I stared down at my plain day dress, smelling the sweat beneath my arms, my scalp itchy from the day in that thankless and bleak room, was serve to worry me that he'd realize I would never be elegant enough to hold his arm in a city such at Paris, and that he would meet someone else.

I kept thinking my situation would get better. I even tried to talk to Mr. Billings. But he'd merely said I was lucky to have such a coveted job and waved me out of his office.

It had become clear to me in my third week on the job why Dean had actually asked me to come. My sewing roommates were workhorses. They did the smaller jobs. The easy sews. Leaving the more intricate stuff to me. I was still sitting in that room with my mother, watching her fly through sewing on buttons and fixing up a ripped hem, while I camouflaged, reattached a tricky bit of fringe, and reconfigured the entire lower half of a dress.

The following day I was deep in repairs on a feathered headpiece when I heard the distinct sound of Michele Cleménte's voice.

"Hey!" She snapped her fingers.

I blinked and looked up, shocked to see the diminutive designer standing in the doorway looking rather perturbed.

"Me?" I asked.

She huffed out a breath and nodded.

"Yes. You."

"I'm sorry." I set the feathered cap in my lap. "How can I help you?"

"Follow me."

With a quick glance at Ruth and Betty, I set the headpiece carefully on my table and hurried from the room after her, catching a glimpse of her heel as she rounded a corner ahead of me.

I arrived to her office a few seconds after she did and stopped when I saw Greta Garbo standing half clothed on a low pedestal in the center of the room. She smiled at me, her eyes darting to the designer who was flipping through a notebook of sketches and muttering to herself.

"What do—" I started.

"Shh!" she said, holding up a hand.

I pressed my lips together and waited while Miss Garbo stared at the ceiling, her hands clasped in front of her as the silence stretched on.

"Dean said you know a thing or two about designing," Cleménte said and I snapped to, realizing once again that she was addressing me.

"I do."

"Well then, what would you do with that?"

She pointed to the back of the dress and I walked slowly around Miss Garbo, taking in the too-high neckline, the gathered side, and the pattern wrapped around her middle until I got to where she was pointing and could take in the entire thing as a whole.

It was meant to be the highlight. A ball gown for the romantic climax of the film. But it was all wrong. The high neck looked like it was choking the starlet, the length of the sleeves was awkward and unflattering, the gathered sides and pattern across the middle of the dress distracting and made her look wider than she was. And at the back there was a long train that looked completely out of place. It was as if the designer had taken different elements from several dresses and patched them together.

I circled again. I couldn't suggest starting from scratch, it wouldn't go over well and I knew my place in this situation. All I could do was observe the silhouette and try and make it more flattering.

"What if you lose the train?" I asked. "Flare the bottom, giving the shape more balance?"

She stood beside me, trying to see what I was seeing. And then she nodded and wiped a tear from her cheek.

"Sorry," she said, sniffing delicately. "It's just, I've never worked like this before. It's so much pressure. When I design a collection, I have all the time in the world. This is..." She shook her head. "Not me. I need time to sit and think and... Well, you must understand."

"I do," I said. "I need quiet and space. I need to make a mess before the ideas come together."

"Yes! There's a process to it, even though others don't seem able to see it. And this is..." She looked around the room, the costumes on mannequins, the drawings tacked to the walls. "Chaos. This isn't how I work. It's too fast. Normally when I design, I do it for me. What I want to see, but I'm having to design for an audience. Not just the one that will see it on-screen, but the behind-the-scenes folks, as well. I don't want to let them down."

She sniffled again and I met Miss Garbo's eyes for a moment before turning back to Cleménte.

"I'm sure you won't," I said. "Do you need me for anything else?"

She took in a long inhale, let it out, and shook her head.

"What's your name again?" She looked embarrassed, and for the first time she felt human to me. Real. Not just another Hollywood bigwig that was far and beyond what I could ever hope to be. I could see the fear in her eyes. She was worried of failing. I knew that feeling well.

"Zora."

"Zora. Right. Well, thank you Zora. A fresh set of eyes was exactly what I needed. I can see it now and you're right. The balance is off."

I bid the two women goodbye then and hurried back down the hall to my feathers.

"Did you mention anything about me?"

I gave Jessie what I hoped was a grin as I dropped a letter to Harley in the mailbox on our way in to the studio.

"I did," I said. "I told him you and Rose are thriving and your costumes are divine."

I'd also told him about meeting Greta Garbo the previous week after being called into Michele Cleménte's office to help hold up a costume she was hand stitching onto the actress to check the fit.

"It was extraordinary," I said. And it had been, though I'd been less impressed with the gown she was wearing. It did nothing for her shape and I cringed at how it would look on the big screen. Cleménte, was a wonderful designer, but her signature style did nothing to accentuate Garbo's figure.

"What else did you tell the dashing Mr. Aldridge?" Rose asked and I shrugged.

The words had felt forced as I'd glossed over my misery, choosing instead to focus on how busy I was and how good the pay. It was incredible that I was able to both support myself and my family better than ever before. And I told him how pretty the city was no matter the time of day.

It was a letter written out of a sense of duty, not by a woman madly in love with a man. Even my "I love you" felt as though it were stamped on, not carefully and deliberately drawn onto the paper as it should have been.

It had taken me longer than usual to write this latest letter. I felt guilty for being untruthful. For the lack of emotion on the page. The omission of details that would've spelled out the truth of how I really was. And in doing so, I realized I was creating even more distance between us. More than just hundreds of miles of land and an entire ocean.

I feared losing him. Hated the thought of letting go of the happiness, safety, and love I'd found in his arms. But as I lagged behind the others, a voice inside me whispered that he deserved better. Someone elegant. Intelligent. Someone who would make him proud. And I was afraid I would never be that person.

As preproduction neared its end, the feeling in the studio became one of electricity—the actors' lines memorized, the choreography perfected, and the lights and sound finally working in sync.

It was at once hard to grasp we'd been there four months, and yet easy to believe as my weary body and lackluster spirits could've sworn it had actually been years.

"You don't sound yourself," Harley's letter said. As usual I lagged behind Rose and Jessie as we walked to work, the two of them chattering about their night's plans as I read the latest from England. "It's worrying. Talk to me, my love. Don't act as though I don't know you. I do. Every inch. Head to toe, and all the delicious bits in between. Please, tell me the truth. Let me help if I can."

But there was nothing he could do. I'd made the choice to stay and I would see the job through. All nine months I'd signed on for. After that, who knew.

I followed Rose and Jessie through the studio door and then ran into the back of Rose who had stopped walking.

"Hey," I said.

"Shhh," she said, waving a hand and putting a finger to her lips.

And then we heard it. Someone shouting. A woman.

There was a series of crashing sounds that made us jump as we exchanged nervous glances.

"Who is that?" Jessie whispered.

"Garbo?" Rose asked, but I shook my head.

"That's Cleménte," I said, recognizing the woman's pinched voice.

We inched farther down the hall, flinching at the sound of another crash, the yelling getting louder as a man joined in.

"Is that...?"

"Crawford," Rose whispered.

Mel Crawford was the director.

"Come on," Jessie said, pointing back the way we'd come. "Let's go around."

We hurriedly backtracked, the shouting fading behind us, as we took the long way around to the commissary where several people were huddled in groups, talking about the commotion on the main stage.

"What's happening?" Rose asked the nearest person as we each grabbed a plate and started loading food onto it.

"Apparently," an extra called Chap said, "Cleménte and Crawford are having an affair. She's mad he won't leave his wife and is threatening to leave the production unless he does."

The three of us exchanged a look. This wasn't good. Production was set to start soon and three of Garbo's costumes weren't finished. Two more weren't even cut out of the fabric yet because the designer wasn't sure she liked them.

"Excuse me!"

We all turned to find one of the producers clapping his hands to get our attention.

"Ladies and gentlemen," he said. "You are dismissed for the day due to uh...circumstances. Please take some food on your way out so it doesn't go to waste, and we'll see you all tomorrow at the regular time."

He turned and hurried out of sight before anyone could ask a question.

"Well," Rose said, grabbing a piece of toast and slathering it with jam. "Pool day, girls?"

I opened my mouth, ready to object out of habit, and then laughed.

"Pool day!" I said.

For the first time since we'd arrived, I relaxed, lazing poolside, the sun glorious on my skin, hair wet from something other than sweat or the cool shower I took every night to wash the day away.

We went out to eat, stopped by a club for a couple hours, talking to friends and waving to familiar faces we saw from across the room, and got home at a reasonable hour.

"You off to bed?" Rose asked, grabbing a pack of cigarettes and heading for the balcony where Jessie was already sitting, her feet propped up on the rail.

For once I didn't mind not being included. I was tired and sated.

"I am," I said.

"Today was good," she said, watching me carefully.

I grinned and gave her a hug.

"It was indeed."

30

I was sitting in the office of the costume manager the following morning, staring at a huge floral painting hanging behind her desk and wondering why I'd been called in. When I'd arrived fifteen minutes before, there was a note on my sewing machine, "Please see Mrs. Thompson." I'd glanced at Ruth and Betty, wondering what they knew, but neither woman returned my look.

"Good morning," Mrs. Thompson said, hurrying in through her office door behind me. "Sorry to keep you waiting. Seems we have a lot of fires to put out today, not the least of which is our situation with Miss Garbo's costumes."

I nodded, understanding now.

"There are two that need to be cut out and put together," I said. "We were waiting for Miss Cleménte's confirmation that they're ready to go. Once we have that, it shouldn't take us long to attach the adornments. It shouldn't take us long at all."

Mrs. Thompson gave me a tight smile and clasped her hands on the desk in front of her.

"Yesterday, after everyone left," she said. "Miss Cleménte made good on her threat to leave. Before she quit, she made sure to destroy every costume of Garbo's that was done, and took her design books with her. Nothing was spared. Not even the costumes you're talking about."

"Oh," I said, my mind whirling as I tried to understand just what that meant. Was the movie no longer happening? Was I no longer needed? Was I being fired? Were all of us? "So..."

"Truth be told, Zora, we are in a bit of pickle. We don't have the time or the money to hire a big-name designer. Nor can we afford the bad publicity if this gets out. I've been informed by Dean Billings that you are something of a designer yourself."

A rushing noise filled my head as I stared across the desk at her.

"Miss Hough?" She raised her eyebrows and tapped her fingernails on the desk. "Is this true?"

"I— Yes. Yes, it is. But—"

The tight smile was back, so rigid I was afraid Mrs. Thompson's face might actually crack.

"Can you do it?" she asked.

I opened my mouth, trying to find words, my mind blank. "I think—"

"No, no," she said, her voice rising in pitch as she got to her feet and rounded the desk to stand before me. "No thinking. Can you do it. It's a simple yes or no."

I took in a breath and forced myself to think.

"How long have we got?" I asked, my mind flipping through the ideas I'd drawn on the train from Seattle based off what Mr. Billings had told us about the script, and knowing adjustments would have to be done now that I knew the full scope of it.

"We can push production one more week," she said.

"So I'd have three and a half weeks total?"

"Yes."

"Nine costumes?"

"Yes."

I looked down at my lap, counting on my fingers the time I'd need for fittings, sewing, altering, adding on any beading or fringe work… It would be a massive undertaking. Unheard of. I'd have to work day and night and I'd need help.

But this was my chance to prove that not only could I do the job, I could do it well, giving me what I needed. A name in the fashion industry.

I met her gaze across the desk.

"I can do it."

"Let's go then," she said, getting to her feet.

I stood on legs that felt like they were made of rubber and followed her out the door.

Within the next few hours, word had spread throughout the studio and anything Cleménte had left behind was pulled from her office and my things were moved in while I sat in a corner chair out of the way, flipping through my sketchbooks, matching old designs I'd done with the new ones I'd created on the train until I had nine looks I was pleased with.

"Here," I said, sliding the designs across Mrs. Thompson's desk.

Her eyes flicked over each piece, taking in the details, the notes on fabric I'd made in the margins, and then looking up at me, her eyes narrowed.

"Stay here," she said, getting to her feet, gathering the sketches, and hurrying out the door.

A half hour later she returned.

"Come with me please, Miss Hough," she said.

I followed her down the hallway and into a room I knew well. The fabric room.

"Off you go," she said, and handed me back my designs.

"They approved all of them?" I asked.

"They did," she said, running her fingers through a roll of fringe. "Not that they had much choice at this late hour, but they're beautiful, Zora. And perfect for the film. You certainly did your homework, even when you didn't need to. Cleménte was never right for this film. It was apparent in both her designs, and the way she worked. But the director insisted so…"

I nodded. We certainly all knew why now.

Besides Ruth and Betty, I was given three other seamstresses to help me get the costumes ready in time. After a brief meeting where I showed them the designs, the fabric I'd chosen, and our timetable, I paced my new office, waiting for my next meeting.

At 4:00 p.m. on the dot she arrived.

"I hear we've had a bit of problem," Greta said, leaning against the doorframe, a twinkle in her pale blue eyes.

"Miss Garbo," I said, wiping sweaty palms on my trousers. "It's so nice to meet you again. I'm Zora Hough."

"Zora Hough," she said, offering her hand. "I'm told you are going to save the production."

"I'm certainly going to try," I said. "But I can't do it without you."

"Then by all means, let's get started."

She stood for hours, letting me pin, drape, repin, and hand stitch until I was satisfied with the first two pieces.

"How did you do all this so fast?" she asked as she changed back into her clothes.

It was after nine and it was just us, her behind the folding screen set up for her modesty, and me cleaning scraps of fabric and bits of thread off the floor.

"Well," I said, sitting on the edge of the desk. "This was the job I'd been told I'd be doing in the first place."

"Oh," she said, coming out from behind the screen as she adjusted the many necklaces she wore. "Don't tell me. Dean Billings exaggerated."

"I gather from your tone he does this a lot?"

"Oh, honey. They all do. It's like a disease in this town. They couldn't help it if they tried." She picked up her purse. "See you soon?"

"See you soon."

She put her hand on the door handle and then stopped. "You know, I already like you much better than that Cleménte. I have a feeling this is all working out for the best. For all of us. Plus, her designs were terrible. She made me look like a certified heifer!"

I pursed my lips as she winked and gave me a wave, the only trace left of her a whisper of perfume.

The late nights I worked before were nothing like the ones I had now. Every stitch counted, every thought was calculated. I had no time for interruptions and forgot to eat half the time, one of the seamstresses assisting me bringing food from the commissary on her way out for the day.

I left every night around eight o'clock, long after everyone else, the lot deserted, the walk home almost an annoyance for the fifteen minutes of time it wasted when I could've been sewing or addressing an issue that had arisen with one of the costumes.

That first Saturday, I awoke, threw on clothes, and hurried back to the studio. There were no days off until the job was done. With Garbo set to arrive at noon to try on the first finished costume, minus the sequins that would be put on as soon as we knew it didn't need additional alterations, I set about working on the next two.

"Zora?"

I jumped and nearly poked myself with a needle.

"Sorry," Deirdre said when I turned. She was the studio's receptionist and was waving a small piece of paper. "Garbo's assistant called. She can't make it in."

"What?" I said and blew out a breath in frustration.

"Her meeting got shifted. She's wondering if you can come to her. She said she'll send a car."

"Fine," I said. "Yes, of course."

A half hour later I was standing in the grand entrance of a house unlike any other I'd ever been in.

"Miss Hough?" the butler said, standing to one side, his hand outstretched to show that I should follow him.

"Right. Sorry," I said, staring up at the chandelier hanging at the center of the foyer, the fountain bubbling in one corner, an arrangement of flowers the size of a small shrub dwarfing the table it sat on.

"Oh, Zora," Greta said as I entered a beautiful room with white-on-white striped wallpaper, a gold settee, and several other pieces of furniture that looked as though they'd never been sat upon. "Thank goodness. I'm so sorry for all this. Please do have a seat. Jimmy? Get her a drink, will you?"

I glanced at the butler who smiled. "What can I get you, miss?"

"Just water please. Thank you." He nodded and was off.

Two hours later, full from an extravagant lunch, my soul replenished with good old-fashioned Hollywood gossip, girl talk, and what felt like a new friend, though I knew she couldn't possibly be, I left Greta's house. The first dress fit perfectly and she'd sworn she was going to steal it when shooting was done. The second, held together with the bare minimum of stitches, draped just as I'd envisioned and would look like something from a dream when it was finished.

"You are going to be a star in your own right after this," Greta said as she walked me to the car. "Mark my words, Zora Hough." She stopped then and frowned. "Do you have a middle name?"

"Lily," I said and watched her pale eyes widen.

"Zora Lily." She snapped her fingers. "That's it."

"You think so?"

"Take it from Greta Lovisa Gustafsson," she said in a thick Swedish accent as she winked. "See you tomorrow?"

"See you then."

Another letter from Harley marked day thirteen of the twenty-five I'd been given to design and construct nine costumes for Greta Garbo in what was sure to be MGM's most talked about motion picture to date.

"I count down the days, quite literally, until I shall see you again, my love. I dream of showing up on your doorstep one day and whisking you back to our home where we belong. Please write soon. I miss you so," he wrote.

But as much as I wanted to tell him about the recent turn of events, I didn't have the time to go into it all, and instead dashed off a hurried letter while I ate a late dinner standing at the kitchen counter and sketching out an idea to add on to one of the costumes.

"He's going to be so proud of you, Z," Rose said when I dropped the letter in the mail the next morning on our way to work.

I reached over and squeezed her hand.

With three days left we had two costumes to finish. A modern trouser suit I wished I could keep for myself, and a gown that stunned even me, regardless of the fact that I was the one who imagined it into existence.

"I'm almost afraid to touch it," Greta said, staring at the white satin gown in the full-length mirror—its stark shimmering fabric in contrast to the large beaded star on the hip, the skirt falling in a cascade of overlapping layers to the floor like something from a dream.

"It looks like it's from another world," someone whispered as Greta turned, the lights catching the beads, giving the impression that the star itself was moving all on its own.

"You've outdone yourself," Greta said, catching my eye in the mirror.

We finished the last piece at ten thirty-two on the night they were due.

"You should be very proud," Mrs. Thompson said, eyeing each of the nine costumes hanging on their respective mannequins. She'd stayed late as well, waiting for me to tell her we'd done it. We'd finished on schedule as promised. "They're stunning."

She ran a light hand over the white dress and then turned to me with a smile.

"Filming starts Monday," she said. "We'll need you to return to the sewing room, but should any adjustments be needed on any of these costumes, you'll be called on specifically to mend them."

I nodded my understanding.

"Also," she continued. "I've requested, and have had granted, a paid day off for you on Monday."

"Thank you."

"It's well-earned, Zora. The studio thanks you."

I looked around the office I'd gotten to work in for the past few weeks, gathered my things, and went home.

Filming took just over three months, the days flying by with little to no breaks in work for everyone as they acted, danced, sang, and we in the back mended and hemmed, the hum of the sewing machines droning their own little tune.

Some days I took a piece I was working on and lurked in the shadows just out of sight, stitching as Garbo spun her magic or Rose and Jessie and the dozens of other women danced beneath the hot can lights over and over until they got it just right.

My weekends finally my own, I began to spend more time with the girls again, taking in a club every so often, and going to the cinema.

And I wrote to Harley. Finally sitting down to tell him all the details of what had transpired.

"It felt amazing," I wrote. "To design for a motion picture and work with Greta Garbo herself. She called me a star. I will remember that moment always."

His response was nothing short of blinding in his excitement.

"Garbo! Zora, my love, you have made it! I didn't doubt it once. And I'm beginning to wonder if I should start looking for a home for us in Los Angeles?"

I grinned and pressed the letter to my breast, leaning back into one of the patio chairs on our balcony.

"What did he say?" Rose asked, handing me a drink as she sat down in the other chair. Jessie was off for the afternoon with a man she'd met and for once it was just the two of us, something I hadn't realized I'd missed as much as I did.

"He's wondering if he should buy a house here."

Rose eyes widened. "Yes!" she said and I laughed.

But while it was tempting, the weather and palm trees, the glitz and glamour of the town fun, I wasn't sure I wanted to make it my home permanently. Getting to design for the studio had been an experience, one that could open new doors I'd previously never considered, but seeing how it affected Cleménte was sobering. Did I want all that pressure?

"What did Ellis's letter say?" I asked.

Along with my letter from Harley, Rose had received one from Ellis, something that had surprised her and sent her quietly to our room, where she closed the door and didn't come out for a long while.

She handed me a piece of paper that I unfolded to reveal that it was a flyer for a show.

"The Oscar Holden Band" it said across the top. "Featuring Ellis Jones."

It was for Doc Hamilton's Barbecue Pit.

"This is fantastic!" I said, looking from the flyer to Rose. She nodded, but I could see something was bothering her. "Are you okay?"

"He's met someone," she said.

"Oh. Oh, Rose. I'm sorry."

"It's fine. It was bound to happen. I just… I guess I thought maybe it would happen to me first. Or that it wouldn't hurt so bad. I hate thinking of him with someone else. I hope she's ugly."

I laughed and she gave me a teasing grin.

"You do not," I said.

"I do! And I hope she has two left feet and a terrible ear for music."

"Rose!"

Now she was laughing too, the two of us cracking up in a way we hadn't in a long time.

After a while we calmed down and she reached over and took my hand.

"I'm glad he's happy," she said. "He's such a good man. It hurts though. I can't lie."

"Love is hard," I said.

"And confusing."

"And heartbreaking."

"I'm never doing it again," she said.

"Yes you are."

"I know."

Halloween came and went with a costume party at one of the clubs and Jessie and Rose convincing me to dress up with them as cats. I sent a picture of us in costume, taken by a club photographer, and a letter written in a hurry to Harley a few days later. I mentioned nothing of his idea of buying a house in California, just that work was busy, time was flying, and I missed him dearly.

His return letter arrived two weeks later, filled with talk of his last business trip, to Spain this time, and telling me to be on the lookout for a package arriving that was not to be opened until Christmas.

The Monday after Thanksgiving, I was standing behind one of the cameramen, careful not to trip over any of the cords, when a gasp echoed through the studio.

"Stop!" someone yelled. "Stop the music!"

I peered through the dark, trying to see around the bodies suddenly rushing around, my heartbeat speeding up at the sound of someone crying.

"Who is it?" a voice whispered.

"Can't see."

"She okay?"

I stood on tiptoe and sucked in a breath when I saw Rose kneeling. My heart sank and I rushed forward, pushing through the crowd to my friend. But when I finally got to her I saw it wasn't her that was crying, it was Jessie, her foot turned at an odd angle, her ankle rapidly bruising.

31

"Six weeks!" Jessie shouted from where she lay on her bed, her leg propped up in front of her.

Her face was puffy from crying, her new cast covered in scrawled words from her fellow dancers wishing her a quick recovery.

"You'll still be in the movie," Rose said, handing her a bowl of soup.

"But not the last big dance number!" Her face crumpled.

She'd broken both leg bones right above her ankle, having rolled it taking a step down the stage stairs, and then the dancer next to her stepping on it as Jessie pulled her down with her. Nearly every evening as she recovered, there was a small parade of well-wishers who came by with food, flowers, and gossip to lift her spirits and keep her feeling included.

Christmas came with the three of us remarking on the strangeness of spending the holiday with palm trees rather than our beloved and familiar evergreens lit up for the holiday. We spent Christmas Eve at Sophie's apartment, playing games and drinking alcohol she snuck in for the occasion. And in the morning Rose, Jessie, and I opened the gifts we'd gotten one another.

"What did Harley send?" Jessie asked from the sofa, where we'd propped her leg up and piled gifts on the table beside her.

For weeks the gift he'd sent sat on my bureau, beautifully wrapped, the card sitting on top. I'd promised not to open it until Christmas morning, and I hadn't. But as soon as I woke, I quietly carried it to the balcony and sat outside as the sun came up and carefully pulled the paper off.

Inside the box was another box constructed of butter-soft, periwinkle leather with a starburst clasp. When I opened it I gasped. It was a sewing case, complete with the finest threads in a variety of colors, needles of several gauges, a pin cushion in the shape of a French poodle, and other thoughtful implements that would make house calls a breeze.

But it was what I found in a smaller velvet box at the bottom that made my heart skip a beat.

"By god that man is romantic," Jessie said, staring at the black pearl hanging from a fine gold chain nestled against white satin. "What's wrong with American men, anyway? They need to take lessons from those Brits."

For Harley's gift, I'd splurged, thrilled that for the first time in my life I could do such a thing. A handsome pair of leather gloves, a silk tie in a shade of blue that matched his eyes, and a little travel clock I'd been delighted to find, that folded up in a neat little case and that I'd had engraved with his initials.

On January 17, 1927, *The Star* wrapped. There was a lot more work to do, mostly for the behind-the-scenes crews, but filming was finally done and the film was set to release the following year. A big party followed, alcohol that had been secreted in flowed, and Jessie hobbled around hugging all the dancers tearfully. She'd made the decision after Christmas to go back to Seattle.

"What?" Rose had shouted when Jessie told us.

We were lounging around our apartment, playing cards, since Jessie still couldn't go out.

"I'm sorry," she said. "It's been on my mind awhile. Even before the accident. I miss home. And while this has all been fun, it's also been stressful. All the measuring and remeasuring to make sure we haven't gained a millimeter. The constant scrutiny and long hours. I miss the days of waking late, working a half day, and then dancing in a show at night. And with Lorraine deciding to hang up her dance shoes, maybe I have a chance at the lead spot at the Alhambra."

"But…" Rose's face fell.

"I know," Jessie said.

Rose sighed and then looked to me. "Have you decided what you're going to do? Have you asked around about doing more design work? I'm sure the studio will give you a glowing reference, unless they want to keep you for themselves."

I shrugged. I had no idea what my plan was. Rose already had another job lined up and I knew at the very least I could stay on at MGM sewing in the back room with Ruth and Betty until another design opportunity came along. But there were no guarantees that would happen. Not when the studios could bring in a high-profile name.

By the following week, Rose was deep in rehearsals for another movie, I was deep in costume making and repair, and Jessie, free of her cast, had begun to pack her things.

It felt strange starting over on a new bunch of costumes designed by someone else after my marathon of designing and creating with Garbo. My pride in doing the job had quickly become overshadowed with disappointment. As though the opportunity had never even happened. Some of the other seamstresses teased me about it.

"Slumming it again," they'd say.

It was supposed to be good-natured fun, but it stung.

"Ah, don't mind them," Betty said one day. "They're just jealous because they've never been asked to do what you got to."

I nodded, threading a needle and looking at the two older women.

"Have either of you ever designed for a motion picture?"

"Ha!" Ruth said. "No way. We know our place. And we're good at what we do. All that—" she gestured toward the door "—is unnecessary stress. I like to do my job and go home. And if I have to bring a little with me to work on in the evenings sometimes, that's fine. At least I don't have studio heads, directors, and starving actors and actresses yelling at me."

I nodded. That was part of what had stalled me from trying to find more work designing. I'd seen how the stress had stolen away the joy of what Cleménte loved.

"Checks are in!" someone shouted as they hurried by the sewing room.

"Want me to grab yours for you?" I asked Ruth and Betty. They nodded without bothering to stop talking about Ruth's son-in-law, that ungrateful bastard.

I wandered up the hall to Mrs. Thompson's office where the seamstresses received their paychecks. This would be the last one from my job on *The Star*, making it feel bittersweet as I walked past the office I'd gotten to call my own for a few brief weeks. Inside now were the garments I'd designed, each one tucked away in a special protective bag. I ached to see them one last time. To run my hand over them and feel the expensive fabrics against my skin, remembering—in case I never got the chance to do such a job again.

"Good morning," I said, knocking on Mrs. Thompson's door.

"Zora," she said, a hesitant smile on her face. "Please come in and shut the door."

I raised my eyebrows but did as she said, and then took a seat in one of the chairs she motioned to.

"How's the old sewing room?" she asked.

"Too warm," I said with a laugh. "The usual."

"Good…good…"

I sat quietly, my hands folded in my lap, waiting for whatever it was she wanted to talk to me about, my nerves starting to spike as the silence stretched.

"Oh. Here," she said, sliding an envelope across the desk to me.

"Thank you."

"Mmm-hmm..." she said, avoiding my gaze.

"Mrs. Thomps—"

"I have to ask something horrible of you," she said quickly and my body froze as my mind raced.

"What is it?" I asked.

I was surprised to see her eyes fill. She swiped a hand across them and took a breath.

"Zora," she said. "I have to ask you to remove your name from your designs."

My mouth opened but no sound came out.

"The problem is," she rambled on, "you never signed a contract. Not to make Garbo's costumes anyway. And Cleménte did."

"But—" I frowned, thinking back. I shook my head. "I was never asked to sign a contract."

"I know," she whispered, closing her eyes. "We were all so frantic. It was an oversight. It was *my* oversight." She blinked and stared down at her desk, unable to meet my gaze, and then took a breath. "The problem is, Cleménte is threatening Crawford and the studio. Her name is on the only contract we have for Garbo's costumes and the studio is worried about the pub licity issue this will assuredly create. Bad publicity. That could affect future funding of projects. Though it was a breach of contract when she walked, they're willing to overlook it. And since you're listed only as a seamstress... If we don't comply with her wishes, she'll go to the press and say the designs are hers and were stolen. Regardless of the truth, the studio doesn't want the trouble."

"But they're mine!" I said.

She sighed. "In truth, as per the contract you *did* sign when you took the seamstress job, they're the studio's. All costumes you have made, assisted in making, fixed, altered, and hemmed are the studio's."

My body quaked, fury raking its way through my limbs and clawing up my torso.

"Is there anything I can do?" I managed to ask.

"No."

I nodded and got to my feet.

"Zora," Mrs. Thompson said. "I'm so sorry. If there were anything I could do..." She rubbed her brow. "Also, I have to ask something more of you."

"Don't talk to the press?"

"Well, that. But something else, as well."

I didn't speak to anyone. Didn't go to the back room to tell Ruth and Betty I wouldn't be back for a while. I walked directly from Mrs. Thompson's office to the room I'd once spent three and a half weeks working in, and where each of the nine costumes now waited for me to remove my name from their delicate fabrics, to erase myself and all of my hard work from the film.

It was cruel what I was being asked to do. Cruel, unfair, and apparently, as Mrs. Thompson had said in a last attempt to try and make me understand, not personal—just how business worked.

The tags were where she'd said they'd be, a spool of thread and needle beside them on the desk. I picked up the tag on top and ran my finger across it.

In tiny print at the top it read "Designed by." Beneath it, Cleménte's name. Not mine.

I sniffed and then turned and unzipped the first garment bag and carefully removed the sheath dress from it. Sitting in the chair at the desk, I laid the dress across my lap, threaded the needle, knotted the thread, and reached for a tag. As I pulled the front of the garment away, exposing the lining inside and my name, stitched in small, sweeping letters, my eyes filled with tears. How many times had I practiced that signature at night on scraps of fabric. The one Garbo had suggested I use. Dozens? Fifty? And now it turned out it was all for naught. No one would ever know that these clothes were made by me, for Greta Garbo, for what would be MGM Studios' first talking picture. It would make its mark in the world of film, cast Greta into the American motion picture stratosphere. Rose and Jessie would make their film debut. And I… I would only ever be known of as one of the women who sat behind the scenes, stitching holes and blown-out hems, attaching buttons, fringe, and beads in a dim, too-hot room in the back.

I stared at my signature a moment longer, then set the tag in place above it, slid the needle into the fabric, and said goodbye to Zora Lily.

"You're sure?" Rose asked three days later, her big, blue eyes full of tears.

I nodded, my own eyes dry. I'd cried enough tears. My body was weary, my mind numb, and all I wanted now was to go home.

But where was home? My parents' house? Harley's?

"This is all a bunch of banana oil," Rose said, pouting, her arms crossed over her chest. "Can't you find another job? At another studio? Or maybe at one of the fancy boutiques?"

But I wasn't interested. Hollywood had lost its shine.

And then there were the doubts that had dimmed for a time, but had managed to find their way back with each stitch of the tags bearing Cleménte's name. The thoughts that I wasn't good enough for Harley. I hadn't "made it" as he'd said in his letter. I wasn't smart enough or successful enough. That I wasn't someone he could be proud to have on his arm. It was those thoughts that led me to choose my parents' house, sending a letter to let my mother know to expect me soon.

A week later, Sophie drove Rose, Jessie, and me to the train station. Sophie had been looking to move out of her apartment for ages, and with Jessie and me leaving, she'd happily taken Rose up on her offer of Jessie's room. The two women hugged Jessie and me goodbye, with Rose swearing she'd write often with news.

"I want all the good gossip," Jessie said, hugging Rose goodbye.

"Give my mama a hug for me?" Rose whispered in my ear as she held on to me.

"I will. Knock 'em dead, you hear me?"

She nodded, unable to say more, and then Jessie and I grabbed our suitcases, boarded the train, and waved goodbye.

Jessie fell asleep almost immediately, but I found I couldn't do the same, my mind playing like its own motion picture, suddenly remembering every detail of my stay, from meeting Sophie, to my first day in that too-warm back room, dressing as cats for Halloween, and measuring Greta Garbo while she cracked jokes and asked about my love life. It had been a thrill, Hollywood. But as I pulled out my old sketchpad, skipping past the torn remains of the pages I'd been requested to hand over to the studio, I began to draw. And by the time the train pulled into Union Station in Seattle, I had a dozen pages full of new designs and an idea I had no clue if I could pull off.

But I was sure gonna try.

32

The path to the front porch, once a plain dirt row with small, muddy gullies Harrison and Eva used to play in, now lay flat and neat with stone pavers leading the way and flowers lining either side. The porch itself was still slanted, the paint on the house faded and chipped, but the front door was new and there were two rocking chairs off to the side with a small table between them. It was welcoming. Friendly. And a comforting change.

The Hough family was doing okay.

"Zora!"

The front door flew open and little Eva, who was not so little anymore, her eight-year-old body long and lean like mine, came flying down the steps. She threw herself at me as I laughed.

"I'm happy to see you too," I said, holding her to me and taking in the scent of hair that had recently been washed. Oh, the wonders an indoor bathroom held.

Since I had money from Harley, I'd sent almost every cent earned from the studio home to my mother, who had asked hesitantly if she might use it to have the bathroom put in. And electricity.

"Wait until you see the house," Eva said as I looked her over head to toe. She'd grown several inches since I'd last seen her, but rather than the ankle-exposing pants she'd normally be subjected to due to the family's financial situation, Mama was able to purchase new ones that fit.

"Is there so much to see?" I asked.

"So much!" Eva shouted and dragged me toward the house.

Before I could see any of the changes though, I was greeted by every family member but one.

"Where's Pa?" I asked quietly. I'd read in a letter from Sarah that he was doing better and had gotten a part-time job a few months ago doing work on automobiles, but this was a weekday evening. Surely he wasn't at work now.

"He was able to pick up a few more hours today," Mama said, giving me a reassuring smile. "He should be home any minute now."

"You probably won't even recognize him," Harrison said. He too had grown. At nine he was nearly as tall as Hannah who was sixteen and still as diminutive and delicate as ever.

"Well," I said. "I can't wait to see him. Now. Who wants to give me a tour of the house. I believe I see…is that a new sofa?"

While Lawrence took my bags upstairs, Eva and Harrison each grabbed one of my hands and showed me every single new addition to the house, from the sofa to the rug in front of it, an ironing board and hanging rack for the sewing jobs, toys, pots and pans, a set of dishes—"They all match!"

I admired the new bathroom, watching as Harrison flicked the light on and off until Mama yelled at him and I excused myself to use it.

Harrison showed me his and Eva's two pairs of shoes each. "Look!" he said. "The bottoms are attached all the way around!"

I ran my hand over the new quilt on Sarah's bed. "I'm gonna share with her while you share with Hannah," Eva informed me. And then sat at the dining table where a bowl of fruit, just like the one always filled at Rose's house, was placed in the center for any and all to snack on.

"What do you think?" Sarah asked, sitting across from me in her usual spot. "Did we do a good job? I mean, it's not the Harringtons' or Hollywood but—"

I reached across the table and took her hand in mine. "It's better," I said.

She looked around doubtfully, but I shook my head and squeezed her fingers.

"Believe me," I said. "This. All of you. It's way better than anything I found in either of those places."

"Is that why you came back?"

I inhaled and then slowly let the breath out, my mind ticking through the many reasons I sat here in this house again now. The pain of what I'd had to give up. The ache of failure. Of not persevering or fighting for what was mine. Of once again being fooled into thinking "maybe this will be the place for me" and finding out, in horrid fashion, that indeed it wasn't.

"It's part of the reason," I said.

She raised an eyebrow, but I merely smiled. The wound was still too fresh to talk about. Maybe one day I'd tell them what I'd done. What I'd accomplished in record time. And what had been unceremoniously taken from me. Sure, I'd been paid handsomely to keep my mouth shut. To stand down. To give up whatever accolades rightfully should be mine. But what would the cost be to me internally? Would regret flag me for years to come? Or would I—could I—pick up and move forward in a way that made sense to me? A way I could accept what I'd given up. There was only one way to find out.

"You okay with me being back in the bedroom for a while?" I asked.

"Only a while?" Mama asked from the kitchen.

Sarah grinned at me and I shook my head.

"I can't stay home forever, Mama," I said.

"You just got here though," she said, moving to the doorway, a knife in one hand, a potato in the other.

"I know," I said. "And I'll stay for a bit, but I need to figure out what's next for me. I have some ideas..."

"Like?"

"Mama!" Sarah said with a laugh. "Let her breathe. She just got home. And for gosh sake. She's a grown woman and doesn't want to live with her parents forever."

"I know that, but what about Harley?" Mama asked. "Does he know you've come home?"

"I haven't written him yet, so no, he doesn't."

"But you will, won't you?"

"Of course, Mama."

"You didn't have a falling out, did you?"

"No. I just, need some time before I tell him. I'm embarrassed about what happened. And sad."

"I sure wish you'd talk to me about it."

"I know. I'm just not ready yet."

"Well, don't let him go too long without hearing from you. He'll start to think you found someone else."

"I know, Mama. I won't. But I need to focus on me right now. What I want. What's next for me."

And part of that was feeling I belonged somewhere, not because I was on someone's arm or because someone had allowed me in, but because I was so sure of myself, my capabilities, and my talents, I didn't care if anyone thought I *didn't* belong. I wanted to be *my own*. Before I was someone else's. I knew it was hard for my mother to understand, this new, modern way of thinking by women, but I needed more than to just get by on the bare minimum or be someone's wife. And I was determined to find a way to get there.

Sarah, Hannah, and I were in the midst of making dinner when Pa came home. I heard him before I saw him, and waited to hear the familiar stumbling about as he mumbled incoherently before making his way to something he could pass out on. But the sounds never came. Instead, there was a hearty, "Good evening, family," and tears welled in my eyes at the deep voice I remembered but hadn't heard in years.

"Zora's home," Mama said, and a moment later he appeared in the doorway.

He stood taller, his hair was cut and clean, his clothes fit, and he was wearing shoes. But it was his face that made me want to cry. Gone was the unkempt beard, the bleary gaze, the ruddy skin. There was still some wear from the toll of so much drinking, but this was the face that had smiled down as he'd tucked me into bed at night. The face that had whispered reassuringly as he'd tended to scraped knees, stubbed toes, and a bruised heart when once again I'd been made fun of in school.

"Hey, Pa," I said, my voice soft.

"Hey, girl," he said, and then in three long strides he reached me and pulled me in for a hug. "Sure glad you're home. I missed you something awful."

"I missed you too."

We stood staring at one another, a lifetime of memories flashing between us, and then he nodded, kissed Sarah's and Hannah's heads, and went to wash up for supper.

"He's doing really well," Sarah said quietly as she checked the potatoes boiling on the stove top. "Home every night for supper, up early every morning, ready to help whenever anyone needs it."

"He fixed up the front path to the house," Hannah said, peeking in on the rolls baking in the oven. "Planted the flowers and everything. Even asked Ma what colors she wanted before buying them."

"That's good," I said. "He was such a wreck after his accident. And then when Tommy died... I thought we'd lost him forever."

"Well, it's thanks to you that he got better," Sarah said.

"What do you mean?" I asked, propping a hip against the counter and watching as she poked at a potato with a fork to check for doneness, the steam reddening her face.

"You going off to Hollywood. I think he thought you'd never come back. That you'd had it with him and us and having to be the one supporting the family. It scared him. He'd already lost Tommy—he couldn't lose you too."

"He was a mess at first," Hannah said. "He didn't know where anything in the house was and kept calling us by each other's names, mumbling and swearing, his hands shaking something awful. But he was determined. Your leaving, as hard as it was for all of us, was a godsend, and if you hadn't gone, he'd probably be dead."

I nodded. The day I left, after kissing my barely coherent father goodbye, I'd feared it was the last time I'd see him alive. And although in the letters I received from Ma, Sarah, and Hannah spoke of him doing better, I'd assumed they were just saying it so I wouldn't worry as much. But now…

"The job he's got is an honest one?" I asked and both girls nodded. "And the drinking?"

"The shaking was so bad at first, Mama got a prescription from the doc. She doled out the prescribed amount for him three times a day, then two, then one," Sarah said and then reached into a cupboard and pulled out a nearly empty bottle of whiskey. "This little bit has been sitting in here for the past two weeks. He hasn't touched it. Hasn't even mentioned it."

I sighed, my shoulders sagging, the anxiousness I'd been carrying for years dissipating like the steam from the boiling water cooking our dinner. We had our pa back. I only wished Tommy were around to see it.

Dinner was a raucous affair as my siblings talked over one another to tell me what was new in their lives while our parents grinned at one another from across the table.

Afterward, Sarah and Hannah helped Mama clean up, Pa took the trash out, and the younger two hurried off to finish their homework, while Lawrence carried my bags up to my old bedroom.

"Not sure where you're gonna put all this," he said, standing on the threshold and eyeing the small tidy room.

I laughed. I still didn't have much to my name, but it was more than I'd left with.

"Maybe just slide them under the bed for now?" I said and watched as he bent his long frame to do just that. "Thanks, Lawr."

He grinned and stood, pushing his hair back from his eyes. He was twenty now, and broader, taller, and more handsome than the older brother he'd always wanted to be like. But where Tommy had been confident and outspoken, Lawrence was quiet, contemplative, and shy.

"How's the job?" I asked.

He lifted his hands to show me his ink-stained fingertips.

"It's good. I like the work. But it's hard at times. Physical. Lots of moving parts. I'm hoping to move upstairs one day."

"What's upstairs?"

"The newsroom."

"You've always been good with words and telling stories. You'd be great in the newsroom."

"I think so, but most of the guys in there are college educated."

"So? Did they grow up here like you did? You're local. An original. You know the people. The city. Better than most of them I'll bet. And if you really wanted, you could go to college. Things are well in hand here now. There's plenty of money coming in."

He shrugged and gave me a sheepish grin. "I've thought about it. But to be honest, it's never been a dream of mine. I just want to write and sell stories. I'll live at home forever, take out the trash, get the younger kids where they need to be, just so long as I can find the stories I want to tell about the city and the people in it."

"Then what are you waiting for?"

"I don't know," he said. "Maybe I was waiting for you to get here and boss me around like you used to."

My jaw dropped in feigned shock and he laughed.

"See? Telling stories already." I grinned. "I think you should do it. What have you got to lose? At least you're still at home and the chance you'll be taking won't mean having to pack up and take your bruised ego home from another state."

He frowned. "What happened in California, Z?"

I inhaled long and slow, a cascade of images filling my mind, hurt and disappointment resonating throughout my body and lodging in my throat.

"Nothing," I said. "It just wasn't for me."

"Too many fancy parties?"

"Not nearly enough."

He laughed. "Fine. You don't have to tell me. I'm just glad you're home. I never thought Hollywood was for you anyway."

"I don't have that spark like Rose has."

"That's not it, Z," he said. "You're plenty sparkly. But that place just seems like it would be full of fake people. And you… you're too real. Too earnest and good."

"Thanks, Lawr."

"You're welcome." He shoved his hands in his pockets then and I was surprised to see a blush creep up his neck and color his cheeks. "Now, I have to get. I'm to pick Caroline up soon and she hates when I'm late."

I raised my eyebrows and he smiled.

"You'll like her," he said as he passed me and headed for the stairs. "She's bossy too."

His laughter echoed down the hallway and I couldn't help but smile, relieved that his suffering after Tommy died seemed to be in the past, his present situation made him smile, and his future looked bright.

I looked around the small room I'd grown up in. It hadn't changed much since I'd left. There were still the two beds with the same mishmash of quilts and blankets and pillows. The same chest of drawers to hold the clothes of several young ladies. The floor was worn but swept clean, the window smeared with tiny fingerprints near the bottom, the rest of the glass providing a view of the backyard. Save for some new things that had been adhered to the walls, it was comforting to see it look the same.

I moved in closer, looking at the things my younger sisters had found important enough to display in each of their spaces. For Sarah it was newspaper clippings of Clara Bow. Always one for a dramatic display, it hadn't surprised any of us when she'd started asking to be taken to the theater and putting on little plays in the living room.

Above the place where Hannah laid her head at night were taped page after page of favorite quotes she'd pulled from the books she'd read and written down. Beside the papers filled with her perfect penmanship, were slightly wrinkled drawings of bears—or were they dogs?—flowers, and the moon and stars. I smiled at Eva's attempts, picturing how she must've looked, her wide eyes narrowed in concentration, the tip of her tongue poking out. How I'd missed that little face. How I'd missed them all.

By habit, I bent to blow out the candle that normally sat on the tall slender table near the door, but in its place was a lamp. I shook my head, marveling at the changes that had come to the Hough house in the past year, then pulled the little chain to turn off the light.

As I walked down the stairs to the main floor, the sounds of my family filled my ears. Harrison and Eva, done with their homework, were playing a board game while lying sprawled on the new rug. Pa was reading the newspaper, Hannah and Sarah were still washing up in the kitchen, and Mama…

"That's quite the rack of clothes," I said, running my hand over the hangers of the garments lined up like soldiers awaiting their turn with my mother's needle and thread. "What are the tags for?"

Each item had a tag affixed, some were pink, others blue, and a few white.

"Pink is for things that need to be done urgently—within two weeks' time. Blue for four to six weeks, and white for whenever I can get to it—no rush, just sometime this century."

"I like it," I said. "A good system is important, I learned."

"Sarah goes through them every night before bed, checks the dates I promised they'd be done, and shifts them accordingly."

"And how are her sewing skills coming along?"

"Good. She's gotten fast and sure of herself."

I watched her sew for a minute, placing my hand on the sewing machine. It was the one Harley had bought me and that I'd had moved here after he'd left for London.

"It sews like a dream," Mama said. "Sarah gets up early most days to beat me to it."

I laughed and then looked at the rack of clothes once more, a particularly pretty blue bit of fabric catching my eye.

"Can I help?" I asked.

"You want to get your hands on that blue piece, don't you?" she said without looking up.

"How did you know?"

"Because I know you, Zora Lily. And I made sure it was hanging just so, so you would see it. It has a ripped shoulder and needs some reworking down the front."

I pulled the frock from where it hung. Whoever owned it looked to have caught her pearls in the fringed neckline and, rather than patiently untangling it, had pulled and taken apart the seam, snagged some of the fringe, and popped a hidden button.

I slid into the chair I'd spent hours in over the years. Mama adjusted the lamp she was using so that it was between us, and handed me a needle from her sewing box, a pair of scissors, and a spool of thread.

Our fingers brushed as I took the items from her and our eyes met and held. She gave me a soft smile that spoke volumes and I nodded, my eyes welling. I was home. It wasn't necessarily where I wanted to be, or even where I belonged anymore, but it was familiar. And right now, after the foreign feel of Los Angeles, familiar was what I needed most.

I sat back, wiped away a tear, cut a long line of thread, and fed it through my needle.

33

Summer began, the Seattle gray parting to give us blue-filled skies and warm, lazy days. The front and back doors slammed constantly as the youngest members of the family wandered in and out, looking for something to do, someone to spend time with, or a chilled drink and a cool spot to drink it in.

"I'm bored," Harrison whined from where he sat on the front steps watching a line of ants march by on the path before him.

I looked up at Mama, who was scowling at a ruffle that wouldn't bunch right.

"Mind if I take a break and provide some entertainment?" I asked, setting down the trousers I was hemming and wiping the sweat from my brow.

"Mmm," she said, pulling out the thread and starting over.

I stood and stretched my back, then hurried up the stairs to the bedroom to grab my coin purse from the shoulder bag I'd yet to unpack. I'd been home two weeks, and while it would have been easier for me to stow my clothes in the half-empty closet and the old dresser drawer that used to be mine, I feared doing so would feel like giving up. Though, as I took in Eva's toys and clothes that always seemed to be lying in piles in front of the beds beneath which my suitcases were stowed, at least I wouldn't have to keep shoving her stuff out of the way.

As I reached inside my bag for the blue-beaded coin purse, my fingers brushed my sketchbook. Grabbing that too, I went back downstairs.

At the front door I slipped on my shoes and opened the screen door.

"Who wants to go to the shop for an afternoon treat?" I asked. Harrison's eyes widened and he got to his feet, dusting the dirt from his clothes.

"Me?" he said and I laughed.

"Are you sure?" I asked and he nodded.

"Well then, let's go see what kind of trouble we can get into."

A half hour later we were on our way back to the house, each of us sipping from our respective bottles of soda, his a grape Nehi, mine a root beer. In his back pocket was an orange Nehi for Eva.

He burped loudly and I shook my head, looking at him out the corner of my eye.

"Hey, wanna check out the pond?" he asked.

"We can go for a bit," I said. "But then I have to get back to work."

He took my hand and led the way.

"How come you came back from Hollywood?" Harrison asked as we meandered toward the small patch of wood where the pond was tucked between evergreen trees and rhododendron plants, their limbs heavy with spent blooms in red and pink and purples, wilted petals clumped on the woodland floor. "Was it not fancy enough?"

I grinned and ruffled his hair. He'd be tall, like his brothers before him, and was already just as inquisitive.

"It was too fancy for me," I said. "I like things a little simpler."

He nodded as though that made perfect sense to him, and then knelt to pick up a worm in our path and place it off to the side.

"Last one to the pond has to take out the trash tonight?" he asked.

I pretended to think about it then yelled, "Go!" and we were off, tearing through the shrubs, kicking up dead leaves, pine needles, and flower petals until we were free of the trees and running across the small patch of grass that led to the little pond where I'd learned to swim and fish when I was younger than the boy beside me was now.

I waded in to my knees while he set down his soda and pulled off his shirt, dropping it to the dirt embankment before turning and running into the water, sending up a splash that rained down on me and made me shout as the cold droplets hit my skin.

"I won!" he yelled.

We walked home, the pond water dripping from our clothes and beading on our skin before evaporating beneath the sun's bright rays.

After a quick bath in the new indoor bathroom, a welcome addition I thought I might never get over, I changed into a fresh summer dress I'd sewn myself the previous week from a ream of fabric Mama had gotten on sale and handed to me.

"What am I doing with this?" I'd asked, running my hand over the lightweight material. It was pale blue with a white flower print, perfect for the season.

"Make yourself something," she'd said. "Make something for all you girls. Whatever you want. It's yours."

"But—"

"Gertrude gave it to me at a bargain. It has a stain, see?" She'd turned over the ream and showed me a small patch of brown. "I think she thought it went all the way through, but it doesn't." The sparkle in her eyes made me laugh. She and Gertrude had been in competition for years, the latter also a seamstress.

I'd stayed up every evening the past week cutting pattern pieces and sewing for my sisters and me, plus a secret project for Mama, as well. A dress for myself—something easy to slip on, but that hit all the right fashion notes of the day: dropped waist, higher hemline, slender straps. I made another version of the same dress for Sarah. Hannah got a blouse to go with the cotton overalls she'd begged me to make her the day after I returned home. Apparently, a female character in one of her books wore a pair and she just had to have them. She'd worn them nearly every day since. And for Eva, a simple dress that was a near mirror image of mine, save for the dropped waist.

"What's this?" Mama said when I'd handed her the creation I'd designed for her.

"Every woman should have something she puts on that makes her feel a little bit fancy," I said.

She'd given me one of her suspicious looks and taken the folded material, setting it on the table before lifting it by the shoulders and letting it unfurl before her.

"Oh," she'd said, her voice barely a whisper.

I was a girl when I overheard her tell Pa that one day we'd have enough money for her to afford such things as more than two pairs of shoes and a dressing gown. She still only owned two pairs of shoes, but now she had a dressing gown.

"Oh, Zora," she'd said. "It's beautiful."

The inside was lined with white satin from a wedding dress someone had brought to us, begging me to cut off the train and reconstruct the body to reflect today's style. There had been yards of cast-off material that I'd cut to not only line the dressing gown with, but also used to add wide cuffs to the sleeves, lapels and a sash, and trim for the pockets.

It was demure, elegant, and looked like the ones I saw in the windows of the department stores in Los Angeles. But better.

I gave myself a once-over in the mirror now, admiring the pretty dress, then hurried downstairs to my seat beside Mama and got back to work.

The summer days were long, the sun shining through the

windows, turning the small house into an oven. Oftentimes I took my sewing out to the front or back porch, and a few times, when it was something for one of my siblings, I put it in a fabric bag with my sketchbook and took Harrison and Eva to the pond. They'd sing the songs they'd learned in school and teasingly tell me I was as slow as an old mare as I meandered behind them, reveling in the rare breeze that lifted my hair from my shoulders and almost but not quite dried the beads of sweat on my forehead.

Nights were warm, the walls of the house holding on to the heat of the day and continuing to bake us long after the sun had gone down. We stayed up late, trying to wear ourselves out before climbing the stairs to the overcrowded bedrooms above where the air was stifling, and then waking early after restless hours of tossing and turning and trying not to touch the hot skin of the sibling beside us.

"How long have you been up?"

I turned at my mother's voice from where I sat on the front porch in a castoff summer dress of Rose's that I'd relegated as a nightgown.

"Too long," I said with a wan smile. "Eva flung an arm into my face. I couldn't get back to sleep after that."

"That girl has always been overactive," she said, sitting beside me. "Even in the womb. I swore she was going to come somersaulting out of me when the time came."

I laughed, remembering how we'd all stared in awe and a bit of fright as our mother's belly moved and stretched with her last child's movements.

"Looks like you're nearly done with Mrs. Mason's dress."

"I'll finish it today," I said.

"It came out beautifully."

"It started out that way," I said. "I just embellished a little."

"Your eye for what works is unrivaled, Zora. Have you drawn any new designs lately?"

"Here and there."

I didn't want to admit that, while I'd sketched several new ideas on the train home, and a few more at the pond while Harrison and Eva played, worry that I'd never see my dream become reality had returned in the past couple of weeks, causing me to feel paralyzed. The crushing blow that was the end of my Hollywood experience still shook me to my core whenever I thought about it. Which was often. And I worried I was fooling myself.

Mama grabbed my hand, her papery-soft skin cool against my mine.

"There's something different about you since you returned from Hollywood. A hesitation I've never seen in you before when it comes to your work."

"Yeah..."

She started to pull away, but I tightened my grip.

"I'm not ready to talk about it. At least not yet."

She nodded. "Perhaps you should go into the city. Visit your friends there?"

My eyes widened. "I never expected those words to come out of your mouth."

She shrugged. "When you were there, you were full of ideas. I'm not sure what happened in Hollywood, but I pray they didn't steal your desire to do the thing you were born to do. I've never seen anyone be so good at something so effortlessly. I'd be infuriated if I weren't so damn proud."

I sighed and leaned my shoulder against hers.

"I'm mad," I said, my voice soft. "I let myself down. What the studio did to me in the end was terrible, but I should've stood up for myself."

"It's hard to trust yourself after being betrayed by someone else."

I looked over at her and was surprised to see the tears in her eyes.

"Oh, Mama," I said.

I knew she was talking about Pa. He'd betrayed her by succumbing to his feelings of worthlessness, leaving her to pick up the pieces. I imagined having him better again was wonderful, but also worrisome. What if she trusted him again and he let he down again.

"You just need to decide, Zora," she said. "Decide what you want and find a way to get it. You can't worry about other people. If you do that, you'll never try anything."

She got up then and a few minutes later the scent of coffee wafted out the screen door. The sound of small feet running down the stairs, shaking the house, made me smile as sleepy voices asked about breakfast and dining chairs scraped against the hardwood floors.

"Mama wants to know if you want toast with your eggs," Hannah said from the doorway.

I turned and looked up at the young lady standing on the other side of the screen. The girl in her was quickly vanishing, the woman she was to be taking hold, sharpening her facial features and rounding her breasts and hips. She was lovely. Willowy and graceful with a mind full of interesting ideas and stories. I knew she was teased in school for her constant daydreaming, but something was brewing in her, I could feel it.

"I do want toast," I told her and got to my feet. "Tell me about the story you're reading while we eat?"

Her face lit up. "Okay!"

The day went like so many before it. Breakfast, cleanup while Sarah, Lawrence, and Pa left for their respective part-time jobs, work on the next garment on the rack, lunch, an hour spent entertaining Eva and Harrison so they wouldn't tear up the house, more sewing, and then preparations for dinner. Every day was the same, the only differences the items of clothing I was working on, the food we ate for lunch, and the things I found to do with my two youngest siblings. So, when there was a knock on the screen door at half past four, we all looked to one another before glancing at the woman standing on the other side.

34

"Zora?" a hesitant voice called through the screen.

The shadow from the eve cast the woman in darkness. I looked at my mother and gave her a shrug before setting the wooden spoon in my hand down on the table and hurrying to the door.

"Yes?" I said and then smiled in confusion at the familiar face. "Jessie? What are you doing here?"

I opened the door, noticing a garment in her arms. It had been just over a month since we'd parted ways at the train station, and while I knew she was going to try and get her job back at the Alhambra, I hadn't been downtown since we'd returned to find out if she had or not.

"I'm so sorry to barge in on you like this. I was grabbing my costume from the hanger and it split. If I don't get it fixed I can't perform and—" She blinked quickly, a tear falling to her cheek. "I need the money. The new seamstress is out of town and I don't know what to do."

"Let me see it," I said, taking the costume and gesturing for her to come inside. Her eyes widened a little as she took in the many faces staring back at her. "Uh, this is my family. There's a lot of us." I laughed. "Everyone, this is Jessie. She's a friend of Rose's and mine."

There was a smattering of "hellos" and then we sat down so I could get a better look at the problem, Mama standing beside me.

"It's down the seam at least," she said. "But the beading..."

I nodded. Several beads had flown off when the garment ripped, leaving a bald strip. I grabbed the metal toolbox I used to keep odds and ends I'd removed from clothing and kept to find a home for elsewhere. There was beading, fringe, ribbon, and more. But no beads that would match the ones she'd lost.

I grabbed a long stretch of champagne-colored ribbon and held it up to the dress.

"It'll look slightly different from the other girls but—" I said.

"I don't care," Jessie said. "Just so long as I can wear it."

I nodded and got to work, carefully ripping the seam on the other side, leaving those beads intact and sewing four-inch strips of the slender ribbon to each side of the separation, making slits on either side of the dress that would show off even more of Jessie's long legs as she danced.

"Oh," she said, watching as I worked. "Golly. The other girls are going to be so jealous when they see this!"

I smiled, snipped the last thread loose from the sewing machine, and pointed to the stairs.

"Bathroom is at the top, first door on the right. Hurry so I can make sure it hangs right."

I followed after her and when she opened the door a few minutes later, she was beaming.

"It looks great," she said. "Thank you so much."

"Of course," I said.

She scurried back into the bathroom to change, and when she came out we walked down the stairs together, her catching me up as we went.

"Harry hired me back. It's not Lorraine's old spot like I wanted, but I'm dancing and that's all I care about. You should come down. I miss you. Most of the same faces are there. And Ellis and Oscar have a great set list. Everyone would love to see you."

"I'd love to," I said. "I'll get down as soon as I can."

She left moments later, waving to my family before pressing some money and her new address into my hand.

"You're a godsend," she said. "Come and see us soon. We all miss you."

I could feel Mama's eyes on me throughout dinner, but every time I looked over, she averted them and pretended to be overly interested in whatever food was on her fork. After cleaning up, I found myself restless, my gaze returning repeatedly to the metal toolbox I'd forgotten to put away.

"It was a perfect solution," Mama said, her voice quiet, as I returned what was left of the champagne ribbon to the box.

"I don't know about perfect," I said. "But it worked quite well."

"I don't think you realize that your brain doesn't work like the rest of ours," she said.

"What do you mean?" I asked as I closed the lid of the toolbox and clicked the latch shut.

"It would've taken me ages to come up with a decent fix for that dress, and it would've been a patch job that would have needed to be redone later. You redesigned it in a way that not only will hold, but looks fashionable. The only reason she'll need that costume mended again in that same spot is if the owner doesn't like that it doesn't match the others. I could not have come up with such a simple, easy, and elegant fix that fast. Nor could most others. You have a gift, Zora Lily. I keep telling you."

I shrugged. "I just saw it in my head. Like a picture. I could see the way it would move. How it would give her more freedom to dance. How it would show off her legs."

"And that's because you've spent time with them. You've watched them move." She sighed. "You need to go back. Go visit. Go be in that world again. I think it would do you a world of good."

"Can I come?" Sarah asked from across the room.

We turned, not realizing we had an audience. That the entire family had been sitting quietly, watching and listening.

"Are you going to leave us again?" Harrison asked, his eyes too big in his head.

I smiled and shook my head.

"No, sweetheart. Mama just means I should have a night out. For now."

"For now," Mama repeated. "But she can't stay here forever, Harrison. She's a grown woman. Eventually we are going to have to let her go again."

"Not far though," I said, more to myself than to them.

"Not far," she said with a searching look and a sad smile for the secret I still didn't feel I could tell.

As night fell, the cooler air seeping into the too-warm house, my siblings made their way upstairs to take turns using the bathroom before going to bed. I tousled Harrison's hair and smiled at Hannah as they waited in line in the hallway, waiting for Eva to finish brushing her teeth.

"You coming to bed already?" Sarah asked, when I entered the bedroom.

"Not yet," I said.

She watched as I picked my sketchbook up from the top of the bureau.

"I can't wait to see," she said. "When you're ready."

"I can't wait to show you. When I'm ready."

I went back downstairs, curling up in the corner of the couch. Sitting there, my legs tucked in beneath me, reminded me of evenings spent with Harley. I closed my eyes, images of him, his legs stretched out beside me, his eyes flying across the page of whatever book or newspaper he was reading, or making notes if he was listening to Aunt Viv on the radio. My heart ached for him. My soul missed what it was to share space with him. To feel his energy emanating from his being. His confidence, his kindness, his clever quips and delicious smile. His beautiful words, written on the page just for me.

All I had to do was write him. Let him know where I was and what happened and I'd once more be cradled in the embrace of his encouragement and love.

But I couldn't bring myself to do it. Not yet. I was still too fragile from what had happened. And much too embarrassed. I would tell him one day. Just not yet. I needed more time.

I flipped through the pages of my sketchbook, watching the drawings fly by, remembering how I'd been inspired to draw those trousers, that blouse, a cape with an oversized bow, a hat, a handbag… I stopped when I got to the remnants of the pages I'd had to tear out, remembering how I'd drawn and redrawn a diaphanous white evening gown with a beaded star that was to be the pinnacle of the costumes worn by Greta Garbo herself, and now had another designer's name on it. But rather than feel sad this time, I felt determined. I'd been mulling over what to do next for weeks, and tonight's visit from Jessie had only bolstered my resolve.

For the next few days, I went through every design in my current book, then pulled out old sketchbooks I'd left behind, and pored over those, as well. I tore out pages, ripped the tops of dresses from their paper skirts, mixed and matched, and sketched new cuffs and hems and collars, until I had fifty designs I was pleased as punch with.

"What do you think?" I asked Mama, chewing my lip as she looked through the stacks of drawings.

"I think they're lovely. Intricate, daring in some cases, elegant, and expensive-looking. Are you going to make them all? Will you wear them? Sell them?"

She looked concerned. We didn't have nearly enough fabric

in our meager supply for me to make even half the designs I'd shown her. But I had my Harley money, plus more I'd tucked away from the film job.

"This is the beginning of a plan," I said. "Every designer has a signature style. This is mine. How I want my clothes to look. See how they're all similar in some way? The necklines? The cuffs…the cut of the blouses and jackets and skirts?"

Mama took another look and nodded, a small smile on her lips.

"They're elegant," she said. "But also understated. Not too flashy, which you know I prefer. I hate a lot of fuss."

I laughed. "I know, Mama. I'm the same. Mostly." I sat beside her at the dining table, looking over the sketches I'd done and then turning to watch her work. "After seeing what people wear out, watching how dresses move, the way the lights hit the fabrics, which materials hold in heat and which ones breathe, I think I have a good sense of what works and what doesn't for the different pieces I want to make."

"So, what's your plan?"

I stared at her for a long moment, worried she'd think the idea ridiculous. Lofty. And unattainable.

I took a breath.

"I want to open a shop. A small boutique. But not quite yet. I have a few more things to figure out." I gathered the drawings, placed them inside the sketchbook and closed it, placing my hands on top of it, fingers spread, as if casting a spell or making a wish. Willing my dream into creation. "I've been looking in the paper for jobs."

"What kind of jobs?"

"Jobs doing what I do here with you. Sewing. But in the city, where I might get the attention of management and garner some connections. If I do well enough, I could potentially gain notice from more notable people. The Dennys. The Harringtons. The Olmsteads. People whose referrals could make me a household name, leading to better money and, eventually, my own storefront. So far I haven't found anything though. At least nothing in the area those kinds of people would frequent."

"Have you spoken with Mrs. Tiller?"

I hadn't seen Rose's mom since returning. I knew from Sarah, who saw her often, that she was still up to her old tricks, keeping her eyes and ears open, playing matchmaker for those seeking work with those looking for good employees. But after being fired from the incredible job she'd found me before, I felt bad returning to her for guidance and resources. Also—

"I want to do this on my own."

She nodded. "Good for you. It will mean more to you that way anyway."

I returned the sketchbook to my bedroom, smiling at Hannah asleep on the bed she shared with Sarah, her face in yet another book. If that girl didn't become a writer, I hoped she'd at least find a job where she was surrounded by books. A librarian perhaps. Or maybe a bookshop clerk. She'd certainly be able to make thoughtful recommendations to her patrons due to her extensive list of books read already in her young life.

I moved closer so I could read the latest quote she'd written on the new page she'd adhered to the wall. It was from Jane Austen's *Persuasion*.

"She hoped to be wise and reasonable in time; but alas! Alas! She must confess to herself that she was not wise yet."

I took a step back and looked to my sketchbook and the newspaper I'd looked for a job in this morning.

"Alas," I said.

For the next few days I worked tirelessly beside my mother while using my lunch breaks to search the local paper for something promising in the workforce downtown. There were plenty of calls for dancers, the location listed always a bit mysterious. Musicians, cooks, maids, loggers and the like, but nothing for a young woman interested in designing and making clothing for the middle to upper classes.

And then I saw it.

"Oh." The sound was barely more than a gasp.

"Did you find something?" Mama said, looking up from one half of a set of drapes she was sewing.

"I think...I might have... It may be..."

"Zora. Words!"

"Huh?" I looked up at my mother's exasperated expression. "Oh. Sorry. It's just—"

I handed her the paper, pointing to the ad I'd just scanned, read, and reread a third time.

"Seamstress," Mama read aloud. "Must be proficient and quick. Able to alter, mend, modify, and construct garments according to customers' specifications and needs. Possible future window space available for fee."

She frowned and looked at me over the top of the newspaper. "What does that mean? About the window space."

"It means if my designs are good enough, I could get window space to show them off in!"

"That's perfect, Zora. And the address is in a good location. I wonder what shop it is. It doesn't say."

I took the paper and looked at the address, something I hadn't paid attention to before, and sucked in a breath.

"That's Nellie Carman's store," I said.

"Who's that?"

It was my turn to give her an exasperated look. I dropped the paper to my lap.

"Mama. She owns the leading women's apparel shop in town. Mrs. Harrington shops there." I leaned back with a sigh. "It's so elegant. The sitting area where the dressing rooms are has this beautiful pale blue carpet and is bigger than my bedroom. I went in with Rose and Jessie a few times when they were buying stockings. And Harley bought me a beautiful cloche from there last spring."

"With a reference from the studio and another from your former employer..."

"Mama—" I shook my head. "I don't want to mention the job at the studio. They'll want me to talk about what I did there, and I just can't. It's too painful. And Mrs. Harrington fired me."

"Do you want the job, Zora?"

"Yes."

"Then never mind your pride. You did good work for both of them. Ask."

She wasn't wrong. But I didn't like it. Regardless, the next day I took the streetcar into the city and walked up the hill toward the Harringtons' house.

"Zora?" Mrs. Harrington said, her voice entering the room before her.

I'd been led to her study by Smith, who had looked surprised and delighted to see me, and was left to wait nervously for the lady of the house.

"Well," she said when her eyes landed on me. "Don't you look fetching."

I wore one of the few dresses I'd bought for myself during my time in California. A souvenir from a life that had barely had time to form. It was casual yet sophisticated, perfect for afternoon tea, an interview with a prospective employer, or even an impromptu meeting with a former employer who had fired me for bringing a stranger into their house.

"Thank you," I said, getting to my feet. "I'm so sorry to just drop by. I hope I'm not interrupting."

"You're not. I'm happy to see you. But to what do I owe this surprise?"

"I'm embarrassed to say that I've come to ask a favor, which I know I have no right to do." I said the last part hurriedly, taking in her raised eyebrows.

But then she shook her head and waved a hand. "Nonsense. You wouldn't be here if it weren't important to you. Though truly, I am still mad at you for giving me cause to let you go. It was inconvenient and the new girl..." She lowered her voice.

"Lord help me. She is far too shrill. She makes the neighbor's dog bark worse than the children ever did!"

We shared a laugh and she gestured to the sofa, taking a seat beside me.

"Tell me what you need, Zora."

"You are far too generous," I said. "And I understand if you have to decline. But I'm hoping you might put in a good word for me with Nellie Carman? There's an advertisement for a seamstress at her shop and—"

Mrs. Harrington placed a hand over mine. "Consider it done, Zora. No need to say more."

"Really?"

"Really." She sighed. "As you know, I have to set a precedent in my home or everyone will think they can do as they please, but you weren't the one I wanted to fire. And I made that one take your place until I hired the new gal. Oh, you should've seen Elsbeth try and keep up with the children." She pursed her lips and snorted delicately. "Any wrongdoings they did went practically unnoticed by me for the joy it brought to see her so miserable. I fired her not long after. Caught her sneaking around in her nightgown late one night, hoping to seduce a guest's teenage son."

"Oh no," I said.

"Oh yes."

She stood then and I followed suit.

"I will call Nellie this afternoon. I hope to see you next time I'm at the shop."

"Thank you, Mrs. Harrington."

At home I slipped out of my dress and hung it up to wear again the next day. If I got the job, it would be the next crucial step in my plan.

35

"Zora?"

I looked up from the jacket I was sewing into the worried eyes of Hazel, my coworker at Carman's as of a month ago. We'd been hired within minutes of one another, each of us sitting in the seating area outside Nellie Carman's office, awaiting our fate after our interviews. She had worn a brown suit that I'd thought looked awfully professional, while I wore the pale green frock. We both admired the other's clothing, commenting on our favorite bits of detail while we waited, the little clock on the wall ticking away the seconds until I thought I might burst from the anticipation.

She was called into the office first, exiting a few minutes later with a smile and worrying me that her look of relief meant my disappointment. But then it was my turn.

"Yes?" I said now, looking to the collar in her hands.

"Does this look right?"

I took the piece and examined it from one end to the next.

"It's right," I said and handed it back. She sighed and nodded and hurried back to her seat.

I took a moment to stretch my back, looking to my right at

Lydia, whose eyes were on what looked like her fiftieth cuff of the day, and then turned back to my own machine, where I had just finished my tenth body of the blouse Carman's would reveal the following week.

We worked in teams. Some doing collars, some doing cuffs, others the body. There were women sewing dresses, others trousers, and still more stitching together coats and dressing gowns and skirts. In another room hats were being formed. The one beside it, shoes. Carman's was full-service when it came to women's apparel, providing high-end fabrics and designs made to order for not just Seattle's elite, though that was most of the clientele, but also for the middle classes who could afford the less extravagant material made into the same designs.

Around the main sewing room of the largest women's shop in Seattle, were fifteen of the city's best seamstresses. We worked from nine to five in a windowless space filled with the hum of sewing machines, the metallic snip of scissors, the whisper of fabric being whisked into place, and the snap of snaps and zip of zippers as they were fastened and unfastened to check for workability. We were allowed two short breaks and a half hour lunch, and the opportunity to have our own work featured in a select corner of the shop's large window where shoppers walked and gawked. Though we were all kept so busy during the day and were so tired at night, no one had yet had the energy to produce anything outside of work.

I removed the garment I'd been working on from the machine, labeled it, and put it in the basket at my feet. Nellie had gotten in fifty-three pre-orders within the past two days for the new blouse and we were scrambling to fill them all in a timely manner, as well as stock the racks.

Lydia sighed, sat back, snipped a thread, and tossed a cuff into a basket labeled Small. She was working on the store's stock, as opposed to the pre-orders that came with very particular sizing instructions.

"That's thirty-four," she said. "Only..." She squinted her

eyes and counted on her fingers. "Six more to go!" She glanced at the other two women assigned to cuffs then back at me. "I have them beat."

"Oh, put a sock in it, Lydia," Miriam said, making us laugh.

A moment later the clock ticked twelve and we hurried to grab the lunches we'd packed or our purses so we could go buy lunch as quickly as possible.

Thirty minutes later we were back inside our airless workspace we'd not so affectionately named The Cave, which reminded me a lot of the sewing room back at MGM Studios with Ruth and Betty, who were probably still chattering away about their ungrateful relatives while half-dressed starlets and dancers hurried in and out to get fit and refitted for costumes. But in other ways, in important ways, The Cave was different. The women were friendly. The air around us less stressed. And there was a camaraderie among us as we helped one another out. Plus, our boss, Nellie Carman, made sure to come by at least every few days to check our work and give encouragement and compliments.

At the day's end, we packed up our things, winding thread back around its spool, poking needles and straight pins in pincushions, folding fabric, and pushing in chairs before gathering our personal belongings from the lockers we were assigned and filing out to find our respective ways home.

"See you tomorrow," I called to Lydia and Hazel as we went our separate ways at the corner.

They waved and disappeared with all the others leaving their jobs for the day while I hurried to catch the cable car home, noting as I went the sign in a window for a room to rent. *Soon*, I thought.

After dinner I helped wash up and then sat beside Mama, watching her work while trying to keep my eyes open.

"You should go on up to bed," she said, leaning in to watch as she fed fabric to her own sewing machine while I tried to stay awake using mine.

"I want to work on my dress," I said, covering my mouth as I yawned.

The dress was the first design in my sketchbook. The first step toward my own line of clothing. Should I ever have a business of my own. But every evening I'd come home too exhausted to pull out the material I'd bought with my first paycheck, a splurge, and begin to even cut the pattern pieces.

"The dress can wait."

"You keep saying that, Mama," I said. "But if I keep putting it off, it will never get made and I'll never get it in that window, people will never see it, and I'll never have my own shop."

"Well then, ask Sarah to help you. She can do the cutting."

"No. It has to be me," I said. "It's my dream. I need to see it through start to finish."

"Well then, my love, stop using what's left of your energy to explain that to me and start cutting."

She leaned forward, pulling me to her, and kissed my forehead. I made a face like I used to do as a small child, making her laugh, and then stood and collected the bag keeping the fabric safe. A moment later the material was spread across the dining table, the pattern pieces I'd drawn pinned to it. I began cutting.

"There," I said a half hour later, nodding at the pile of cuttings, the scrap material gathered and put in our remnants basket.

"Good," Mama said. "Now go to bed and get out of my hair. I have work to do. Oh. And you have a package."

"I do?" I asked, looking around.

"I think Sarah put it on your bureau."

I hurried upstairs and found the package where she said it might be. The return address was one I knew well. The package had come from Rose. Smiling, I grabbed it and my nightgown and went to the bathroom where I sat on the toilet seat lid and pulled apart the brown paper to reveal a small stack of letters. The one on top was from Rose, the four beneath from Harley.

I ran my finger over his name, tears filling my eyes. With my whole body I wanted to confess to him everything. What had happened in Hollywood, how sad and disappointed and angry I was. How I felt I'd let myself down. I wanted to feel his arms around me as he comforted me and told me it would all work out, the solid feel of his body making me feel heard, protected, supported, and safe.

But I couldn't. Not only because he was so far away, but because there was a voice inside me that had grown stronger in the past few weeks. A voice that said the person I needed to lean on was me. And though no one else might understand, not even Harley, I needed to do this on my own.

I tucked Harley's letters back inside the paper they'd come in, changed into my nightgown, and went to bed.

For the next month, anytime I had enough energy and could stay awake long enough to do a little bit of my own sewing, I sat beside Mama like I had so many times before and worked. With every stitch that brought the dress to fruition, the fabric sliding between my fingertips, the design taking shape beneath my hands, I felt the old excitement of ideas coming to life. And as it neared completion, I found myself rushing home and hurrying through dinner so I could work, the fatigue brought on by long hours in The Cave left at the door.

It was a Tuesday night in early August when I snipped the last thread, arched my back in a long-needed stretch, and then stood, pulled the garment from the sewing machine, turned it right side out, and held it out before me.

"It's done," I whispered.

I heard the scrape of the chair my mother was sitting in and then her presence just behind me, her breath soft and warm against my shoulder.

"Oh. Oh, Zora..."

We stood there for a moment and then she grabbed a hanger and took the dress from me, sliding it on and hanging it on the hook she used for finished garments waiting to be retrieved. And there, in the light of the one lamp and two candles we'd used for extra light so as not to run too much electricity, I stared at my creation and saw for the first time, promise for my future.

"Will you ask tomorrow?" she asked. "About the window space?"

A tremor of excited anticipation ran through me.

"I will," I said.

The following morning, the dress in a castoff garment bag from MGM over my arm, I caught the cable car down the hill to work.

"Is that it?" Lydia whispered as we stood outside, waiting to be let in.

I nodded, chewing my lip, nervous for what Mrs. Carman would say. If she'd like it. If she'd like it enough to feature in the window.

Others gathered around me as they arrived, wanting to see but respecting my privacy and nerves. I stood off to the side with Hazel and Lydia, who acted like my bodyguards, shielding me from the prying eyes of our coworkers until the familiar sound of the door being unlocked got all of our attention and we filed in and hurried through the back hallways of the shop down to the basement.

I hung the garment bag in the coat room, retrieved my metal toolbox from my locker, and sat beside Lydia in my seat. Ignoring the glances I felt bouncing off me, I pulled out my scissors and resumed work on the jacket lining I'd started the day before.

At half past ten the bell for our first break rang. I looked up and caught first Hazel's eyes, then Lydia's.

"You ready?" Lydia asked.

I inhaled, nodded and exhaled, then rose from my seat, pulled the garment bag off its hook, held up fingers crossed for good luck to my two best work friends, and strode upstairs to Mrs. Carman's office.

"It's stunning," Hazel said.

It was 5:02 in the evening and the entirety of The Cave had

run up the stairs, through the shop, out the back door, and around the building to see the dress as soon as the quitting bell rang our favorite tune.

In the front window, in the far-left corner, set next to a fetching tennis outfit, was the dress I'd designed, sewn, and presented to Mrs. Carman. It looked glorious on a mannequin set in an elegant pose, the early evening sun glinting off the window just so.

"You made that?" an older woman named Carlotta asked.

"She sure as sugar did," Lydia said, linking her arm through mine.

"It's beautiful," someone else said, followed by several "mmm-hmms" and a "sure is."

"If someone doesn't buy it first thing tomorrow, I'll be shocked," Hazel said.

I just shook my head, flattered by the compliments and thrilled to see something I made on display in the window at Carman's, but worried with all the other pretty outfits in the window that no one would even notice it. Maybe it wasn't as special as I'd first thought after all.

The group began to dissipate, everyone hurrying off to get home, but I couldn't move. Couldn't stop staring at something I'd made being featured in Carman's big picture window.

"You okay?"

I turned and saw Hazel still standing beside me.

"What if no one buys it?"

"Well, that's just not possible, Z."

"Why?"

"Because it's special. And it outshines everything else in the window."

She squeezed my hand then and, after a moment more, we waved goodbye and parted ways.

The next morning when I arrived, there was a line of customers waiting for the shop to open.

36

"Zora?"

The door to my office opened a crack and one of Lydia's gold eyes appeared in the narrow space.

"I keep telling you, you don't have to knock," I said for what had to be the dozenth time. "Just come in."

"But she's watching me," she whispered, tilting her head toward where the secretary guarding Mrs. Carman's office and those of us lucky enough to be given our own small rooms to conduct our work in.

I shook my head, my eyes once more on the drawing before me as she stepped inside my small but cozy office and snooped around through boxes of fasteners and reams of fabric stacked on shelves lining one of the walls.

"She's fine," I said. "She doesn't care who comes to see me."

"But she might tattle that I'm not at my station."

"It's your break time. You can't get in trouble for visiting me on your break."

"I'm disturbing you though. Mrs. Carman won't like that."

As she said this, she rustled around through a pile of tissue paper in a box, looking for what was inside.

"Indeed, you are disturbing me," I said with a laugh. I covered my mouth as a yawn escaped and arched my back in a stretch. "Speaking of breaks, I need one too. Come with me to get a cup of tea?"

"I can't believe you get to use the kitchen," Lydia said as she followed me down the hall to where tea, coffee, and water were provided for those who worked on the upper floor with Mrs. Carman. Oftentimes I came in in the morning to find freshly baked muffins or cookies had been brought in. There was always a bowl of fresh fruit, and on Fridays she had lunch brought in for us from a restaurant down the street.

As Lydia's wide eyes took in everything from the expensive china to the fruit, the homemade molasses cookies to the shiny silver kettle I was boiling my water in, I grinned to myself. It really was incredible that in a matter of a couple months I'd ended up here. And now, three months after that, I'd had seven different designs grace the front window of the leading women's apparel shop in Seattle.

It was exhilarating to have my own office, complete with a beautiful desk and lamp, a comfortable chair, a plant I was just barely keeping alive, two dress forms to hang my designs on, drawing paper and pencils, every kind of fastener in every possible color, and expensive fabrics at my fingertips every day.

My designs were beginning to be sought after, Seattle's elite finding me as I hurried to get lunch with Lydia and Hazel, and offering money to have me make them something one of a kind. But Mrs. Carman and I had an exclusive deal and a contract had been signed.

Two designs a month for six months and then we'd speak again. She was convinced she could keep me on for longer, while I was already impatient to find my own little shop. But for now, it was a good deal and got my name out there. Since that first dress that had caught the eye of Seattle's elite, I'd designed a pajama set, a dressing gown, a blouse, a skirt, and a lightweight cape for a summer evening on the town. Each design could be modified in a number of ways so that no two were the same and clients would get something custom to them. Fabric, collar shape, cuff size, buttons or snaps, pleats, hem length, etc. could all be chosen from a book of images I'd drawn and that had been professionally bound and printed. And while Mama had initially worried I was giving up pieces near and dear to my heart, I was quick to reassure her that the designs featured at Carman's were all created specifically for the retailer and had none of what I intended to be my signature style, which was being saved for the future shop I was that much closer to obtaining.

At five on the dot, I set down my pencil and gave the sketch I was working on a last once-over. It was another dress, this one for a special evening out. An anniversary, maybe a New Year's party, perhaps for a mother of the bride. More structured than the last dress that was strictly for a daytime stroll by the waterfront or a luncheon, it had a wide neckline to show off the wearer's collarbones and elegant little pleats that began three quarters of the way down the skirt, giving the frock movement with a hint of sass. The neckline was the closest I'd allowed myself to veer toward the designs I was saving for myself and the future shop I was determined to have. It would be a signature feature in all my dresses, as I'd always found that part of a woman's body particularly beautiful and, as Harley had said one night as he'd slowly kissed along the slender bones stretching from my neck to my shoulders, "They are delicate, innocent, and sexy all at once."

Harley.

My breath caught in my throat and I closed my eyes, picturing the way I used to find him looking at me from the other end of the sofa. How had I refrained from writing him for so long?

But I knew. Shame. Embarrassment. Feeling like a fool in a world he'd warned me might not be honest.

I looked at my desk, covered in drawings, and then stood and slid into the coat I'd bought with money I'd earned from my new job. I would write him soon. I was nearly there. The dream was at my fingertips.

But not until I was there. Until it was in my grasp, I wasn't ready to talk to him.

Despite my resolve not to write to Harley, I was distracted through dinner with thoughts of him, barely registering Hannah's excitement as she told the family about the day she'd had at the pond with her best friend, Ruth, and Ruth's mother. Sarah had a good day at work as well, and Lawrence finally submitted a story and had it accepted at the paper. Even the younger kids were in good spirits, having spent the day with Pa who had taken a rare day off to ride the streetcar downtown with them and treat them both to sodas.

"We sat at the counter on swirly red seats!" Eva said, her cheeks pink with excitement, eyes wide as she seemed to relive it in her mind.

Harrison merely nodded, his mouth full of green beans.

"And how was your day, Zora?" Mama asked. "You're awfully quiet tonight."

Usually I was full of tales from the day. The customers I'd met as they picked and chose the details they wanted on the garment I'd designed. Stuffy older women looking to appear younger by way of fabric draping. Middle aged women trying to hide widening hips and thickening thighs. And the younger ladies, barely into new marriages that had seen them enter a phase of wealth that decried a certain way of dressing as they vied for the newest and most stylish clothes one could find this far from California, New York, and of course, Paris.

"It was fine," I said, pushing Harley from my mind and smiling around the table at the expectant faces waiting to be regaled. "I was on my own most of the day, sketching and looking at some new fabrics that came in."

"How did the latest design go over?" Pa asked.

I felt myself soften at the question posed to me by the man who had been so absent in recent years, but was now once again part of the family, offering the attention we'd craved from him.

"Mrs. Carman loved it," I said. "And the women are all clamoring for it, most asking for two or three in different fabrics and with modifications. It's so busy, I've been making some of the blouses myself, just so we can keep up with the orders in a timely manner."

"I hope she knows what she has in you," Mama said.

"She does, Mama."

"And doesn't try to hold you back." Her eyes narrowed. After what happened in Hollywood, we were all a little wary of people not being as they seemed and taking more than they'd promised.

"She won't," I said. "I'll make damn sure of it."

"Good girl."

After dinner, instead of offering to help wash up like usual, I let Sarah and Hannah take the reins and retreated to our bedroom to retrieve my pen, ink well, and the stationery set I'd purchased in Los Angeles when I'd first arrived. But as I stared down at the gentle flower design at the top of the page, I put the lid back on the box and grabbed one of my sketchbooks instead.

"Are you going to do some work?" Mama asked, noting the notebook in my hands as I opened the front door.

I nodded and slipped out the door, taking a seat on the top step, my glance swinging, as it always did, to where Tommy used to sit.

"Miss you," I whispered, then opened the sketchbook and stared down at the blank page.

But the design ideas didn't come. No collars to be had. No hemlines or bodices or sleeves. Just the thought of Harley and the worry that I'd waited too long. Perhaps after all this time, he wasn't even waiting to hear from me. Perhaps he'd simply moved on.

I stared out at the horizon. The sky was crisp bluc onc moment, softened with lavender the next, the edges marled with fuchsia where the two colors met and deepened as night crept in.

A cool breeze swept over me, causing the hairs on my arms to rise. Summer was coming to an end, autumn making her intentions clear. A car went by and the sound of laughter erupted from a house somewhere down the street. The happy jingle of the bell on someone's bicycle, the wail of a baby hidden beneath a carriage hood as its young parents took an evening walk. I had once imagined a similar scene with me and Harley. The two of us, a pram sent from England, an adorable baby asleep inside with his father's eyes and my nose. I blinked back tears. I had certainly ruined that dream. Harley had most likely found someone else by now with whom to share those moments. And I would be alone, forever wondering what might have happened if I hadn't been so hurt, my ego in such a shambles, and had just written back.

I looked over at Tommy's spot on the front steps.

"I need to know," I said.

With a sigh I uncapped the bottle of ink, dipped the metal nib, and wrote Harley's name across the top of the page.

37

Autumn brought sideways rain and blustering winds that sent fallen orange and yellow and brown leaves skittering across the pavement, plastering to my shoes and ankles as I hurried from the streetcar to work.

With only a couple more months on my contract to Carman's, I made the most of it with a beautiful tweed jacket and skirt set, a coat in a gorgeous mahogany color with a bright orange satin liner, and a dropped waist dress in aubergine velvet that had the women of Seattle clamoring to be the first to buy it before even seeing what other colors it came in or modifications had been set to make theirs stand apart from their neighbors.

"You're a smash hit."

I looked up from the fabric I was pinning, a dozen straight pins in my teeth, and gave Mrs. Carman a bashful smile.

"And that looks like another piece of brilliance," she said, taking in the draping of an evening gown I intended to be the final garment of our contract that was up in November. It would be perfect for the upcoming holiday season, and a great way to say goodbye.

I removed the pins from my mouth as my eyes swept down

the fabric. It was going to be a beautiful dress, the alterations I'd offer minimal. Only a few would get this one, and they'd have to pay.

"I quite like how it's turned out," I said.

I started at her abrupt guffaw of laughter.

"Oh, Zora," she said. "I think on some level you have to know how good you are. But if you don't, well, maybe I should keep it a secret from you so I can convince you to stay on."

I knew it was coming. The discussion of possibly extending our agreement, but I did know how good I was. I had proven it time and time again with each line that formed when a new design debuted, each woman who chased me down on the lunch breaks I dared to take outside of the safety of the shop, and every paycheck that showed just how much I'd made from commission on one of *my* garments.

I had interest. I had the money I'd saved from the settlement with MGM. And I had a plan. All I needed now was a space to rent when my contract with Carman's was up.

"Do you have a few minutes to talk?" Mrs. Carman asked, looking around for somewhere to sit. But the only chair was the one at my desk. "Shall we move to my office?"

"Of course," I said and followed her down the hall.

Mrs. Carman's office was the size of the main floor of my parents' house, with high ceilings, light-colored furniture, expensive art and vases and flower arrangements, and a small kitchen all her own.

She motioned for me to sit on the cream-colored sofa and then stepped into the kitchen.

"Tea?" she asked. "Water?"

"Water please."

She served it in an etched crystal water glass, the fanciest I'd ever seen, with three large ice cubes that bumped the tip of my nose when I took a sip. As I delicately wiped it dry, she poured cream into her tea and sat across from me in one of two plush pale blue armchairs.

"Have you given any thought as to what you'd like to do next?" she asked, getting straight to it—something I'd always liked about her. "We can extend your contract, if you like the agreement. Alter it to meet whatever needs you might have now that you've been doing the job for four months." She took a long sip and then tilted her head, as if considering other alternatives. "You can have a new title if you like."

My current title was listed as Designer. I didn't know another title that would fit me.

"Lead Designer," Mrs. Carman said, as if reading my mind. "I, of course, have two other leads who do the bulk of the garment designs here, so maybe something special for you. We can work out the language later if need be."

But a new title wasn't what I wanted. At least, not a new title here.

"The thing is, Mrs. Carman," I said. "I don't want to be the lead designer. I want to be the *only* designer. I want my own shop."

She was quiet for a moment as her eyes narrowed and she seemed to take in everything from my hair to my subtle makeup, my dress, and shoes. Slowly she began to nod.

"I suppose I always knew it was too good to be true, keeping you on here. You're too good. I hoped we'd have a few years together before you realized your potential though. You are going to cause me a lot of angst, Zora dear."

"How do you mean?"

"I've had no competition until now. But you're going to give me some. Which means I'm going to have to work harder than I've had to in the past couple of years."

She winked and I laughed. Nellie Carman was one of the hardest working women I'd ever met.

"Do you have any thoughts for what's next?"

"I have a lot of thoughts. And a lot of questions I need to find the answers to."

"Well, I happen to know a little something about starting from scratch, so if you ever want to talk...my door is open. But while I still have you, get back to work!"

I grinned as her laughter followed me down the hallway.

My new apartment was two blocks from the tiny shop space I'd noticed on my way to and from work at Carman's every day. I'd leased both within a week of each other, with one month left to go on my contract with Mrs. Carman.

"Where do you want this?" Lawrence asked, standing just inside my front door, a box of sketchbooks and pencils in his ink-stained hands.

I looked around the spare studio apartment with a partial view of the Smith Tower and pointed to the only table in the space. He set it down and then disappeared to grab something else from the truck his friend had loaned out for the occasion, crossing paths in the hall with Pa, who was carrying a new lamp I'd purchased.

There was a lot of new in this space that was all mine. A bed, a small settee, a kitchen table with two chairs, the lamp, and bedding and towels that were so soft I almost didn't want to use them for fear they'd wear too soon.

Two pots, a pan, a set of water glasses, a plain tea set and kettle, silverware, a set of dishes, and some cleaning supplies. It had seemed so much as I'd nervously checked and balanced and checked my funds again and again. But now that my family didn't need my income, I could afford it. The Hollywood money, as painful as it was to take at the time, had served me well. So far. The next step was yet to come.

When the household items were all delivered, boxes left here and there to be sorted by me later, we loaded back in the truck and drove the two blocks to the shop I'd leased for the next seven months.

"It's an odd number," the owner had said when I'd requested not six months. Not twelve. But seven.

"I'd like a month to prepare," I'd said. "And then six to see if I can turn a profit."

He'd looked me up and down, shrugged his shoulders, and handed me the contract.

"Good luck to ya, miss," he'd said, and then shuffled away.

Luck. I would need it.

Three hours later, I stood alone in the small room where my future as a designer would begin.

The main room was spare, painted white from top to bottom, with a wide picture window, a door with an etched glass inset, and a bell above that chimed whenever it opened or closed.

The back had a long counter I planned to use as a break area, a large room I'd use for storage and cutting fabric, and a bathroom. It was tiny in comparison to what had been available to me at Carman's. But I didn't care. It was mine.

"It's...very white," my dad had observed, squinting as the sun shone through the etched glass, splintering and sending rays every which way.

"We could paint it," Lawrence said.

But I shook my head. It was perfect. A perfect canvas for my work. Where Carman's clothes were set against warm, soothing colors, giving off the feeling of luxury, I wanted my store to feel fresh, bright, and exciting. The white would give the colors and designs of the moment the floor.

I'd decided to feature two outfits at a time in the window, each one complementing the other. Like I'd done for Nellie Carman, I would have a book for each one that showed the modifications that could be made and the fabric choices. Each design would be available for as long as it sold well, but the window would change every month, if not sooner, to feature the next outfits.

"There will also be a single rack," I'd told my mother and Sarah when they came to see the shop space for the first time.

"A rack?" Sarah asked.

"Of ready-made clothes," I said. "I'll make each design in a larger size, with room to take in, a few of each, and sell them for less. Customers won't get the modifications, but I'll size it for them."

"Will you have time for all that?" Mama asked, ever the worrier but also, I'd come to learn, the realist.

"Well," I said, chewing my bottom lip as I surveyed the two women. "I was thinking that if things go well, perhaps I could hire one or the both of you to help."

But while Sarah's eyes lit up, her hands clasping together at her breast, Mama shook her head.

"There's not enough room for all of us here. We'd be in each other's hair and stomping on toes. Poking needles into elbows."

"You're so dramatic, Ma," Sarah said. "Obviously we'd either take the clothes home with us, or Z would deliver them."

"Oh," Mama said, her cheeks coloring. "Well then, I suppose if you need me..."

"I may not," I said. "But let's hope I do."

I walked around the shop now, running my hands over the metal bars my father was coming back to install the following day. I'd hang fabric from them in one of the two back corners to create a dressing room. A box with a tray, kettle, teacups, and some fabric napkins my mother had made sat on the counter in back, two mannequins Ms. Carman had given me at an amazing discount were ready and waiting for their first garments near the window, and the sewing machine Harley had given me beckoned from the table that would become my workspace.

I poked around in some of the other boxes. There weren't many, and most were filled with fabric, thread, and other sewing implements. I found a plant in one and removed it, smiling at the hand-printed pot. Hannah had clearly had fun painting flowers and trees for the little green-leafed plant I worried I'd kill. I was not known for my green thumb, but she'd insisted, thanks to a book she'd read, that a space needed a plant.

I set the plant on my table and glanced back in the box it had come from. There was a stack of papers and I grinned as I spied artwork from Eva and Harrison. "Gud luk!" one said, a wobbly happy face beside it, Eva's name below. The other I was pretty sure was supposed to be a truck—art wasn't Harrison's strong suit. If he didn't grow up to either own a truck or work in a job that allowed him to drive one, I'd be shocked.

Under the hand-drawn pictures were a few pieces of mail. Advertisements mostly, a good luck card from Mrs. Carman, a letter from Rose, scented with her signature dousing of perfume, and—

My heart stopped when I saw his name.

Harley.

I inhaled, excitement and worry coursing through my body together. And then I frowned. The handwriting was mine, not his. The return address my family's home in Ballard. This was my letter to him—not a letter from him.

I stared at the ugly markings marring the front and then turned the envelope over, my heart sinking when I saw the stamp reading RETURN TO SENDER. OCCUPANT NO LONGER AT THIS ADDRESS.

A breath escaped in a small, defeated puff. I leaned against the table, turning the letter over and over in my hands, my fears now solidified. I'd waited too long.

My eyes filled. I had no other contact information for him. I knew no one in England I could reach out to, and I was sure anyone who'd known him or done business with him here had long since lost contact. I knew his father's furniture business was still bringing pieces in, I'd seen them in shop windows. But the men on the trucks wouldn't know how to get a message to a man they'd never met who lived so far away. Who knew if he was even still working for the family business. Perhaps he'd moved on to something else. Maybe he'd decided to live out his dream to go to Italy after all, and was now living in a small fishing village, sitting on a terrace that overlooked the sea while drinking wine and reading.

Or perhaps he'd fallen in love with another woman. The kind of woman I always imagined was better suited for him. Someone posh, with fine manners. Educated, witty, and from a family that could stand alongside his and not bring them shame with their humble dwellings and too-large brood of children.

As much as I hated to admit it, it was the more likely scenario. And the mere thought of it made my chest feel as though a weight was pressing against it, restricting my breathing as it painfully crushed my heart.

Tears spilled over and down my cheeks. How stupid I was. How selfish to think he was just sitting, waiting for word from me. Of course he'd moved on. I'd given him nothing. Nothing but silence in return for his beautiful and encouraging words. What else was he supposed to think but that I'd moved on first?

Memories of our time together weakened my knees and pulled me downward until I sat on the floor, a heap of misery and acceptance. I'd lost the man I loved. And it was my own damn fault.

I touched the black pearl he gave me on Christmas that had hung every day since beneath my collar. "This is just the beginning," his note had said.

"The beginning and the end I guess," I said to the empty room.

My eyes swept the room, landing on the mannequins in the window.

"What do I do now?" I asked them, a sob catching in my throat. My gaze slid over their forms, devoid of garments, and with a sigh, I knew.

I nodded and got to my feet, then turned to the sewing machine and the reams of fabric stacked beside it.

Taking in a deep breath, I pulled my shoulders back and lifted my chin. I hadn't come this far to give up.

"I guess I get to work."

38

The grand opening of Zora Lily was beyond anything I could've imagined.

I woke the morning of to blue skies and the sun shining bright, bathing the city in its glow. A long, luxurious bath, my hair, freshly shorn into the era's fashionable bob, and I was dressed and out the door before noon to prepare.

"Nervous?" Sarah asked when she'd arrived a few minutes after me.

"Yes. And excited. But mostly nervous."

"It's going to be wonderful, Zora. I just know it."

The appetizers and miniature desserts I'd ordered were to arrive at two, a suggestion by Ms. Carman who had promised she'd be in attendance. Also coming was a reporter from the *Times*.

"How do they know about me?" I'd asked no one in particular when I'd gotten the news. I'd assumed that was also the handiwork of Ms. Carman.

While Sarah and my mother took delivery of the food, I hurried to the back to do my makeup and get dressed. The shop looked perfect; there was nothing more for me to do but get myself ready.

The dress I wore was one I'd sewn myself after painstaking deliberations. All eyes would be on me. I would need to show what I was capable of, but stay in keeping with what I personally hoped to portray.

Color was the biggest question. Black was too austere, white too bridal. Red wasn't my style. Pastels too lacking of color for the occasion.

"You need some sparkle," Sarah had insisted, but I'd shaken my head. It was a daytime event and I was more subtlety than shine.

And then I found it.

It was the shade of blue that the sky turns right before it goes navy. Structured cap sleeves, my signature wide neckline to accentuate the collarbones, and then faint scalloped stitching that started at the top and turned to beads midway down before cascading to my knees in overlapping pieces that fluttered prettily when I walked.

"I want one in every color of the rainbow," Sarah declared.

"Me too," Hannah whispered, reaching out a hand to touch the skirt. It was the first time I'd ever seen her impressed by a piece of clothing.

"You look..." Papa said, stopping as his eyes reddened and filled with tears. "Incredible, sweetheart."

"Thanks, Pa," I said and kissed his cheek.

"Not bad, sis," Lawrence said, coming in for a hug while Harrison and Eva gave obligatory smiles, more interested in the tantalizing little cakes sitting on trays than my dress or the shop.

"Thanks, Lawr," I said. "Is Caroline coming?"

"You think she'd let me get away with not bringing her?" he asked. "Is Rose going to make it?"

I shook my head. "She's in the middle of filming, but she sent those." I pointed to a gorgeous bouquet of flowers.

I moved away to give the shop one last look, the minute hand on my new watch ticking down the time, my heart racing as I tried to ignore the people outside the window looking in.

At three on the dot, I opened the door.

The food I'd worried I'd have too much of was gone within the first hour of opening. There were dozens of familiar faces and even more that I'd never seen before. At one point the reporter for the *Times* asked for a minute of my time and we stepped into the back room so I could answer questions about my hopes for the boutique and where I got my inspiration. When I emerged again, Mrs. Harrington was standing beside Sarah, putting in an order.

"Zora Hough," she said when I approached, and then corrected herself. "Pardon me. Zora *Lily.* What a secret you kept. This is…magnificent."

"Thank you for coming."

"How could I resist?" she said. "You're going to give Nellie a run for her money."

I grinned, seeing the woman she spoke of holding court across the room. Nellie Carman was too big a name to be worried about me.

"I could use a little friendly competition," she'd told me before giving me her blessing when I'd left her store.

I made sure to talk to everyone, even if just for a moment. I answered questions, made suggestions, accepted lunch and dinner and party invitations, introduced family to friends, and friends to acquaintances.

"You're a smash hit."

I turned at the familiar voice and threw my arms around Jessie's neck.

"I was wondering where you were," I said.

"Sorry I'm late. I was waiting to catch a ride with a friend." She pointed and I followed her finger to see Ellis standing awkwardly near the door, someone's purse in his hands.

Linking my arm through Jessie's we weaved through the crowd.

"Ellis!" I said, and threw my arms around his neck.

"Damn, Zora," he said. "Rose always told me how good you were but I had no idea."

"Thanks, El. I like your clutch."

He blushed and nodded at a statuesque Black woman dressed in a beautiful emerald day dress and looking through a book of fabric samples, my mother beside her, pointing to a swatch.

"That's my girl," he said. "Anna. She dances at the Alhambra and when she saw the invitation you sent well…there was no getting out of coming." He gave me a look. "Thank you. For inviting me." He looked around the room, taking in the mostly white faces.

"I invited all my friends, Ellis. Why should you be an exception?"

"You should come down to the club. We sound better than ever."

"Ellis. I would be delighted."

By the time I locked the door that night, the moon had replaced the sun and the stars winked down at me.

I was exhausted but exhilarated, my feet sore, my cheeks aching from smiling so much, my voice hoarse from so much talking. But I was happy. Happier than I'd been in a long time.

Inside on my worktable were flowers and gifts, and more orders than I could've hoped to get. They would take me the next month to fill.

I could hardly wait to get started.

39

"Your ten o'clock is here," Sarah said, poking her head into the back room where I was leaning a hip against the counter, sipping tea, and perusing a catalog of new fabrics that had been sent over this morning from my favorite textile retailer.

I looked up to see her taking in my of outfit for the day with an appraising look.

It was part mine and part Carman's, a good luck gift from Nellie. My part, a fitted black waistcoat and long, wide-legged cuffed trousers, which were a daring fashion statement, but I'd found working in them to be liberating as I kneeled and bent to measure and pin. Nellie's part of the outfit was a white blouse with thin black stripes and a large bow tied at my neck beneath the vest. In Carman's, they'd paired it with a prim, pale pink suit, something someone my mother's age might wear to a business luncheon. But for someone my age and with my long legs, the menswear look was a more fitting and fashionable choice. Add to it the men's bow tie I'd fashioned as a headband around my newly bobbed hair, and I looked straight out of a movie. At least, that's what Sarah had proclaimed the moment she walked in the shop this morning.

I nodded at my sister, drank my last sip of tea, rinsed the cup, and set it in the sink before checking my outfit in the full-length mirror my father had hung on the back of the storage room door. With a confident grin, I headed out to the main room.

There was always a flutter of excitement in the shop when Nellie Carman came by. Her name was synonymous with elegance and success, which was why when she'd offered a way to keep my foot in the door at her store, just in case things didn't work out, I'd said yes.

The offer was a year contract we'd revisit after twelve months. I'd provide one design a month to be featured in the main window and earn a commission on every garment sold. Basically exactly what we'd been doing, but with one less design a month. The pattern would be exclusive to Carman's—I couldn't do a different version for my own store. And she would retain the rights to it.

"Should things not work out with your own shop," she said. "Though I fully believe they will, you'll still have a place here that you can come back to, or I'll keep you on merely as a contracted designer."

I signed the deal that afternoon. I knew if Harley were around, he'd have advised to do it. As a salesman, he knew the advantages of having your product in more than one spot. "But not too many," he'd once told me. "People like to feel they've purchased something special. Something not everyone has. Exclusivity is everything to those with money."

But, unlike Carman's, I didn't only want to cater to the upper classes, thus the rack. And so far the idea had gone over well. I only made a handful, so the likelihood you'd run into someone wearing the same thing was small and, thanks to the keen business mind Sarah had, we made them in different colors. If you purchased one, you still couldn't get the modifications of the more expensive, custom option, but you would get it sized to fit you for a small fee.

The shop had only been open a day when I realized I needed to hire extra hands immediately. Sarah quit the secretarial job she'd started a couple months before and showed up the next day to find me smiling but panicking, a clipboard in hand and a line out the door as I took orders and measurements on a pad of paper.

"Here," she said, taking the clipboard and looking over what I was doing. "I've got it, Z. You measure, I'll write."

That night she organized a new system using a ruler. For each garment she listed a place for the customer's name, measurements, address, and date it was ordered and when it was to be finished, as well as fabric options and modifications offered.

"This way, after we do our part, they can scour the book and mark what they want themselves."

"You're a genius, sis," I said.

Two weeks in, my father became a full-time employee again, half the day working for me, running errands and fixing things, and half the day at the auto shop. Mama came to the shop one full day a week and hung out in the storage room that Pa had fashioned with a fold-down table and another sewing machine I'd bought on sale. She and Sarah took over the rack clothing fittings, ordering from our suppliers, and keeping the break room stocked with tea and cookies for our guests, while I sewed the custom jobs, our clients wanting only my hands to touch what would become one of kind pieces.

"We need more tags," Mama called from the storage room where she was working late one evening.

"Already?" I asked.

Unlike the professional yet elegant sewn-on tags Carman's clothing had, with its little insignia, store name, and the city, I'd decided, after much thoughtful contemplation, to emulate what I'd done in Hollywood. I wanted a more personal touch for my garments. I wanted the people who bought and wore my clothing to feel as though they'd gotten something special.

And so, with a trembling hand one night, I'd threaded a needle with fine white thread and slid it through a swatch of dove gray satin lining.

The first batch was terrible. I was nervous, thoughts of everything that could go wrong, how I could fail, stacks of boxes and swaths of tissue paper never used. Over and over I sewed my name on that swatch until the very last one looked how I'd remembered. With a sigh of relief, I picked up a fresh swatch, threaded the needle again, sat up in my chair, and began again.

I made the tags in every color of lining we had in stock to be sewn into each piece made. They were delicate, each Zora Lily signature done in white or gray or black thread, and I'd done three dozen, a lofty goal for one month. At least I'd thought.

A month in, business had slowed, but barely a tick. The designs in the window were still selling, but had mostly seen their day and were ready to be retired to the storage closet. Everyone's breath seemed to be held in tight as they waited to see what would come next. Would it be as good? Could I do it again?

"Are you ready?" Sarah asked.

We were standing in the breakroom the night before the new set of garments was to debut, with a bottle of wine spirited beneath bread and cheese and other treats in a congratulatory gift basket from Mrs. Carman, who had visited the shop not once, but three times in the first month.

"She just wants a first look," Sarah had said when she read the card that came with it while also eyeing an expensive box of chocolates.

I handed her the chocolates.

"Whether or not that's true," I said, grinning and shaking my head at my sister. Sarah was wary of everyone's motives and I'd had to remind her several times that most of these women weren't used to the word *no*. "It's a lovely gesture from a lovely lady who has been a wonderful customer. Now—" I lifted my glass and waited for her to do the same. "Cheers to one month down and the beginning of another."

"May it be as profitable as ever," Sarah said.

We clinked glasses, took one sip each, then set down our glasses, grabbed the hangers holding the next month's designs, and made our way to the two waiting mannequins she'd pulled from the window as soon as the door had closed for business earlier that evening.

"The women are going to flip," Sarah said, her voice breathless with anticipation as she slid the folds of fabric into place.

I prayed she was right.

And now here we were, four months in and I was standing in my very own successful shop with the woman who had given me a shot, watching her have a look around, eyes wide, taking in the mannequins, the rack of premade garments, the fabric samples Sarah had organized on a rope ring made of braided thread so women could easily flip through them and feel them against their skin.

"How will I ever convince you to come back now?" she asked, a grin playing about her brick red–painted lips.

"You had your chance," Sarah said with a wink as she rushed by, clipboard in hand.

"It's perfect," Nellie said. "Reminds me of when I started, but with so much more style. Have you extended your lease yet?"

I had. I'd asked for five more months, bringing it to a full year. Sarah thought I should try and lease it for far longer, but I was hesitant. Just because things were going well now, didn't mean they'd last. Someone else could open a competing shop. Maybe their designs would be better.

"Not likely," Sarah had said, ever my champion.

"I have," I told Nellie.

"Good," she said. "And meanwhile, keep your eyes open for a bigger space for when the lease runs out. I think you're going to need it."

"I'm not sure I want to go bigger," I said, glancing around the little space that brought me such joy every day. "But we'll see. Now, what can I do for you? To what do I owe the honor of you making an appointment with me?"

"Look at you getting down to business," she said with a wink before checking the delicate watch on her wrist. "But yes. I have to get back to the office myself so let me tell you what I'm thinking. I'm going to Paris in three months' time and I want you to make some pieces for me. Five day dresses, two evening, and a dressing gown."

My jaw dropped.

"You want to wear my designs…in Paris?"

"I do indeed. And—I don't want to see them beforehand. I trust you implicitly. I'm here today for you to say yes and take my measurements, and then will leave it entirely to you to decide what you want me to advertise in the fashion capital."

"Nellie," I whispered, my mind already mentally flipping the pages of my sketchbooks and remembering every fabric we had on hand. "You're sure?"

"Positive. Shall we get started then?"

40

The morning sun poured through the window of my bedroom, bathing the quilt I'd kicked to the footboard in warm, golden light. I smiled and stretched, then bounced from my bed and padded to the bathroom to wash my face and brush my hair.

I loved mornings in a way I never had before. The quiet while I enjoyed a cup of coffee and breakfast as I read whatever book I was currently immersed in, my feet bare on the warm hardwood, my day stretched out ahead of me, waiting to be filled with customers and ideas, fabric deliveries and the hum of the sewing machine.

Glancing at the outfit I'd laid out the night before, I contemplated switching out the cloche I'd chosen for another headband fashioned from a man's bow tie. It had become a bit of a signature style for me, the bow sitting just behind my ear, against my neck. I'd even begun to see women on the streets emulate it.

"You're a trendsetter," Sarah whispered to me a few days ago when a customer came in, the same style of headband fashioned around her head.

I'd merely laughed and hurried to the storage room to retrieve another client's order. But the warmth in my cheeks gave away my pleasure.

Finished with my breakfast, I set the dishes in the sink to be cleaned later, and set about getting ready for the day. Unlike so many women these days, I still kept my beauty regimen quite simple. A bit of rouge, a touch of mascara, a light sweeping of lipstick.

I smoothed my hair, slid the headband in place and slipped out of the menswear pajamas I'd made that were similar to a pair Harley had owned. I'd loved the way the shirt felt the many times I'd stolen it from the foot of the bed and put it on on my way to the bathroom, and had wanted something like it for myself. But unless I shopped in the men's department, I couldn't find anything like it for women. And so I'd made my own. To which Sarah exclaimed upon seeing the finished product, "Make me some too!"

The shop now carried a handful of sets that sold out almost as soon as they made it on the shelves.

I dressed in a simple white day dress with a dropped waist and gentle tiers down either side of the skirt. It was sleeveless and had my signature wide neckline, this one dipping into a shallow V in both the front and back.

After putting on my shoes, checking my headband was still in place, grabbing the sketchbook I'd been working in the night before, and my purse, I hurried out the door.

"Good morning, Miss Hough," Mrs. Parker, my neighbor across the hall said as we passed in the stairwell.

"Good morning," I said and leaned down to pat her dog, Smith, on the head. "And good morning to you, fine sir."

The sun hit my face as soon as I exited the building and I stopped for a moment to soak it in.

"Good morning, Zora!"

I turned and smiled at a young man carting a box of vegetables out of his family's corner grocery store to be placed in bins.

"Mornin', George," I said and then waved as I checked the street for cars and hurried across.

As soon as I saw my shop my heart gave a little jump. It never ceased to thrill me.

Passing the window, I noted that one of the mannequins seemed to have gotten bumped, causing the shoulder of the sleeve to slide off a bit. I'd ask Sarah to fix it when she got in. Unless she was already here. But had she been, I knew she would've noticed and fixed it before I even got a chance to see. She took as much pride in the shop as I did.

I slid my key in the door and the happy jingle of the bell greeted me. I wondered if Nellie still got excited when she entered her store.

"Probably not," I chuckled, walking across the main room's floor, my eyes taking in everything from the rack of clothes that was nearly empty to the swath of fabric I'd forgotten to put away that Sarah had thoughtfully folded and left on the corner of my worktable, as I went.

I was making my first cup of tea for the day when I heard the bell again and then the scrape of a mannequin being moved.

"Good morning," I said as Sarah entered the break room.

"Good morning," she said and yawned. I laughed. She'd never been much of a morning person. "Someone must have bumped one of the mannequins yesterday."

"I saw," I said. "I knew you'd fix it first thing."

"I hate when my ladies are out of place," she said with a wink while adjusting her bosom.

"Sarah!"

We burst into a bout of uncontrollable giggles. Sarah's chest size had gone from nothing to a lot in the blink of an eye when she was thirteen, bypassing a need for my flimsy hand-me-down brassieres and going straight into one of mother's spares. It had been a source of amusement between us ever since, as I'd never had much in the chest area to speak of and oft joked I could stand to borrow some of hers.

One of my favorite things about opening the shop was having

my sister come work with me. She'd always been more driven than me. Louder about it anyway. And seeing her here, using the skills she'd learned in school and then honed at her first job was something to behold. The clients loved her, she was organized, remembered every detail of someone's order without looking at her clipboard, and she'd made more friends in the first week than I'd made in all the months we'd been open.

"You seem happy," I told her one day as we reorganized color swatches after a particularly frenzied day.

"I am," she said. "I love working in the city. Watching your business grow. Seeing you do well at what you love. And I've kissed so many cute boys!"

"Sarah!"

But I'd laughed along with her. It was what she'd always wanted. Friends, a social life, and male attention. The fact that she happened to be a savvy businesswoman on top of it all was the cherry on the sundae.

As usual, the morning was busy, clients popping in to pick up orders, peruse previous design books, review the modifications they'd chosen and change one or two, or just come to see if the pajama sets had been restocked.

"Darnit," a middle-aged woman named Doris said, noting the empty shelves. "I was hoping today would be my day."

"Is that Doris?" Sarah called from the back before appearing in the doorway, a measuring tape hung around her neck. She smiled when she saw one of our most loyal customers. "Doris, don't you fret. I've been waiting for some fabric I ordered to come in and it's here. I intend to make a set just for you. They should be done next week."

"Oh!" Doris looked from my sister to me, her hands clasped at her chest. "You two are absolute dolls. What day should I come?"

"How about Wednesday," Sarah said.

"Wednesday it is. Thank you, dear. Ta!"

"Ta!" Sarah waved.

I shook my head, grinning at my sister who shrugged.

"I am very fancy and say 'ta' now," she said, making me snort.

"You are very fancy indeed. You're going to work extra hours just to get those done, aren't you," I said.

Sarah shrugged. "I am. But I don't care." She checked her clipboard. "Don't forget you have a lunch date at noon."

"How can I forget?" I asked. "You've been reminding me every day for a week."

"I'm excited you're finally seeing a friend," she said. "You never get out. What would Rose think?"

"Probably the same as you. That it's high time. And I'm sure wherever she is, which is most likely on a set somewhere being fabulous, she is applauding me."

I drifted to my worktable then and began cutting pattern pieces for the next garment on my list while thinking about my friend. I missed her dearly. Missed her laughter, that twinkle in her eye when she was up to no good. And the way she always stood by me. But she was where she belonged, and so was I. And we'd both finally come to accept that. Her last letter had even said as much, right before she'd asked me to design a dress for her first acting debut. There would be a premiere and a party after.

"I want your piece in the papers," she'd written. "So make it glamorous. I'll wear it on the red carpet before the picture premieres."

The fabric for the gown was already cut and the detailing sorted. I'd been working on it after hours and planned to spend this evening on it as well, just as soon as the last client left and the door was locked behind them.

At eleven fifty I pushed away from my sewing machine, checked myself in the full-length mirror in the back, grabbed my purse, and kissed my sister's cheek as I passed her on my way to the front door.

"I'll be back in an hour," I said as I left.

"Have fun!"

I nodded and left the shop, the echo of the door's bell jingling behind me.

Fun. My idea of it and my sister's were two different things. For me, fun was sitting cross-legged on my very own sofa in my very own apartment dreaming up clothing designs. Fun was splurging on a bottle of bubble bath and spending an evening soaking in the tub with a good book. I loved walking through the city in the early hours as the corner grocers flipped their signs to Open and the smell of coffee began to waft into the street. Rain or shine, I was inspired in those moments as the sun was just coming up. The day was still full of possibilities at that point, and I was a sponge, soaking it all in.

But Sarah insisted it wasn't enough. "You need friends," she said. "Activities outside the shop."

Sarah's idea of fun was being social. Lunches with friends. Dinners with friends. Nights out dancing with friends. Things that had once been a part of my life too, but were now mere memories.

She still lived at home, but there were many times I'd wake to her knocking discreetly on my door, pleading with me to let her sleep on my sofa.

"Mama will be worried if she wakes and finds you not home," I'd told her the first few times it happened. But we were long past that now. Mama now knew if Sarah wasn't occupying her usual spot in the bed she now had to herself, Hannah sharing with Eva, then she was with me. Most of the time. I didn't mention the mornings she showed up to work having clearly not gone home, and had definitely not spent the night on my sofa. She always just gave a coy smile and a shrug while straightening the outfit she'd worn the day before.

"At least put on something fresh," I'd say, pointing to the back room where we now kept a surplus of items.

"I'll pay for it!" she always said, to which I grumbled something rude, knowing she wouldn't and I'd have to dock her pay.

But her being social was both good for business, and for me. The women she socialized with often frequented the store, usually coming in small groups that exclaimed over the items, making other customers curious, not wanting to miss out on something so exciting. I was constantly asked out to lunch these days by women wanting to thank me for something extra I'd done free, asking me to design something for a special occasion, or, and this shocked me the most, just wanting to be seen with me.

"You're a celebrity," Sarah said one day when I'd mentioned a dinner I'd gone to, the woman who'd invited me constantly waving people over to meet me while I hurried to chew my food, swallow, and smile warmly.

"But I'm not," I'd insisted.

"You are. A local celebrity. And they all want to say they know you personally."

I'd wrinkled my nose at that.

"That makes me feel used."

She'd waved a hand. "Feel flattered instead. They love you. They're in awe of you. You should hear the things they whisper to me about you."

At that, I'd put my hands over my ears, shook my head, and backed up into the break room until I could no longer see her; I could only hear her laughter.

Thankfully, my lunch today was not with a customer, but with Jessie, who I'd barely seen since the store's opening. She'd come by two weeks ago and asked me to lunch to catch up.

We spent the hour laughing, recalling dance mishaps, costume disasters, the time one of the musicians was so drunk he fell off the stage, and our time in Hollywood.

"Remember that couple that got so sauced they fell over and passed out?" Jessie asked.

"And then the police showed up and some of the guys propped them up on chairs to try and make them look normal?"

We giggled into our napkins as two older ladies seated beside us tsked at our mirth, which only served to make us laugh harder.

We parted with a hug on the sidewalk after with promises to get together again soon, and I returned to the shop with a bounce in my step and a lightness I hadn't felt in a long time. Sarah was right. I did need something outside the shop. I'd tell her later though. I wasn't willing to see her look of satisfaction just yet.

My lunch with Jessie, it turned out, was the beginning of a shift. Rather than spend every evening either working late in the shop or designing on my sofa at home, I began to meet up with friends again, old and new, for dinner, a movie, and finally to the Alhambra.

I brought Sarah, whose stare of awe the first time she saw me in my more glamorous nighttime look made me blush with delight.

"You absolutely glow," she said, taking in everything from my lined eyes to my shimmering dress, down to my shoes. "I mean, you're a beauty without a hint of makeup. But this...is this how you looked when you met Harley? Because no wonder he said he never looked at another woman after seeing you."

I furrowed my brow at the mention of his name. It was like a tiny dart to my heart to hear it.

"Sorry," she said quickly.

I shook my head and plastered on a smile. "It's okay. And no. I wasn't nearly as refined that night. I was only just getting started, wearing one of Rose's old dresses that didn't quite fit, my hair unfashionably long and tucked under, and my shoes... Oh, they were horrid! Remember those old scuffed black cast offs of Mama's?"

Sarah nodded, laughing. "They were so ugly. And yet I'll bet you were still the prettiest girl in the club."

"I was never that."

"You've always been that, Z. You're the only one who doesn't know it."

"You're just saying that in hopes I won't notice you're wearing *my* shoes now."

"I am not!" She laughed, reaching out to shield my eyes.

"Anyway, it's the absolute truth. Even in school I'd always hear people whisper about how pretty you were."

"Then why did they treat me so bad?"

"Because pretty doesn't make up for being poor as dirt with a drunk dad and six siblings, half of which don't have shoes that fit, wearing patched-up threadbare clothes, and eating sandwiches with no fillings. Pretty doesn't make people be kind to them. It often makes them meaner, angry for what they don't have. For what they have to work for when you come by it so easily." She gave me a sad smile. "They hated you because despite what you came from, you were still better than them. And they knew it. They knew they'd never be as kind or smart or pretty. They knew that your prettiness went deeper than your looks, and their ugliness came straight from the heart. They had ugly little souls and the only way they could try and make themselves forget was to torture you."

My eyes filled.

"Do you really believe that?" I asked.

"I do."

"Funny that they're nice to me now." I'd run into several old classmates in the past few months, most of which fawned over me and my shop.

"Sure they are. They want to be able to brag that they knew you when."

"That's awful."

"It is. And that's why you smile politely when you see them, and then charge them double!"

The Alhambra was just as I remembered it.

Frankie gave me one of his huge hugs, nearly swallowing me whole, and then pointed out a table whose occupants were just leaving.

I grabbed Sarah's hand and led her through the crowd, trying to ignore the ghost of Harley that resided everywhere in this space. Seated at a table, leaning against the bar in back, lounging on one of the sofas…

I ordered Sarah and me both a Mary Pickford, and waved to Jessie when she emerged from backstage, laughing as her eyes widened and she ran across the dance floor to greet us.

Ellis hadn't been lying. The new band Oscar and he had put together was one of the best I'd ever heard, and when they took a break, I left Sarah, who was talking with a wide-eyed young man, to slip down the back hallway.

"You guys sound great," I said from the doorway of their breakroom.

"Zora!" Oscar said. "Thought that was you I saw in the crowd."

He gave me a hug and offered me a chair as Anna, Ellis's girlfriend, and Jessie entered.

"How's the dress?" I asked Anna.

"I'm almost afraid to wear it it's so beautiful," she said. "But El took me out last weekend and I got so many compliments. Expect some new customers on your doorstep soon."

"I appreciate it," I said. "I'll take as many as I can get."

I left the band members then, Jessie wanting to introduce me to a new beau, and then made my way back to the table to watch the cabaret show with my sister.

We took the streetcar back, Sarah dozing on my shoulder. I nudged her at our stop and hurried her along back to my apartment where she slipped off her shoes, dropped her purse to the floor, and lay down on the sofa.

"Do you still think about him?" she asked.

"Who?"

But I knew who she was talking about.

"Harley."

I wanted to say no. That I'd moved on. But for some reason I couldn't lie.

"Every day, Sarah. Every damn day."

41

"Tell Jess hi for me," Sarah called after me as I hurried out the door on a warm summer day in early July.

I waved and then clapped a hand to my head, laughing as a breeze tried to sweep away the cotton cloche I wore.

Jessie and I now had a standing weekly lunch date. Usually in a different spot each time, as she heard from club customers about new places, or I heard from my clients about a fun new dish being served somewhere we already loved.

I hurried down the sidewalk, breathing in the warm air and smiling as I weaved around meandering pedestrians waving paper fans or hiding beneath the shadows of their umbrellas, the heat making everyone move slower than usual.

I arrived before Jessie and the hostess's eyes widened when I gave my name.

"Oh hello, Miss Lily," she said, her big blue eyes fluttering over me from hat to shoes.

I was wearing a new dress I'd designed for myself, something I did often to gauge the reactions it received. If it got a lot of attention, I did a version for the shop window. If only a little attention, I made a few for the rack and Sarah kept note on how it sold. This dress I was particularly fond of because it was made in a lightweight, white fabric perfect for the warmer temperatures, and combined several features I'd previously only used by themselves. A wide draping neckline, inch-wide shoulder straps, a loose-fitting bodice, and a dropped waist that hugged the hips rather than hid, the hemline mirroring the neckline with its raised sides.

When the hostess's gaze met mine again, her cheeks colored.

"I love your dress," she said, barely unable to keep her eyes on mine as they flicked over the details again.

"Thank you," I said. "It's a new design. I'm unsure if it's one I should feature. What do you think?"

The big blue eyes got wider.

"Yes!" she said. "Absolutely. I'd buy ten if I could afford them. In every color you offer. It's sweet but also..." The big blues narrowed.

"It has a touch of sex appeal, right?" I asked.

"Yes." She breathed and with a last wistful look, grabbed two menus. "This way, Miss Lily."

When Jessie arrived a few minutes later, a vision in a frothy pale pink number, her blond hair sleek and tucked behind her ears, she made me stand and turn.

"This is so embarrassing," I said, turning quickly and then taking my seat again and ducking my head.

"Why?" she asked. "I just made you about a half a dozen sales. And that doesn't include my own order. What other colors will it come in?"

"I'm thinking a pastel palette. Maybe a couple of slinkier prints, as well."

"Perfect. I'll take two. And that hat. Wherever did you get it?"

I lifted a hand to the little folded brim and ran a finger up the feather attached to the side.

"I made it last night with some leftover material," I said.

"Of course you did."

I felt my cheeks warm, which made Jessie grin.

"How you can still be so modest I'll never know," she said.

We ordered lunch and, while we waited, she asked about my morning at the boutique and the family. Her usual order of business.

"The shop is busy as ever," I said. "It's still hard to believe how well it's all going. And the family is great. Nothing new to report. Sarah is still a dream to have at the store. I swear half our clientele is due to her talking us up at the clubs. Lawrence got another article published in the paper and is close to quitting the printing side of the job. Hannah got an award at school for a poem she wrote and started a book club with some of her friends. They meet twice a month to discuss whatever new book they're reading. She loves it. And the younger kids are driving my mother up the wall. They've both grown like weeds the past couple of months and she can barely keep them clothed. Thank goodness I've made friends with the woman who owns the children's clothing shop two blocks from mine. We've swapped discounts."

"Old Lady McCarthy?" Jessie asked. "I cannot imagine her wearing anything more stylish than an old potato sack. What's she want with your shop?"

I smacked Jessie's hand and pursed my lips to keep from laughing.

"She uses the discount for her daughter," I said. "Apparently she's up-and-coming in society. Anyway, now Mama can buy clothes for the younger two kids at much more affordable prices, which helps, even though she and Pa are doing so much better these days in regard to money."

It was a relief. A weight off my shoulders. I hadn't realized just how heavy until it had been lifted. It had been so long since things had felt so settled and comfortable at my parents' home. We'd come far since Tommy's death. I liked to think he'd be proud—if not a little bit sad to not be participating in it. It made me wonder sometimes though, would we be here had he not died? I'd never have taken that nanny job for the

Harringtons, which led to me living downtown, frequenting speakeasies and meeting the dancers whose costumes needed mending. All of which led to meeting the producer who offered up Hollywood. Perhaps without the heartbreak that followed, I'd never have found myself home again, with a quiet determination to redeem myself. Which had ultimately led me to this moment now.

It felt terrible to think that Tommy had needed to die for any of the good stuff that happened after to come true. But it was a curious thought.

"So now that you've settled into being Seattle's darling, what's next?" Jessie asked.

I scoffed at the "darling" and shrugged, taking a bite of food.

"Any men catch your eye lately?"

"Not a one."

"Zora. That is just disappointing. There are several eligible bachelors who would look gorgeous on your arm. I can introduce you to any of them. Just say the word."

"If I were even remotely interested, I would," I said. "But the truth is, I'm not. Not even a little bit. I'm focused on the shop right now. I'm thinking about looking for a slightly larger space."

Her eyes narrowed and she watched me for a long moment.

"Are you still holding out hope to hear from Harley?" she finally asked.

Despite how painful it had been to admit, I'd come clean to Jessie about the letter I'd sent Harley being returned. About how long I'd taken to write him back in the first place. About how sad I'd felt.

"Hollowed out. Empty. Bereft," were my exact words.

"No," I said now, my voice soft. "He's gone. Probably married and living a very glamorous life somewhere on the other side of the world with someone much more refined than I."

"Hmm," Jessie said, narrowing her eyes at me. "Maybe that's how he'd have ended up had he never met you. But I saw him with you, Z. That was never his style. If anything, he's out there right now trying to find a way to replicate the feeling you gave him. And not with another woman, but with experiences and places."

Again I imagined him on the balcony of a small Italian villa, staring out to sea, a drink in his hand. Maybe Jessie was right. Maybe she wasn't. But whatever he was doing now, I decided then and there that's how I would picture him forevermore.

"It is a shame though," Jessie continued. "You were so well suited to one another."

I smiled and shrugged, folding and refolding the napkin in my lap, trying to forget how it had felt to lie in the crook of his arm, hold his hand, feel his lips on my collarbone as he breathed me in.

"Yes, well," I said. "I just hope wherever he is, he's happy. He deserves that at the very least."

She nodded and then mercifully changed the subject.

"So, I have a question for you," she said, pushing her plate to the side and leaning forward, her words coming fast. "We've put together a new show at the Alhambra and we desperately need new costumes. Barb is a good seamstress. She does great at sewing up our dresses, but she's not so keen on design. I know you're plenty busy, but maybe you could at least come down and see what we're doing and give her some ideas? Something to work with? A pattern to go off of? You were always so good at listening to the music, seeing how we move, and putting it all together in a costume to reflect the feeling."

My heart gave a little flutter of excitement.

"When are you thinking?" I asked.

"Tonight?" She chewed her lip, watching me as I considered.

I was planning to work on Rose's gown that evening, but I could do that the following night, and I had all day Sunday, as well.

I nodded. "Okay. I'll be there."

"Yay!" she said and clapped her hands for a second time, causing the gentleman at the next table to jump in surprise.

★ ★ ★

A half hour later the bell above the shop door jingled, announcing my return.

"How's Jessie?" Sarah asked, poking her head out from behind the dressing room curtain, a pencil in her mouth and a tape measure hanging from her neck, a familiar sight when she was taking someone's measurements.

"Lovely as ever. You should join us sometime."

"And miss out on the sandwiches Ma packs?"

I snorted and rolled my eyes. Our mother, despite having more money than she'd ever had, still scrimped on the insides of a sandwich. Every day Sarah would pull hers out of the bag it was packed in, peel the two slices of bread apart, and hold them up for me to see the meager bit of cheese and the see-through slice of meat.

"Really?" she'd say, then smash them back together and take an indecently huge bite I was sure she'd choke on.

"You could make your own," I said for what had to be the hundredth time, to which she made a face and went back to measuring.

I grinned at two women browsing fabric samples.

"Can I answer any questions for you ladies?" I asked, stowing my purse behind my worktable.

In an instant I forgot about Jessie and going to the club that night when one of the women pointed to a soft green swatch of material. As we discussed the design she wanted it for and where she'd be wearing the garment, I became absorbed in my work, envisioning how the client would look and what modifications would work best for her figure.

When they left a half hour later, smiling with excitement over the orders they'd placed, a feeling of contentment washed over me. For the first time in my life, I realized I was in the place I was supposed to be. And not only that, I was the person I'd always wanted to be.

42

When the last customer had gone, I turned out the lights in the window and began the task of tidying my desk, clearing the fabric reams, scraps, thread, and pins that had accumulated during the day.

"You aren't staying?" Sarah asked, winding a measuring tape into a circle and setting it in its holder. "I thought you were working on Rose's gown."

"Jessie wants me to come down to the club and check out their new show. They want new costumes that match the feel of it and I said I'd take a look and give some suggestions."

Sarah's eyes widened. "Are we— Do we get to make costumes?" She laced her hands together and held them at her chest. "Please say we're making costumes."

I laughed. "I don't know yet. It takes so much time, especially if there's a lot of bead work. And it doesn't pay particularly well."

"Maybe not before," she said. "But now you're Zora Lily *of* Zora Lily's."

"They still have a budget they have to adhere to and a seamstress on staff."

"I'm happy to work at a discount. And she can help!"

I held up a hand. "I'm excited at the thought of doing it too.

I miss making costumes. But we have our hands full, so let's just wait and see how extensive the job will be first."

"Fine." She pouted prettily. "I wish I could come with you tonight, but I have a date."

"Bill?"

"Who?" She furrowed her brow and then wrinkled her nose. "Ew. No. I cut him loose last week. He was a terrible bore. This one's name is Jay."

"This one," I repeated and shook my head. "You're too much. Well, have fun and don't do anything I wouldn't do."

Our eyes met and we burst out laughing. Sarah was freer than I was in the romance department, and had experienced much more much faster than I had at her age. But one night a few months ago, over another of Mrs. Harrington's hidden bottles of wine, we'd sat in my tiny apartment and I'd divulged, whilst blushing profusely, that I had a naughty side too. I hadn't provided many details, but enough that after that night she'd looked at me in a whole new light.

"I promise I'll behave," Sarah said now, raising her right arm. "Mostly."

After cleaning up, we walked out of the shop together, I locked the door, and then we hugged and parted with promises to see one another bright and early the next morning.

At home I slipped out of my shoes, shed the black-and-white polka-dotted satin scarf I'd worn knotted in a big looping bow at my throat, and pulled out ingredients for dinner.

I ate while sitting on the sofa, my legs curled under me, a new book beside me, grinning to myself thinking about how my mother wouldn't approve. It wasn't proper. Men wouldn't think highly of a woman sitting and eating in such a fashion. She'd be surprised to learn eating like this was something I'd learned from Harley, who'd enjoyed eating a meal from the comfort of his living room.

When I finished, I washed the dishes and then set about getting ready for a night out. I didn't plan to stay long. One drink, a bit of the show, some discussion with the women about color ideas and what they wish their current costumes would do for them, and then back home.

I stared at my rack of clothes, running my fingers across the hangers as I peered at and dismissed dress after dress, finally choosing a modest, forest green sleeveless number with a pleated skirt and beaded geometric design around the bodice. A long gold-plated necklace with a tassel charm, black Mary Jane's, and my signature bow tie headband in a matching shade of green completed the look.

After coating my lashes, rouging my cheeks, and dabbing on a touch of rose-colored lipstick, I grabbed my handbag and was out the door.

I could feel the music before I could properly hear it, the beat reverberating through my body from the soles of my feet to the top of my head. The slot in the door to the Alhambra slid open, music bursting from the slender space. A pair of familiar eyes glanced at me and widened.

I held up a folded piece of paper, prepared to slip it through to him, but Frankie was too fast, throwing the door open and wrapping his arms around me.

"Miss Zora," he said when he released me and smiled into my eyes.

"Hey, Frankie."

"You're here!"

I turned at the sound of Jessie's voice and she threw her arms around me in a tight hug.

"I saved you a seat at the other end," she shouted, grabbing my hand and pulling me toward the crowd.

I nodded, tightening my grip on her hand as bodies Charlestoned nearby, arms swinging, legs kicking.

Immediately upon taking my seat I was accosted by two men asking me to dance, each one trying to sell me on the merits of their skill.

"Shoo!" Jessie said, waving them away. "She ain't for sale, boys. Get lost." She glanced apologetically at me. "Sorry. There's a small group of men that watch for fresh meat and swoop in as soon as they notice you're not with a man. It wouldn't be so bad if they offered to buy you a drink first, but they never do."

While Jessie flagged down a waitress and ordered me a Mary Pickford, I looked around the room, taking in several familiar faces, noting with pleasure a few women wearing dresses I'd created, and letting the music fill me.

Our drinks came and we sipped while talking over the music and watching the dancers move around the floor.

"Shoot," Jessie said, checking her watch. "I need to get changed. Will you stay for the whole show?"

I hadn't planned on it, but now that I was here, the music wooing me with its sultry horns and playful piano trills, why not?

"I will," I said.

"I'll see you after, then," she said and then disappeared into the crowd.

The show was great; the dancing girls, flashy good fun. The crowd whooped and hollered as the musicians leaned in to their instruments, invigorated by the newfound energy in the room. But my attention was on the costumes. The movements. The leg flicks and hand waves, twisting torsos and swiveling hips.

"What did you think?" Jessie asked, chest heaving as she caught her breath afterward, dabbing at her brow with a towel.

We were standing in the narrow hallway behind the stage after the last dance number was over.

"You've gotten even better," I said.

"Thanks, Z. And the costumes?"

"I have several ideas. I'll draw something up and give it to you at lunch next week?"

She clapped her hands. "I can't wait! The girls were so excited to see you in the crowd. They can hardly believe *the* Zora Lily might be designing our new costumes. Don't worry though.

I told them it's not for sure. I know your time is precious and management probably can't afford you."

"We might be able to work something out," I said. "Depending on how much detail you're looking to have."

"We'd actually like something lighter," Jessie said, smiling at one of the other dancers who hurried by, nodding her agreement. "The beading is heavy and makes it hard to move. Especially near the end of the show when we're exhausted."

"Noted."

"You're a doll, Z."

"I've missed getting to do this kind of work. Thanks for asking me to come down. And for the drink. See you next Friday?"

We kissed cheeks and I made my way slowly out of the club, smiling as the music echoed around me in the stairwell until the heavy door thudded shut and I was left with only the sound of the base thumping in time with my heartbeat.

It was strange standing outside on the sidewalk, the quiet jarring compared to the noise of the club. They were like two different worlds, each one bleeding into the other, while not wanting to admit the other existed. As if by doing so, one would have to come back to a reality they didn't want to face, and the other would succumb to a truth about themselves they weren't ready to admit to.

Tucking my purse beneath my arm, I began the walk uptown toward home. Halfway there I realized the sketchbook I wanted was at the shop and turned on my heel, picking up my pace.

The bell jingled as I opened the door, the sound never ceasing to make me smile. It was the jangle of hope. Of hard work and a dream. *My* dream come true.

I stepped inside and locked the door behind me, the sight of my worktable luring me to sit. I switched on the desk lamp and looked through the pile of sketchbooks until I found the one I wanted. Unlike the others, the designs in this book were ideas for me, my family, and friends. It was personal, with notes beside each drawing detailing the occasion it might be worn for. There was a sixteenth birthday frock for Hannah, the red carpet gown for Rose, a wedding dress for Sarah for if that girl ever settled down, and a mother of the bride dress for Mama. There had even once been the beginnings of a wedding dress for myself, but I'd long since removed that page and tucked it away in a shoebox at the back of the bedroom closet shelf at my parents' house.

Flipping past the filled pages, I found an empty one and set the book on the table, a pencil at the ready in my hand. I closed my eyes and pictured the dance girls at the Alhambra tonight. How they'd shimmied their shoulders, swung their arms, and spun their bodies. I heard the music, remembered the way their dresses had bunched and creased, catching on their stockings, pulling at the seams, and then picked up the sketchbook and began to draw.

I was on my third page of sketches when I stopped to stretch my back and make a cup of tea. As the kettle warmed, a new idea pushed forth and I tapped my foot, staring impatiently at the appliance, waiting for steam to appear so I could pour the water and let the tea steep at my desk while I got back to work.

I was on my fifth page when I checked the time and saw it was nearly eleven. My seventh when I drained my second cup of tea and pondered eating one of the cookies someone had brought in earlier that day.

Chewing the sweet molasses treat slowly, I wandered the shop, a small smile playing about my lips as I took in the cozy, bright space, the mannequins in the window dressed in clothing I'd created, the painted shop name—my name!—scrolling across the window, my worktable, the dressing room, and the racks and shelves of clothing for sale.

How far I'd come in so little time, nudged out of the comfortable space I'd become so accustomed to despite not feeling I'd belonged there, but not knowing how to get myself out. Move forward. Make changes.

But I'd made it. I'd taken chances. I'd believed in myself and my talent. And that was all that it took.

I knew something now that I hadn't before. Life would always throw challenges, but it was up to me to consider each and every one and make a choice about how I would take it on. And I was up to the task.

So many times I could've given up. Tucked the dream away for good. Done what so many other women did and searched for a man to be her salvation. But I hadn't. I'd refused to use even one cent of the money Harley had left for me. Not even to help my family. I'd sent every dime I didn't need to survive in Hollywood to my mother so that they could put in the bathroom, buy a new sofa, and afford enough food for everyone. I would perhaps regret for a long time what might've been with Harley, but I knew I never would've been happy with him if I'd allowed myself to just be a pretty piece on his arm, rather than a woman in charge of her destiny.

I wished he could see me now. I knew he'd be proud, just as I knew he wouldn't be surprised.

"You're a woman who will do things," he'd said once from across the room as he watched me get dressed for the day. But I hadn't known what he meant. Didn't know what he saw. Didn't believe. Not then anyway. I hadn't been forced yet to own up to what I knew could be mine—should I only reach, and work, and strive just a little bit harder.

I smiled at the memory, finished the cookie, and sat at my worktable, taking a sip of tea as I flipped through the drawings I'd done that evening. They were good, and it felt good to know that.

Setting them aside, I checked the time, unsurprised to see it was nearing midnight. I knew I should get home since I was due to meet Sarah early the next morning before the shop opened, but the fabric for Rose's dress caught my eye and before I knew what I was doing, I'd threaded a needle and begun to sew.

With each slice of the needle through the dove gray fabric,

the silver thread snaking along the back of my hand, my confidence in the ambitious design grew. It was unlike anything I'd seen and I hoped she'd like it.

I hummed as I worked, knotting off one section and moving to another, as always, feeling a bit like a magician as I created elegant garments from swaths of plain cloth. I was so immersed in the intricate stitches I sewed, careful not to tear the delicate fabric beneath my fingers, that I didn't notice the man in the window. Had no idea how long he'd been standing there. And might never have looked up if not for the gentle knock, knock, knock on the pane.

At first I ignored it. More often than not, when I found myself working late on a Friday or Saturday night, a group of young men would wander by on their way to or from one of the clubs and find it good fun to tap until I finally gave them a smile and waved them on, refusing their shouts to join them. But this wasn't the tapping of obnoxious boys out for a good time, and so when I looked up and saw a familiar pair of blue eyes staring back at me, I was confused. And then the air slid from my lungs as my heartbeat sped up and the gray fabric in my now damp palms slipped off the table to the floor.

I stood as if pulled by an unseen force. An invisible puppeteer lifting me by the top of my head, the strings connected to my limbs too slack to be useful as my arms hung limp at my sides. It was only realizing the look on his face was one of uncertainty, of worry and perhaps fear, that the feeling returned to my lower extremities.

As I moved to the door, he moved with me, the two of us shadowing one another until our eyes met on either side of the windowed door, never wavering as my one hand slid to the lock and the other pressed the latch on the handle, the bell jingling above us.

My eyes searched his as I breathed in his scent and felt his presence, the power of him, as his own gaze traveled over my face, taking in every inch, every detail, every freckle he knew so well before returning to meet my stare.

The glimmer of a smile. A new emotion sweeping over his features as he looked down at me. Into me. Was that hope? Longing?

Love?

My lips moved of their own accord, rising at the corners, unable to hide the joy I felt at seeing him. It was the only encouragement he needed.

"Hello, Zora," he said.

His deep voice reverberated through me, plucking at nerve endings, thrumming through my veins.

In an instant a million little memories filled my mind. I was both there, standing on the threshold of my shop, and somewhere else entirely. I remembered evenings in the clubs, the twinkle of lights sparking off our cocktail glasses, his voice in my ear as he spoke to me while the music played and the dancers danced. Nights with us sitting at either end of his sofa, reading, our feet meeting in the middle. Holding hands while walking through the park. Staring at one another across the table as we dined. Nights where he left me breathless, his beautiful hands moving over my skin followed by his lips. Long, lazy mornings, our legs entangled beneath the covers, his warm breath on my neck as he whispered good morning.

As a cool breeze swept past him and over me, the images in my head shifted. A future I hadn't dared hope for before now stretched out in endless possibilities. Us. Together. A home. Two? One here and one in England? That villa in Italy with a view of the sea? Summers traveling. A growing circle of friends. Family. Our own? Tiny dresses with bows. A son with his father's one shallow dimple?

It was all there. Right in front of me. Ours for the taking, should I just say the words.

And so I did.

"Hello, Harley."

43

Washington, DC, 2023

"Are you nervous?"

I glanced over my shoulder at Lu, who was standing, her dark hair pulled back in its usual no-nonsense ponytail, arms crossed over her chest, looking as anxious as I felt.

"Not at all," I said, chewing one side of my lower lip and cracking the knuckles of my fingers one at a time as I turned back to stare out the windowed doors facing the museum's front steps.

"Liar."

I snorted in response. She knew my tells.

Weeks. I'd had mere weeks to pull together what would probably go down as the most complicated exhibition of my career. But also the most rewarding. The pride I felt at what my team had accomplished was indescribable, and the party I'd planned to thank them barely did justice for the gratitude I felt.

The finding of that hidden stitched tag had unraveled a mystery I at first didn't think I was equipped to deal with. So daunted by the task of getting to the truth, I'd almost thrown in the towel thirty minutes into it.

A Google search had shown nothing. At least on the first page.

Everyone knows if you move onto the second page of a search engine you're grasping at straws, but I thought I'd just have a peek. Just in case there was a tidbit. A mention.

A whisper.

And there it was. A name. A snippet of information so old and forgotten, Google hadn't cared to add more. But that tiny bit of information was something, and I'd pulled the thread.

Zora Lily had been a fashion designer and the owner of one of Seattle's finest women's boutiques from the late 1920s until she closed the door in the 1950s. Lauded for her elegant and trendsetting designs, she'd built a store catering to the wealthy, but with something for the middle and lower classes, as well.

"Everyone should have the opportunity to look good," she'd said in an interview for the *Seattle Times*. "Not just those with means."

Her success spanned decades, and she'd had to move the shop twice over the years to accommodate the demand for her designs. But the store was only one part of her story. What I wanted to know—*needed* to know—was how her name ended up behind the tag of renowned designer Michele Cleménte. Because it hadn't just been the one dress. I'd checked every single gown, dress, and suit in that back room that night. Zora Lily's name was in all of them, hidden behind the much more famous woman's.

I'd left the room, leaving my worktable a shambles, and hurried down the hall to my office to begin what often seemed like a wild goose chase and a waste of time. We had a show coming up in less than a month. This last lot of costumes, the oldest of the bunch, had so much work yet to be done. But I couldn't stop myself from looking, typing in every possible scenario I could think of. Was Cleménte's real name actually Zora Lily? Was the fabric previously used for something else and repurposed? Or, more likely and the worse scenario of all, was Zora Lily, a woman who I now know had made a name for herself as a fashion designer in Seattle in the 1920s, the creator of those garments—and Cleménte, for reasons unknown, had put her name on them?

I typed in both women's names, one after the other. Nothing. I typed in *Garbo*, *Lily*, *Clemént*e, *Hollywood* in every variation I could think of. Nothing. And then I typed in Zora Lily's name again, followed by the *Seattle Times*. There was the article I'd already seen, and then another, this one reporting on the grand opening of her shop, and identifying her further as Zora Lily Hough.

My search began anew, and this time, more information popped up, complete with several images of a dazzling young woman standing in front of her very first store, at what looked to be a club, and in a wedding announcement with a man that could only be described as dashing.

"Get it, Zora," I whispered, my eyes taking in her impeccable style. A style I'd seen repeated on the costumes down the hall. Dropped waists, wide necklines, gathering on the hips, tiered hemlines, and on an outfit that was used for a travel scene, a suit with a headband, the bow attached to it worn behind Garbo's ear.

It was after midnight when I left the museum, visions of a willowy woman with a sparkle in her eyes and a smile of quiet confidence floating through my brain. Who was this woman who had risen from, at least from what the paper reported, poverty, tragedy, and disappointment. Had she been poor, or had her early upbringing been sensationalized? And what tragedy? What disappointment? All I saw was a well-dressed woman, her fancy boutique, and a handsome man on her arm.

I woke early the next morning after a fitful night of sleep, Zora's name running through my brain like a reader board. There was nothing I could find that connected her to Hollywood. No reason her name should be in those clothes. It made no sense. Had the studio purchased them from her shop and slapped another designer's name on them? The dates didn't line up. Zora Lily didn't open her shop until after the movie would've been filmed.

I was two hours early to work and stood staring at the gown I'd been working on the night before. The design aspects I'd been confused by, the style not usual for Cleménte now stood out even more. It didn't fit. Michele Cleménte had not made these clothes. I looked at the photo of Zora I'd printed off at home.

She had.

A pit opened in my stomach. I could not show these costumes as part of the exhibit and post signage claiming them as Cleménte's. I couldn't lie. I was going to have to tell my boss.

"You have proof?" Merritt Braeburn, my employer and infamous stickler for detail asked without looking away from her computer screen after she'd seen me sitting outside her office when she'd arrived.

"Well. Sort of?"

She'd looked at me, her dark eyes searing.

"You want me to potentially scrap a major part of the exhibit on some 'sort of' proof?"

"Hear me out?"

"Oh, believe me," she said. "I'm all ears."

And so I told her. About the tag falling off and the hand-stitched name beneath. How I'd peeked beneath the tags on all the other costumes from the film and found the same silver, white, or black thread spelling out a name that was then hidden behind the well-known designer's tag. How the style of each garment hadn't matched up with Cleménte's well-documented details. And then the online search. A young woman in Seattle and a boutique bearing her name in a script too similar to the stitched signature in the garments in the back room not to be one and the same.

"She's passed," I said softly. "In 1993. But there are descendants. Two daughters and a son. All still alive. Grandchildren.

Great-grandchildren. Most are still in the Seattle area. I was planning on reaching out."

"I'm surprised you haven't yet," she said, tapping the tip of a pen on her desk.

"I wanted to speak with you first. But regardless of what you decide about the show, I'd like to find out what they know."

"What if they don't know anything? What if there's nothing to know?"

But Merritt wasn't stupid. And like me, she loved knowing the truth of the pieces that graced the halls of our museum.

She shook her head and sighed. "Dammit. There's always something with these exhibits. Call them. Go see them. Whatever it takes. Let's get it right. We don't want to be made fools of. And now I need to know too. The garments are still in the back?"

I nodded.

"I'll come down to see them myself after my meeting."

"I was hoping you would."

Each person on my team was informed of the situation immediately.

"So," Carmen said, pushing up the thick glasses constantly sliding down her upturned nose and staring at the green tweed three-piece suit she'd spent long, back-breaking hours leaning over to mend the cuffs, lapels, and trim over the pockets. "Are we stopping?"

"No," I said. "The pieces will be shown, there's just a mystery surrounding them and I'm on the case."

"Can we help?" Maggie, my youngest conservator, asked, her dark eyes wide with excitement at the prospect of solving the puzzle.

"Put down the magnifying glass and stay in your lane, Sherlock," Lu said, causing the room to laugh. Maggie spent every break from work with her nose in a mystery novel.

"I will let you know," I said. "Right now though, I need you all to stay on task while I go make a few phone calls."

"Do you want me to work on your gown?" Lu asked.

I glanced over at the diaphanous gown with its beautiful star. None of its parts had made sense to me before. Not with Cleménte's name on it. But now, imagining Zora Lily's pretty head bent over it, her nimble fingers wielding the scissors and painstakingly cutting the delicate fabric and sewing on the beads, I understood it. It all made perfect sense. These designs were an extension of her, and it would be a disservice to her, her family, and anyone who set their eyes upon them to not let the truth be known.

"No," I said. "I want to do it."

A few minutes later I was back at my desk, the phone numbers I'd managed to find, thanks to a good old phone directory, on a notepad before me. With my breath held, I dialed the first one.

44

It had taken several calls, dozens of emails, one trip to Seattle, and some legal forms to be signed for the moment now before me to happen.

"I'm a little nervous," I told Lu, my eyes glued to the street out front. "Excited. Anxious. I just want them to love it."

"There's no way they won't," she said.

"But what if they think *she* wouldn't have loved it?"

Lu turned to me and put her hand on my arm, making me meet her gaze.

"Sylvia," she said. "You love your job. No one would ever say otherwise. You love every piece of art that crosses your desk and take such care with each item as if you created them yourself. But what I have seen you do in the past few weeks is beyond anything you've done before. Anything you've *had* to do before. You worked tirelessly to right a tragic wrong. You refused to give up, willingly giving up your precious sleep..."

I laughed—everyone knew I needed at least nine hours of sleep to function, though ten was preferable.

"To make sure this woman's work was known. And what you have created—" she pointed in the direction of the exhibit room where we'd oh-so-carefully placed each gorgeous piece of fashion history on display "—is a respectful, thoughtful, and elegant show that makes my blackened heart practically weep every time I walk through it."

"I love your tiny charred ticker," I said.

"Shut up and listen to me," Lu said.

I saluted and she rolled her eyes.

"I understand you like to play it cool and loose like me so that no one will know you have real feelings," she said. "But I need you to unhinge that body armor for a minute and take this in."

"Is this where you make me cry?"

"Yes. If only you'd shut up."

I pressed my lips together and pretended to lock them and throw away the key.

"Zora would be so proud of what you've done," Lu said, her usual sharp, quick way of speaking rounding and softening, pulling tears from the dark recesses of my eyes and making them well. "She'd be so proud of *you*, Sylvia. The care you've taken. The attention to detail. The research and interviewing and all the extra hours you've put in to make sure the way her work is shown is like walking into a storybook of her life, complete with those gorgeous pictures the family gave us to use. It's perfect. It will probably go down in history as your best ever work." She shrugged her diminutive shoulders then with a smirk. "You've peaked. It's all downhill from here, baby."

I snorted. I could always count on Lu to build me up and then playfully smack me down.

Regardless. She'd gotten me and I wiped away the tears I'd tried valiantly to hold back so as not to ruin my makeup for the big day.

"Jerk," I said, patting gently around my eyes and holding still as my friend reached forward to swipe a finger beside my eye.

"Just a little smudge of mascara," she said.

I stared at her, my chest doing a small, shuddering heave.

"Thank you," I said. "For all your help and support, keeping the others going while I stowed away in my office for hours on end and flew out to Seattle on a moment's notice."

"It was my pleasure," she said. "Except when Carmen broke down after that sleeve fell apart once again and threw her pin cushion at the wall where it stuck. Actually, that was quite enjoyable to watch. I take it back."

"I'm sorry I missed it."

"Have Harry in security pull the tape for you. It was a brilliant moment and you deserve nice things."

I grinned and then movement outside caught my attention.

"They're here," I whispered, watching as the limousines I'd ordered pulled up to the curb.

"See you in a bit," Lu said, backing away from me.

"You're going?" I asked, panic filling me tip to toe.

"This is your show, babe. Knock 'em dead."

I ran my hands down the front of the twenties-inspired loose-fitting, dropped-waist dress I'd found at a favorite vintage shop on Connecticut Avenue, took a breath, and opened the door to welcome Zora Lily's family and friends to the Smithsonian National Museum of American History.

There were twenty-six of them in all, the youngest a five-year-old; the oldest eighty-eight, Zora and Harley's firstborn daughter, Helena Rose. Twenty-one members of the Aldridge family came, and five members of Zora's best friend Rose's family, who had provided even more information, letters Rose had received from Zora, and photographs of the two women through the years.

"Helena," I said, as the older woman reached the top of the steps with the help of a hot pink cane. "Welcome."

Like their parents, all three of the Aldridge children were tall and slender and shared striking resemblances to the couple they'd been born to. They also dressed with impeccable style, something I'd noticed immediately upon being greeted by almost the entire brood when I'd flown out to Seattle.

It was Helena I'd first spoken to, finding her number in an online phone book and crossing my fingers before dialing. When I'd told her who I was and the reason for my call, she was quiet for so long I feared we'd been disconnected. And then…

"Can we meet?" she'd asked, her voice cracking with emotion. "I'd love to tell you the story in person."

I flew out the following day. Upon arriving at the Capitol Hill home that had been Zora and Harley's, passed down to their eldest child who had raised her own family there, I found myself immersed in the history of the woman at the heart of a mystery I was determined to get to the bottom of.

"Our mother was a brilliant designer," Helena said, looking to her sister, Maureen Zora, and their younger brother, Elias, both of whom nodded their agreement. "But naive in the early days of her career."

What followed was a tale of a young woman given an opportunity anyone in her position would have jumped at. A chance at the big time. An opportunity to make a name for herself in Hollywood.

"What she was sold on and what she got were two different things," Helena said.

"It was basically a higher-paid version of what she'd been doing with Grammy," Maureen said.

While her best friend, Rose, was working and making friends, going out at night, only to return in the wee hours of the morning, Zora was also getting little sleep. But not for any of the fun reasons Rose had. She was worked to the bone, expected to either stay late or take work home with her if she hadn't finished what she was working on for the day.

"They had a little apartment they shared with another gal near the studio," Helena said.

"But then how did—" I started to ask.

"The costumes?" Helena said and I nodded. "According to my mother, the studio had signed a contract with Michele Cleménte. As you obviously know, she was a big name in fashion design at the time. But just as she was supposed to start, she had a big blow-out with the director. Apparently the two were having an affair. He was married, told her he wasn't leaving his wife. You know how that kind of tale goes. She shouted the whole tawdry story on set for all to hear and then walked off, leaving them with no one to design the costumes. With Garbo as the talent, they were scrambling. Mama quietly offered up her design book. Looks she'd been working on when she thought the job would be hers. They loved them, of course, but more importantly, Garbo loved them. Mama was a genius when it came to reading a room, a scene, a feeling that needed to be conveyed. And she was hired."

"At far less the salary Cleménte was to be paid, of course," Elias said.

We all chimed in, echoing his "of course."

"She got her own office and spent hours with Garbo, measuring, remeasuring, doing fittings and more fittings until each piece was done."

"And then what?"

"Everything was shot, the edits wrapped, and they were preparing for the movie to come out when Zora was called into her manager's office."

My hands grew damp and I clamped one around the other.

"Mama had never signed a contract when she took over the job, and Cleménte's had never been torn up. She threatened to spill the affair to any news site that would listen if she wasn't given credit for Garbo's costumes. The studio wanted a famous name attached and couldn't afford the bad publicity so…" Helena's voice trailed off.

"No," I whispered, an ache in my chest for the young woman whose work, so distinct and thoughtful and ethereal at times, had become a pawn in someone's selfish game.

"Yes," Maureen said. "Like Helena said, Mama was naive in those days. She'd been so excited by the opportunity, she'd forgotten the most important thing one has to know about Hollywood. You have to watch your back." She shared sympathetic looks with her siblings before continuing. "Because there was no contract, except for the original one naming Mama as one of the seamstresses on the film, she was pressured into keeping quiet. Cleménte would be credited with designing the costumes. Mama would be given a large amount of money to keep her mouth shut."

My eyes welled imagining the heartbreak, not only for the opportunity taken from Zora, but her work being stolen, as well.

"As you can imagine," Elias said, shifting in his seat, a whisper of the man who had been his father in his facial features. "Our mother was devastated. As soon as the job was complete, she packed up and came home."

"She was devastated indeed," Helena said. "But she didn't come home completely at a loss. She had a bunch of money and an idea. She just needed time to figure out the how and when of it all."

"And so the boutique was created," I said.

"And it was a success," Maureen said. "Oh, how we all loved visiting the shop with Daddy. He'd bring us by and she'd hug us and swath us in fabric and put on a British accent, mimicking him, and tell us how fabulous we looked, dahhhling." I grinned as the other two siblings chuckled. "She'd put us in hats and slip off her heels and let us clomp around in them. I'm sure her clientele thought we were a nuisance but she didn't care. We were hers and she loved sharing her world with us, showing us different stitches and new designs she was working on, asking our opinions..."

"'What do you think of this pouf, Helly?' she'd say," Helena said. "'Mo—put on this fringe and have a spin, will you? I need to see how it splays.'"

"'Elias Walker Aldridge, should the bow go here? Or here?' She was always asking our opinions, making us feel a part of it all, making it ours too."

"It was a sad day when she closed the store," Maureen said.

"Like we were at a funeral," Elias said.

"An era gone," Helena chimed in, her voice low as they all sat, the memory playing out in their minds, exchanging sad smiles, remembering.

"She was ready though," Maureen said. "She'd done so much in the years it was open. Helped the community in times of need, gave sewing classes and so much of her time to work and to others."

"Did she quit designing completely?" I asked.

"Of course not," Maureen said and they all laughed. "She designed for us, for friends, and other family members."

"And for herself, of course," Helena said, giving her brother and sister a look I didn't understand until she followed her statement with, "She even sewed the dress she wore for her funeral."

My mouth dropped open and then I laughed. "But of course she did."

I stayed the night as a guest in the large historic home, Helena giving me free rein to wander the rooms as I pleased after giving me a tour and introducing me to family members, some of whom lived there, some who had come just to meet me and share their own stories of the woman I'd come to seek more information about.

The house was elegant, filled with expensive pieces of furniture from Harley's father's collection, paintings, and finishings, but not too precious that the some of the knobs weren't worn in spots, or scuffs didn't appear on the hardwood floors. There were nicks in the woodwork, penciled markings and names for the children who had grown here going up one doorway and down the other side, and smudges on some of the windows where small hands had pressed to them as little faces stared out.

I could feel Zora's presence here. See her in my mind's eye, gliding down the curved staircase. I pictured her seated at the dining table or the armchair I was told was her favorite spot to sit and read and design. On the walls were some of her sketches that had been framed, images of her, her and Harley, and so very many of both parents with their children.

I smiled as I stared at one such picture, taking in the hilarious scene.

"We were to be taking an elegant photo for Christmas," Helena said from behind me.

I turned with a grin. "Looks *very* elegant indeed."

In it, Elias was lying on the floor, eyes closed, tongue hanging out as though he were playing dead. Helena, standing beside her father, was lifting the front of her dress, showing the underskirt and covering her face. And little Maureen was literally hanging from their mother's neck. In the center, both parents smiled as though nothing was amiss.

"This picture," Helena said, "was what it was like in this house, in this family, every day. It was a beautiful way to grow up. We were surrounded by love. Mama's brothers and sisters were always coming by, sometimes staying a night or two, sometimes dropping off their kids, our cousins, so they could get a weekend away. It was loud and busy and filled with laughter. That was the legacy our parents left us. And that's why, even though she could've tried her hand in Hollywood again with all the success and the fame she'd gained here in Seattle, she never sought to go back. You should know that. Whatever you decide to put in your exhibit, I hope you'll show people that Zora Lilly lost nothing of herself when all that happened. She only gained."

I looked back at the silly photograph of the family of five, then let my eyes wander over several more. The three children together, Zora with her own siblings, her parents, Harley and a handsome fellow who looked like a softer and younger version of him with the same wavy dark hair and light eyes, an image of Zora in a dressing gown, standing on a balcony, a city sprawled out before her, the couple at their wedding, holding hands while walking away from whoever was taking the picture, and dancing, his hand on the small of her back, a small smile on his face, her head tucked beneath his chin.

Helena was right.

So often we sit in the "what-ifs" of life, wondering, lingering, drowning in a future that may never have been. Zora could've tried to fight. Could've hinted in the press when they interviewed her about her shop, drawing someone's attention to Hollywood, the dresses, and the betrayal.

But that wasn't her style. The style in which she lived her life, much like her dress designs, was steeped in a quiet dignity one could see in every photo taken of her. Rather than seeing the dresses and the opportunity with MGM as things that were taken from her, she chose to look at them as a gift, and move on to a place where she and her talents were wanted. A place she belonged through and through—as soon as she decided to make it so.

"We've only seen the costumes she made once," Helena said, a wistfulness in her voice. "She had a copy of the movie and played it for us."

I turned wide eyes onto her.

"Did you ever see the drawings of them?" I asked.

She shook her head, her soft white hair brushing against slender shoulders.

"She had to leave them behind. It was part of the deal so that she couldn't later use them to prove they were hers."

Anger pressed the air from my lungs.

"Well, you will see them now," I said, looking at another photo, this one of Zora and Rose standing beside a train, their suitcases at their feet, another young woman standing off to the side. Rose was blowing a kiss; Zora looked straight at the camera, one eye closed in a wink. "I don't believe in a lot of woo-woo stuff. But somehow, I think she sent me here to make sure you did."

45

We stood inside the grand entrance of the museum together, their faces expectant, excited, my insides trembling and anxious as I was about to lead Zora's family to see for the very first time the costumes their matriarch had sacrificed.

"I'm excited," Helena said, gripping my arm with one hand, her other clutching her cane as we led the way.

"I hope you like what we've done," I said, a tremor of anticipation coursing through me.

I'd never been nervous about one of my exhibits before. Not even my very first one. I always had a very clear vision of what I wanted to show people and how to do it. This was no different. Except that it was completely different. I was invested this time personally. I cared not only that this woman's story was told, but that it was told in the way her children felt described her best. She hadn't been a sad woman. She'd never felt she'd lost out or been wronged, even though it was clear she had been. She'd been happy, smart, persevering, and most of all, generous.

"I'm glad it happened," Lu said one day as we sat, just the two of us, after hours working on the Zora Lily costumes.

"You're glad what happened?" I asked, my lips carefully clamping down on the straight pins between them as I spoke.

"The whole thing with Cleménte. I don't think Zora was built for a life in Hollywood. She'd never have been happy."

"Agreed," I'd said.

"Although," Lu said, sitting back in her chair, a needle raised as if she were going to poke the air, making her next point quite literal. "She could've been the American Chanel."

"Humph," I said, defensive of the woman whose truth I had fought to uncover. "Chanel would've been the French Zora Lily."

"Ooh," Lu said, narrowing her eyes. "Point to you." She stabbed the air with her finger.

Besides the museum's employees, no one outside had seen the exhibit yet. Opening day was tomorrow, but today, for as long as the family needed, this part of the museum was theirs and theirs alone.

I led the way, walking slowly for the elders in the group, and when we rounded the corner there were audible gasps as the family took in the spectacular display before them. From the sparkling sign announcing The Hollywood Glamour Exhibition, to the velvet and silk backdrops, the lights, and of course, the costumes. It was a feast for the eyes.

Beautiful, expensive fabrics in gorgeous colors, bejeweled necklines and cuffs and risqué draped backs. And along with each costume-wearing mannequin was an enlarged photo of Garbo wearing it in *The Star.*

I watched as the family spread out, each of their interests drawn by something in particular.

"Look!" one of Zora's great-nieces gasped, pointing to one of Hollywood's most iconic gowns.

I smiled as she stood staring for a long moment before suddenly turning her back to the mannequin, raising her phone, and taking a selfie.

"They never get tired of taking pictures of themselves," Helena said.

I patted her hand and grinned as she continued her thought.

"I'm actually a bit jealous," she said. "There are some moments from my past I wish I could've documented. Alas, no one was around to take my picture and the memories have faded. But oh how I'd love to be able to show you this great two-piece swimsuit I once owned and the handsome lifeguard I kissed behind a palm tree on one of our trips to Spain."

The family finished up in the main room and then we headed down the wide hallway that led to what Lu referred to as my crowning achievement.

"Oh," was all Helena said when she saw the sign above the doorway leading into another room that originally wasn't supposed to be part of the exhibit, but that we'd been allowed to use when the mystery around *The Star* was revealed to us.

"History Uncovered: The Zora Lily Story" the sign read.

"Oh my goodness," someone behind me whispered, followed by several more family members murmuring with wonder as they stepped inside.

Like the rest of the Glamour Exhibition, the costumes were gathered together with images on stands of the star who wore them and a description of the gown or outfit beneath it. Unlike the rest of the exhibition, the remainder of the room surrounding the main event wound along the perimeter by date with enlarged images of Zora Lily, her work, the different shop spaces she'd owned, framed sketches of her designs, glass boxes with tape measures, her favorite pin cushion, a thimble, worn from use, and letters exchanged between her and Rose, her and Greta Garbo, and even one particular letter to Harley.

I had spent hours above and beyond my usual nine to five, collecting, sorting, and compiling. The marketing team was brought in to discuss the setup, public relations on how to advertise our findings, and family members and friends of Zora, Harley, and Rose interviewed for a video that played on a large television screen on the back wall, two rows of benches set up in front of it for ease of viewing.

"Shall we?" I asked Helena, smiling as her hand tightened on my elbow.

"Yes, please," she said, her voice a whisper, her eyes red with emotion as we led the way into the room.

It was organized by decade, starting with the few early photos there were of Zora as a child, her little brow crooked with worry, as if wondering who this person was taking her picture. Beside her in every picture from her youth was her older brother, Tommy. It was only when he had an arm slung around her diminutive shoulders that she dared to smile. From there the story moved to her teenage years. A slender young woman with delicate features, too-big shoes below skinny ankles, and a best friend happy to steal the show with silly antics and poses. But even Rose's theatrics couldn't pull one's attention to the beauty blooming next to her. Zora was stunning.

As she entered her twenties, it was clear from two pictures in particular that something had happened. A life-altering change shifting something in her eyes. The timidness from one photo replaced by the stark loneliness in the next. In the first, she was sitting beside Tommy on the top step of the family's front porch. In the second, she was sitting in the same spot, but now she sat alone.

A framed newspaper story of Tommy's death hung below the two images.

Another shift and here was Zora out on the town, smiling, her arm linked with Rose's, a band in the background, and handsome young Harley looking on as the two women posed. Early photos of Harley and Zora as he courted her, and then some early drawings as she began to dream again of a career in fashion design.

An image of her cutting the ribbon to her first shop, standing below the little bell above the door, posing with the mannequins, and working alongside her sister Sarah.

In the 1930s, the Depression hitting the world and sending it into a recession, Zora posted flyers in the shop. If you had textiles you could donate, she, her mother, sisters Sarah and Hannah, and anyone else they knew who could sew, would turn scrap material into blankets they would then give to those in need. The boutique's clientele was asked to consider donating clothing they no longer wore so that it could be given away for free, or deconstructed and cut to make children's clothing. Soup kitchens were organized, shelter sought and provided for those who had lost their homes or were transitioning to somewhere smaller they could afford, and jobs offered when they became available.

A decade later, with the United States entering the Second World War, Zora and her family stood on a pier and waved goodbye as Harrison was shipped out to fight in the Pacific. Fearful of losing another brother, Zora kept busy by partnering with the Red Cross, often closing the shop early to host other women volunteering their time to put together nonperishable food packages to be sent overseas. Harley would come by with refreshments, receiving adoring glances from the women, his and Zora's young children happily offering to fetch twine and packing supplies.

Thankfully, as shown in the last photo dedicated to the decade, Harrison made it home with only a missing finger, but with plenty of unseen battle wounds he never talked about.

All the while, the boutique flourished. From the 1920s to the '30s and '40s, hemlines dropped and rose, waists flowed and cinched, sleeves draped and poofed. Bias cuts became the rage, backless dresses with jeweled details, tiered hems, tea dresses, and chiffon chiffon chiffon. From there clothing became more structured. Shoulder pads and nipped-in waists, simple blouses with sensible skirts, dark-colored dresses with bright white cuffs and collars. But always with Zora's flair. She had a way of making the simple elegant, interesting, and special.

The boutique entered the 1950s on a high note, but Harley was anxious to travel more with his wife by his side. And so, after a many long talks she came to the decision that 1953 would be her last year. She'd be fifty years old and, though she and Harley had traveled a lot in their years together, she wanted longer trips. More time to just sit with the man she loved in the places they'd come to enjoy.

That last year was graced with some of Zora's most beautiful and intricate designs to date.

"I want to go out quietly," she'd told the *Seattle Times*. "Elegantly. And giving my clients and this city my best creations yet."

Possibly my favorite part of the exhibition were some of those pieces. Helena, Maureen, and Elias owned nearly every single garment Zora had ever designed, and a dozen of them hung in near-perfect condition on mannequins around the room.

"Are these…?" Lu had asked, her jaw dropping open when I'd pulled the first piece from its protective covering upon my arrival back in DC.

"They are," I'd answered, and then continued to reveal to my coworker and friend, some of the most beautiful clothing either of us had ever set our eyes upon.

"How?" she'd asked, gingerly touching a layered chiffon hemline. "Oh my gosh. Is this what it's like to touch angels' feathers? Fairy wings? Glinda the Good Witch's ball gown?"

"I don't think it was a ball gown, technically," I'd said. "It was like her everyday dress."

"Whatever. Did you *feel* this fabric?" she asked. "It's otherworldly."

"I did. Just wait. It gets better."

Zora, her eye always on the future, had made sure to make herself one of each of her most favorite designs done for the boutique. Each one was worn only by Zora, and when its time in the sun was over, she had it professionally cleaned and stored in a protective garment bag for safekeeping.

"She had no idea if anything would ever come of them, understand," Maureen had told me, running a hand over a gorgeous blue and orange tweed jacket and skirt set. "But she thought perhaps one day, because fashion and art are an important part of human history, we might be able to donate them to a museum for money should we ever need it."

"Well," I'd said. "I don't know if you need it, but the museum will give you money and you don't have to donate, just let us borrow. I'm prepared to offer a contract saying as much."

When we'd circled the entirety of the room, Helena let go of my arm and wandered off with her siblings to look again, look closer, reminisce with family members and friends as they stared together at the old pictures, remembering a time, a place, a moment shared from each of their individual perspectives. I smiled as they posed next to life-size pictures of the woman who had raised them, loved them, and given them a legacy to be proud of.

Interestingly, none of Zora's descendants had pursued fashion themselves.

"Maureen had a real eye for it," Helena had told me when I'd visited Seattle. "But no desire to create anything herself. When we were kids, she loved to go with our mother to fabric shops and pick something out. She would then say what she wanted it made into and stand very still so Mama could drape and pin the material she'd chosen, and then sew it into creation. To this day she loves to peruse fabric stores, though she usually just looks now and doesn't buy."

I meandered, stopping now and then to admire a photo, read a description, or take a picture for someone. At one point I found myself standing beside a glass case displaying three pieces of stationery placed side by side, each one covered in Zora's careful handwriting. Behind the letter was a framed photo borrowed from the massive picture wall in Helena's home. In it, Zora was standing on a balcony, Florence laid out before her, the Cathedral of Santa Maria del Fiore in the distance. Her dark bob was tousled, and she was wearing a dressing gown, one sleeve slipping off a shoulder, her back to a camera held by her new husband.

"They were on their honeymoon," Helena had told me when she'd noticed me staring at it in her home. "Father took this photo moments after reading a letter she'd written to him years before. It had been returned to her, unopened and with a stamp across the front. 'Return to Sender. Occupant No Longer at this Address.' She was bereft. She'd thought she'd lost him forever. But she'd saved it anyway, just in case, and gave it to him their first morning in Italy.

"When they were courting, she'd had a hard time telling him how she felt, the deep feelings of inadequacy she'd had all her life, and the fear of being rejected making it difficult to be honest about such things, despite him freely giving his words of love to her. This letter said it all and Father treasured it. He kept it in a special box in his bedside table. I was fourteen when I found it. Such an impressionable age. He saw me with it and didn't even get mad for the intrusion on his privacy. Just told me it was the most beautiful gift our mother could ever have given him."

The clothes and the items that had belonged to Zora were my favorite part of the exhibit. It was my job after all. To appreciate the physical, tangible remnants of the past. But the letter was special.

The words were poetry. Zora's feelings an ocean, swelling, pulling, splashing onto an unseen shore before gathering the fragments left behind and churning anew with another emotion, idea, or hope. She had laid bare her soul on those pages, giving everything she never had before, and my heart ached knowing how devastated she must've been when the letter came back to her, unopened, her feelings of love and devotion never to be known. At least, that's what she'd thought at the time.

My gaze went back to the photo. One could almost feel the

love coming from this woman who no longer wondered, but knew, this was where she belonged. With this man, in this place, in this life.

I moved toward the entrance of the room and turned, taking it all in. My heart filled with something that went beyond love of an art form and my typical satisfaction at seeing a plan fall into place. This feeling was different. It was more than appreciating the intricate patterns, the thoughtful details, the designers that created them, and the techniques used to bring them to fruition. These garments told a story aside from where they belonged in the history of fashion. They told the story of a woman.

Art, I understood now, was so much more than the sum of its brush strokes, curved clay appendages, or intricate stitching. There were stories woven, kneaded, and scratched into each piece. Blood, sweat, and tears intermixing with charcoal, textile, and canvas. Hopes, dreams, anger, fear, heartbreak, redemption, romance, and the thrilling sensation of falling in love all resided in an artist's work, the admirer of such pieces never knowing what emotions and story had shaped it.

I was hit suddenly with sadness, thinking about how, when the exhibition was over, all the pieces and photos and costumes would be archived away, out of sight, enclosed in airtight containers in a temperature-controlled room, cloaked in darkness and slowly forgotten. I'd always been fine with the process, never even giving it another thought. We were preserving the artefacts for future generations after all. But in removing them from sight, in hiding them away from society, the stories behind them were lost. The reason they'd been created in the first place pushed further and further away until eventually, no one would remember them at all.

Seeing Zora's descendants sporting bits and pieces of her work, a cape on one of her nieces, a flared skirt on a granddaughter, the white scarf with black polka dots knotted at the neck of her eldest daughter, clarified that art wasn't to be hidden away. It was to be admired not only for what it was and the timeframe it was made in, but the emotion the artist had borne it from.

The family began to disperse, wandering back through the rest of the exhibition toward the front doors of the museum. I caught Helena's eye.

"Well?" I asked, almost afraid, but sensing there was no need to be.

She looked to Elias and Maureen who had come to join us, standing on either side of their older sister.

"She would've loved it, Sylvia. You recognized the love in her work and have honored her memory with such care and detail, telling her story through her designs and photographs in such a thoughtful display. It's—" Her voice caught and she wiped a tear with the back of her hand. "It's as if she's in this room with us. I can feel her presence. You did that." She reached for my hand. "We are indebted to you. Thank you."

My eyes welled and the three siblings moved in, encircling me in a hug. When we parted, I walked them to the doors, promising to meet them for dinner before they left town, and to keep in touch.

"You come visit should you ever find yourself in Seattle again," Elias said. "You're family now."

"That you are," Helena said.

I waved goodbye from the steps and then walked back through the exhibit on my way to my office, sighing, a mixture of relief and gratefulness filling my body. I no longer cared what anyone else thought about the show. Had not one worry about what the reviews would be. I had pleased the only people who mattered, and honored a fashion icon the world had nearly lost without ever knowing her.

As I opened the locked drawer that stored my purse, I noticed a slender square box no bigger than my hand sitting in the center of my desk. There was no card. No note to say who it was from or why it was there. Just as a simple navy blue box with a white ribbon tied around it.

I sat and pulled one end of the ribbon, watching it fall away before lifting the lid. Folding back the silver tissue paper inside, I gasped.

Inside was a black satin bow tie headband. *The* black satin bow tie headband.

"She had them in every color of the rainbow," Helena had told me when I'd noticed the one wrapped around a lone mannequin bust that still sat in the home office where Zora had designed her last two decades of clothing. "And several prints. But eventually they all went by the wayside. She'd give them to Maureen and me to wear or play with when we were girls, to our daughters when we'd grown, and to our granddaughters. Eventually, they all but disappeared. All but this one. We would've buried it with her, but she'd given explicit instructions not to. 'Save it for someone who will appreciate it,' she'd said. The three of us siblings all appreciated it, and so here it sits getting dusted once a week, away from the sunlight so it doesn't fade too much too fast."

And now here it was, in my hands.

It wasn't until I'd turned it over several times that I saw the envelope and photograph tucked beneath where it had lain.

The photo was of Zora, "age twenty-eight" the back read. In it, she stood proudly in front of her first shop, wearing one of her first creations and the very headband I held in my hands. I grinned, taking in her name written in elegant script across the front window, imagining the sound of the bell above the door as customers came and went.

I pressed the picture to my heart and then set it aside and slid the card from the envelope.

"Some things don't belong in a museum," it read.

I smiled. Helena knew me too well. Part of me wanted to rush back out to the exhibition and place it with the rest of the items. In the glass case with her tape measure and thimble perhaps. Or maybe with one of the dresses she'd worn. But another part of me, a bigger part of me, knew that while she would've understood it, Zora would've been disappointed. That's not why it had been given to me.

I propped the photo and note on my desk and then exhaled and stood, turning to the round mirror hanging on the wall beside my office door. Ducking my head, I slid the band over my hair, tucking the bottom beneath the bun I wore and sliding the rest up over the top, adjusting it so that the bow sat just so behind my ear.

"Well done, Zora," I whispered.

I gave my reflection a nod then grabbed my things, turned out the light, and shut the door behind me.

ITALY

1932

He watched her, as he always did, with a hint of a smile on his face and wonder in his eyes. From the first moment Harley had seen Zora, he knew she was the woman he'd been waiting for. The way she moved, her careful demeanor in juxtaposition with the fire in her eyes, the kind smile and easy laugh. And then later…her skin, like silk against his, her voice husky as she lay tucked in bed beside him.

She sat now, bathed in the golden Italian morning sunlight, on the balcony. She was a picture, her dressing gown slipping from one shoulder, dark hair piled on top of her head, a bouquet of flowers in a ceramic vase left by the hotel staff beside her.

Sipping from the delicate cup in her hand, she looked over her shoulder at him, a shy smile on her lips. Her eyes lowered then met his again and his chest ached with the beauty of all that she was, remembering the fear he'd felt when he'd had to leave her, when her words and then letters became sparse. Until they'd stopped coming altogether. And then the memory of the moment their eyes finally met again through the shop window.

He looked down once more at the letter in his hands. It had been on her pillow when he awoke, above the imprint of where her head had lain. He'd looked questioningly around for her, finding her where she was now, awake, watching him, waiting.

"Read it," she'd said.

"What is it?" he'd asked, pushing himself up and leaning against the headboard before reaching for the envelope. A crude stamp across the front read, "Return to Sender," his name beneath, her name in the upper left-hand corner.

"Everything," she'd said, and then turned away to look back out at the city beyond.

He'd never minded the absence of words, understanding her fears and the trauma she'd experienced as a young girl at the hands of others. She showed her love for him in other ways. Like how she always reached for his hand, ran her fingers through his hair while listening to him talk as they sat on the sofa or lay in bed. It was clear in the way she looked after him, asked about his day, his family, and how he felt about any given thing. He didn't need her words, he told her. But he wanted them. One day. When she was ready.

And then of course, when she finally did, the letter was returned. Unopened. Occupant no longer at that address.

Despite the letter never finding its way to him, Zora hadn't been able to throw it away. She wanted to keep it as proof. For herself. That she could love. And that she *had* been loved.

He finished reading and laid the pages on his chest, placing his hands over them and watching his wife as she got to her feet, staring out at the sun-bleached structures they'd undoubtedly find themselves wandering through later, in search of a meal and a drink, and much later a sunset.

He wished, in her moments of doubt, she could see herself as he did. A formidable force. A whirlwind of ideas and mystery, grace and laughter. And then, in the next breath, she would transform into something else, tucking herself away, as if exhausted by her own effervescence. She'd become contemplative, shy, moving about their life like a whisper of herself. He found her intriguing in all her forms, and was excited to learn who else she was in their years together.

Setting the letter aside, he stood and joined her on the balcony, breathing in the scent of lemon trees, the Mediterranean beyond…and Zora.

She looked up at him then with questions in her eyes, but he just smiled and sat, pulling her onto his lap, the two of them staring out at the world together.

"I can't imagine it ever being better than this," he said.

She smiled and snuggled into him.

"Oh. But, Harley. It will be."

★★★★★

Acknowledgments

As always, the creation of this book was a journey, starting with my partner in crime and agent extraordinaire, Erin L. Cox. Your belief in me and my stories is priceless. I will never be able to thank you enough. Never. But I'll keep saying it anyways. Thank you.

My forever gratitude to the amazing team at MIRA. Your continuing support, hard work, and gorgeous covers are a dream for this author. Thank you. And to April Osborn, my editor. Our path together began with this book, and you stepped in like the pro you are, with wonderful ideas, thoughtful notes, and encouragement. Thank you for making this book sparkle and shine.

Without writer friends, I'd probably toss my laptop out the window. Writing is often a lonely journey. Having people to turn to, commiserate and laugh through the tears with...people who understand the roller coaster this job is, is priceless. Jamie Pacton—I love you, V. Chris Panatier, Kate Quinn, Rob Wolf, and Sara Ackerman—thank you for checking in on me. For sharing your own words, methods, and wisdom.

Dan Hanks. Thank you. For the writing sprints. For believing in me even when I'm swearing up and down that I can't, and shouldn't, write another word ever. For always making me laugh. And for the sfogliatelle. *jazz hands*

To my kids, Jackson and Dylan. Thank you for your patience with me as I disappeared once more into one of my fictional worlds. Thank you for being interested in my stories. And in me.

To Danny for your never-ending support and emailed articles whenever I ponder a subject out loud.

To my parents and siblings, who never falter in their excitement that this is my reality. I still can't believe it either!

Of course, I can't write an acknowledgments page without mentioning Zora Lily, my great-great-grandmother whose name inspired a book. I wish I'd known you. Thank you for having existed. I hope you would've liked this book.

And of course, dear reader, thank YOU. I hope in this story you found a little fun, a dash of music, a bit of a romp, and a whole lot of hope. Thank you for reading.

Author Note

What's in a name?

Unlike my first two books, this story was born simply from a name. Zora Lily. The real woman who possessed this moniker was my maternal great-great-grandmother, whom I'd never heard of until one fateful afternoon a few years ago. I was instantly smitten by the glamorous-sounding name, and a woman who, with her husband, Horatio, moved from Canada to Seattle and became part of the great logging boom, living with her family in a logging camp in Ballard, WA.

She was the mother of eight. Barely educated. Illiterate. That's what we know. But I like to think she was so much more than that. That she dreamed big, laughed hard, adored her children, had wonderful girlfriends around to support her, and that her love with Horatio was a great, big love. And I hope she'd be proud to have her name on this book, even though it's not her story. Just a tale inspired by a name. Her name.

Zora Lily.

Further Reading

The Roaring Days of Zora Lily would not exist without the help of a handful of books I researched for a variety of details to build my 1920s Seattle. Please see the list below for the works of several authors that helped inform the music, the musicians, the partygoers, and the fabulous women.

Jackson Street After Hours by Paul de Barros

Beautiful Little Fools by Jillian Cantor

Flappers: Six Women of a Dangerous Generation by Judith Mackrell

Seattle Prohibition: Bootleggers, Rumrunners & Graft in the Queen City by Brad Holden and Paul de Barros

Lost Roadhouses of Seattle by Peter Blecha and Brad Holden

Discussion Questions

1. Zora's impeccable eye for fashion has her observing every hem and neckline, ruffle and fringe, in every room she enters. What passion or expertise do you have that makes certain details impossible to ignore?

2. The Hough family's station in life is marked by not having an indoor bathroom and residing in a neighborhood that uses candles instead of electric streetlights. How does the wealth inequality of the 1920s differ from the present day? In what ways is it the same?

3. Elsbeth Pritchard's abuse and harassment mars what would otherwise be an exciting new chapter of Zora's life, and she largely keeps her head down and refuses to engage. Do you think she responded appropriately? How would you act in her shoes?

4. In spite of Prohibition, alcohol is freely enjoyed throughout the novel by characters from all walks of life. Can you think of any laws that are as flagrantly ignored today?

How might the consequences differ, depending on the person who is caught and made an example of?

5. Both Jessie and Ellis long to hit it big in the entertainment industry but find themselves hindered by their "foreignness" and skin color, respectively. How are they able to overcome their hurdles, and what obstacles might prove impossible to bypass?

6. Zora waits months and months to write Harley back and attributes it to the intense shame she feels after being taken advantage of in Hollywood. How do you feel about her decision to put it off until she achieves her dream?

7. Through Sylvia's efforts, Zora is finally recognized for designing Greta Garbo's costumes in *The Star*, years after her death. Given her successful boutique, steadfast husband, and loving family, how important do you think it would have been to her if she had survived?